REBIRTH

A glancing hit from the Terminator's chainfist sent Ky'dak sprawling and half-wrenched his helmet off. Ky'dak did the rest, tearing away the seals between helm and gorget with his gauntleted hand. Eyes like burning coals glared back at the monster. Like all sons of Nocturne, Ky'dak's skin was onyx-black. It was almost invisible in the darkness. In his anger, his eyes became dagger-slits of blood red.

The Terminator charged Ky'dak, and at the same time Va'lin pushed himself up into a run, tossing a frag grenade in the monster's midst. The close detonation staggered the Terminator, but not for long. He also turned, his hellish glare fixed on Va'lin who stood his ground and braced his flamer.

With a brief spurt of ignition, Ky'dak leapt onto the Terminator's back and thrust downward with his chainsword, finding the gap between gorget and neck. Pipes, cabling and servo lines were all shredded. Spitting machine oil quickly became blood as the churning teeth bit into flesh.

'Burn it!' Ky'dak snarled, shouting to be heard.

To see the complete range of Salamanders stories, eBooks, MP3s
and audio dramas, please visit our website at blacklibrary.com.

A WARHAMMER 40,000 NOVEL

BOOK ONE IN THE CIRCLE OF FIRE

REBIRTH

NICK KYME

BLACK LIBRARY

For my beautiful girlfriend, Stef. Without you, none of this would have been possible...

A BLACK LIBRARY PUBLICATION
First published in Great Britain in 2014 by
Black Library,
Games Workshop Ltd.,
Willow Road,
Nottingham,
NG7 2WS, UK

10 9 8 7 6 5 4 3 2 1

Cover illustration by Cheol Joo Lee.

A CIP record for this book
is available from the British Library.

UK ISBN 13: 978 1 84970 614 8
US ISBN: 978 1 84970 674 2

See Black Library on the internet at
blacklibrary.com

Find out more about Games Workshop
and the world of Warhammer 40,000 at
games-workshop.com

Printed and bound by
CPI Group (UK) Ltd, Croydon, CR0 4YY

It is the 41st millennium. For more than a hundred
centuries the Emperor has sat immobile on the Golden Throne of
Earth. He is the master of mankind by the will of the gods, and master
of a million worlds by the might of his inexhaustible armies. He is a
rotting carcass writhing invisibly with power from the Dark Age of
Technology. He is the Carrion Lord of the Imperium for whom a
thousand souls are sacrificed every day, so that he may never truly die.

Yet even in his deathless state, the Emperor continues his eternal
vigilance. Mighty battlefleets cross the daemon-infested miasma of
the warp, the only route between distant stars, their way lit by the
Astronomican, the psychic manifestation of the Emperor's will.
Vast armies give battle in his name on uncounted worlds. Greatest
amongst his soldiers are the Adeptus Astartes, the Space Marines,
bio-engineered super-warriors. Their comrades in arms are legion:
the Astra Militarum and countless planetary defence forces, the ever-
vigilant Inquisition and the tech-priests of the Adeptus Mechanicus
to name only a few. But for all their multitudes, they are barely
enough to hold off the ever-present threat from aliens, heretics,
mutants — and worse.

To be a man in such times is to be one amongst untold billions. It is
to live in the cruellest and most bloody regime imaginable. These are
the tales of those times. Forget the power of technology and science,
for so much has been forgotten, never to be re-learned. Forget the
promise of progress and understanding, for in the grim dark future
there is only war. There is no peace amongst the stars, only an eternity
of carnage and slaughter, and the laughter
of thirsting gods.

DRAMATIS PERSONAE

ADEPTUS ASTARTES

Salamanders Sixth Company

Drakgaard, Ur'zan	Captain
Her'us	Champion, 'Serpentia'
Sepelius, Kratus	Apothecary, 'Serpentia'
Onagar	Pyroclast, 'Serpentia'
Zetok	Pyre warden, 'Serpentia'
Tul'vek	Banner bearer, 'Serpentia'
Kaladin	Battle-brother, 'Serpentia'
Tseg'un	Battle-brother, 'Serpentia'
Vervius	Battle-brother, 'Serpentia'
Elysius	Chaplain
Zantho, Akadin	Veteran sergeant, tank commander
Kor'ad	Venerable Dreadnought, 'The Warmaker'
Kadoran	Veteran sergeant
Kessoth	Sergeant
Vah'gan	Sergeant
V'reth	Sergeant

Salamanders Fourth Company

Iaptus	Sergeant, 'Wyverns',
Va'lin	Battle-brother, 'Wyverns'
Dersius	Battle-brother, 'Wyverns'
Naeb	Battle-brother, 'Wyverns'
Ky'dak	Battle-brother, 'Wyverns'
Arrok	Battle-brother, 'Wyverns'
Xerus	Battle-brother, 'Wyverns'
Illus	Battle-brother, 'Wyverns'
Vo'sha	Battle-brother, 'Wyverns'

| Sor'ad | Battle-brother, 'Wyverns' |

Bar'dak, Goran	Sergeant, 'Targons'
Amadu	Battle-brother, 'Targons'
Ush'ban	Battle-brother, 'Targons'
Ramadus	Battle-brother, 'Targons'
Nerad	Battle-brother, 'Targons'

Salamanders, Third Company

Agatone, Adrax	Captain
Exor	Techmarine
Xarko	Librarian
Zartath	Battle-brother, former Black Dragon

ECCLESIARCHY

Angerer, Maelisia	Canoness Preceptor, Order of the Ebon Chalice
Laevenius	Celestian Sister Superior, Order of the Ebon Chalice
Stephina	Seraphim Sister Superior, 'Archangels', Order of the Ebon Chalice
Avensi	Seraphim Sister Superior, 'Shrivers', Order of the Ebon Chalice
Cassia	Seraphim Sister Superior, 'Sanctifiers', Order of the Ebon Chalice
Helia	Seraphim Sister Superior, 'Exculpators', Order of the Ebon Chalice
Revina	Non-militant Adepta Sororitas

'CURSED' ASTARTES

Urgaresh	Champion
Thorast	Apothecary
Ghaan	Former vexillary
Skarh	Black Dragons Chapter, the 'wrath'
Haakem	Black Dragons Chapter, the 'wrath'

ARCHENEMY

Faustus, Heklion	Warlord, Black Legion
Gralastyx	Daemon Prince of the Eye
Vorshkar	Champion, the 'Chosen', Black Legion

Children of Torment

Kargol	Terminator
Kaid	Terminator
Lufurion	Champion, Warlord of 'The Incarnadine'
Klerik	Renegade Astartes, 'The Incarnadine'
Preest	Sorcerer, 'The Incarnadine'
Juadek	Renegade Astartes, 'The Incarnadine'

MORTALS

Redgage	Colonel, Cadian 81st
Issak	Medicus
Makato, Kensai	Lieutenant Armsman on the *Forge Hammer*
Jedda	Master-at-arms on the *Forge Hammer*

THE OTHERS

Kinebad	Archeotech hunter
Scar-borne	Mercenary, former gladiator

PROLOGUE

An old lie

It began with Sejanus. It began with his corpse and the corpses of his Glory Squad red-carpeting the throne room floor of the High City. They had died invisibly, by unseen hands. Retribution for the treachery that had laid them low would be ostensibly more visible. It would come at the hands of Hastur's brothers, vengeance for a favoured son.

A speartip was formed, oaths sworn. A legion descended on Sixty-Three Nineteen with one desire in its heart. It wasn't compliance. It was a desire for blood, a way to level the scales of treachery balanced against it.

It began with Sejanus. It ended at the induction gate.

Faustus skirted the edge of the main battlefield with a company of genhanced warriors in tow. The Twenty-First Velites were armour-light compared to the majority of their Luna Wolf brothers. Designated reconnaissance, they carried bolters and long-barrelled viper-class sniper rifles, scoped and modified for mass-reactive ammunition. They moved fast, quietly and without fuss.

Thirty led by a Centurion roared up an exterior stairway appended to one of High City's flanking sub-towers. In ruins, half flattened from cursory bombardment, it nonetheless clung to life and though much of the tower structure was destroyed, a large section of wall had endured. Klaed had spotted the vermin through his scope. Hooded and cloaked, but with the tiniest scrap of flashing silver on magenta giving them away. Careless. One man's laxity had signed his entire unit's death warrant.

'How many, Klaed?' asked Faustus, pausing. He had been pacing the steps three at a time, a characteristic spring in his motion. The Centurion loved war. He lived for it. There was but one thing he placed above it: the warriors in his charge.

A broad-shouldered Luna Wolf, muddy-white half armour clamped around his bulky torso, lowered the scope. 'Thermal imaging puts them at eighty-six. Give or take.'

'It is give or take, brother?' asked the warrior directly behind Klaed, whose pepper-stubbled jawline never betrayed a smile.

'Easy there, Klaed,' said the warrior, clapping a meaty hand on Klaed's shoulder. Ahenobarbus was half a head taller and a shoulder width broader. He wore a leather skullcap, strands of his long hair allowed to flow freely from beneath it. His combat shotgun was low slung, his finger rested alongside the trigger.

'What does it matter, Clod? Eighty-six, one hundred and eighty-six. These men are walking dead anyway.'

Ahenobarbus half turned so he could scowl at Narthius.

'That is not my name, pup.'

The young Luna Wolf beside him grinned. 'But it suits you so well.'

Narthius's face was gaunt, but handsome where most of his brothers' were blunt and flat. A shorn crest of dark hair cut his cleanly shaven scalp in two even hemispheres of tanned skin. Ahenobarbus thought Narthius over-preened and had remarked so on more than one occasion. In turn, Narthius described Ahenobarbus as a lump of heavy meat, blunt but useful if pushed and aimed in the required direction.

Both had saved each other's lives more times than they needed to count. That tally paled in comparison to how many times Faustus had saved the lives of all of his men. Reconnaissance units faced a harder task than most. Though admittedly not always at the brunt of the fighting, they were often without support nor as heavily armed or armoured. Quick minds, decisive action. It was a greater shield than any power armour or even Cataphractii plate, or so Faustus believed.

'You two will have time to spar later,' he said, cutting the banter short. 'With me, if this operation doesn't go smoothly.'

As they moved out again, Narthius patted Ahenobarbus on the back. 'Don't worry, Clod. I won't let them kill you today.'

Ahenobarbus kept up the act for a few more seconds before his scowl faded. Laughter lines crossed with his numerous scars, as perfect white teeth were exposed in a feral grin.

'Let's hope they don't spoil your youthful good looks whilst you're saving my life, eh, pup?'

Faustus had reached the summit of the stairway, a wide but pockmarked path of cratered stone with one side facing a granite wall, the other a partially destroyed iron railing. It was high up, the wind catching his cape and causing it to flap spasmodically. It also offered a good vantage of the larger battlefield.

On the left flank, Abaddon was driving First Company hard. Faustus couldn't see the Centurion individually but recognised his vexilliary's banner. Evidently, Ezekyle wanted the honour of breaching High City before anyone else, but Tenth were already approaching the gate. Their vanguard was engaged with the gate's guardians. Strong-looking men, well armed and equipped but not the equal of a legionary. Titans roamed at the battle's periphery, drawn back from the fighting companies of Luna Wolves now the need for men, not machines, took precedence. A fake dawn was still fading in the distance from the sundered starship that had crashed in the border districts. It threw light across the three kilometre-wide mass of Legio Astartes battleplate battering successfully against High City's door. False Emperor or not, Sixty-Three Nineteen's potentate was about to learn a lesson in the ephemeral nature of rulership.

The covered gallery of the stairway had led 21st to overlook the induction gate. An enfilading position.

'Velites!' Faustus cried out so as to be heard above the thunderous battle. At the summit of the stairs, the hair fled from his face in streaks of white as the wind tugged at it, and his eyes flashed sapphire-blue in the reflected flare of distant lightning. It was easy to follow men like Faustus, and Faustus knew the importance of never being afraid to demonstrate that. He raised his drawn gladius. Come the assault, he would sheath it again, but for now it served a solid purpose in cementing his image and invigorating his men. 'We blood them now!'

At Faustus's bidding, Brother Ezekus came forward and attached a pair of melta bombs to the gallery's access door. It was barred, bolted and evidently well fortified but the wrought iron sloughed away in seconds against the violent burst of microwaves. Shroud bombs were thrown through the growing aperture in advance of the Velites. Faustus stepped through first, amidst smoke and scanner-foiling electro-static. His enemies appeared as monochrome green spectres through his night vision goggles. A cough from his rifle and the man closest to him went down, throat exploded just as he had begun to turn. Two more shots in rapid succession killed near-identical targets.

The gallery was long but also narrow. A parade of firing slits lined its east-facing wall, overlooking the battlefield. Fixed weapon mounts lay in every alcove, an array of energy carbines, solid-shot cannons and high-powered sniper rifles.

Faustus fired quickly and on the move, vacating the breach so the rest of the Velites could file in behind him. The legionaries fanned out across the width of the gallery as they entered the tight space, their rifles whispering promises of death to the enemy. Men collapsed in droves, soon too many to be ignorant of, folding up as if their bones were suddenly turned to paper and could no longer support them in their armour.

One turned, a flash of magenta armour revealed as his cloak parted with the rapid movement. He gaped at the apparitions emerging from the sea of fog that had suddenly risen up around him, but had little time to concern himself. The soldier was about to raise the alarm, but found he could only quietly choke with the combat blade suddenly embedded in his neck. He fell without further sound. Faustus was on him before his cooling corpse hit the ground, kneeling and then retrieving his blade in one swift motion.

Twenty-four were dead, the first eight teams, before the enemy realised they were under attack and attempted to counter. By then, Faustus and his men were amongst them, knives drawn for close quarters. In the tight confines of the corridor, the gurgling refrain of slit throats merged with the raucous discharge of legionary combat shotguns and bolters as the secondary units moved in.

At the end of the gallery, the survivors had marshalled a makeshift defence. They broke some of the cannons out from their concealed nests, rolled in whatever they could to fashion a barricade and set up behind it, weapons blazing.

'Grab cover!' Faustus bellowed across the vox, though his voice carried down the gallery well enough without it.

The Velites reacted as one, vacating a fire corridor where energy rounds and solid shells were chewing up the gallery floor. Glass and mosaic spat upwards in a cloud of shrapnel. The gallery had once been an artful place but war had rendered it into something entirely uglier.

Faustus rolled, chased by a fusillade of enemy fire that chipped stone and made the dead bodies jerk in animated parody. He moved rapidly out of the central aisle and up against the nearest alcove set into the wall. They were shallow but offered some protection.

Ahenobarbus took a hit to the leg, some kind of phase-weapon. Pain bled out of him in an angry roar as his flesh was burned black, and Narthius had to drag him clear.

'Told you I wouldn't let them kill you, Clod,' he said, replacing a spent clip.

Ahenobarbus grunted, pressing his muscular body into the wall.

'Flesh wound, pup. Takes more than something like that to kill me.'

'Our limits will be tested soon enough,' Faustus told them both with a dark smile. He and the other two Luna Wolves were holed up together, hunkered down behind a granite column being chipped back by aggressive suppressing fire.

'You want us to take that barricade, sir?' asked Narthius, forced to shout above the din.

'I know you would if I ordered it, brother. But no. As robust as even Ahenobarbus here is, a headlong rush into those guns is suicide. I'd have a more heroic death for the Velites, and this isn't it. Not this battle. Not this day.' He turned his attention across to the opposite side of the corridor, through the hail of bullets and energy beams, to where Klaed was taking cover with Ezekus.

Faustus opened up the vox by tapping the bead embedded in his ear.

'We need to divide their attention. Can you fashion me a diversion, Rakon?'

Rakon Klaed nodded, not bothering with the vox. He tapped Ezekus on the shoulder, who was kneeling down in front of him, acting as spotter for the rest of his unit but with mixed success, and asked him a question.

The demolitions expert nodded curtly once and went to his bandoleer.

Faustus turned back to Ahenobarbus and Narthius, sizing up the big warrior first of all.

'Can you walk?'

'I'll run if you ask it of me, sir.'

'I only need a kick, brother. A hard one.' Faustus gestured to the firing slit. It was damaged from an errant shell explosion or some such and cracks lined the stone around the broken slit, promising a much wider aperture if forced.

Ahenobarbus lashed out with all his considerable strength and the slit broke apart, sundered stone sent tumbling from the ruptured aperture. In the noisy carnage of the battle no one paid it any attention. It was also now large enough to accommodate a fully-armoured legionary.

Faustus strapped his rifle over his shoulder so that he could draw a pair of combat blades. The edges were serrated and shone dully in the gloomy light of the gallery. Narthius was watching, and followed suit.

'Three volunteers,' Faustus said to the others in the two adjacent alcoves. 'Not you, brother,' he added to Ahenobarbus when he tried to offer. 'A kick is one thing, but a climb…' He gave him a conciliatory pat on the shoulder.

Eight Luna Wolves, all the legionaries in ear-shot stepped forwards. Faustus picked three – Kern, Faek and Henador – and passed Ahenobarbus to hang out of the gaping hole the hulking warrior had made for him.

'Fifty metres,' he said to the others, who had crept forwards to get as close as they could to their Centurion. 'We won't have much time. We'll need to move quickly. Charges?'

Kern proffered his captain a pair of krak grenades. He was a veteran warrior, greying hair tied back in a pony tail that snaked down the back of his neck.

Faustus thanked him.

'On my mark then, blades at the ready.' He looked across the gallery floor through a gulf of unremitting enemy fire but found Klaed waiting for his signal. Faustus gave it and in his next movement plunged through the gap in the wall and back outside into the battle proper.

Klaed simultaneously patted Ezekus hard on the back and the squat demolitions expert flung a cluster of shroud and frag grenades he had bound together with wire.

Smoke and fire filled the confined gallery space, which rang with the thunder of explosives.

Outside, Faustus was already moving.

A shallow ledge, nothing more than a lip with room enough for the edge of his booted toes to snatch purchase, ran along the exterior gallery wall. Faustus had leapt onto it and then swung, pivoting on one foot and plunging his first knife into the rock. It sank in deep, the monomolecular edge retaining optimum sharpness. In under a second, he had swung again, using the opposite foot to pivot on and the embedded knife as a makeshift handhold, swiftly rolling his body across the gap from back to front. He crabbed in this manner across the entire length of the wall, using one blade then the other, pivoting off right foot then left, back over front until he had reached the firing slit beyond which he had judged the enemy forces to be barricaded.

The magenta-armoured warriors were so intent on the Luna Wolves pressing them to the front, they missed the five commandoes almost in their midst.

Faustus paused at the edge of the firing slit, sparing a glance at his four legionaries who had followed their captain's example precisely and now awaited his next order. Sheathing one of the blades, Faustus attached the krak grenades, moving over to the opposite side of the firing slit before he primed them.

He gave one last look at the others, before mouthing, 'Three, two...'

On one the incendiaries went off, erupting in a storm of stone shards, fire and pluming smoke. The men on the other side in the gallery choked on it. Those closest to the wall who had foolishly abandoned their posts were ripped apart in a flare of harsh, white light and knew nothing of their deaths. Others were mauled by the razor-edge stone shards. Some also caught on fire. Bodies were thrown inwards and bludgeoned into pieces by sheer concussive force.

But this was as nothing compared to what came in the wake of the explosion.

Faustus and his men were upon the enemy, the epitome of their savage namesake, howling and slitting throats with their blades.

Seeing the enemy stricken and distracted, Klaed ordered the headlong rush into their dwindling guns. The Luna Wolves took some hits but weathered the storm and struck the enemy mass like a threshing machine.

None were spare, but the slaughter was brief. In under thirty seconds, every man wearing magenta armour in the corridor was dead.

The last one who died was cut down by Faustus. He had been a sniper, his weapon resting in the next alcove along from where the Centurion had made the breach. It was locked on a tripod, its firing position fixed. Out of curiosity, Faustus looked down the scope. Just moved into the crosshairs, having broken through the induction gate was the captain of Tenth. Faustus didn't know his name and the warrior was gone in seconds anyway.

He smiled, though, amused at the fact this unknown officer would never realise how close he had come to death.

'You're very welcome,' whispered Faustus, before looking away.

Ten thousand years later…

CHAPTER ONE

Heletine, at the outskirts of Canticus

Three contrails from a trio of gunships scored through the dark sky over Canticus.

The city was burning. Ash and smoke from the fires had brought on premature night. War had transformed this place. In the grubby brown half-light, once regal statuary writhed in imagined torment, proud temples hung open like cracked corpses and the gilded streets turned black with spilled blood. It was, in every respect, a haunted landscape. Death stalked the streets, death and the nightmares that brought death with them – a legion in black, a legacy most foul and one that still yearned for some scrap of its former power and prestige.

The Thunderhawks wove through the chaos, banking and turning to keep the buildings between them and the torrent of flak fire spitting from the gun emplacements entrenched somewhere below. They were snub-nosed, boxy-looking vessels, their Salamanders green begrimed by the war. And they were not alone. The polluted sky over Canticus was choked by more than smoke alone – a battle equal in ferocity to that being fought on the ground was being contested in the air. Stormtalon interceptors engaged in sporadic dogfights with the draconic, winged daemon-engines of the Archenemy, as they tried to shepherd the larger landers. The enemy vessels were more like beasts of ancient myth, steel and dark anima combined. Their name 'Heldrake' was well earned.

The Thunderhawks lost their last outrider when the Stormtalon was set upon from above, a daemon-engine seizing the interceptor in its

17

claws and bearing it down into smoke and oblivion below.

Boosting their engines, the gunships increased speed, risking a more direct approach through the latticing flak fire to put some distance between them and the Heldrake. Wing-mounted bolters flaring, they strafed a landing zone ahead, committing to a rapid deployment dive.

From the roof of an old preceptory, an armour-clad warrior watched the gunships make their cargo drops into the heart of one of the city's war zones. Seven identical drops had taken place in the last hour. More would follow. Each transporter went in hot. The first carried a single war machine – a hulking Redeemer-class Land Raider, named for devastating heavy flamers – for only in fire could true repentance be found. The others had two battle tanks apiece, Predators. Ubiquitous amongst the Adeptus Astartes' armoury, these two were the less common Annihilators, armed with lascannons. In short, they were tank-killers.

The tracks of the five vehicles were already rolling at combat speed before touching down, weapon-targeting systems active and tracking movement. They hit the ground running with no break between land-ing and combat, before the Thunderhawks pulled away sharply, banking around with throaty pulses from their engines and disappearing intermit-tently behind great plumes of smoke.

Of the Heldrake, there was no sign. Perhaps it had been destroyed in the crash, or perhaps it had simply found other prey.

Drakgaard's focus was elsewhere, on the tanks and their mission. It had been a sacrifice to redeploy the armour. They would pay for that, and lose some of the bitter ground they had gained with blood and sweat. Canti-cus, even the world of Heletine itself, was demanding like that. She was a warren, a dark labyrinth. Little was taken for granted in such theatres of war, save for the vastness of the death toll.

Despite the massive destruction already wreaked against it, a proud and pious city stretched out in front of Drakgaard. Temples stood silhouetted against the gloom, and beneath their columnar and statued glory lurked a sprawl of streets and avenues. If the monolithic temples and shrineholds were the flesh, then the streets were its veins and arteries. Though those arteries were shedding freely and spilling lagoons of blood, there was still artistry to the city's claustrophobic design.

Possessed of a grim mien, the brother-captain seldom found much to enjoy in beauty. Some in the Chapter had whispered an iron hand would suit him better than a drake-scale mantle, but Drakgaard was Salamander from skin through to marrow. Yet, in spite of his quiet detractors, Drakgaard did wonder at what Canticus would have looked like before war had engulfed it.

With the fires that had broken out, very little remained of the city's geography that wasn't contested. Much of it was now in ruins, partly from brutal urban engagements and partly from the preliminary bombardment that had lasted four days and yielded little in the way of tactical traction for the allied Imperial commander.

Drakgaard looked upon his works from his vantage on the roof and saw only a long war of attrition ahead.

He had committed almost all of their strength to the taking of Canticus and the driving out of an entrenched enemy. Sixth Company's entire complement as well as assault elements from Fourth made up the Salamanders infantry and Sergeant Zantho had assembled a sizeable division of battle tanks to neutralise the heretics' heavy armour. Yet despite all of this formidable strength, the war was still a bitter grind.

It suited Drakgaard, it suited the Chapter. Meet them eye to eye and burn them out of their holes. The Salamanders had waged this way of war for centuries. None were as tenacious or as committed as the sons of Vulkan. He had been at Badab and Armageddon, Drakgaard knew the full meaning of 'attrition' – his body bore the scars in testament to the fact.

Were he able, Drakgaard would have smiled at the thought of past glories but his face was drawn up into a permanent snarl because of old injuries. He had several, and wore them proudly, more proudly than the many honours he had received in a long and distinguished career. A warrior was measured by his scars not his medals, or so the captain of Sixth believed. It was a trite belief, but one he clung to when the ache of old wounds became pronounced. Much like this day.

A three-dimensional representation of Canticus projected from a hololithic device revolved in front of Drakgaard. The transmission was poor, which made the image grainy and prone to breaks in resolution, but the story it told was clear.

Five major war zones across the world of Heletine, all being fought with fang and claw. To the equatorial south a predominantly Cadian force fought a guerrilla war for dominance of the Centari Mountains. Drakgaard had lent the Astra Militarum forces several squadrons of Stormtalons to leaven their war burden. Judging by the skies over Canticus, he might need to recall them soon. In the east, at Veloth, Sergeant V'reth of Third Squad held the fringe of the barren desert region and its few remote temples, supported by some minor Cadian armour and Sentinel squadrons. The city of Solist was all but destroyed, and only a token force skirmished over its remains now. Escadan was firmly in Imperial control and served as a muster point for the other major cities. An industrial region in the main, the heretics had paid it no mind, presumably deeming it of little tactical significance.

The rest had come to Canticus. It was here, Drakgaard was convinced, that the deadlock would finally break. He had but to find a way. He accessed a dispositional feed from his battle-helm prompting force organisational data to scroll down his left retinal lens.

The Cadian 81st were almost down to bare bones after being first responders to the crisis and bearing the brunt of the heretics' wrath and martial strength. The local defence forces were all but depleted or had defected. Drakgaard had witnessed sixteen separate firing squads that morning as the dogmatic Cadians sought to excise further traitors from the allied ranks. A thankless task, but one that fortunately did not burden the brother-captain.

The Salamanders held firm. They did so with honour, and according to the Promethean Creed. As commanding officer, it was Drakgaard's opportunity to expunge the stain on the Chapter's glory brought about by the troubled Third. Agatone had not taken kindly to his warriors being taken off the frontline. It had been five years since Nocturne, five years since a Lexicanium named Hazon Dak'ir had nearly destroyed them all. After the deaths of two captains and a verified record of renegade defections coming from within the ranks of the company, Drakgaard was not surprised when Chapter Master Tu'Shan had demanded a period of investigation and spiritual restoration.

It was the fire-born way, and now Drakgaard's star was in the ascendency. He resolved to conduct himself with honour, and bring glory back to the Salamanders. First, he had to win the war on Heletine.

His thoughts were disturbed by the sound of heavy boots tramping up the stairwell behind him.

'Chaplain,' said Drakgaard, recognising his visitor without needing to see him.

Elysius acknowledged the greeting with a nod. The black-armoured Chaplain stood a little taller than the captain, but not as wide, though the presence of a power fist served to bulk out his frame. Unlike Drakgaard, he wasn't wearing his helmet and had it mag-locked to his belt instead. His head was cleanly shorn, all the way down to the scalp. It shone like a smooth nub of onyx.

'I can't recall the last time I saw your face, brother-captain.'

Drakgaard didn't even spare Elysius a sideways glance. 'We are at war. Such things as helms are necessary when bad men are trying to kill you.'

'You know what I mean. Much is revealed by the face, the eyes in particular.'

'You of all of us should know something of the desire to hide one's face.'

'I did it out of shame and respect,' Elysius replied. 'What's your excuse?'

'Very well...'

With a hiss of escaping pressure, Drakgaard unlocked his helm from his gorget and lifted it off. Then he faced the Chaplain. He was a mess of scars and exposed muscle, only partially healed. In his left cheek, his molars were visible through the sizeable gouge in his skin.

'What do you see?' Drakgaard asked.

Elysius's expression softened marginally.

'Pain, a legacy of it.'

Drakgaard snorted, unimpressed with Elysius's attempts at camaraderie. He returned his helmet to its proper place.

'Is that all? By your sermonising tone I was expecting you to reveal some revelation of my character.'

'I need only hear your voice for that.'

Drakgaard didn't answer.

Since they had been talking, vox reports had been feeding in to Drakgaard's comm from the various battlefronts. None were directed at him personally, he just liked to keep abreast of developments. What he was hearing far from satisfied the captain. Despite their difficult relationship, he allowed himself to vent in front of the Chaplain.

'They are a horde, Elysius,' said Drakgaard, gesturing to the amorphous enemy below. There was little to see, even from the roof. The cultists and their dark masters had become little more than a homogenous mass. Now day was finally turning to night, vision was further impaired. Though, with all the smoke, the transition was difficult to appreciate. 'We should have broken them by now, and restored this world to the grace of the Throne.'

'Quite the pious sentiment, brother.'

'I am not without faith,' Drakgaard quickly replied, as if his pride had been wounded.

'Indeed, I apologise. Dug in, with knowledge of the terrain… They are more than just a horde, brother. Black Legion is a formidable enemy. They were like us once.'

'No longer,' Drakgaard scowled, unhappy with the direction the conversation was taking. 'And I have seen precious few actual Renegade Space Marines amongst the heretics to warrant considering them our main enemy here.'

'Rest assured, they are here and have been brutalising Cadians and turning what's left of the Heletine militia against us.'

'I am far from assured.' Drakgaard folded his arms. 'How easily some can fall to ruin…'

A strained silence fell between them that lasted a few seconds before Elysius replied.

'Have you set yourself in judgement too? Did your eyes see more than my own during Dak'ir's trial?'

'I have great respect for you, Elysius. Your record is beyond reproach but Third Company was ill-fated ever since the day it lost Ko'tan Kadai. Some believe that curse spread to all associated with it.' Drakgaard turned, his helmet's faceplate ever-snarling as if echoing his mood. 'I am no gifted dissembler–'

'Nor am I, brother. What are you insinuating?'

Drakgaard raised a placatory hand. 'Nothing. I merely speak and see plainly. There was something cankerous at the heart of the Third, and you were closer to it than most. Perhaps Agatone can reforge what has been broken, perhaps not…'

'And if not, then who? You, Ur'zan Drakgaard?'

Whatever Drakgaard felt at Elysius's intentional snipe was left unsaid as the low thrum of thrusters interrupted them.

Their attention was drawn skyward to another vessel. Not a gunship this time, but a lander.

Elyisus narrowed his eyes.

'You recognise that vessel,' said Drakgaard.

'I do. I've fought alongside their kind before. Although not this particular order.'

Like the Chaplain's armour, the ship was also black but that was where any affiliation ended. Through occluding smoke, the icon of a chalice became visible. The stylised cup dominated the underside of the lander and was depicted holding a stark white flame like a brazier.

'What was your appraisal?'

Stabiliser jets flared as the main engines died off and all forward momentum slackened to nothing. Eddies of dust and swirling smoke spun away as if retreating from the vessel as it hovered into a slow descent. Below, Imperial engineers and labourers scattered as a Salamanders command squad approached the landing zone with weapons at ease but ready.

'You have not fought with the Adepta Sororitas before, then, brother-captain?' asked Elysius.

'You mean beside.'

Elysius looked confused.

'Beside, not with.'

'I know what I meant.'

Drakgaard shook his head.

'They are good fighters,' Elysius continued. 'Not Adeptus Astartes, but resolute, determined.'

'That all?'

As the ship emerged through the smoke, so did several others, all armoured in black with the sigil of a chalice on their flanks and underside. Some were smaller with the aspect and armament of gunships.

'No. They're fanatics. Only their brand of fanaticism is sanctioned.'

'Brand? Is that supposed to be humorous, Brother-Chaplain?'

The ships touched down on the landing field, a host of ground crew hustling back and forth in the resultant dust storm kicked up by a host of descent thrusters. Whilst the ground crews coughed behind their sleeves, trying to keep the grit from their eyes and waving to their comrades in an attempt to exert some order on the unexpected arrivals, Drakgaard's warriors stood and watched. To the practised military eye, they had formed a defensive perimeter.

'Believe me, brother, there is nothing amusing about the Order of the Ebon Chalice,' Elysius concluded.

Then they descended the stairs from the preceptory, and went to meet the Sisters of Battle.

CHAPTER TWO

Heletine, Canticus southern war zone

The ambush had come swiftly, leaving Va'lin and his brothers pinned down and estranged from their commanding officer.

Sergeant Iaptus was further up the street, shouting vainly against the din of exploding shells and solid shot raining down on half his squad. Even through the carnage, Va'lin could see Iaptus had his storm shield raised and was using it to ward off the worst of the frag.

From a distance he looked angry, the hammer in his gauntleted fist rippling with energy to match his rising temper. No warrior ever liked to be trapped by his enemy, especially when he was used to soaring across the battlefield on jets of fire.

Va'lin activated the vox-feed in his battle-helm. Comms had been scratchy ever since the last hit. He saw Iaptus nod then smack the vocaliser of his own helm and after a few seconds of crackling static, the sergeant's voice bled through.

'Push up with the rest of the squad...' He battle-signed to a tower forti-fied by flak board and razor-wire. From it, a static cannon emplacement was ripping up most of the plaza where his squad were currently hemmed in. 'Neutralise that gun nest then we re-take the high ground and move west along–'

An explosion interrupted the sergeant's orders, forcing him back into cover as the heretics brought up a pair of rocket crews.

Two infantry squads in varying degrees of combat efficacy were currently stymied until Iaptus could establish territorial dominance.

A burst of flame drew Va'lin's attention as Brother Herador maintained the small cordon the Salamanders did control.

With the Space Marines essentially penned in by heavy artillery from above, the heretic infantry forces were attempting to overrun them on the ground. They hadn't reckoned on Salamanders' tenacity.

The street where the fire-born hunkered down was broad and long, offering little in the way of cover. They had been marching in dispersed formation when the attack came. The area was supposed to have been cleared, but something got through. A battalion's worth of something.

As soon as the ambush hit, after Agrek and Nemis went down, the rest of the Salamanders darted into alcoves and doorways. Black Legion Havocs in the buildings overlooking the road were quick to establish a punitive firing pattern. Hard, barking chatter from autocannons and heavy bolters became a constant drone.

Three separate breakouts were attempted. All failed. The last one had killed Kra'tor. He was lying face down in the middle of the road, his armour shot to pieces.

Snatching glimpses of their enemy between salvoes, Va'lin counted three squads of legionnaires. The rest were cultists, a ragged band of half-armoured but well-supplied human soldiery. Some, judging by their scratched out livery, were ex-Heletine defenders. Man was easy prey for Chaos. His fear and selfishness made him weak. Va'lin tried not to despise the turncoats for that – they had merely succumbed to instinct. It didn't mean he would find any impediment to ending their lives, however. For once on the path to damnation, even a single footstep cannot be taken back. Zen'de had once said that, and all Salamanders heeded his wisdom. Chaos was a moral choice, not a disease. The mind had to be willing, for the spirit to suffer.

'Must be close to fifty or sixty up there.' The voice that came from Va'lin's left belonged to Naeb and was altogether too eager. He wore a Mark VI battle-helm with an extended nose cone. Part of the helmet's structure had also been altered to accommodate a bionic eye in place of the left retinal lens.

'Are you concerned for your safety, brother? I can protect you.'

Naeb laughed, the humour suited him. 'Your protection? Now that is something to be feared.'

In the wake of the explosion, the smoke concealing Iaptus and the rest of the squad was clearing. They were less than twenty metres in front of them, but with the amount of solid shot and las-shot stitching the rock-crete between the two halves of the squad it may as well have been a gulf. Va'lin's tactical display reported no casualties.

Iaptus's comm-rune lit up again, interrupting Va'lin and Naeb.

'Belay order to advance, and hold position. Air support inbound.'

'He's pinned,' said Naeb, afforded an enhanced view through his bionic. The explosion had been a marker and now every targeter the Black Legionnaires had was aimed at Iaptus and his half of the squad.

Va'lin scoured the rooftops. The jump pack felt heavy on his back. He had not been an Assault Marine long, but he already felt the same frustration as the veterans in his squad at their wings being metaphorically clipped.

'We're useless down here,' he muttered.

Still no point of entry presented itself through the enemy's defences, but amidst the smoke he did see a third squad of heavies moving up. More power armour, toting lascannons and plasma guns, enough to wipe out all three Salamanders squads.

'How long for that air support, sergeant?' Va'lin asked over the vox.

'Soon, just be ready.'

Va'lin switched the feed to Sergeant Kessoth, who was leading the stalled infantry wave on the opposite side of the street.

'Sergeant Kessoth, can you advance and concentrate fire on that roof?' Va'lin rune-marked the location on his tac-display and transferred it to the sergeant's feed.

There was a slight pause before Kessoth's deep voice responded.

'In Vulkan's name, we will try, brother.'

In the street, the other squad intensified their return fire but it was largely ineffective. Seven muzzle flares roared into life, while at the same time Kessoth led his men out into the open, pushing for an advanced position and a better line of fire.

'If he makes that run, we must be ready to move,' said Va'lin.

Naeb nodded, then battle-signed to the rest of the squad who were strung out along the street in alcoves and doorways. Two crouched down behind Kessoth's upturned Rhino that the sergeant's squad had been quick to vacate before it exploded. The wreck was still burning, and spewing smoke.

Above the stricken Imperial troops came the unmistakable engine drone of a Stormtalon.

On the rooftop, the third Havoc squad rushed into position, trying to put some cover between themselves and the aerial threat. Several cultists turned and levelled weapons at the gunship. The high-pitched whine of an assault cannon superseded the engine drone. Fourteen cultists were sprayed across the adjoining rooftops, rendered to bloody chunks by the Stormtalon's spinning nose-mount.

The gunship hove into view, weapons flaring. It chased down a second group of cultists who had fled at the sight of their disintegration and were headed for a way off the roof.

Kessoth pushed up. His squad was taking fire, and through the carnage Va'lin thought he saw one of the fire-born crumple from a direct lascannon hit but his view was obscured and uncertain.

He glanced back to Sergeant Iaptus, still hemmed in and taking heavy fire.

'Get ready,' he voxed to the others.

They would need to break cover and quickly boost jump packs. A single thrust should provide enough elevation to climb the first roof. From there they could–

A sudden, ululating screech shattered Va'lin's battle plan.

Something fast, a flyer, swept in overhead.

The Stormtalon saw it too. Its left turbofan switched to maximum rotation as the gunship tried to turn. The underslung assault cannon was pivoting on its limited axis when a shadow descended on the gunship. In seconds its glacis was ripped away, the pilot with it. Va'lin saw his flailing body fall to the ground somewhere below. His eyes met those of the pilot's slayer.

Neck craned over its kill, wings at full span, it was akin to some immense but metallic bird of prey. The uglier truth was this was a daemon-engine, something that had once been a man and machine but had been turned, through the ruin of Chaos, into an abomination.

Shrieking a war cry, the monstrous Heldrake cast the wreckage of the Stormtalon down and soared up into smoke and shadow. Distant las-fire chased it from somewhere deep in the city. It was enough to force the monster to disengage but too late to save the Stormtalon.

It fell like a dying angel, striking the ground with lethal finality. A second explosion rocked the embattled Salamanders as the burning gunship hit Kessoth and his squad, who were scattered by the blast.

The cheer that went up from the cultists dragged down on Va'lin's resolve like an anchor as did the sight of Kessoth's squad being so brutally neutralised.

Before the smoke had cleared, heavy fire came down again from the towers and forced what was left of the battered Salamanders who were in the open into retreat.

'Merciful Vulkan…' Naeb watched the beleaguered warriors drag their sergeant with them, leaving two more for the Apothecary's reductor.

Va'lin's attention was on the second Havoc squad, scrambling back across the rooftops now the threat of the gunship had been ruthlessly dealt with. There was no sign of the murderous Heldrake, but its contribution had been telling. Unmolested, the Havocs could circle around and find a vantage over Iaptus's position. Without cover, the sergeant and the fire-born with him would be annihilated.

'Sergeant Iaptus, enemy high to your flank–' Va'lin's warning stopped short when the dead return came back. The vox was down again. 'Blood of the primarch...' he swore. Driven back into cover, neither half of the squad had a good sight line to the other.

Va'lin half turned, careful to give the bulky jump pack he was wearing some room.

'Battle-sign ineffective...'

'Plan beta?' asked Naeb.

'Two krak grenades on this wall. We effect an insertion, work our way up through the structure.'

'If this fails, brother, we bring the wall down on top of us, reduce our cover to rubble and become target practice for those Havocs up there.'

'Then hope it does not fail.'

'Affirmative.'

Both pinned their charges in place and primed them. Then they hunkered down, Va'lin on one side, Naeb the other. The rest of the squad waited as the tactical feed through their retinal lenses divulged the strategy.

'Sergeant Kadoran,' Va'lin addressed the only officer he had comms with who was still conscious, 'we are effecting an insertion and will attempt to gain a counterattacking vector through the structure. Hold firm.'

'Holding, brother,' replied Kadoran. 'Bring them hell.'

'Firing!' cried Naeb a second later. An explosion rippled across the street but not from enemy incendiaries this time. Hot air, dust and debris plumed out in a wide, expanding cone from the point where the Salamanders had attached their krak grenades. As the smoke began to clear, a ragged hole large enough for a Space Marine was revealed.

'Ingress now!'

Naeb led them in, Va'lin hanging back to usher in the rest.

Once far enough inside, the noise from the street lessened but only marginally. It was dark, the city evacuated several weeks ago, and cluttered with debris. Part of the upper floor had caved in after some previous bombardment. A wide lobby area was dominated by an ornamental prayer fountain. Clouded by dust, the water in the fountain was rimmed at the edges where a ruddy scum had developed. Pieces of broken masonry, timber and brickwork from the sundered upper floors jutted from its shallow basin.

Quickly establishing a perimeter, the five fire-born led by Va'lin tromped noisily across the lower floor. Debris crunched underfoot and they smashed bodily through the remains of a narrow doorframe. Urgency fuelled their steps, and the certain knowledge that if they delayed their sergeant and the rest of their squad were dead.

Across a long hallway a shaft of light indicated a breach in the ceiling and a possible route onto the roof.

'Move up,' Va'lin said quietly across the vox.

They moved in single file with Ky'dak at the back maintaining rear-guard. Targeters bled grainy red sight lines into the darkness but picked up on nothing. By now, the squad had switched to low light vision through their retinal lenses, but so far nothing stood out. It was a large space, badly damaged and that meant a lot of places to hide.

Reaching the shaft of light, the Salamanders found themselves in a stairway large enough to accommodate the squad. A few splintered timbers and the odd broken balustrade intruded into a potential jump route that led all the way to the roof.

Brother Sor'ad stepped up to clear the wreckage and put a larger hole in the ceiling through which the light was filtering. He got his bolt pistol to head height when something hit him... hard, and flung him across the room.

Sor'ad hit the wall, his bolt pistol up and firing. Brass shells bounced off a hide of hulking war-plate, its servos groaning with the effort of propelling a Terminator-armoured monster across the room.

Va'lin reacted, releasing a jet of promethium from his flamer just as Sor'ad's hand was severed from his wrist, taking his sidearm with it. The burr of the Terminator's chainblade sounded like a challenge as he turned to declare his allegiance to his enemies in some dark tongue.

Clad in thick black battleplate with a stiffened topknot of indigo hair rising from the crown of his head, the Terminator was massive, easily twice as wide as the power-armoured Assault Marines and half again as tall.

Though he wore the Eye of Horus and sigil of the Despoiler, the Terminator was not a pureblood warrior of the Black Legion. Human flesh stretched across his immense chest plate, strips of skin like gonfalons hanging from his greaves and shoulder guards. Each cured and leathery offering was daubed with the crescent rune of Slaanesh, the Chaos god of carnal pleasures and excess. Many warbands had gone on bended knee before the one they called 'Warmaster', and he had accepted them all and seen his legions grow. This particular horde called themselves the Children of Torment, revelling in the torture and pain they had subjected Heletine to.

That legacy of pain continued with Sor'ad.

With a growl that came closer to ecstasy than fury, the black-clad Terminator plunged the churning teeth of his chainblade into Sor'ad's torso. Driven by the traitor's immense strength and mounted to a power fist, the Salamander was brutally gutted.

Naeb roared, voicing his anguish at the sight of a brother slain so callously, and went in with his chainsword. None could fault Naeb's bravery but he was outmatched and the Terminator swatted him aside even as he lifted Sor'ad off his feet, impaled on the still turning chainblade. Blood fountained against the monster's graven armour, drooling into sigils and the simulacra of screaming faces. For a moment as they drank in the blood, it was as if they actually were screaming and Va'lin shook his head to banish the image from his mind.

He triggered his flamer again, sending a gout of promethium over the monster and forcing him back a step. Time was slipping away, precious seconds that could make the difference between life and death for Iaptus and the others, but this monster had come as if from nowhere.

'Naeb, the roof...' Va'lin gestured to the upper floor.

Naeb was back on his feet and eager for vengeance but duty prevailed.

Dersius and Ky'dak were circling the monster. He had no helmet, his face ravaged by conflict and the entropy of the warp. Spiked chains hung from his battle-gear, which was ancient and war-beaten. Mounted to his wrist were two bolters, combined to fire in unison. It was archaic, not as potent as the storm bolters used by the Chapter Terminators, but could still tear an armoured Space Marine apart with enough concentration of firepower. Muzzle flash brightened the gloom, and the heavy boom of bolter shells accompanied it.

Ky'dak boosted to avoid the storm of rounds spitting from the combi-bolter. Dersius was about to attack when Va'lin stopped him.

'Go now!'

Ky'dak was grounded where the ceiling jutted over him, but Naeb and Dersius soared upward on tongues of flame, their twin fusillade clearing the wreckage above. The backwash from their boosted jump packs spilled down into the room below, filling it with a conflagration.

Va'lin crouched and let the fire wash over his armour, seeking Ky'dak through the heat haze.

A glancing hit from the Terminator's chainfist sent Ky'dak sprawling and half-wrenched his helmet off. Ky'dak did the rest, tearing away the seals between helm and gorget with his gauntleted hand. Eyes like burning coals glared back at the monster. Like all sons of Nocturne, Ky'dak's skin was onyx-black. It was almost invisible in the darkness. In his anger, his eyes became dagger-slits of blood red.

The Terminator charged Ky'dak, and at the same time Va'lin pushed himself up into a run, tossing a frag grenade in the monster's midst. The close detonation staggered the Terminator, but not for long. He also turned, his hellish glare fixed on Va'lin who stood his ground and braced his flamer.

With a brief spurt of ignition, Ky'dak leapt onto the Terminator's back and thrust downward with his chainsword, finding the gap between gorget and neck. Pipes, cabling and servo lines were all shredded. Spitting machine oil quickly became blood as the churning teeth bit into flesh.

'Burn it!' Ky'dak snarled, shouting to be heard.

Va'lin fed the Terminator a burst of promethium, dousing the monster's torso and face. Ky'dak snarled as the flames lapped up and over him too, but clung on as his foe flailed and stomped. His hair was on fire, but Ky'dak would not relent and roared through the pain.

Bellowing, trying to dislodge the Salamander on his back, the Terminator brought up his combi-bolter. As his arm came around, brass shells roaring from the gun mouth, Va'lin charged. Boosted across the room by his jump pack, he hit the Terminator hard and forced his aim. A shell clipped Ky'dak, tearing him off the monster's back, but three more punched through the Terminator's skull and detonated.

Decapitated, combi-bolter still chugging out rounds into the floor, the Terminator staggered one more step and then fell.

Ky'dak's chainsword was still lodged in the stump of what remained of the monster's head. He was getting to his feet and going over to retrieve the weapon when Va'lin asked, 'Where did that thing come from?'

Ky'dak shook his head, wrenching his blade free. It was damaged, some of the teeth were broken and the motor had given out.

'Machine-spirit be damned,' he hissed.

Va'lin peered into the shadows from where the attack had first come but could see nothing of significance. When he was certain nothing else was coming out of the dark at them, he looked up.

'Are you injured?' he asked.

'Just wrathful.'

Ky'dak's eyes blazed without his battle-helm, but it was something cold and hollow that burned behind them.

Craning their necks towards where Naeb and Dersius had forced a path through the ceiling, both Salamanders got into position then simultaneously engaged their jump engines. They burst up through the roof, trailing fire into a murky night clouded with smoke. They found their comrades quickly. Naeb and Dersius were already amongst the Havocs, having joined up with Iaptus and the others.

A second squad of renegades had moved into position after Va'lin's battle-brothers, intending to bracket them in, but were surprised when two further Salamanders emerged amongst them.

Ky'dak was first to react. He impaled one legionnaire in the neck, ramming his dulled chainsword through the warrior's gorget like a pike. Va'lin torched the other two with a short burst of fiery promethium, letting his partner finish them as they cooked in their armour.

'Fire and blood, they're everywhere,' snarled Ky'dak, searching for the next fight.

From his vantage on the rooftop, Va'lin's gaze was drawn downward.

An armoured column was moving in from the west. Five vehicles. He recognised the tank commander riding up in the cupola, Akadin Zantho. Two more, heavy-armoured Vindicators, rolled in from the north as well as a pair of massive Redeemers. In the streets below, what Va'lin could see of them, the cultists panicked. The legionnaires held on grimly, the other Havocs turning their autocannons and heavy bolters on the Salamanders tanks.

One of the Predators ground to a halt, its turret rising as solid shot ricocheted ineffectually off its hull. Twin-linked side sponson mounts angled in unison to meet the same target. The hum of power generators grew to a shriek as the capacitors reached a critical mass and unleashed laser death on the Havocs. Power armour shredded apart like flakboard as three more equally potent salvoes lanced from the other Predators.

In a few violent, energy-charged seconds, the Havocs were gone with only a faint crackle of corposant to mark their destruction. The cannons swung around on their turrets, tracking fresh targets and vaporising cultists with every energy discharge.

With a command Va'lin couldn't hear over the battle, Zantho unleashed the Redeemers. Avenues and tunnels, all the clandestine crawl spaces the heretics had used to effect their ambush were filled with flame. He'd seen enough.

Va'lin urged Ky'dak onwards and as the burning below commenced, the Assault Marines leapt into one of the heretic gun nests and cut down its crew. Most were already running anyway, and the Salamanders snarled at the backs of their foes as they fled. It didn't stop either one shooting them down. An enemy unwilling to fight face to face and eye to eye was worthy only of contempt and so would be put down thusly. The deaths of the crew were scarcely footnotes in an ongoing saga of the war on Heletine. After that, heretical resistance crumbled as the will to fight bled from them.

It bled all over the streets in runnels.

Scraps of the fleeing cultists survived, as vermin always did even when faced with a cleansing fire. Some reached tunnels, hidden culverts and side streets. Their escape would afford them a little more life. It would be measured in minutes or days only. Salamanders were patient. They could wait until the fire became a conflagration for all these thrice-damned souls to burn in.

Zantho rode down the rest, watching impassively from his Land Raider's cupola as cultists fell screaming beneath the tracks. It was not music to his ears, as some warriors might claim; it was merely war. But that did not make it any less satisfying. He had a vengeful streak, the tank commander. He found it amply slaked in those final moments of the battle.

* * *

Va'lin watched as Ky'dak wrecked the autocannon that had been strafing the road. With the battle over, there seemed little else to occupy his fading need for violence. Below, the remnants of Kessoth's and Kadoran's squads had moved into the open and were laying down fire on the other towers and weapon emplacements. One tower collapsed, seemingly capitulating against the onslaught. Another simply fell silent, an empty shell haunted by terrified ghosts who had looked true fury in the eye and blinked. Salamanders had that effect.

'With Zantho here,' said Ky'dak, stepping up to the edge of the cavernous hole they had used to breach the tower, 'that means he has either secured the northern district of the city in much shorter order than any of us could have hoped or...'

Va'lin absorbed the scene below too and guessed at the other warrior's inference. 'He has surrendered it on Captain Drakgaard's orders, to pull our souls from hellfire.'

'Takes the edge off, doesn't it.'

Va'lin did not answer. Sigils daubed in what he assumed was blood on the walls had caught his eye.

As a Space Marine, he was largely immune to such debased iconography, but it sent a twinge of unease running through him.

He doused the sigils in fire, before muttering, 'Strange...'

'What is?' asked Ky'dak, turning around to face him.

Even Chaos sigils had a pattern. They were each fashioned in such a way as to show and garner allegiance from some daemonic patron. The blood-graffiti in the nest conflicted, as if more than one potentate of Ruin were being called upon. It led Va'lin to speculate how many enemies were on Heletine and which of those had yet to reveal themselves. Ever was it the way with Chaos in his experience. Nothing was ever as it seemed, a fact that extended to an incident during his Scout training back on Nocturne. The memory grew sharp in his mind. Distant gunfire, the last echoes of a battle fought and won, brought him back. No sense in lingering on that now.

'Nothing,' he lied, letting his suspicions rest. Master of Recruits Ba'ken had always remonstrated Va'lin for his over inquisitive mind, and here he was again. Part of him wished Ba'ken were here now – his wisdom would be greatly appreciated – but Va'lin had left him behind on Nocturne. That door was closed to him. It wasn't even his home world. That too was gone, and how he missed it.

He rejoined Ky'dak as he looked out of the sundered gun nest.

The battle was over, the tanks had seen to that and Salamanders infantry was quickly mopping up what little resistance did remain.

'What happened in the stairwell, brother?' he asked.

Ky'dak looked confused.

'We fought and killed an enemy combatant. I don't follow.'

'There was a death wish in your eyes,' said Va'lin. 'I've seen rage like that before and *his* path was far from glorious.'

'Speak plainly, Va'lin. We have been battle-brothers for only a short time but you've never been cryptic with me. Don't start now. Who do I remind you of?'

'Very well. He was a Firedrake, a sergeant before that. Zek Tsu'gan.'

Ky'dak recognised the name. 'The defector?'

'No one has said he defected.'

'But they're hunting him?'

'Yes.'

'And you're likening me to him?'

'You are as reckless as he was. You fought as one, not a squad. You defied every combat doctrine.'

Ky'dak scowled, abruptly disinterested.

'We are alive, he is not. You're a pragmatist, Va'lin. I've heard you don't always follow orders directly. I thought you would understand.'

'Improvisation and adaption, not a reckless desire to kill or die in the attempt no matter the cost.'

'When Iaptus takes issue with my tactics, then I shall listen. Until then…' Ky'dak shouldered Va'lin out of the way, and put one foot on the lip of the ragged window crater. 'I follow my own doctrine, brother. It's simple,' he said, half turning so Va'lin could see the coldness of his eyes again. 'Do whatever it takes to win.'

Iaptus was below with the others.

'Time to regroup,' said Ky'dak and leapt from the window.

Va'lin followed, descending from the seven-storey tower on heat hazing jets of thrust from his jump pack.

Rockcrete split underfoot as he landed hard, sending out a web of impact cracks across the roadway.

He saw Ky'dak nod to their comrades, who returned similarly restrained responses. Taciturn, perceived as maudlin, even distant, Ky'dak had few he would consider friends. Va'lin, however, was welcomed back warmly. Dersius clapped him on the shoulder. Even Naeb, who was suffering with an injury from where the Terminator had struck him, managed a half-embrace.

'In Vulkan's name, brother.'

With the battle effectively over, Naeb had clamped his war-helm to his thigh. His breathing was a little laboured but he smiled broadly at his friend.

'You led us from that death trap, Va'lin, and Iaptus knows it.'

Iaptus, his ornate weapons now sheathed to his armour, approached. His face was as stern as always but he allowed a tiny crack in his stony facade.

'Well met, Va'lin.'

Unlike the others, Iaptus wore a veteran's battleplate. His Mark III, so-called 'iron armour' had scales worked into the cuirass and greaves. Even his jump pack was ornate, each of the exhaust vents crafted to resemble a drake's snarling mouth.

Every time he saw him, Va'lin was reminded of everything he wanted to be and how he wished to serve.

'Brother-sergeant.' Va'lin's tone bordered on reverent, and he bowed his head before meeting Iaptus's gaze again.

'You have my gratitude and the gratitude of this squad, brother. I shall see to it Captain Drakgaard hears of your bravery and ingenuity.'

'I was not alone. My brothers,' Va'lin gestured to Dersius, Naeb and Ky'dak, 'were alongside me.'

'Shoulder to shoulder,' said Naeb proudly.

Dersius nodded.

Ky'dak gave a faint sniff of what might have been contempt. Va'lin bristled but let it go.

'I was merely doing my duty, sergeant,' he said instead.

'Aye, and well,' Iaptus replied.

'As my masters have instructed.'

'Not well enough for Sor'ad,' said Ky'dak, somewhat acerbically. 'He lies dead, his duty ended.'

Iaptus turned to the other Salamander.

'And he will be missed. Sepelius will be here soon.' Iaptus gestured to Naeb. 'Get him to the Apothecary as soon as Sepelius has harvested the fallen. I don't want us to be further under strength for whatever our captain would have us do next. I must convene with Sergeant Zantho. Va'lin… The squad is yours until I return.'

Iaptus turned to go to speak with Zantho, leaving Va'lin with the others.

Dersius pointed towards the edge of the city district where a host of Rhinos was making its way along the crater-strewn road.

'There,' he said. 'Sepelius will be amongst them.'

'Then carry me, brother,' Naeb replied, staggering, 'for I think my Larraman's cells have been overly taxed already.' Blood was still leaking freely from his damaged plastron, but he managed to smile thinly.

'You will need a Techmarine to look at that armour too, brother,' added Dersius, supporting Naeb under the shoulder. Together, the two began limping towards the oncoming entourage of support vehicles.

'Does your stoic pragmatism ever meet with empathy or sympathy, brother?' Naeb gibed with good humour. 'Or are you simply absent those parts of your personality?'

Dersius was a broad-shouldered warrior, easily the stockiest in the squad. He was a methodical thinker, dogged and determined but not predisposed towards command. For a few seconds he stared blankly at Naeb until he realised he was gently being made fun of.

Va'lin was certain his booming laughter would be heard all the way back at camp.

Ky'dak was about to follow, when Va'lin grabbed his arm to stop him.

'You and I will speak again, Ky'dak.'

'Oh yes? Have you not already said your piece, brother?' He didn't look remotely concerned about being physically restrained. Privately, Va'lin wondered how far he could push this before Ky'dak reacted.

'Whatever your issue towards me, I won't have it mar the efficacy of this squad.'

'Mar the efficacy?' He lowered his voice. 'Do you hear yourself, Va'lin? Iaptus's backslap has gone to your head, brother. This squad is ninety per cent efficacious. It has been thus since we lost Sor'ad. I have no "distemper" towards you. I am angry for reasons you could not understand, but I assure you, brother,' he leaned in close and slowly removed Va'lin's hand from his arm, 'they have absolutely nothing to do with you.'

A little on the back foot, Va'lin let him go.

Questions could wait. Some had waited years, ever since the fire canyons on Nocturne and what he had seen amidst the smoke. Ky'dak and the Terminator they had killed, and the conflicting sigils in the gun nest were the latest but also the most pressing. As he followed after Ky'dak, a thought went through his head.

Vulkan ward us from whatever is to come.

An ill feeling was growing within him. Ever since they had set foot on Heletine, it had been there, almost like a premonition.

CHAPTER THREE
Elsewhere

Xarko smelled the burning. It surrounded him, emanating from a sea of fire.

A spur of dark rock like an unfurled tongue stretched out from the safety of the bank over endless magma. Xarko was standing upon its precipice, looking down into grey palls of pyroclastic smoke.

Above, there was no sky, no earth. Only darkness reigned – eternal, amorphous and unnatural.

No armour, no protection of any kind covered Xarko's body, yet the flames spitting up at him did not burn. Not even when they touched his naked skin and sizzled against flesh before dissipating into formless smoke did they cause him harm.

This raiment of fire had become his mantle. He embraced it, and the sheer destructive power of the mountain. Her name was Deathfire. The ancient tribes had called it so, and thus it ever was and would be. Surrounded by its heartblood, Xarko stood at Deathfire's subterranean epicentre and exulted. He closed his eyes. With the shimmering heat haze and the smoke he was almost blind anyway. The fire became a sudden omnipresence, a sentient and blazing ocean. In many ways, more than Xarko realised in that moment, it was.

Senses now fully engaged, he drank in the heady atmosphere and used it to marshal his thoughts. Waves churned and roared. Ash and earth were redolent on the hot breeze and borne aloft on eddies of steam. Xarko wished to rise with them but knew his destination was below, deep within the merciless currents.

With the rock sharp and gritty underfoot, his bare skin prickling at its touch, Xarko committed his mind and soul… and leapt from the spur.

For a fleeting moment, he felt peace. Suspended in midair, as if held in aspic, a strange transcendence overcame Xarko. Then the fire sea opened its maw wide and swallowed him. There was no pain, only reluctance as if admittance into these lower depths was uncertain. But after overcoming this brief inertia, Xarko began to descend.

In spite of the preparations he had made, the experience was disconcerting at first. Eventually, he allowed the currents to take him. As he sank into endless flame, he recalled the myths of old Nocturne, like Ullyus dragged down to the hell maelstrom by his anvil, or Kar'dra, who failed to outswim the drake Bhaargal on the Acerbian Sea, or Gheliah, who sank to his doom in the Gey'sarr Ocean wrestling the serpents of Okesh.

Xarko was no mythic hero of Nocturne, though he relished recalling their deeds. Yet, here he was on the fire sea, cut adrift just like in those sagas of old. The memories armoured him, more potent than any suit of ceramite and adamantium ever could in this place. With a final push, he reached the bottom of the ocean and almost simultaneously breached the surface, emerging into a twilit world.

Hard iron chains wrapped around his ankles, the weight of their small anvils dragging at him but also anchoring him. The stronger his mental state, the more inviolate the chains became, the tougher each link would be. By anchoring his body in this place, they were also anchoring his mind. Seeing and feeling the mental tethers, however illusory it all was, made it easier to believe they were actually there. In this place, belief was reality. Without the anvils… well, he did not want to consider what kind of fate that could lead to.

Alone, he beheld a night-black ocean, one that reached to the edge of sight and beyond. A storm was rising, driving the sea into turbulent waves with their crests ablaze. Firelight dappled the water like frenzied flecks of pigment. Images resolved, painted on this dark canvas by an unseen hand.

To Xarko they resembled faces. Some, he knew, were old; others, yet to be. Boundless, formless chronology unfolded before him. He had but to swim in it to learn its secrets.

The storm was perturbing, though. He had not expected it. Turmoil was common in this other realm but not like this. Something was wrong; something external was trying to exert its influence.

Xarko swam, braving whatever tumult had seized the ocean. Fear was an enemy he could ill afford. His training and conditioning had rendered the concept alien. Here, both would be tested. Despite the tempestuous waters, he knew these straits and their perils. Predators did not take long to come. Drawn by Xarko's soul-flame they appeared as shadows at first, a darker sliver on an already black background. Three shapes resolved soon after, spear-tips of coal knifing through an ocean limned in red.

A great swell of water was rising. Xarko went perpendicular to the tide, swimming hard against the edge of a growing wave. The anvils, rather than hold him down, began to slip. Only force of will kept them manacled. Driving furiously, arm over arm, legs beating hard, he risked a glance over his shoulder… and smiled.

The coal-black hunters were following.

He swam on, all the while the currents shifting below him, the tide ever pulling. As he raced, he heard voices, half snatched before the roar of the flaming sea carried them hence. In the fiery-wreathed depths, he half glimpsed faces that were about to resolve before they too were dashed by the ocean's fury.

The wave was rising, curling, and in a moment it would break.

Xarko rose with it, his body screaming. The hunters gave chase, darting after him like flung spears. Xarko reached the wave crest just as it crashed. He crested the peak with a last surge of strength and the hunters, fractionally behind him, were smashed apart. Gasping, Xarko rolled gently down the back of the wave. The tumult ended, and the sea was calm again.

Taking a few moments to gather up his depleted strength, Xarko heard the voices return. One rose to prominence amongst the clamour. Whomever it had, did or would belong to cried out in anguish. The tides began to rise again, this time a reflection of the mental turmoil expressed through the twilit ocean rather than the incursion of neverborn entities.

Xarko turned, trying to discern a pattern to the images painted in fire upon the water. He thought he saw a face, locked in a silent scream before it grew too wide and ate itself in a fount of spume.

An echo faded with the image, two words, difficult to grasp.

Ferro ignis.

Yes, that was it.

Fire sword.

Xarko had no idea as to its meaning.

He wanted to delve deeper, find truth within the tides, but another voice wrenched him back. Unlike the cry he had heard across the ocean, Xarko recognised this one and allowed his mental tethers to unravel. One by one, the chain links around his ankles unpicked themselves and fell into the sea where they dissolved like ash. Slowly, deliberately, Xarko detached mind and body from this realm and awoke in another… aboard a spaceship.

Transition from the other realm to the one of matter and substance was not immediate. Xarko first became aware of the chamber around him. His psychically heightened senses slowly faded in a diminishing pulse, like an echo reaching its aural terminus. He felt the ship, the souls aboard, his Librarian's eye seeing everything in a burst of psychic sonar.

Engines were at full stop, anchor was laid and the low thrum of life support systems barely intruded on the quietude. Serfs roamed the corridors, performing such circadian rhythms as was required of them, but it was almost ghost-like on the *Forge Hammer*.

The ship was slumbering. Ever since the seekers had departed, a state of dormancy had descended upon those left behind as if their existence was held fast in amber until the others returned to report their findings.

In his darkened chamber, Xarko drank in the silence and absorbed the shadows. His crouched form exuded steam. Wisps of white vapour rose up into the air filtration systems of the frigate. On his perch nearby a *drygnirr* with blue scales and a yellow crest cawed and snapped.

'I see it, no need to shout, Kraelish,' Xarko murmured, still coming around from his journey across the fire tides.

A vox hail lit up the console in front of him.

'Speak,' said Xarko.

'It's me,' a stern voice answered. 'We've found the ship.'

The feed was a little broken, unclear. Atmospheric interference had been fouling communications. Either that, or Agatone was leading his men further down into the hive.

'Anything else?' asked Xarko.

'Just ash, brother.' Agatone left a short pause before saying, 'Your voice is slurred, Codicier. I thought Vel'cona advised you to limit your time trawling the fire tides.'

'I'm just tired, brother-captain,' Xarko lied. 'No need for concern.'

Another pause as Agatone considered his response.

'Have you heard anything from the others?' he asked.

Xarko used the console to activate a screen. Weak light bled from it, illuminating his features. They were sharp, angular. Not uncommon in Nocturnean psykers. His eyes glowed a deep crimson but there was the faintest trace of cerulean blue there also, as his recent exertion of power had yet to fade completely.

Three sigils were lit up on the screen, one of which was active. Below each sigil, lines of biorhythmic data identified each individual member of all three hunt-teams. A chrono-stamp indicated their last recorded communication. Two had been silent for several hours.

'Nothing. They made planetfall, but all quiet since then. Yours is the first voice I've heard in a while, brother-captain.'

Agatone paused to give orders to the other warriors in his hunt-squad, before resuming his conversation with Xarko.

'Lok went west into the tunnel complex, Clovius north to the silos.

Down here, taking any direction is like entering a labyrinth.'

'Our father faced a similar trial, or so legend says.'

'Not like this. It's like trawling in a sea of effluence. Whatever prompted him to seek refuge here, I cannot say. Sah'rk nests have more charm.'

'Will you keep looking? What if he's already gone? Or dead?'

'If he's dead there'll be a mess, and we can track it. Warriors like him don't die easily. I think we're close. Zartath claims he has his scent.'

'You trust him, the mutant I mean?'

'You realise he can hear you, Codicier?'

'He knows my feelings. I have voiced them often enough to his face.'

'Consider yourself fortunate he has yet to cut yours open.'

'I shall bear that in mind, brother-captain,' said Xarko, smiling at an empathetic snarl from Kraelish. 'And so your quarry, will you keep looking?'

'I must.'

'Then I shall continue to monitor you from the *Forge Hammer*.'

'All quiet up there?' asked Agatone, as the conversation began to wind down.

'Peacefully so.'

'And the tides, Xarko… what did you learn from them?'

Now it was Xarko's turn to pause as he considered the question.

'Unsure, but they are fickle. There was… some turmoil.'

'I am not a psyker, Xarko.' Agatone chafed. 'What exactly does that mean?'

'That something is going to happen, something important. Soon, I think.'

Agatone took a few seconds to respond.

'Stay out of the tides, Xarko,' he said eventually. 'Some mysteries are best left alone.'

'As you wish.' Xarko bowed to the shadows and cut the vox-link.

Silence was restored and darkness reasserted. He closed his eyes to cast his consciousness out amongst an ocean of thought and began to roam. Serfs went about their duties, the decks were quiet with bulkheads sealed and all systems were running normally. For now, they remained undetected.

But Xarko's psychic awareness stopped at *Forge Hammer*'s armoured hull. It failed to reach into space. For if it had he would have known that all was far from normal. He would have perceived the small ship gliding slowly towards their anchorage in the upper atmosphere and he would have felt the homicidal intent emanating from the few determined souls aboard.

'Lieutenant Makato,' Xarko spoke down the vox-feed to his chief armsman.

'My lord,' came a firm reply a few seconds later.

'I am entering my sanctum, and not to be disturbed.'

'Understood, my lord.'

Xarko severed the link, closed his eyes and re-entered the fire tides.

CHAPTER FOUR

Sturndrang, the underhive of Molior

The crash site reached at least fifteen metres in all directions. Debris littered the ground, great streams of it like mechanised intestine. In the hive levels above, detritus hung from girders and gantries, serving as evidence of the ship's difficult landing. Ship no longer, it was now a partially destroyed wreck. Scorch marks blackened its flanks, deeper and longer on the right-hand side where the engine had exploded. Dust, grit and dented fuselage, half-exposed to the bare metal, obscured much of the gunship's iconography. Its flattened nosecone, shattered glacis and ruptured right wing made even identifying its class a challenge.

It was a Thunderhawk, a gunship with a winged lightning bolt symbol described in black on its side amidst a field of bile-yellow. The amount of damage inflicted on the ship, together with the obvious hostility of its impromptu landfall, made it even more surprising that at least one of its occupants had survived.

Exor emerged from behind the ship, having been to examine the engine damage.

He shook his head, the mechadendrite tools he had been using to perform the rituals of function retracting in their haptic implant sleeves as he breathed, 'Omnissiah… I have no idea how he landed this ship and lived.'

His shock betrayed his youth, as did his voice. It had the mechanised cadence of most Techmarines, only lighter. Exor was far from being a veteran, unlike his two much more grizzled companions.

43

'What else?' asked Agatone, his deep voice slightly muted inside the folds of his hood. He looked sidelong at the dead hivers they had left in their wake and considered hiding the bodies. As Space Marines, they had little to fear from the underhive's inhabitants but in a large enough pack they might prove problematic and dead always brought carrion in a place like this.

He returned his attention to Exor.

'It won't fly again,' declared the Techmarine. 'One engine is gone, along with the wing on the right-hand side. Weapon systems and all forms of cogitation are defunct. Landing stanchions are wrecked and the hull's structural integrity needs a complete re-armour before it could ever be considered for atmospheric flight. In short, the ship is dead, captain. Machine-spirit and all.'

Agatone grunted as he considered the ramifications. With his own visual assessment, he added what he could to the information Exor had provided.

Scratches marred the exterior hull that were not a result of crash damage, stripping the paintwork to bare metal in places. As well as the crushed forward aspect of the ship, the rear was also badly damaged, its exit ramp ripped away and long gone. A gaping hole where the ramp should have been provided access to a charnel house of bodies within. Some looked like battle dead, ferried from Nocturne but dying before their Apothecary could minister to them or retrieve any gene-seed from the truly lost causes. Like the ship, they wore armour of yellow livery with the black winged bolt symbol on their shoulder guards. Closer inspection had revealed the dead had been gnawed upon where the flesh was exposed, as if by whatever carrion-eaters lived this far down in the city's underhive.

Agatone approached the rear hatch. Zartath had gone back inside the ship, disappearing through a ragged hole in the fuselage that led to darkness and the reek of blood. Trusting the dead gangers had no other scouts in this section of the underhive, he drew back his hood. It itched, and he was used to being bare-headed. Even the stifling confines of his battle-helm would have been preferable. But they had left their armour aboard the frigate that had laid anchor in Sturndrang's upper atmosphere. Agatone had insisted; they would be less conspicuous that way. He felt almost naked without his full battleplate, having to settle for body-carapace and half greaves normally reserved for sparring. A storm cloak completed the 'disguise', concealing their armour but unable to mask the Salamanders' sheer size. Their equipment also came without battle-helm, which meant ear beads for vox, no tactical data-feed and no respirator.

So there was no filtration of the underhive atmosphere, which stank. It was redolent of petro-chem, fycylene and low-grade promethium, amongst other synthetically produced combustibles. Despite the rank odour, it failed to conceal the stench of putrefaction emanating from inside the ship's hold.

Agatone scowled. 'Reeks of decay.'

'Fecal matter also. Sections of the hold are swimming in the crud.'

'Indigenous?'

The voice of Zartath snorted with amusement. 'I doubt the Malevolents soiled their armour, though with your errant drake amongst them and bent on killing some may have.' He snorted again, in derision this time, 'They don't know from savagery…'

Agatone ignored the feral boast, though it was becoming all too common since they had made planetfall. 'Was our quarry wounded?' he asked. 'Beyond whatever injury he sustained during the crash.' If he was struggling with an injury, it would make hunting him easier, his pattern more predictable. He would seek out a medic, or whatever sawbones passed for thus in this decrepit burrow.

A low snarl answered. 'Unlikely. Everything I see suggests he took them by surprise. He killed them quick, but painful.'

Exor joined Agatone. The Techmarine activated his auspex. 'Bio-scan reads negative. Blood's all theirs. Some samples from the hold might yield more though…'

'As I said,' Zartath growled, unable to disguise the contempt he felt towards the Techmarine, 'I don't need the artifice of your Martian masters to tell me that.'

Despite his youth or possibly because of it, Exor rose to Zartath's slight as he emerged from the hole in the fuselage.

'Every day I am reminded of how much of a beast you are, Zartath. Cursed, I've heard some say. Half human.'

Where Zartath was wiry and gaunt, Exor had flatter, plainer features. In keeping with the traditions of the magos of the Adeptus Mechanicus, he carried several augmetic and cybernetic implants that gave him a partially mechanised appearance, and these were made all the more apparent because of the stripped-down armour he was wearing. But this was not the only marked difference between them. Exor's skin, much like his captain's was onyx black and his eyes a deep fire-red.

Zartath's skin was pale under his cloak and armour. Although he had sworn fealty to his adopted Chapter, even undergone its 'rite of pain' to become one of them, he was still not of Nocturne. His eyes still blazed, though, but not with the captured fire of a Nocturnean heritage and a genetic First Founding ancestry, but with an intensity of purpose and spirit that had seen him live where others had perished in the slave arenas of the dark eldar.

In the earliest years, not long after the war on Nocturne, the great Dragon Strife as some referred to it, Agatone had found it difficult to trust the mutant. He questioned his inclusion in the Chapter, an issue deliberated over for years in the Pantheon Council, but now he was forced to admit that if properly directed and motivated Zartath could be a loyal and potent asset.

Even so, he still needed a strong hand now and again. A leash, according to his more vocal detractors. Agatone did not like to think of him as some hound – it felt disrespectful. But it was not always easy.

Zartath bared his teeth, and claws.

'Let him up,' said Agatone, brooking no argument. 'Sure or not, Exor needs to examine the ship.'

Bone claws retracting into his gauntlets, Zartath leapt down. The ossified growths were the physical manifestation of his mutancy, a gross distortion of the radius or ulna; only surgical x-ray or autopsy would reveal which with any certainty. Exor had expressed which methodology he would recommend to discern an answer. Zartath's mandible bone and teeth were also unusual, the canines overlong and pronounced like fangs. His mouth, both inside and his lips, was black. So too his tongue which tapered to a sharp point like a dagger.

Some Chapters, such as the Marines Malevolent, would hunt down and execute what they regarded as deviations from the Emperor's genetic design, a template that had regrettably been diluted over the millennia since its initial perfecting. None now existed who could restore it, and so there were those amongst the Adeptus Astartes regarded as 'cursed' and although the Salamanders did not ostensibly count themselves amongst these puritans, there were still some for whom the presence of such an obvious mutant element in their ranks was not only distasteful, it was also dangerous. It had made the ex-Black Dragon's transition to the Salamanders difficult.

As if to emphasise the fact, Zartath glared at the Techmarine as they passed each other, his body almost shaking with repressed violence.

'Shall we see who is the more human, brother?' Zartath snarled, showing his savage nature again. 'Let me cut the metal from your flesh. I doubt the remainder would amount to much. Certainly, there'd be no spine amongst the offal.'

Exor had climbed halfway into the ship when the augmetic replacement of his right eye flared, crosshairs interleaving over the iris and cornea as he accessed an internal targeting matrix. His right hand, a bionic, strayed towards his holstered bolt pistol.

'Cease,' Agatone told them both. The two had been at each other's throats since planetfall, and it was trying the captain's patience. In truth, each now came from a different world. Zartath, though he had adopted the Salamanders as his Chapter now and wore their deep green livery, was still a Black Dragon. Not merely that, he was also a mutant and still prone to volatility. Exor was younger, not long returned from Mars where he had been privy to the secrets of the Adeptus Mechanicus and emerged a fresh-forged Techmarine. Like Zartath, his loyalty was irrevocably split, partly to Nocturne and the Chapter, partly to the red Martian world.

Conflict, Agatone reminded himself again, was inevitable.

'I brought you here to hunt, Zartath,' he said. 'So, hunt. Find his trail.'

Like a hound brought to heel, the ex-Black Dragon nodded and obeyed.

Alone for the moment, Agatone considered their surroundings and the likelihood of the success of their mission.

Sturndrang was a heavily industrialised world of vast factorums and massively overly populated hive cities. Utilising the rich mineral deposits of its mines and other subterranean works, the majority of its populace served the Throne through intense manual labour in the production of materiel for the never-ending Imperial war effort. Shells, tank armour, glacis for aircraft, vulcanised rubber, plastek, fuel, teeth for chain-weapons, even rivets were all manufactured on Sturndrang in one of its twenty-three hives.

When they had made their descent through low atmosphere, the Salamanders had been granted their first proper look at their hunting ground, a smog-choked vista of blister-encrusted spires on a plain of irradiated wasteland.

Sturndrang was a war world in many respects, and a standing army was garrisoned on it to protect its highly valuable assets. Amongst the domes and blisters, the sub-spires and annexed mezzanine levels jutting from the ugly sloped flanks of the hives, Agatone had seen bastions and blockhouses. Landing pads, even a sizeable orbital dock were in evidence. Search-lamps strafed the night that gripped Sturndrang in an eternally clenched fist and patrols in light gun-cutters or atmospherically-sealed speeders made regular passes to ensure continued compliance and maximum civilian efficiency.

Agatone had come from a world of industry too. Nocturne, although much less stable than Sturndrang, an alpha-classification death world in fact, was not so dissimilar in its industrial endeavour. It was, however, entirely less like a sprawling slave camp. As they had made planetfall, careful to avoid the patrols and the strafing lights, Agatone found the idea of Sturndrang disgusted him. A quirk of his humanitarian nature, he supposed, but to inflict such squalor and deprivation on a populace seemed little better than tyranny to his mind. It was then he was reminded of just how large and unruly the galaxy was. So many worlds, so many interpretations of the Imperium's law.

'So much corruption...' he had muttered angrily, and without the taint of Ruin in sight.

And beneath these very literal hives of industry were the substrata, those sectors that had been constructed upon to serve the fervent desire of Sturndrang's overseers for greater production, larger output. Over centuries and millennia, they had sunk deeper and deeper into the earth until few alive could recall what their original purpose and function had been. Here and there, as the Salamanders had descended into the underhive, experiencing the squalor and desperation of its underclasses for themselves, was evidence of former glories. A mosaic floor, an ornate fountain long parched, a marble staircase, a grand hall stripped of its gilding, a begrimed sign bearing some proud industrial motto or rubric. Wars, natural disasters, power grabs, all and more had served to transform Sturndrang during its long history of Imperial fealty. Fortunes and landscape had changed – one thing that had not was the production of materiel.

As Agatone stood by the wreckage of the Malevolents' ship, one his former battle-brother had somehow guided to this devastated landing his Techmarine now examined, he considered the warren they were searching. Labyrinthine did not even begin to describe its complexity.

He hoped Tsu'gan was dead. He would wish he was dead by the time Agatone finally caught up with him.

CHAPTER FIVE

Heletine, Canticus, Imperial held territory

They reached the laager of armoured personnel carriers where Sepelius had set up his apothecarion. Ahead of Va'lin, Dersius and the injured Naeb, trails of wounded snaked from various medical stations. Most were Cadians, battered and brutalised, tramping wearily in long trains like a coffle of slaves. Some travelled via stretcher; others were covered from sight, being taken for the pyre not the medicae. Entire troop holds of Chimera transports were filled with the dead. Va'lin had seen their bodies. White Shields, troopers, Kasrkin, even commissars. None were spared the Black Legion's wrath or thirst for blood.

Overhead, the low turbine thrum of engines was a constant drone as slow-moving Stormravens ferried the Salamanders dead and injured. As he looked up at the shadow of one passing over them, Va'lin wondered if Sor'ad was aboard. He also caught Ky'dak's eye for a moment, following a few steps behind the others, and glanced away.

Munitorum clerks would record the latest Canticus engagement as a victory, but Va'lin and the others who had fought in the battle knew it was a pyrrhic one at best. Zantho's armoured intervention had cost them ground elsewhere. Where one point of pressure was relieved, another was redoubled. So far, during these first weeks of engagement, all the Imperium had managed to achieve was a grinding stalemate. Va'lin wondered why, and also what the Black Legion wanted with this world, beyond mere bloody conquest. Speculation would have to wait. As they reached the edge of the laager, Sepelius awaited.

Va'lin had already sent the others back to barracks for weapons and armour repair. Without Iaptus, who was still on the recently won battlefield with Zantho, there were only four of the original squad present.

Upon seeing the battered assault squad tramping through his 'gates', the Apothecary asked, 'More meat from the grinder, brothers?'

Dersius handed over Naeb to a pair of medical servitors Sepelius had sent to meet them. The servos of the cyborganic creatures strained audibly as they took the injured Salamander's weight. Naeb knew little about it. He had been going in and out of consciousness for the last few minutes. Va'lin was relieved his brother would finally be getting some medical attention.

'Seems I have a butcher's lot already,' added the Apothecary in a sibilant voice.

The improvised medical station inside the laager's armoured boundary was capacious. Warriors from Sixth stood sentinel in stormbolter turrets, and small squads of Cadian 81st patrolled the periphery with fingers poised next to lasgun triggers. An air of unease pervaded on account of a battle barely won.

Nearby, a large area had been staked out and delineated as a landing pad. The Stormraven Va'lin had seen flying overhead earlier had just finished unloading its mortal cargo and was cycling its turbine engines as it prepared to get airborne again.

'Is that what we are to you, Sepelius... Meat?'

Dersius could not keep the distaste out of his voice.

'Anything other and I fear the trauma of seeing so much death would unhinge me, brother,' Sepelius smiled, but it was cold and utterly without humour.

The Apothecary wore predominantly white armour, though it was stained by now with blood and dirt. One shoulder guard displayed his allegiance to the Chapter. Unlike the assault squad's green drake head sigil on a field of black, Sepelius was part of Drakgaard's command squad and wore the same drake head against a backdrop of fiery yellow. His face was long, his forehead pronounced. An ugly man in many ways, not that this concerned Sepelius remotely. He was tall also, and marginally looked down on the warriors before him. His hair was shorn close to his scalp, and winter-white much like his demeanour.

'Just patch him up, Brother-Apothecary,' said Va'lin, cutting through the needless posturing. 'I have need of him, as does the grinder.'

The servitors were carrying Naeb away into a busy throng of medics and walking wounded. Sepelius had already established a system of triage and was prioritising Adeptus Astartes over Guard. From the sheer number of injured against the amount of medical staff present, it looked like they had a long night ahead of them.

'He'll be ready for death again come the morning, Va'lin,' Sepelius replied as the other three Salamanders turned to leave. 'Tell me,' he called, 'are your thoughts still troubled?'

Va'lin cursed under his breath, but kept on walking. Against his better judgement, before he knew how caustic Sepelius could be, he had gone to the Apothecary about his experiences in the fire canyons back on Nocturne. Upon meeting the man, Va'lin's instincts had warned him against saying too much but now Sepelius would not let it go.

'What's he talking about?' asked Dersius with a scathing glance over his shoulder at the Apothecary.

Ky'dak said nothing, and kept his eyes forward, but Va'lin could tell he was also intrigued.

'I confided in someone I shouldn't have, brother. There's no more to it than that.'

A spit of flame overhead and the aggressive roar of jump jets interrupted as the descending figure of Sergeant Iaptus prevented any further awkward questioning.

He seemed agitated.

'Dersius, Ky'dak, rejoin the rest of the squad back at camp. Brother Va'lin, you are with me.'

Iaptus boosted away again immediately and Va'lin followed.

'Brother-sergeant?' he asked across the vox, which was now fully functional again.

'Captain Drakgaard has recalled all officers not currently in the field. Apparently, there has been a change in our war footing on Heletine.'

'Because of Canticus, and Zantho's redeployment?'

As they soared over the city, leaping from one ruin to the next, Va'lin was afforded a good view of the fires and the wreckage the war had wrought so far. Canticus appeared as if it had been ransacked, and he wondered again at the motives of their enemies.

Through the darkness and drifting smoke, Va'lin picked out the phosphor lamps of a hexagonal landing pad and the bulky Stormraven there with engines idling.

'That and something else,' Iaptus replied as they touched down thirty metres from the waiting gunship. 'Allies,' said Iaptus, speaking without the vox as they tramped across the earth. 'Sisters of the Ebon Chalice.'

'Sororitas?'

Iaptus turned his gaze on Va'lin.

'The Ecclesiarchy's warrior-zealots have come to Heletine for Throne only knows what reason.'

The front hatch of the Fourth Company Stormraven descended to form a ramp. Iaptus and Va'lin climbed aboard to make the remainder of the journey to Escadan and the Imperial encampment.

CHAPTER SIX

Nova-class frigate, *Forge Hammer*

The ship drifted, night-black against a starless void. Battle-worn, its hull was ragged and bore stark evidence of a recent hostile engagement. Its engines were dormant and without function, cold like a dead star. Its port and starboard facings were dark and no heat trace was present in its systems that, for all intents and purposes, were inert. Ostensibly, the Hunter-class Destroyer that had recently come into close proximity of the *Forge Hammer* was dead.

Lieutenant Makato's face betrayed his consternation as he glared at the sensorium feed that described the foreign vessel that had just strayed into their vicinity. His mood failed to improve as he regarded the scratchy pict captures. Incongruity displeased him, and everything about this ship, its sudden appearance and condition, was incongruous. Like a slow-moving ocean predator that plays dead whilst drifting on the currents with the other flotsam, the dark ship had crept up on the larger frigate, as innocuous on the sensorium as an asteroid. It wasn't until the ship could be seen and identified that the alarm had been raised.

'How long have you been aware of this?' Makato asked pensively, smoothing his moustache and beard.

He was looking over the shoulder of a young officer, overseeing the ship's eyes and ears. The *Forge Hammer* was currently at 'silent running', so the bridge was quiet, the many consoles sparsely attended by a skeleton crew and under-lit with softly glowing lumens.

'A few minutes, sir. I hailed as soon as I was sure.'

'Sure of what, ensign?'

'That it was a ship, sir.'

'And what's your assessment now?'

The officer seemed nonplussed. 'It's a wreck, sir. A carcass of a ship, really. It must have drifted into the planet's gravity well and been drawn to us.'

'You've detected no motive power at all?' asked Makato, whose eyes had yet to leave the screen.

'No, sir.'

'No life signs?'

'Not that we can tell, sir. Biorhythmic activity is difficult to accurately gauge at this range, though, and our instruments are not–'

'Then we should take a closer look.'

'Y-yes, sir.'

Makato lifted his gaze from the console at last.

'Not you, ensign,' he said, and turned his attention to the broad-shouldered armsman standing at ease behind him.

'Jedda, summon three of your men trained in atmospheric combat.'

Jedda saluted crisply and departed as ordered. The uniform he wore, like all those sworn to the fire-born aboard the *Forge Hammer*, was coal black with his rank markings described in grey. Makato's insignia, as befitted his station, was silver.

'You,' said Makato, facing the officer, 'will vox for Enginseer Utulexx to join us on launch deck six. I want a craft fuelled and ready in twenty minutes.'

'Us, sir?'

'Yes, I need to stretch my legs.' Makato was stalking away when he paused. 'And tell him to bring the Thallax.'

'Sir…' the ensign ventured somewhat hopefully.

Makato paused again. Though he had his back to the lad, the stiffening of his shoulders intimated his annoyance.

'Should I contact Lord Xarko with news of this discovery?'

Makato seemed to consider this, relaxing for a moment, before stiffening up again and trooping on his way.

'No, do not. The lord is in his sanctum – we don't need to disturb him with this.'

An Arvus Lighter was prepped and waiting on launch deck six for Lieutenant Makato as per his orders. So too was a squad of armsmen, all kitted out in atmosphere suits. They stood at attention outside the small atmospheric craft, armed with heavy-gauge lasguns and hand-held plasma-cutters. The atmosphere suits were enhanced rubber and plastek, ugly looking things and cumbersome but they were effective.

Also present was the enginseer. Utulexx had brought his watchdog, which loomed large and threatening behind the robed servant of the Martian Mechanicus. The Thallax was a battle engine, a hulking cyborg that cradled an immense rifle across its armoured torso. It was called a 'lightning gun', a blunt yet accurate appellation. Through a series of capacitors and power relays slaved to the Thallax's cyborganic systems, the lightning gun was capable of producing a devastating energy beam that could incapacitate mechanical targets via an extreme overload of power. For organic targets, the effects were somewhat messier and more permanent.

Between Jedda's squad and the combat-droid, there was a lot of firepower. In his many years of service aboard the *Forge Hammer* and the *Triumphal* before that, Makato had learned to be cautious, especially when stepping into the unknown.

Apart from the lumen array which was lighting up the area around the Arvus, the rest of the deck was dark. There were sixteen launch bays on this deck in total, all lined up on the flanking wall. All but one were sealed and in shadow. Aft launch bay theta-seven was lit by a ring of flashing amber emergency lamps.

This was Captain Agatone's ship, and while he and the rest of his warriors were off-deck Lord Xarko was in command. In his absence, Kensai Makato ran things. Though by any military standards his rank was modest, he took great pride in his appointed task. He was in service to a Chapter of the Emperor's Angels; in his mind that was a great and unimpeachable honour. Every serf from armsman to brander-priest was his responsibility. In many respects he was this ship's major-domo, its custodian and gamekeeper. Any potential threat to its smooth running Makato regarded as his duty to deal with.

This ship was but the latest.

And besides, as he had told the ensign, he needed to stretch his legs. The last bit of excitement they had experienced was several weeks back when the *Vulkan's Wrath* had docked with the *Forge Hammer* letting Agatone and eight of his men aboard. Xarko was already on deck, the Librarian had joined them earlier via shuttle craft. A course was plotted to Sturndrang and the rest was kept need-to-know. For Makato that meant their destination but nothing else. Agatone and his charges had seemed agitated, though, but that was the extent of what was shared with any non-Adeptus Astartes personnel.

It didn't matter to Makato. He knew his duty, and would prosecute it to the fullest. If that meant breaking up the monotony of twiddling his thumbs in low orbit above some dirt world he had never heard of and was less than inclined to visit then so much the better.

Descending via pneumatic pressure lift, Makato reached the deck promptly.

'All is in readiness, Jedda?' he asked as he reached the others.

'Aye, sir,' replied the gruff master-at-arms. 'All pre-flight checks have been conducted. Ship is fuelled and at your command.'

'Then let's get this done.'

Makato paused on the lighter's access ramp before going in.

'You know why you're here?' he asked Utulexx.

'Explorative mission aboard apparently scuppered Hunter-class vessel that has drifted into our immediate vicinity.' The enginseer spoke through a vocaliser grille instead of a mouth. Underneath his hood, a single optic glowed as its tracking rings focused and refocused on the lieutenant. He was hunched, a result of the heavy cybernetic augmentation his body had undergone during his long tenure, but most of his mechanised enhancements were concealed by expansive brown robes. A Mechanicus sigil, unique to his dominions back on Mars and echoed over the Thallax's black and gunmetal grey carapace, adorned his priestly vestments.

'You wish to know what is on board, lieutenant,' Utulexx concluded.

'Correct.'

Makato glanced up at the 'head' of the Thallax. He had to crane his neck quite far to do so. A diode where its eye might have been glowed green, signifying passivity.

'Keep that thing quiescent unless it's needed,' he warned Utulexx. 'If there are survivors, I don't want them eradicated before I've had a chance to question them.'

'And if they are hostile, lieutenant?' asked Utulexx.

'Defend us.'

Makato led them inside without further preamble. He had already decided he would fly the craft himself and once aboard quickly got strapped in to the pilot's station and commenced start up protocols.

The others filed in after him, Jedda in front, and likewise strapped themselves in to the crew compartment. Each man checked the rebreather and function of the atmosphere suit to the man on his left. Once satisfied, Jedda gave the signal for the launch to commence.

Seeing that the enginseer and Thallax were also now aboard, Makato began ignition. Through the lighter's glacis, he saw the amber lumens around the launch portal turn to green as he provided the requisite launch codes. The landing strip was lit. He boosted the shuttle's engines and fired up into launch. Eight seconds and they had cleared the landing strip and emerged from one of the aft launch ports into the void.

Twenty-three kilometres in front of them loomed the dark and lightless shape of the stricken destroyer.

As he made course for the massive vessel floating listlessly through

space, Makato found it hard not to think of it as a tomb. He was no cow-
ard, far from it. Makato had served with the Imperial Navy for almost a
century, and was considered a veteran. But deep down in his marrow, he
prayed for the ship to be empty and that nothing was lurking aboard.

A damaged fighter bay allowed the Arvus untrammelled access to the
Hunter-class vessel. Within seconds of touching down onto an ice-
bitten, debris-strewn deck it was obvious that atmospheric conditions
aboard had been severely compromised. Mag-locking the landing stanchions of the lighter, Makato lowered the ramp and gave the order to
disembark.

The Thallax led them out, its targeting matrix hazing the zero atmosphere of the deck. Engaging luminator banks on its chest carapace, it
spread a thin wash of magnesium-bright light over the void-dark interior.

'I am no expert, sir, but I'd hazard this bay has been damaged by a tor-
pedo impact,' said Jedda through the contrivance of his atmosphere suit's
vox. He cast his own lamp pack over the expansive deck, made larger by
depressurisation and the subsequent evacuation of all men and materials
not bolted down. Evidence of fires rapidly extinguished could be seen
marring some of the walls, which were also riddled with tiny craters the
size of Makato's fist.

'Some kind of fragmentation warhead...' he posited out loud, 'shredded
the whole deck.'

Each man had locked his boots with a moderate magnetic charge.
Enough to hold on but not so much that he could not advance. As an
additional safety precaution, Makato had insisted each man be tethered
to another. If one experienced magnetic failure, the other would anchor
him down until further help could arrive.

Only Utulexx went without, trusting to the manifold apparatus of his
cybernetic implants to keep him grounded. The Thallax had its own terrain adaptive systems that included void combat. It could have traversed
the outside of the ship if so commanded.

'Sergeant,' the enginseer began, using voice amplification and modula-
tion to be heard by the atmosphere-suited humans, 'I have located a route
further into the ship.'

Makato turned, slowed by the lack of gravity, and saw the access port
Utulexx was referring to.

It looked like a maintenance hatch, a crawlspace just wide enough for
the Thallax if it was crouched down. The rest of them should not have
any trouble, and there was no way their plasma-cutters were going to get
through the larger gates and sealed bulkheads that had come down, too
late it seemed, to seal off the launch bay.

'Make it safe, enginseer. We'll proceed in that direction.'

Utulexx nodded and with a blurt of binaric cant sent the Thallax up to take point.

At Makato's order, Jedda brought up two armsmen with plasma-cutters. 'Make it quick,' he voxed.

Six minutes and they were through the hatch and into the corridor beyond. During that time, Utulexx scanned for life signs but found nothing.

The Thallax would have been compromised in the narrow access corridor, so Jedda went in first with his carbine primed. It was snub-nosed and compact, perfect for boarding actions. At close range, Jedda was confident of its stopping power.

On one wall in the eight-metre corridor was a cogitator panel. Utulexx force-accessed it using his mechadendrite implants and gained access to some of the ship's onboard systems. First he rebooted the life support, which had been inexplicably suspended, then used what little emergency reserves remained to provide minimal lighting and motive power to some of the lifters. He then sealed the maintenance corridor behind them with a secondary blast gate that dropped down from the ceiling. Yellow lumens in both walls flickered once and stayed on. The light was weak, but at least it was lit and better than abject darkness. A hissing sound presaged re-oxygenation and in just over eight minutes the corridor and the immediate section of the ship beyond it – a small maintenance deck – was habitable again.

The corridor was wide enough for two abreast, so Jedda and Makato were shoulder to shoulder when the exit hatch opened and admitted them deeper into the ship.

Jedda went first, breathing slow and steady through his respirator, blowing out gusts of carbon dioxide through the filtration vents at the sides of his mask. He moved low and stealthy, almost feline, the carbine tucked into his shoulder and panning across the deck.

Like the rest of the ship, it was deserted. Squalls of mist ghosted across the floor, obscuring it from view. Lamp packs still flickered as they tried and failed to maintain a consistent link to the ship's recently resupplied emergency power. In the half-light, they saw chains hanging from a vaulted ceiling. A swaying phosphor globe sporadically illuminated a squadron of power-lifters, their cabs bowed down as if in reverence, lifter arms hung slack by their sides. No crew, though. There were no bodies anywhere, only crates and laid down tools.

Advancing close on Jedda's heels, Makato paced out the deck in his mind. He guessed two hundred and sixty metres. Definitely a sub-deck, but the lifter tube at the end of it would grant them further access. He reasoned that any survivors still on board would either be on the bridge or in life support.

According to Utulexx's scans, this meant heading upwards to the higher decks.

Roughly halfway across the maintenance deck, Makato clenched his fist then raised it to order an all-stop. The boarding party were moving in a column, and there was plenty of space between them and the shadowy confines of the wider deck either side.

'Enginseer, I'm reading some temperature fluctuations.'

'The ship is still normalising its environment,' Utulexx replied, his Thallax watchdog standing dutifully over him.

'Are we safe to remove respirators?' Makato asked. They were fouling his peripheral vision, and if the ship was atmospherically stable from this point, he would prefer to be without the handicap.

Utulexx took a few seconds to collate and assess the data from across the activated decks.

'You may disengage atmospheric redundancies, sergeant.'

Makato unclipped the dome-like glacis from his head and removed it along with his respirator. The air smelt stagnant, still in the early stages of filtration and recyc but at least it was air.

Jedda and the others did the same, breathing deeply and relieved to no longer be stifled by their masks. They still needed the suits, however. Temperature levels were sub-zero and clouds of low-lying coolant still thronged some parts of the deck, encrusting stanchions and gantries with artificial hoarfrost.

Pulling a data-slate from a pouch in his atmosphere suit, Makato said, 'According to this, we can take the lifter up three levels and come out in cryogenics. If there's anyone still alive on this ship, that's where they'll be.' He tapped the slate and the haptic implant in his glove blanked away the schematic and transferred it to a retinal lens independent from the suit itself but worn by Makato in a circlet around his head. The rectangular lens was transparent and flicked over his right eye where it displayed the schematic layout of the ship and superimposed it over his current destination. Now he had a living map of their route to cryogenics.

Thusly prepared, he moved the column out again.

'How many saviour caskets does a vessel this size have?' he asked Utulexx, who consulted his datacore for the answer.

'Between three and five hundred, intended for essential personnel only.'

Makato nodded.

'So there could be as many as five hundred souls up there?'

'With the amount of damage this ship has sustained, the amount of time it could have been adrift in the void, I would posit that number to be significantly less.'

'But five hundred at most?'

'Potentially, yes.'

Makato began to wonder if he had brought enough men. Too late now. He decided they would get to cryogenics, assess the situation and then determine if further rescue teams were needed.

They crossed the remainder of the maintenance sub-deck without incident. The lifter was large enough to accommodate the entire team, so they went together. After three decks, they reached cryogenics.

As the gates to the lifter opened, a long corridor was revealed, stretching away into half-darkness. Two other corridors lay either side of it, but were only accessed through the central aisle, making five in total. Makato's schematic showed each corridor had two rows of fifty cryogenic saviour caskets. This was the ship's cryo-vault and, according to its chrono-stamp, it had not been accessed in several days.

Five hundred souls. Alpha through epsilon, with the main access corridor marked as gamma.

As they stepped from the lifter and onto the deck threshold, it became clear that not all of the caskets were functional. Some were broken, the activation lumens within dark and non-operational. Each casket was identical, arranged vertically and shaped like a glass cocoon mounted to a power generator slaved to the cryo-vault's power array. They were large too, large enough to accommodate a human host with ease. Pipes and tubes fed nutrients and maintained hydration. A simple face mask rebreather provided oxygen. During cryo-sleep, a host should want for nothing and be left to dream. But some of the inhabitants lodged in this ship's cryo-vault had been anything but quiescent. Closer inspection revealed that most of the caskets were empty but some contained desiccated, even skeletal, remains of human crew.

None of these men or women had died well.

Jedda made the sign of the aquila as Makato led them down the main access corridor. Lamp packs stabbed into the darkness, shining into each casket, as their bearers checked for survivors.

'The long sleep…' said Makato, trying not to imagine waking from cryostasis locked inside one of those caskets, unable to breath, barely able to move, slowly freezing to death as the process of vitrification broke down. The terror-etched faces staring hollow-eyed back at him made it hard to refute the image. Hands curled into claws, scratching ineffectually at glass. Fingertips blue with cyanosis. Lips peeled back over ice-rimmed jaws and teeth, mouths outstretched in silent expressions of fear and anguish…

'Something very bad happened here,' Jedda murmured. It was the first sign of internal doubt he had shown since mission start.

Makato found he could not argue, so said the only reassuring thing he could think of, 'Whatever went wrong and condemned these poor souls to a cold death has passed. Stay vigilant.'

They moved slow, two by two with one man as rearguard.

The air was chill, and getting colder by the second. Their breath ghosted in long, white plumes of exhalation. The hard deck clanked underfoot with every booted step.

Nothing on the schematic.

'Are you getting any bio-signs, enginseer?'

Makato had left Utulexx and the Thallax at the entryway, where a command console was linked to all five hundred caskets.

'The ship's entire complement of cryogenic stasis caskets has been activated. None are registering life signs but the control functions of this facility have been compromised.'

'Compromised?'

Makato, Jedda and his men were reaching the end of the first bank of caskets. Frost crusted their boots from the expulsion of cryogenic gas leaking from several damaged units that crept across the floor in a white fog.

'Sabotaged,' Utulexx replied. 'Cryo-freezing should not be able to occur if a unit is damaged or its hermetic seal has been breached. This facility is currently violating that protocol.'

Hence the air, and the frost underfoot.

Makato gripped a support stanchion of one of the caskets to test it. The metal cracked and split with only a minor application of force. Shortness of breath, acute headache and nausea: Makato did not need to be a medicus to recognise the early stages of hypoxia.

'Helmets on,' he ordered, feeling his skin start to prickle.

Encased by the domed glacis, Makato experienced a stifling of his senses but the temperature readout on the glass and the increased nitrogen in the air's composition suggested some minor factional distillation had occurred with the large-scale release of several broken caskets. Prolonged exposure would be harmful to both him and his men.

At the end of the first bank they had discovered sixteen operational caskets, another twenty without power and fourteen with hermetic breaches spilling out cryo-gas into the localised atmosphere. Eight had been occupied by members of the crew. All were dead, their stasis arrested or having failed completely.

Four more banks awaited them, but Makato was growing impatient. As a Navy veteran, he had learned to trust his instincts. Here they were telling him to perform whatever due diligence he needed to in the cryo-vault and then get himself and his men off the ship.

'Jedda, split your men into two teams and have them cover the port-facing caskets. I'll take the starboard.'

Jedda nodded and went to his task.

Makato went right. Before heading down the next bank of caskets, he checked the load of his carbine; there was frost occluding the ammo gauge and he had to wipe it with his glove several times before it cleared.

He had yet to fire it, so he knew the weapon held a full charge but the sight of the flashing readout was absurdly reassuring.

'Enginseer, any life signs?'

'Still none, but I am reading increased heart rate and respiration in your biorhythms, lieutenant.'

'I'm fine, just keep your attention on the cryo-vault. I don't want any surprises.'

The next bank of cyro-caskets was dark and what little light that came from the deck lamps underfoot was obscured by the vaporous atmosphere created by the leaks. About halfway down the corridor, one of the caskets spewed thick gouts of freezing mist into the air from a ruptured pipeline. It was hard to tell in the conditions, but the cable looked as if it had been cut.

Giving each casket a cursory examination now, as he subconsciously increased his pace, Makato edged past the badly damaged cryo-unit. As he emerged into the latter half of the corridor, a thought occurred to him.

'Enginseer, what purpose would deliberately flooding the cryo-vault with aerosolised nitrogen serve?'

It took a few seconds for Utulexx to respond. During the short pause, Makato caught the sound of Jedda's voice through the muffled confines of his helmet. He was about to raise the armsman on the vox when Utulexx replied.

'Other than to create a hypoxic atmosphere, I can think of only one: the obfuscation of genuine active bio-signatures within the vault.'

Makato's grip on his carbine intensified, and his pace slowed as his heart rate increased. Each casket was an empty void, most were unlit. The billowing pipeline behind him created a soft, dulcet refrain that scraped his nerves rather than eased them.

'Explain.'

'If an infiltrator wanted to hide their presence from a rudimentary bio-scan, a cryo-vault with a compromised structural integrity would be the optimum location to achieve that.'

'Meaning, the drop in temperature would effectively make them invisible?'

'Precisely.'

'What about the effects of prolonged exposure?'

'In most cases that would result in decreased motive and cognitive function, concluding in death.'

Most cases.

Makato wanted to hail Jedda. He wanted to recall his men, but the next cryo-casket in line was frosted with recent activation, the glass almost impossible to see through. Almost impossible. Something loomed behind the glass. It was large.

'Lieutenant,' Jedda's voice came over the vox. 'We've found something...'

Makato was only half listening as he reached out a gloved hand to wipe away the hoarfrost obscuring his view.

'You said most cases. What could survive in conditions like that?' he asked Utulexx, whilst simultaneously smearing away the frost on the outside of the casket, creating a half-horseshoe window of clear glass through which to observe...

'Only a transhuman subject could survive in a nitrogen-saturated environment for any length of time.'

...power armour.

'Emperor's blood...' gasped Makato, and backed away. From the opposite end of the cryo-vault he heard smashing glass and the shouts of Jedda and his men. Energised carbine discharges followed in a high-pitched whine.

'Who is firing?' Makato demanded. 'Jedda, report!'

Jedda's reply was swallowed up by more las-discharge and panicked shouting.

Makato dared not turn his back on the cryo-casket. In his peripheral vision, which was limited within the dome of his helmet, he saw a second casket was similarly occupied. In the one directly in front of him, something was moving.

Power armour... It took him a few seconds to make the connection.

Through the gap in the frost, Makato saw the casket occupant's eyes open. They were black, like pools of oil.

'Enginseer, we're in trouble. Activate the Thallax.'

Utulexx gave a clipped affirmative. At the same time, a gauntleted hand smacked the inside of the casket, forming a crack in the hardened armourglass.

Makato raised his carbine and fired a three-round burst almost point-blank into the casket and ran. He went straight through the venting gas and felt it bite even through the protection of his atmosphere suit. He got as far as the junction when the crash of sundered glass resounded behind him and something heavy fell onto the deck. He did not look back.

Jedda was coming the other way with one of his men. A third shambled into view behind them. There was blood on this armsman's atmosphere suit and a rent in the hardened material through which Makato could see aggressive heat bleed. The armsman staggered two more steps before collapsing facedown on the deck.

Jedda kept on running. So did the man with him.

Makato did not know their names, only that they were Jedda's men and therefore Jedda's responsibility. Faced with what he suspected was in those caskets, Makato felt remiss in not learning those names, that in this moment of peril, he had disrespected the lesser armsmen somehow and would now not be able to rectify that. It was strange how much that bothered him.

'Where's the other one?' asked Makato, recognising his maudlin thoughts as potentially hazardous to his survival, however remote that might be, and pushing them to his subconscious. Maintain focus now, live to repent later. He, Jedda and the other armsman regrouped in sight of the central corridor. The heavy tread of the Thallax resonated against the metal as it advanced, but was not particularly comforting. Makato wanted it between them and whatever was coming out of the caskets, but his duty made him go and get his men first.

'Dead, lieutenant,' Jedda replied. 'They gutted him soon as they came out of stasis.'

'They? How many did you see?'

To his immense credit, Jedda was managing to stay coherent.

'Three, I think. The first broke out behind us, killed Halder. It was slow, still shrugging off stasis but it tore him apart all the same. We retaliated. I think we wounded it but a second one came out in front, boxing us in, so I gave the order to retreat.' Jedda glanced over his shoulder at the facedown corpse a few metres away. 'Navaar got clipped by the one we wounded.'

Halder. Navaar. Makato would remember them, and would honour their sacrifice if he survived. If any of them survived.

'I've got at least two more in banks delta and epsilon,' he said, then asked the other armsman, 'What's your name, son?'

'Bharius, sir,' Bharius answered, a little confused.

Strange, how the small things mattered when death was crouched within your eye line.

'Are they…?' ventured Jedda, unwilling to voice the name of their would-be killers aloud.

Makato nodded.

He had never fought against Renegade Space Marines before. Despite his many years of service to the Chapter, the scenario had never come about. No fire-born would ever even countenance putting a human life in harm's way whilst they could still be that human's shield. It was their creed. But Makato knew what was in that first casket, even though he had only seen a sliver of its identity, a half-glimpsed plastron, an ice-bitten gauntlet. Those pits of night glaring murderously through the frosted glass.

Armoured in black with eyes the mirror of their battleplate, there were many renegade warbands who answered that vague description. Makato knew only of a few, but had not seen any iconography or markings to narrow that down. It hardly mattered, all were deadly and beyond he and his depleted squad's current capabilities to kill or even incapacitate. Even the Thallax would struggle to overcome an entire squad of transhumans, but it could slow them down.

If Utulexx could then seal them in the cryo-vault... They were sluggish, Jedda had said as much. Even transhuman biology would struggle to return to full efficacy after prolonged cryogenic exposure. It had been the perfect camouflage but had also left them diminished.

'What are your orders, sir?'

Makato could not have wished for a better soldier than Jedda. It crushed his pride to think they might all soon be dead.

'Thallax is inbound. We get it between us and them, hold corridor gamma until Utulexx can seal the cryo-vault.'

Jedda nodded and the three of them ran for the central corridor.

The Thallax was immense and easily filled the corridor with its height and bulk. Capacitors in the cyborganic's micro-reactor cycled up to full ionisation. Coils along the barrel of the lightning gun, sleeved to its left arm and cradled by the three metal digits of its right, electrified with energised promise. A chainsaw bayonet protruding beneath the rifle's muzzle began to turn. The low hum of the blade became a throaty growl.

It halted halfway down the corridor, the single cortex in its skull flaring red, a hound at the extent of its master's leash.

Upon seeing the Thallax, Makato slowed almost to a stop as did Jedda and Bharius. The voice of the enginseer got them moving again with purpose.

'It would be unwise to delay, lieutenant.'

Makato got Jedda and Bharius behind the Thallax a few seconds before the firing began. Glancing over his shoulder as he ran down corridor gamma, Makato saw a burst of energy whip from the coiled muzzle of the lightning gun and into an armoured warrior who had just stepped into its sights.

There was an audible grunt, the strong scent of burned metal as the warrior took a hit that slung him back and slammed him into one of the caskets that then burst apart in a flare of actinic light.

A subsequent salvo of shots ignited the muzzle coil moments after the first, as the Thallax reacted to a second combatant. A third came closely on its heels. Both warriors were carrying some kind of blade, but had no firearms to speak of. It was hard to be certain in the half-dark while trying to fight the sudden rush of transhuman dread that Makato felt creeping into his marrow. The shots went wide of the mark, or rather the warrior evaded one and took the other as a glancing hit on his shoulder guard. Makato saw nothing further, as he needed to look back around or would risk colliding with the caskets or one of his men in the rising panic.

When he did turn again, the Thallax had winged the second warrior, but the third was still moving. A fourth, difficult to discern with the air clouded by the corposant discharge from the lightning gun, had entered the corridor but stooped to help his wounded comrade. According to his rough calculation, Makato reasoned the Thallax had one more shot before the third warrior made up the ground and would be on it.

There was still a quarter of the corridor to go. Makato saw Utulexx waiting at the end for them, entering the activation protocols that would seal the cryo-vault.

When he heard the high pitched shriek of the lightning gun, Makato turned. The shot was good, but even wounded the third warrior swung his blade and forced the Thallax to parry with its bayonet.

'You need to hurry,' came the voice of Utulexx through the vox.

Makato was torn between standing his ground with his carbine and running like hell. They were almost there but the Renegade Astartes were close and they moved so fast...

A fraction too late, he saw Bharius turn and aim high with his carbine. A fifth warrior in black armour had mounted one of the caskets, like a living gargoyle but one poised to attack rather than slaved to stone.

In front of Makato the Thallax had thrown back the third warrior but the second, who had now recovered, went in hard with his blade. With incredible strength he slashed apart a cluster of cabling that put the cyborg on one knee as the mechanised equivalent of its tendons were severed. A point-blank burst from the lightning gun sent the warrior reeling, rolling end over end until he struck one of the caskets and it crumpled inwards against his violent impetus.

In the same moment, a dark spray flecked Makato's helmet glacis and atmosphere suit. Bharius's abruptly clipped scream revealed what had happened.

Something large, much more massive and imposing up close, landed amongst them. Paralysed with the same dread he had been fighting ever since seeing what was inside the caskets waiting for them, Makato could only watch as a black-armoured angel of death tore apart what was left of Bharius. In the same killing stroke, the warrior seemed to point his gauntleted fingers at Utulexx who had begun to seal the cryo-vault. Makato did not even have time to feel anger at this betrayal as the enginseer came apart in a welter of gore and machine components, his blood merging horribly with oil.

Slow, so impotently slow, Makato turned with his carbine.

Reacting to its master's demise, the Thallax was turning too, intent on engaging the enginseer's murderer, who had evidently implanted his watchdog with some kind of vengeance protocol. It was ultimately dooming as, with its guard down whilst it took aim at the warrior that had killed Utulexx, the other two warriors ripped into the Thallax from behind, and destroyed it.

Knowing there was no way out now, Makato put up his hand and low-ered his gun. With a glance, he ordered Jedda to do the same.

Seen behind his retinal lenses, the eyes of the warrior who had dropped down on them from the stasis caskets met Makato's.

'Surrender…?' said a guttural voice, deep and harsh as scoured steel. 'A considerably wise move on your part.'

Now he saw the warrior up close as it rose to its full, awesome height, Makato saw the blades were not blades as such – at least, they were not the kind that are drawn or lacquered or mounted in an armoury. They were bone. A living part of the warrior. Bone protruded through his battle-helm too, a crest of it that stretched across his entire skull all the way to the nape of the neck as far as Makato could tell.

He had the rank markings of a sergeant, and Makato assumed this one was their leader, but carried no visible weapons other than the deadly bone growths. By the way he had torn Utulexx apart, Makato had thought the warrior might be a psyker but again, as he looked closer, he saw the smaller bone 'knives' embedded in parts of the enginseer's sundered corpse.

The two who had cut the Thallax apart, severing both arms and legs before decapitating it, joined the sergeant. The three warriors formed a cage of black ceramite around Makato and Jedda, who had now sunk to their knees.

These two had the same bony growths as their sergeant, only shorter and without the crest. One of the warriors, the one Makato had seen through the glass, was without a helmet. His skin was extremely pale, rimmed with frost, the extremities tinted azure with cyanosis. Whether a result of lurking in unprotected and partial cryo-stasis or some mutagenic quirk, his ears were slightly pointed at the ends, his nose almost beak-like. But it was the eyes that resonated. They were indeed black, as if the pupil had overwhelmed the sclera and clouded the eye with abject shadow.

Makato found he could not hold the warrior's gaze and looked away. Before he did, he saw that all three had the silver icon of a snarling dragon on their shoulder guards.

'We are cursed,' the sergeant told Makato when he saw him looking at the bone growths of him and his men.

Makato was no stranger to being around Adeptus Astartes. The awe they inspired with their mere presence was familiar to him, but there was something different at work in the black-armoured sergeant. He radiated strength and savagery. Something feral and utterly monstrous lurked behind the faceplate he wore, a mask to contain a beast, betrayed by the snarl in his every syllable. There was no pity, no potential for remorse or compassion, only brutality and the prospect of violence.

Despite his terror, Makato found the resolve to speak, though his words were uttered as a rasp through fear-clenched teeth.

'I am Lieutenant Makato of the Chapter Adeptus Astartes vessel *Forge Hammer*.' He was surprised at his own defiance. Jedda's head was bowed, but he raised it upon hearing Makato's proud words.

Makato was fifth generation Navy, and his esteemed heritage extended all the way back into the previous millennium. His was a proud family, a lineage of honour and duty. A silver braid upon his uniform had once belonged to his father, Hiroshimo. Makato had barely known the man, for a life in the Navy is one that seldom comes with the comfort of loved ones, but he still valued that tangible piece of familial legacy like the heirloom it truly was. A ceremonial sword he had in his quarters had once served his grandfather, Yugeti, and though Makato had never drawn it in battle the blade was still sharp. In the memories of these things lay strength. Makato drew on that, on the legacy of Yugeti and Hiroshimo, and yoked it for the courage it afforded in facing down the monster before him with unyielding resistance. He up-thrust his chin imperiously and–

The blow came swift, and a starburst of pain flashed behind Makato's eyes a moment later. He tasted blood, and felt a raw and aching agony in his face. His atmosphere helmet was gone, smashed loose by the warrior's blow. The realisation of that came late as well as the fact Makato had been knocked onto his face. It had been little more than a slap, but he felt the loose teeth in his mouth and spat out a wad of blood.

Jedda made to rise when the sergeant advanced on Makato, but was roughly put down by one of the other warriors. The sergeant paid the armsman no heed, who was doubled over in pain, several of his ribs broken.

'Leave him,' snarled Makato in a half-rasp, looking up from all fours as he tried to get back up to his feet, glaring through blurring vision.

A second blow put him down again, harder than the first and he had to stifle a yelp as he felt something break. Makato was determined not to give his aggressor that satisfaction. With the three black-armoured warriors looking on impassively, Makato struggled to his knees again and grimaced through a cage of missing teeth.

'I am Lieutenant Makat–'

He was struck again, hard enough to send him sprawling this time. Dark shadows crowded at the edge of Makato's vision as he came close to blacking out. Only half-conscious, Makato felt himself seized by a manacle-like fist. The pain of the sergeant's grip was so intense it brought Makato back around.

'I heard you, maggot,' the sergeant uttered in a low growl. 'I am battle worn and half frozen but not deaf.'

'What do you want?'

Makato could smell the sergeant's foetid breath issuing in a cloud of vapour through his helmet grille as he crouched down to answer. It stank of spoiled meat and old blood. Makato imagined fangs behind that mouth grille.

His words came out as a whisper that was more chilling than any battle cry.

'Revenge,' he said. 'But first we want your ship.'

Makato laughed in spite of his rising terror. 'You are mad. There will be retribution for this.'

'Could well be,' said the sergeant before he hauled Makato up by the chin, his gauntleted fingers closing vice-like around the lieutenant's neck. The fingers bit flesh, drawing blood. He raised him until his feet dangled off the floor. 'Now hear me. Your courage is misplaced. You want to live, but above that you want your men to live. I am willing to allow this. The one in the corridor you left for dead yet survives. So too does the one currently bent double at the feet of my warriors.'

The sergeant seized Makato's neck a little harder, spreading his fingers across his lower jaw as he brought him in closer. 'I am Urgaresh of the Black Dragons. You will see us aboard your ship, and on my honour no further hand will be raised to you. Are we in accord?' The one who called himself Urgaresh dropped Makato to the deck, who immediately gasped for air as he clutched his throat.

'Your honour?' said Makato when he could breathe again. 'How can you speak of honour when you ambushed and killed two of my men?'

'We fought. You lost. Do not succumb to vainglorious pride and add to the tally already made. An accord? Do we have one or must I kill another?'

Urgaresh stepped in close, giving Makato the lightest of kicks to urge him towards a quick answer. Pain flared in Makato's chest, but he was still alive. So was Jedda, so was Navaar if what the Black Dragon had said was to be believed. He did not know the name of the warband, what Ruinous deities or warmaster they served. Makato only knew he had no choices left.

He nodded weakly.

Urgaresh stepped back and called to the warrior who had stopped to tend to their injured.

'Thorast, does our brother yet live?'

'He does.'

Urgaresh turned back to Makato. 'That is fortunate for you, maggot. Tend the wounded mortal, stabilise him only,' he continued to Thorast, though his gaze did not leave Makato, who was kneeling again. 'Get these two fit enough to leave this ship on foot. We are bound for the *Forge Hammer* then, and a reckoning with the sons of Nocturne.'

CHAPTER SEVEN

Sturndrang, underhive of Molior

The journey from the surface of Sturndrang and down into the subterranean underhive had not been without incident. Even by shedding their armour and attempting to conceal their true nature beneath capacious storm cloaks, the Salamanders were far from inconspicuous. An underhive was the epitome of a dog-eat-dog existence, except here they actually did eat the dogs… and the rats, and whatever other carrion was unfortunate enough to stray beneath the hungering gaze of the underhivers. Dominance through fear of reprisal, the showing and establishing of strength was essential for anyone to thrive in such lightless, lawless conditions. That often meant as a pack, for even starving wolves are prone towards an instinct to congregate. It was no different here in the deep underground of Hive Molior.

Three men, large in stature, and obviously of a martial leaning had entered an arena without their prior knowledge of the fact. The arena was immense, the length, breadth and depth of the sprawling underhive. They had been stalked, but suppressing their genetically imposed instincts to confront and overcome, the Salamanders had managed to avoid conflict until one of those hiver wolf packs had finally tracked their scent to a place of reckoning. It had gone poorly for the gangers, who had made the fatal mistake of thinking their trio of chrono-gladiators were any guarantee of victory against such hooded and unknown warriors. Hulking and gene-bulked, the chrono-gladiators would fight on regardless of injury, until their death-clocks ran out. For most, at least those that inhabited Molior's underhive, they would be formidable opponents. For most... not all. Their leader had seen three fools lost and out of their depth; his education to the contrary had been bloody and at Zartath's hands, or rather claws. So had it been for all fifteen of these wretched men.

As Exor performed a more detailed analysis of the crashed ship and Zartath hunted for Tsu'gan's ever-cooling trail, Agatone went over to the corpses of the gangers.

He had little experience of hive scum such as this, his wars demanding a much sterner test of the veteran captain, and found them an eclectic mix. There were hazards in these dark, forgotten places of the world, he had no doubt about that, but the threat did not come from such pathetic opponents. They were a far cry from the noble sons and daughters of Nocturne, and Agatone wondered how hard he would strive to protect the lives of degenerates such as these. He considered the morality of that decision, and whether or not it was right to discriminate on the grounds of personal worth as he saw it.

Am I fit to be the arbiter of such a decision? he wondered. And what of Tsu'gan? How should he be judged? It was a dilemma he had faced ever since being charged by Tu'Shan with the errant Salamander's recovery. Others from Third had far more straightforward imperatives. Most remained on Nocturne to help train the scout company and begin the inception of a Seventh Battle Company, an unprecedented undertaking since before the time of the Second Founding. Two much smaller factions had been given unique sanction by the Chapter Master, one to track down Tsu'gan and the other, comprising Firedrakes led by Herculon Praetor, to find whatever remained of the Dragon Warriors. Praetor's mission was simple – retrieve from their cold, dead corpses the missing book from the Tome of Fire.

Agatone was not given the choice of which path to take. In his heart, he wanted nothing more than to track down the Chaos renegades and exact vengeance for their heinous assault on Nocturne, but Tsu'gan had been his responsibility. In the Pantheon Chamber, he had vowed to Tu'Shan to do all within his power to bring the errant fire-born back, or die in the attempt.

And so he and nine others had departed the *Vulkan's Wrath* and secured a more modest frigate to take them to Sturndrang where the last recorded position of the stolen Malevolent gunship had been plotted by Prometheus's sensorium. It was tenuous as trails went, and a planet-wide search grid was far from narrow, but they had found the ship and that in itself was miraculous. Now they merely had to find the man. Agatone was close to beseeching the Emperor for His providence.

'Do you hear that?'

Zartath's voice distracted him from his thoughts. He began to return to the crashed gunship.

Somewhere in the distance, deep in the belly of the underhive, a rough klaxon was chiming. It could mean more hive scum, or something worse.

'It's getting louder,' said Agatone, and reached for his holstered pistol. He slipped a small combat shield the size of a buckler onto his wrist. All of their weapons were small, easy to conceal, but at that moment he wished he had a bolter.

Behind him, one of the gangers was stirring.

'I thought you killed them...'

Zartath's fangs glistened wetly in the faint phosphor light. The klaxons were rising in volume as if one had begun a relay and that relay was now working its way towards them. He had to shout.

'I did!' Spittle sprang from his lips in a chain as Zartath's bone claws snapped loose, first piercing flesh then skin. 'They were cold when I left them.' His martial pride had been slighted and that needed to be answered for, but Agatone was already standing over the dead gangers. The master had the leash.

'Karve don't die so easy, hulk...' drawled the ganger, but he was in a bad way. When he tried to rise, Agatone floored him with a palm-strike to the chest. It was little more than a slap, but cracked at least two ribs.

'Stay down,' Agatone warned.

The one called Karve gurgled, blood frothing from his lips because of a collapsed lung. Aghast at what the warrior had done to him, Karve had enough strength to rip open his jacket and body armour. Beneath the rough apparel was some kind of device. It looked to Agatone like a hexagonal amulet, a piece of crude technology that had as much to do with the arcane as it did with science. Briefly, he wondered where this gutter rat had found, stolen or bartered for it.

Upon closer inspection, he realised that rather than being on a chain, the amulet was actually surgically attached to Karve's chest, just below his heart. There were small notations etched around the edge that could have been runes and it had two hardened glass ampoules inset in a small chamber in the centre. The dual vial of chemicals was empty as the various stimulants and apparently regenerative fluids had already been dumped into Karve's body intravenously. It was how he had come back, with a massive flood of chemicals and perhaps something else if the runes were not just for ornamentation.

Karve tried to laugh but just ended up gurgling more blood. Agatone could tell by his eyes though – they were narrowed in bitter mirth, and the wretch flecked his lips with crimson as he spat and wheezed.

'You're dying,' Agatone told him, his eyes pitiless as they regarded the wretch. 'Whatever you know, speak up now and I'll end it quickly.'

A bone claw flashed past his eye-line, coming perilously close to the ganger's exposed neck and would have cut off Karve's head had Agatone not seized Zartath's wrist.

Heel! The command came unbidden to Agatone's mind and he felt ashamed at it. He chose his actual words more carefully.

'Hold. He knows something. I want to hear it.' Agatone's dour gaze fixed on Karve again. 'What are these alarms? What do they mean?' Seeing it rotating slowly on the ganger's chest, Agatone seized the amulet and stalled its motion. Karve immediately paled and jerked uncomfortably. 'Talk and I release it. You can eke out whatever dregs of life are left in this thing or I can end you. Those are the last two choices left to you now.'

A crude equivalent of an adrenaline shunt, the amulet was no doubt intended to give an enterprising underhiver a fighting chance at finding aid or sloping off to safety should he be badly injured. But Karve's wounds had been so severe that it was merely prolonging his life so he could experience more pain. Agatone was willing to extend that further if he could find out what the discordant noise coming from the klaxons meant.

Alerted by the sound, Exor emerged from the wrecked gunship to find both Agatone and Zartath crouched over the ganger.

'What is it?' he called out. 'Did we trip some kind of alarm?'

'I don't think it's an alarm…' said Agatone, watching the ganger's growing hysteria. 'I think it's a warning.' He released the amulet and let it continue its fatal countdown. There was no negotiating with the wretch now – his mind was crashing even as the cocktail of narcotics flooding his system attempted to jumpstart his broken body. There was no resurrection for gutter scum; for them, death was a way of life. Knowing his end was near, the ganger smiled, showing blood-rimmed teeth, and managed to utter two words before he died.

'Feeding time…'

Agatone crushed his throat with a booted foot.

Zartath growled, annoyed at being deprived of the kill, but a glare from Agatone calmed him at once. Again, the captain tried not to think of the warrior as a wild beast only partially tamed, but evidence was evidence.

'Something is coming,' snarled Zartath, and turned in the direction of the deeper underhive and the darkness smothering it.

Agatone checked the ammo gauge on his bolt pistol. He carried two spare clips attached to his belt, but if he ran dry he still had his combat knife. He eyed the darkness that seemed to have grown more pervasive over the intervening seconds.

'Whatever comes from that tunnel,' he said, using his vox-bead, 'does not live. Am I understood, brothers?'

Both Salamanders responded in the affirmative.

Standing at the periphery of the crash debris, Exor had drawn a lamp pack as well as his bolt pistol and was shining it into the gloom. By now the klaxons were screaming, evidently part of a mechanised relay that fed throughout much of this district.

'What does it presage, Zartath?' asked Agatone, his voice almost a roar by necessity. Over the years, he had learned to trust the savage warrior, but Zartath did not answer. He listened. Agatone cast around for the source of the cacophony but it had to be higher up, above ground level and accessed via lifter or one of the many ladders to the rusted gantries.

Whilst his comrades were rooted, Exor kept advancing with the lamp pack. His bolt pistol panned across the leavened shadows.

The vox-bead in Agatone's right ear crackled.

'I see movement, brother-captain.'

Up ahead, Exor dropped into a kneeling position, setting down the lamp pack so he could aim his sidearm and also draw his combat knife.

'Distance, brother?' asked Agatone, hurrying to reach the Techmarine. Zartath was a few steps behind him.

'Hard to be sure… It's as if the ground is… writhing.'

The great, sprawling underhives below cities such as Molior were fraught with dangers. In many respects they were as war-torn as any of the battlefields Agatone had ever fought on.

Feeding time, the ganger had said.

Food for what, though?

'What do you mean, Exor? Be specific. What can you see, broth–'

Agatone cut off at the same time as the warning klaxons.

In the echoing silence that followed, a different sound established itself. It was the sharp refrain of skittering and the shriek of thousands of bestial voices.

'Name of Vulkan,' Agatone breathed, realising what was upon them. 'Fall back, Exor. That is an order, Techmarine.'

There was no time. Spewing from the tunnel mouth, riming its sides almost all the way to the ceiling, was a vast deluge of vermin. Some had the appearance of rats, others were malformed and only resembled creatures of nature. As he saw what was bearing down on the Techmarine, who stood before it like a man before the crashing waves of a tsunami he knows he cannot outrun, Agatone knew this was a plague of un-nature. Mutation was rife in the swollen tide and Exor was about to be drowned in it.

Exor carried a belt of flares, six in total. He lit and threw down the entire bandoleer, then ran with all haste. The vermin tide screeched angrily as the flares ignited, the light rather than the fire causing them pain. It gave him a few precious seconds to gain some ground.

Agatone and Zartath were coming towards him. He waved them back, shouting, 'Get to high ground!'

Behind him, the shrieking vermin chorus was like a knife drawn over glass. Exor clenched his teeth and fired off a three-round burst blind. The shrieking intensified in pitch for a few seconds, and he realised he had hit something. But then how could he miss?

The nearest gantry was a few metres away – Agatone and Zartath were already climbing its rickety ladder – when Exor felt the creature land on his back. Only half armoured with what amounted to Scout carapace, he was more vulnerable than he would have been in an encompassing suit of power armour. It stank, the creature, of spoiled meat and mould. There was something else too, a taint that disturbed Exor more than the horde itself and suggested a ruinous origin to the mutation affecting the vermin. It bit deep into the back of his neck before Exor could crush it.

Another latched onto his leg but he shook it off before it could bite down. He did not risk another shot, putting all of his effort into running those last few metres. The tide was almost upon him now, its high-pitched squeal deafening and close.

Agatone and Zartath had made it to the gantry. Exor boosted into a final sprint and leapt for the ladder. He scaled the first few rungs before his weight and the impact of his landing wrenched the bolts free and the ladder tore away from its holdings.

Instinctively he reached out and felt a strong grip around his wrist.

'Hold on,' Zartath snarled through gritted teeth, leaning right over the gantry with Agatone clinging to his belter to stabilise him.

Below Exor, the vermin tide roiled and undulated. The diminutive horde lapped against the support struts of the gantry like a dirty sea pounding against the resolve of coastal bulwarks. Blood slicked the Techmarine's arm from a savage bite – with the adrenaline pumping into his system, he had barely noticed it but now it was running freely, something in the bite preventing his Larraman cells clotting as they should do. Zartath felt his hand slipping, and he fought to maintain his grip.

'Climb…' he snarled with the effort of holding on.

Exor reached, determination etched on his nondescript features… and slipped.

The fall was relatively short, and what awaited him below was far more hazardous.

Agatone watched his Techmarine disappear into a morass of furred bodies. Exor was absorbed instantly.

Zartath made to leap in after him, but Agatone stopped him.

'He'll be carried by the flood, end up Throne knows where,' growled the ex-Black Dragon.

'So will you if you jump. Here,' said Agatone, finding a length of chain and hacking it loose from the gantry with his blade, 'we'll drag him in.'

Agatone opened up the vox whilst Zartath gathered up the length of chain.

'Exor,' Agatone began, scanning the vermin tide for any sign of the Techmarine, 'if you can hear me, try to breach the surface and we'll haul you in.'

There was no response, but a second later Exor's outstretched hand burst forth from the tide which had now flooded the entire lower level.

Zartath was whipping the chain around in a circular fashion and was about to launch it in the direction of Exor's hand when he saw what was clenched in it.

A frag grenade primed for detonation exploded in the Techmarine's hand as he released the trigger. Scores of furred, verminous bodies were sent skyward in a welter of blood and bone. The blast forged a crater in the tide with Exor at its epicentre. He was badly wounded, and had lost the hand, but he was alive.

Knowing the tide would reform in moments, Zartath threw the chain. Exor caught it in his remaining hand and Agatone heaved. With Zartath helping, Agatone pulled Exor up and away from the ravening horde. They hauled the Techmarine like a piece of cargo, and when his body crested the gantry's edge they dragged him onto it.

'Vulkan's mercy…' Agatone breathed.

Exor was covered in bites. Every bit of exposed flesh had been gnawed upon, in some cases savagely. His right hand and forearm were almost completely destroyed. Oil and blood were spewing from the shattered cabling jutting from the stump. It was a mercy that the hand had been a bionic. His armour was ruined and though partially shielded from the blast by his attackers, Exor was badly burned.

Agatone would have expected such injuries to already be healing, but something was interfering with Exor's regenerative abilities and he bled from where he should be healed.

'Some kind of toxin…' he rasped feverishly. He was shaking, going into shock.

Below them, the vermin tide was passing, and Agatone guessed it happened in cycles, hence the klaxons.

'What do we do with him?' said Zartath.

Agatone shook his head, sighing deeply. This had not been a part of his plan. Too deep to go back, too far away from help to request reinforcement or extraction, there was little choice left to him.

'Get him to a medic. There must be something down here. Wherever that wretch,' he gestured to where Karve and his men used to be, for the tide had carried them off to feast upon, 'stole that disc from that he wore. Our mission is to stabilise Exor and then proceed as originally planned.'

'Leave me here…' said Exor, but the words were laboured. 'I just need time… to recover, then rejoin you later.'

Zartath had dragged him up into a sitting position but the Techmarine still looked on the verge of collapse.

'There's something in your blood, Exor,' Agatone told him. 'It's preventing you from healing properly.'

'Poison… I can feel it… coursing through me.'

'Not coursing,' snarled Zartath as he tasted some of Exor's spilled blood before quickly spitting it up, 'cursing, brother.' For once, there was no rancour when he referred to Exor as his brother. Zartath looked up at Agatone from his kneeling position. 'Tainted. An unnatural venom.'

Despite being close to unconsciousness, Exor's eyes widened as he despaired, 'Am I damned then?'

'No, brother,' Agatone replied, tasting the blood for himself and scowling as he too spat it out immediately. 'Chaos damnation is not a disease. You cannot contract it by a wound. It is a moral decay, a choice. Those things harboured it, some dark plague, and we must flush it out if you're to heal.'

'You're certain it is… the taint?' asked Exor, face screwed up in obvious pain.

'No, but I can see its effects and it is no poison I have ever encountered. The taste of your blood, it is not… right. It's old, somehow.'

'Then Tsu'gan found more here…' Exor faltered briefly, 'than a hive city. Could he have succumbed to it?'

'Perhaps, but we won't know until we find his body or evidence of his escape,' said Agatone. 'Either way, we're getting you away from here and to whatever help this warren can offer.' Agatone went to lift Exor up, when Zartath stopped him.

'Respectfully, brother-captain,' said Zartath, 'I must carry him.'

'Because you think you let him fall?'

'Because you are the leader of this mission and should not be encumbered and, yes, because I let him fall.'

'You're my hunter. I need you out in front,' said Agatone. 'Exor stays with me.'

Zartath did not argue, he merely helped his captain get Exor onto his shoulders so Agatone could carry him.

'He's heavy,' said Agatone.

'Too much metal,' Zartath replied.

'That metal may well have saved him,' Agatone replied, noting that Exor had passed out. That was good, it meant his body was trying to heal him.

'Are his wounds tainted by Chaos?' asked Zartath.

'You tasted his blood too, what was your first impression?'

'I received a vision, a flash, a fragment, nothing more,' Zartath replied. 'Such tortures were inflicted upon me at Volgorrah by the xenos. They were weapons of the warp, brother-captain. Tainted blades, tainted fangs.

I saw hell in my mind's eye. I hear it still, a keening in my ears. What did you see?'

Hell, thought Agatone, but did not speak it. He did not need to.

'Which way?' he asked.

'Tsu'gan's tracks suggested he went east.' Zartath pointed in the direction of the tunnel.

It was wide mouthed, hung with the broken links of chains and decaying girders. Even in the gloom, they could see it sloped downwards and went deeper into the heart of the underhive. For now, it looked deserted. If the vermin tide did return, the klaxons would sound. Forewarned, even encumbered with Exor's body, they should be able to get clear in time. Tsu'gan was injured in the crash. He would have needed aid too, and Agatone had never met a warrior with better survival instincts than he.

'Then we go east,' he said, and let Zartath lead the way.

CHAPTER EIGHT

Heletine, Imperial-held city of Escadan

Before the invasion, Escadan had been a city that vaunted achievement and excellence in all its forms. Unlike the labyrinthine Canticus, or the towering industrial stacks of Solist, Escadan had been a bastion of light where the great and gifted were exalted like gods. Statues and petroglyphs celebrating the world's luminaries lined the concourses to its many cenotaph and stadia. Historians, scientists, ecclesiarchs and artisans were all honoured in marble, onyx, agate and carnelian.

When war came, the exalted were trampled just as easily as their lessers, bloody conflict ever the great leveller.

A veritable cavalcade of exquisitely detailed statuary punctuated the galleria to the grand amphitheatre Drakgaard had chosen as his headquarters in the city. It was expansive, though its beauty had been no defence during the outbreak of hostilities. It was the first place the allied Imperial forces had secured and liberated, but many of the alabaster renderings that greeted visitors to the arena itself were mutilated in some fashion. Intended to recount the athletic achievements performed here, now they were a stark reminder of what Escadan and, indeed, Heletine had lost because of the war.

Stark magnesium lamps had been erected around a relatively small area in the centre of the amphitheatre. Drakgaard stood within the cordon of light, just breaching the penumbra at its edge as he pored over a hololithic map table whilst awaiting the summoned officers and the new arrivals.

Elysius had joined him, having followed from the preceptory roof.

'Why here, brother-captain, if you don't mind me asking?'

'I do not,' Drakgaard replied stiffly, his attention on the map that showed an uncomfortable number of red zones where the enemy still held territory. Since initial engagement, the pattern on the map had shifted as the Black Legion migrated from region to region, halting briefly to fight before moving on again like ash nomads. As of yet, Drakgaard had been unable to detect any strategy in it.

'It helps me think,' said the captain at length. He looked up, taking a rare break from his strategising. 'Here,' he gestured to the expansive amphitheatre. He did not know its name, for there were none left alive to tell it, at least that he had met, but it hardly mattered. 'In this sliver of light, I am an island. Around me is darkness, obscuring, obfuscating, but here in the light I can see clearly.'

'A little more poetic than I had you down for, Ur'zan,' said Elysius.

'My mind isn't closed off to it as some would believe. I merely find little use for it.'

The Chaplain laughed, and the sound echoed, but there was irony to his mirth.

'Are you sure it isn't metal and cybernetics beneath your skin instead of flesh?'

'Would that it was,' Drakgaard replied bitterly and went back to the map table.

Just beyond the edge of the oval of light cast by the lamps, a small group of serfs and Departmento Munitorum logisticians examined data concerning supply lines, ammunition stores, casualty rates and engagement reports. Drakgaard had them feed him every one through his battle-helm's retinal lens display.

'Canticus is the dam,' muttered Drakgaard as he surveyed the map and the troop dispositions on it again, 'breach it and we will flood this world with our wrath. None could escape it.'

Elysius was about to respond when he heard footsteps echoing from one of the concourses that led into the amphitheatre. They sounded unhurried but purposeful, and lighter than a fully armoured Adeptus Astartes would make.

Three females, tall and armoured in the black of the Ebon Chalice with white chasubles beneath accented by crimson inner fabric, emerged into the arena. Though they were shrouded by shadow, Elysius had some time to examine them as they made their way across to where the Salamanders awaited in the cordon of light.

Two were stern-faced, their age hard to determine. One, a canoness by the look of her trappings, had harder eyes that spoke of centuries of warfare. Votive chains attached to censers trailing prayer incense hung from

her battleplate. A pair of braziers, slaved to a small reservoir of promethium, crested the rounded stabiliser jets of her power armour's generator.
She carried a power mace tied off at her hip by a leather thong and on the
opposite hip wore a holstered fusion pistol. Her hair was cropped short
and the silver of polished gunmetal.

The other was marginally less grizzled but carried a scar down the left
side of her face that must have come close to taking her eye. The scar
extended across her scalp, however, cutting a channel into coal-black hair
that was flecked with white. Across the unmarred side of her face, she had
tattooed an icon of the Ebon Chalice, presumably to guard her sight from
further harm. A bolter was mag-locked to her thigh, the stock modified
and shortened with a combination flamer attachment. On the other side
she had locked her helmet, which was pure white and marked above the
helm's retinal lenses with the same icon she had tattooed on her face.
Her sidearm was a bolt pistol, but in her gauntleted hands she cradled a
leather book and not a weapon. Purity seals adhered to her armour, held
in place by red nubs of wax stamped with the Order's holy sigil.

Not as tall or broad as a Space Marine, the Sisters of Battle still radiated
strength and purpose. Despite his distaste for some of their methods,
Elysius found it hard not to feel a kinship with these warriors. He saw
the reason for his reluctance in their eyes, for they glittered with a hostile
fervour Elysius would not have expected amongst supposed allies.

As a Chaplain, Elysius was no stranger to impassioned oratory. His
sermons were crafted to inspire fury and purpose in his brothers, but
since his time in the clutches of the dark eldar on the Volgorrah Reef and
everything he had witnessed during the battle for Nocturne, his once
brittle humours had veered away from the choleric. He believed he was a
better spiritual leader because of it, but these two still retained an edge of
religious fanaticism that Elysius considered dangerous to any who failed
to share it.

By contrast the third Battle Sister appeared less soul-hardened. She was
younger, her hair longer than the other two, with streaks of velvet red in
the black. She also wore a fluted jump pack, reminiscent of angel wings,
marking her out as a Seraphim. Elysius had fought beside these shock
troops before and knew them to be effective, dedicated warriors. This one
had the rank insignia of a sergeant, or Sister Superior in the less secular
terminology of the Adepta Sororitas.

Striding across the cracked flagstones of the partially ruined arena, the
canoness and her charges were quickly before the two Salamanders.

'Blessings of Saint Dominica upon you, Chaplain,' she addressed Elysius
with a slight bow, recognising his spiritual authority before the actual
secular command of Drakgaard, 'and you, captain,' she conceded with a
nod. 'I am Canoness Angerer, Preceptor of the Order of the Ebon Chalice.'

Though she spoke ostensibly in greeting, the canoness's words were like iron coming from her lips, her voice as stern as her bearing.

'My Sororitas...' she began, gesturing to her retinue who bowed as Angerer's gauntleted hand passed over them as if in benediction, 'Sisters Superior Laevenius of my Celestian Guard,' the scarred warrior glared icily, her fingers seeming to tighten on the book, 'and Stephina of the Order Seraphim.' She nodded to both warriors, hands by her sides and within easy reach of the powerblade she had sheathed next to her jump pack and the plasma pistol belted at her waist.

Elysius hoped it was just habit that made them so war wary, or this alliance that was seemingly being proposed by the Sisters' presence on Heletine would not be an easy one.

Drakgaard made curt introductions, explaining the other officers in his command cadre were either inbound or about to be linked to by hololith. He did not waste time with pleasantries, preferring to explain quickly so he could move on to the obvious question.

'What are you doing here on Heletine, Canoness Angerer? What brings the noble Sisterhood of the Ebon Chalice to my battlefield?'

Elysius sighed resignedly, the gesture hidden by the shadows. The meeting had not begun well.

A difficult alliance it is then.

What the Sisterhood wanted was precious little. As a holy world, and part of the Ecclesiarchy's galactic protectorate, Heletine had several enshrined relics that would be better served far from the war zone and in the custody of the Sisterhood's Convent Prioris on Terra.

Angerer and her Order were here to ensure the acquisition, protection and transference of these relics. They had brought a Preceptory to achieve this sacred task, which included over six hundred Adepta Sororitas, the majority of those of the Order Militant, and a sizeable armoured force of Immolators. According to Angerer, her Battle Sisters were already being deployed in the muster field at the edge of Escadan city along with the flame tanks.

In openly discussing the disposition of her forces, Angerer also pledged her Sister Hospitallers towards leavening the burden placed upon the Imperial medicae by the war thus far. Furthermore, she added, if the Ebon Chalice could lend aid to the Adeptus Astartes in the prosecution of their sacred duty, then they would consider themselves doubly blessed.

'It could explain the erratic occupation of the enemy,' suggested Elysius after he had finished hearing what Angerer had to say about the relics.

Drakgaard nodded, his eyes back on the map hololith.

On Armageddon the orks had deliberately befouled certain sites of religious significance, effectively rededicating them to their own brutish deities. None could say if such vile acts had any bearing on the spiritual conflict being fought across the entire world, if Imperial belief was somehow weakened as a result, but it had dampened morale and sapped the courage of some. Where the orks erected their totems, where their crude sculptures of dung stood like dirty monoliths, blighting the air with their stench, the greenskins were harder to defeat.

The Imperial allies on Heletine had yet to see or hear from the heretic leader – some more credulous individuals believed it could be the Warmaster himself but that was ridiculous – but his strategy might be to fight a war of faith to win a war of blood.

Drakgaard gestured to the areas of confluence on the map hololith.

'Can you determine which of these regions are also sites of religious significance?'

Angerer had a string of votive peals in her grasp, twenty-three perfect white orbs that the canoness would later explain represented all the souls she had saved from darkness and brought to repentance. She had many such rosaries in her possession; this was the only one with a single black opal.

As she smoothed the pearls between her fingers, Angerer's lip curled but the thin smile did not reach her eyes.

'My Sister Dialogus has already begun.'

The Stormraven touched down on a landing strip within sight of the amphitheatre.

Iaptus had said nothing further during their short journey. Va'lin considered mentioning the sigils in the gun nest but had no idea to what they portended, if anything. He also thought about voicing his concerns to his sergeant about Ky'dak but decided the matter was between him and Ky'dak for now.

So it was that they flew from the edge of Canticus to the heart of Escadan in silence but with their thoughts far from quiescent.

As soon as they disembarked, Va'lin noticed theirs was not the only transport to have alighted in such close proximity to the Imperial headquarters. Another, a black-armoured Rhino with an icon of a white chalice on its flanks, also stood idle at the edge of the landing apron. Its engines burred, giving off a faint heat wash, as the vehicle readied for imminent departure.

At a more distant landing zone, the main muster field for the Imperial forces as well as its barracks, a host of those same black ships were in the midst of deployment. Va'lin noticed several tanks amongst the disciplined squads of Battle Sisters.

'Armour and infantry,' he observed. 'The Sororitas are here in force, brother-sergeant.'

Though the main muster field was over a kilometre away, the rituals of blessing and piety being performed by the Sisters were discernible, as were the bizarre war engines that came ambling out of their ships' holds and the zealots who accompanied them.

Blinded, festooned with devotional seals and the red-raw wheals inflicted during self-flagellation, they appeared more like slaves than warriors. The engines were fashioned in the manner of walkers, bipedal and armed with various blades and saws. Some also carried what looked like short-range flamers. A whip-thin, emaciated wretch served as the only crew. Va'lin found it difficult to tell if they were manning the machine or were bound to it as some form of torture.

The others, those who marched sullenly alongside the walkers were no better. They wore hoods in the form of masked inhibitor helms and their lash-grafted arms hung slack by their sides, trailing in the dirt. Barefoot, their reedy bodies were half-naked and exposed to the elements.

'They are the penitent,' said Iaptus when he noted Va'lin's frown. 'See...' He gestured to a cadre of chainblade wielding females and the mistress goading them from the ship with an energised lash. 'Faith can do strange things to the faithful, but it is nothing compared to its potential effects on those wishing to atone or punish themselves for transgression.'

'What kind of army is this?' asked Va'lin, heedless of the disrespect he had just directed at the Sororitas.

Whilst they were talking, they had moved within the shadow of the amphitheatre. Its faded glory and obvious ruination were a microcosm of what was happening to Heletine.

'We are about to find out, brother,' Iaptus replied.

Both Sergeant Zantho and Colonel Redgage, the commanding officer of the Cadian 81st, attended the war conference via hololith. Their forms were rendered in grainy static-laced amber light that emitted from projector ports located in the floor of Drakgaard's command hub.

A third figure joined them via hololith, though his projection was much larger than the other two and, despite the fact his actual presence was many kilometres away in Canticus, entirely forbidding.

'No gains were made during our last sortie into the western districts.'

The voice had once been that of a transhuman warrior, but was now rendered machine-like through Dreadnought vox-casters that trembled the air even via hololith.

Kor'ad was immense, and his sarcophagus was a scaled carapace replete with the honours of his previous incarnation as a brother-captain of the fire-born. Upon his hulking back he wore the spines of the beast he had ritually killed for his ascension to the Chapter. Its hide hung down like a tabard between two piston-driven legs. Twice he had been forced to quit his appointed posting within, initially to perform an undertaking of great honour, secondarily out of necessity and a desire to serve on. Kor'ad did not miss the touch of air upon his face, the feeling of heat against his bare skin. He did not care that he would never witness another sunrise or behold his brothers with his own eyes rather than the sensorium of his Dreadnought tomb. Kor'ad, the Warmaker, had no such misgivings about his transformation. As a flesh and blood Salamander he had lived for battle – now he could fight on forever.

Kor'ad's left arm was gloved in a power fist that in turn clenched a thunder hammer. The right carried a weapon-mount, a Contemptor-pattern heavy plasma, the wide muzzle shaped into a dragon's snout. His flamer would have been more appropriate to the iconography but it lacked range and firepower for what Kor'ad had in mind.

Colonel Redgage, a thick-set man with a neat handlebar moustache and grey hair, was clearly still in the field. The edges of a war tent were revealed at the very extremity of the hololithic projection and the dull, but far off, sound of heavy mortar occasionally interrupted his reports. Kor'ad, though, was at war during the conference, his grainy image showing him in battle. More than once the resolution cut off mid-stream as a nearby explosion broke the link, and it was generally foul with smoke and airborne debris.

'The loss of the armour reduced our efficacy considerably, captain. I strive to hold what we have already taken but it is far from certain.'

Kor'ad led a heavy division comprising half of Sixth Company's Devastators and two other Dreadnoughts. Snatches of missile salvoes and the collimated streamers from heavy energy weapons intruded on the feed. The barrage from the Devastators was intense and unremitting. They were a hammer, a means to pound the entrenched enemy into submission for the spear thrust of Zantho's tanks.

'If you shackle my hands, captain, what else can I do but strain against it?'

The plan involving the heavy weapons unravelled spectacularly when all the Salamanders armour was recalled from the western districts and Kor'ad was left with a static force with no means of actually taking the ground they had spent so long pummelling. It had left the venerable warrior frustrated.

'I am a war-maker, captain, not a defensive bastion.'

The hololith crazed once then blinked out. Whether the link had been cut accidentally or deliberately would likely never be known.

It left Drakgaard seething at only static charged air.

The council had not gone well. Va'lin and Iaptus had arrived in the midst of Zantho's report. Despite their victory at Canticus south, the tanks had achieved little but to shore up a ruin and prevent a slaughter. That in itself was reason enough to redeploy them but it brought the Salamanders no closer to a lasting victory on Heletine. Every engagement had been a frustrated one. Heretics were dug in, and the warren-like streets made for a complex hunting ground.

Drakgaard dearly wanted to burn them out, but he lacked the necessary manpower to conduct a citywide cleanse. Ambuscade complicated matters further, making the execution of a large scale mission difficult. They were spread thin and unable to consolidate.

'You are at an impasse, brother-captain,' said Angerer after she had heard the reports of all the officers. 'And I sense the Emperor's divine providence in bringing us to Heletine to win this war of faith. Your salvation is at hand.'

The physically present Salamanders stiffened at this remark. Iaptus clenched his fists. Even Va'lin felt his gorge rise at the canoness's remarks. Zantho and Redgage cut their holo-feeds. Only Elysius managed to remain neutral.

Drakgaard gave voice to the reason for the sudden hostility.

'Our salvation and inevitable victory shall be won with our blood and courage, as our gains in this war have been so far.'

'Forgive me, brother-captain,' said Angerer, bowing with false contrition. 'I only refer to the ruins we saw upon our arrival, of a city... no, a world in turmoil.' She made the sign of the aquila and never before had Drakgaard found it so repellent. 'The Emperor is with you now, His light shines through us, His daughters. Surely, even the stubborn pride of the Salamanders would yield to an ally sent from the Throne itself?'

With the Adepta Sororitas tanks, with their warriors and materiel, they could launch an effective counter attack. A citywide purge might be possible, but not under these conditions. Drakgaard could not countenance that. He had expected trouble from the Ecclesiarchy troops but not this arrogance and condescension.

'Salamanders yield to no one,' he uttered through clenched teeth. 'Even emissaries of the Throne. You need to choose your words more wisely, Sister.'

Angerer bowed again, but showed no remorse this time.

'I meant no slight or dishonour, but you are losing this war. Whether your faith is wanting or your arm unwilling, it does not matter–'

'Wisely, Sister!' Drakgaard warned her, echoing the belligerence felt by his men.

'It does not matter,' Angerer repeated, and would not be cowed. 'We are here. The Emperor is here.'

Laevenius maintained a mask of austerity throughout, but the younger Sister Stephina could not hide her concern at the sudden turn of events, her gaze flicking back between the Space Marines they had inadvertently annoyed.

Angerer was heedless of both.

'Relics of the holy Ecclesiarchy are at rest beneath the rubble you have made of these temples and sanctuaries. I only pray they are still intact.' And now did she reveal the cause of her passive aggression. 'You are truly the hammer, aren't you Captain Drakgaard? It has fallen here on Heletine, a slayer of relics more than a slayer of heretics, I am afraid.'

Drakgaard half drew his sword. It was a saw-toothed kaskara with one serrated edge and the other a singular flat blade. The hilt was ornate, with a blended tellurium and gold banding for the grip. The pommel was a drake's tooth ripped from the maw of the beast whose hide also served as Drakgaard's cloak. It was sun-burnished and flashed like copper flame as it was unsheathed.

Elysius laid a hand on the kaskara's pommel, preventing Drakgaard from drawing it fully. When the captain glared back at him, the Chaplain lightly shook his head. Realising he was being baited, Drakgaard regained his.

'Do not presume me to be a patient man, Sister,' he said to Angerer. 'I do not bear insult with reproach or restitution. You should know this about me.'

Around the war council, both Iaptus and Va'lin had drawn pistols in their hands. From the shadows, Drakgaard's command squad became more than just bulky silhouettes as they emerged into the light. They too had weapons to hand. None would use them unless commanded.

Drakgaard did not need them to. The show of unity was enough.

'It is the same for my Chapter,' he explained needlessly.

Elysius clutched the icon of a hammer he had bound to his armour with his ordinary hand and stared at the Adepta Sororitas, one servant of the Imperial faith to another. Though his face was as stone, there was a depth of warning in his gaze.

Angerer seemed abruptly aware of her surroundings, all her bombast and self-righteousness having bled away like smoke. She licked her lips.

'Forgive us,' she said, holding up a placatory hand to show her sincerity. 'Our journey from Convent Prioris has been long and arduous. As I said, my Dialogus,' Angerer gestured to Sister Laevenius, who carried a scroll fastened to her armour that she now unclasped and handed to the canoness, 'has already begun the work of charting the position of known relics in Canticus. According to her study, a great many have been lost.' She read out a handful of names from the scroll to emphasise her point.

The shawl of Palatius.

Gerontium's blood.

Saint Acretia's skull.

The reliquary of Naaga Dahl.

None amongst the Salamanders had heard of them, not even Elysius, and none cared much for the recitation either.

'It weighs upon us all, the sundering of such artefacts that can never be replaced. Our religious ideology is a touchstone to this Order, to every Ordos Sororitas... I came to you with closed fist where I should have offered an open palm.'

Acting out her words, Angerer opened her hand before Drakgaard.

'I ask only that we be allowed to try to save our holiest relics.'

Drakgaard sheathed his sword, and braced his hands against the edge of the hololith table.

'Mark here, on this map, the sites of your relics. Have your artefact keepers come and do it if needed. I want to know where they are to be found.' He straightened then, and walked around the map table to clench Angerer's wrist in a warrior's grip which the canoness reciprocated.

'At least one thing you said was accurate,' Drakgaard allowed. 'We are at an impasse, and I am not so prideful that I don't see that or accept help if it is offered.' Angerer was about to speak when Drakgaard tightened his grip to let her know he had not finished. 'Is it help you offer? An alliance, Sister? My duty is to Heletine and nothing will turn me or my warriors from its cause and the cause of its people.'

Angerer showed no discomfort, though she must have been in pain from the Salamanders captain's iron grip. Instead she nodded, her eyes meeting his.

'You are different to other Chapter Adeptus Astartes,' Angerer said.

Drakgaard wore his helm, as always when at war, so Angerer would not have seen his smile but she heard it well enough in his voice.

'We are the epitome of them, Sister.'

Canoness Angerer bowed to the warriors in her midst and took her leave with Sisters Laevenius and Stephina.

Outside the amphitheatre, a black-armoured Rhino APC awaited them with its engines idling. Its hull was chipped and dented from recent combat and there was dirt ingrained in the metal but the icon of the Ebon Chalice still stood out proudly.

Knowing this was where they parted ways, Sister Stephina turned to the canoness and clasped her hands in front of her chest. She was about to bow and receive benediction when Angerer reached out to hold her clasped hands.

'Sister...' she began.

Stephina looked up. She was stern, but could not hide her youth and relative inexperience compared to the more veteran Sisters.

'My canoness...' her voice was soft, but with an underlying strength. Her drill abbot had been a fearsome tyrant in the schola, but he had taught Stephina well. She possessed a determination others lacked, but she had yet to find the true faith of the likes of Angerer and Laevenius. She had yet to witness a manifestation of Saint Alicia Dominica as they had done.

'Are you a Daughter of the Emperor?' Angerer asked her, as softly as her own harsh and grating cadence would allow. Up close, the canoness's votive incense was cloying to the point of almost making Stephina gag.

Stephina nodded.

'And whose will do you serve?'

'I serve the Emperor's will, my canoness,' she answered, still bowed.

'And whose will do you serve on this mortal plane?'

Now Stephina raised her eyes, and saw both Angerer and Laevenius, a step farther back, watching her intently. Though she had served the Order of the Ebon Chalice for several years, proving her piety and devotion beyond reproach, she sensed her next answer to be an important one that presaged something more than the mere affirmation of duty.

The Rhino's engines grumbled, as if annoyed at the delay. Fumes plumed from its exhaust ports that reminded Stephina of grey censer smoke. The cloying incense threatened to make her eyes water.

This seemed suddenly very much like a test of faith. No, Stephina corrected herself inwardly with a hint of shame at the weariness she felt, of loyalty…

'I follow the orders of you, my canoness,' she said, choosing her words carefully.

Angerer smiled thinly, but it was a false thing, a mask to hide a very different emotion.

'You are a dutiful servant, a dedicated warrior.'

'I am as you and my drill abbot made me to be.'

The smile faded like winter sun before a cloud.

'Indeed,' said Angerer. 'I have a duty for you now, Sister. Is your will and your faith up to it, I wonder?'

Stephina was not sure why her will and faith were being put to the question but she answered in the affirmative.

'I need you to watch the Adeptus Astartes.'

Stephina's face wrinkled with confusion.

'Watch them, my canoness?'

'Yes, observe everything they do, every ritual they partake in, and their rites of battle.'

'But why?' Stephina clamped her mouth, realising her error. She had spoken without thinking and had failed her canoness's test. She would be found wanting. Saint Alicia Dominica would not appear before her, even though she was Seraphim.

Laevenius looked shocked and about to rebuke Stephina for her unintended insolence, but Angerer forestalled the Celestian's chiding with surprising sanguinity.

'Because I do not know them,' said Angerer, and now she showed the truth of her emotions at last as her face became hard and unyielding as ice, 'because I do not trust them. We embark on a mission of faith, sacred to His Ecclesiarchy. They are diabolic savages who worship fire and burn the bodies of their dead. We must be mindful. You are my eyes and ears in this, Stephina, so I ask again, do you have the will and faith for this solemn charge?'

Now Stephina nodded at once, glad she had avoided the canoness's ire but fearful any slowness in answering would also condemn her.

'I am, my canoness.'

Angerer looked over Stephina's shoulder, beyond the dark fluting of her angelic jump pack and up into the murky sky crowding Escadan.

'Then go and do the Emperor's work. Fly, my warrior angel.'

Angerer stood back to give Stephina her benediction, before the Seraphim was airborne on wings of ebon night.

The others watched her go, trailing tongues of flame in her wake.

Laevenius drew up alongside Angerer, the book clenched firmly in her gauntleted grasp.

'Should we tell her, canoness?'

Angerer lowered her gaze to ground level again to where the war was being fought in distant Canticus.

'She would not understand, Sister. She does not possess the same faith as you or I.' Angerer paused to turn. She touched her armoured fingers to the vicious scar on Laevenius's face, the one that had nearly taken her eye. It was jagged, as if done with a blunt blade, claws… or nails. 'Besides, we each have a personal stake in this, don't we?'

Laevenius nodded slowly. Her gaze strayed to a small glass phial attached to the canoness's trappings. A clear, shimmering liquid was contained within. Then she too touched the wound on her face, almost absently. The pain of Laevenius's injury, her scarred appearance, it was a daily reminder of how she had once lowered her guard. She vowed it would not happen again. She clenched the book at the memory of her wounding, imagining it to be the neck of the one who had tried to maim her, and lifted her gaze.

'Are you certain, Sister Laevenius?' asked Angerer, nodding to the book. It was not really a question.

'She is in the Book of Names, as prophesied by Saint Dominica.'

'Indeed, she is.'

Though Laevenius betrayed no outward sign, Canoness Angerer felt the question on her lips.

'What is it, Sister? You have served the Order faithfully for many years. You have earned the right to speak your mind.'

Laevenius bowed her head, showing contrition and acknowledging the wisdom of her canoness.

'How do we know? How can we be sure she is here?'

Angerer smiled benevolently, the way a mother smiles at a daughter when she knows her child is being foolish.

'We do not need to know. We only have to believe, and all that requires, dear Sister, is faith.' Angerer maintained her smile but as she narrowed her eyes the tone of it seemed to subtly change as a measure of her hatred for their quarry was revealed. 'Remember Laevenius, hellspawn can wear many masks. Some even clothe themselves in righteousness to ward the faithful sword from their necks, but we are not fooled by such glamours are we?'

'No, canoness.'

'No,' Angerer agreed, a cold glint in her eyes at the thought of that faithful sword doing its holy work, 'no we are not.'

After the departure of the Adepta Sororitas, Drakgaard had dismissed the others too. He was walking back wearily to quarters he had set aside for his own private contemplations when Elysius's voice arrested him.

'Would you have struck her down, brother?'

Drakgaard paused. He was halfway down an unlit corridor, a branch that fed off from the amphitheatre and led to a small barracks room. There was no accusation in the Chaplain's tone, merely matter-of-fact enquiry.

'No,' he lied. 'I meant only to declare my anger at her ill-chosen rhetoric.'

'Was it so poorly chosen?'

Drakgaard turned quickly, the choler of his earlier mood returning.

'You think she was right?'

Elysius stood before him with open palms.

'No, but I think you believe she might have had a point. Salvation? You latched onto that word. I've seen your doubt, brother. This campaign has been overlong and much more arduous than it had any right to be. You question whether we are in need of some divine providence.'

'Perhaps we are. We have yet to even set eyes on their master.'

'He or it is here, Ur'zan, rest assured of that.'

'Then show me to him, Elysius, and I will end this war.'

The Chaplain held up a placatory hand.

'Patience, brother. We must endure as always.'

Drakgaard's shoulders sagged a little, even in his armour and he unfastened his helmet. Even in the darkness, his scar-ravaged features were hideous. His humours rebalanced, veering back towards the phlegmatic.

'Should we not be enough? That is all I ask.'

'Whether this war would have been ended by our hand alone is a moot point now, brother. We will never know. The Ebon Chalice are here and at our disposal.'

Drakgaard's eyes widened incredulously. 'You believe that?'

Elysius conceded the point with a tilt of his head.

'Well, perhaps at our disposal is stating it too strongly. Pragmatically, we are reinforced. And we of Nocturne's heartblood are ever the pragmatists.'

Drakgaard nodded and Elysius saw the weariness in his eyes.

'You realise, of course, that you will have to treat with her again.'

He nodded again, all too aware that both forces needed to agree on strategy before any meaningful blow against the Black Legion could be struck.

'Do you trust them, Elysius?' he asked, a captain to his Chaplain.

Elysius's reply was emphatic. 'No, brother. I do not.'

It was warm in the barracks house, and dark. The scent of burning metal pricked the air, adding to its heat. In one corner, smoke thronged the mouth of a small furnace. The coals within glowed a dull, fire-red. Brought all the way from Nocturne, from the slopes of Mount Deathfire, the coals represented rebirth and transformation.

Fire changes all, as old Zen'de used to say.

'Etar...' Drakgaard rasped, breathing deep of the smoke and cinder smell. It eased him, and acted like a balm.

A hooded brander-priest stepped into view. His head was bowed, the instruments of his sacred calling clenched in thin, wiry hands.

Every fire-born had a brander-priest. It was he or she that would scour the flesh, burn in the deeds of duty and embed forever the ignominies of defeat. For a Salamander's skin was his legacy and his mortal tapestry of remembrances. Like many Chapter warriors had subalterns, minor equerries or auxiliaries, the fire-born had the brander-priests or Incendum Sacerii as some knew them. It was an old term, rapidly growing out of fashion but Drakgaard was an old warrior and had tastes to match.

They were armourers as well as priests, and some amongst the Chapter even called upon them for counsel. Drakgaard had only ever uttered his own brander-priest's name. It was not that he thought Etar was beneath him, it was simply all the communication that was needed between them.

As Drakgaard held out his arms, Etar took it as a signal to stow his branding iron in a rack on the wall and went to his master.

It took almost an hour to remove the armour and Drakgaard grimaced at every plate extracted from his body. A litany of scar tissue was revealed beneath, merging with the brands that also colonised Drakgaard's flesh. He remembered every one, knew every wound and relived it acutely when he was stood naked in readiness for the blessing of the furnace.

He stepped forwards, limping with the knotted muscle and twisted skin of his right thigh. Smoke and heat fell upon him like a purifying veil as he felt the soles of his bare feet start to burn.

A metal plate sat adjacent to the furnace, absorbing its heat. Drakgaard stood on it, arms held by his sides, fists bunched as he breathed deep of the fiery vapours. It was only now, during the ritual of branding, that the dull ache of his injuries abated. Pain to cleanse pain, only this was the purer.

Drakgaard bowed his head, eyes now shut as he entered deep meditation. He heard the scrape of metal against stone as Etar took up the brand again and thrust it into the furnace. It would take a few minutes to reach the temperature he needed it to. Drakgaard awaited its touch, welcoming it.

Bring the fire, he willed, a brief cessation to the dull agony he lived with day in and day out. Let it burn…

Thus far, the war on Heletine had been long. It was to get longer.

CHAPTER NINE

Sturndrang, underhive of Molior

No one else approached them as they delved deeper into Molior's foetid underbelly, Zartath's massacring of Karve and his gang enough to keep others at bay. Through the tunnels, the atrophied gantries and abandoned block-towers, beneath the low grimy fog underfoot and the distant skeletal remains of once-regal domiciles, Agatone was certain that eyes watched from the febrile darkness. He detected fear and a weakness of spirit in the marrow of this desolate place, one he had only found previously in the enslaved. Most other Chapters would have despised the human underclass that dwelled in lower Molior but, as a Salamander, Agatone pitied them.

Zartath had a less humane philosophy.

'They reek of fear, this waste,' he said, his voice a guttural snarl of distaste. 'This pit is ripe with it, that and corruption. I was held prisoner, but I was never a slave. Not like this. Small wonder the taint has crept in – weak minds are ever prey to it.'

Through his belligerence, Zartath betrayed himself. A slight tremor in the cheek, under the right eye, at the memory of his incarceration by the dark eldar. For the longest time, he had scavenged to survive and watched his brothers slain. It had changed him, made him into something that was more animal than man, but despite his savage edge, he still felt.

Back aboard the *Forge Hammer*, after they had left their brothers – Agatone's brothers, in truth, for although liveried in green drake scale and having endured the rite of pain, Zartath still had the feral beating heart of a dragon – Agatone had seen the ex-Black Dragon at prayer. His words were guttural, more like growls and snarls, but they were imprecations and devotions of faith. It was a rare moment of stillness, one Agatone did not interrupt nor reveal his witnessing of later. Zartath had been given a fresh suit of power armour upon his induction to the Chapter, artificered by none other than Forge Master Argos, but he had insisted on keeping his old and battered trappings. A relic, scarcely effective protection anymore, Agatone believed Zartath had kept them to remind himself of who he was and where he had come from. It gave the captain hope that his savage charge was more than just a beast.

Even so, though his assessment of the pitiful wretches they had seen in lower Molior was harsh, it was an opinion likely to be shared by many of the Adeptus Astartes.

'They look starved to me, not tainted,' said Agatone. 'Don't judge so harshly. We don't know how long these people have been the grist for the millstones of their overseers or which potentate has them firmly beneath their heel.'

'Are we liberators now then, captain? Do you wish to save these wretches from themselves?'

Agatone did not answer. On this mission, redemption extended only to one, and he was proving elusive.

There was a plague upon this place, though. Whether a moral or spiritual decay, Agatone did not know, but whatever the source it was virulent. Only now, as they drilled down, was it evident how rotten the core had become. A warrior such as Tsu'gan, even in disgrace, would have seen it had he ventured this way, this deep. Agatone wondered if he had tried to find the source and been outmatched, or had he been too wounded to do anything but stagger hopefully towards aid?

The image was incomplete, a fact that more than irked the Salamanders captain.

They pressed on.

After wandering through a labyrinth of tunnels, walkways and the low-ceilinged sub-hives pressed upon by the multitudinous levels above them, Agatone and Zartath emerged into what amounted to a settlement. It was no more than an industrialised shanty, a few aggregated structures and a populace of dirty-faced, malnourished individuals that huddled in packs around drum fires. There were vendors, selling dubious 'meat', some weapons and crude supplies. All of it was trash, gathered from the refuse of the hive, but none of these would-be entrepreneurs dared approach the newcomers.

The appearance of the bulky, obviously armed and armoured, strangers sent herds of these human dregs scurrying for the dark and further anonymity. Agatone wondered who else had visited these poor wretches and what their purpose might be.

'Eyes and ears, Zartath,' Agatone murmured, but the ex-Black Dragon's awareness was already at its peak.

Exor was a dead weight on Agatone's shoulder, and he noticed some of the bolder inhabitants approach a little closer for a better look at his burden, muttering in hushed whispers to one another when they saw it was a body he carried.

Mercifully, the Techmarine was still breathing and had not yet slipped into sus-an membrane coma. If that happened, reviving him would not be easy. Certainly, it could not be achieved with whatever crude technology the underhivers possessed.

Walking slowly through the procession of rough buildings that shouldered against each other like malformed teeth, their facades badly abraded, Agatone looked for signs that might indicate a medical facility.

He winced. The keening sound Zartath had mentioned earlier was still echoing in his head. It actually seemed louder and he wondered if he had spat out the tainted blood too slowly.

As they reached the square of this frontier settlement, a 'welcoming committee' at last met the two warriors. It was one armed with guns and blades, ten men strong. They looked weak, fearful.

As well they might.

Others, too many to discern numbers, cowered in the shadows cast by the ramshackle buildings.

'C-collection isn't until next cycle,' stammered the leader, an old-looking man with pepper-wash stubble and narrow weasel-like eyes.

One looked much the same as another to Agatone, and once again he railed at the filth and depravity of these men and women. Each wore a haphazard agglomeration of armour plate, plastek and some form of hide that he assumed was flensed from the indigenous fauna of Molior's underhive. Their weapons were machetes or the lengths of sharp metal bent roughly to resemble makeshift blades with taped up grips. Crude ratchet-action shotguns and rusty-looking stubbers served as firepower.

Agatone wondered if they were even loaded as the men moved to encircle them both.

'We're not here to collect,' he told the leader.

'Because we gave up our tithe – we gave up a full flock as ordered,' said the old man. Now he had the strangers in his sights and surrounded, he grew a little bolder. 'You'll get nothing more from us.'

'Tithe?' Agatone asked, intrigued.

The old man looked confused, as if answering a question Agatone should already know the answer to.

'For the Seven Points.'

'We're strangers here,' Agatone explained. 'What are the Seven Points?'

Zartath was eyeing the natives dangerously. Surreptitiously, Agatone held out his hand in a silent signal to stand down. They could kill or incapacitate these men in a matter of seconds, but Agatone needed information, not more bodies.

'Not are,' said the old man with a half-smile, the kind a native gets when he realises he has outsiders in his midst and sees the possibility for exploitation. 'Is. The Seven Points is an arena. Some folks call it the "cross", though Seven Points is more accurate.'

Agatone scowled.

'You'll understand when you see it,' said the leader. 'Silas Krebb and Otmar the Brute own it. They own everything around these parts. Their gangers set up the fights and we, amongst others, provide the fighters. We've only given up dregs before, but this time we had a real prize for 'em.' The leader flashed an ugly smile, revealing three gilded teeth. Agatone also noticed his coat and pistol were of a higher quality than the rest of his apparel. No doubt the spoils of his slave trading.

Despite his best efforts, Agatone found his anger rising.

Zartath was far ahead of him.

'What arena?' Zartath snapped, painful, associative memories resurfacing. 'What did you give them?'

The old man paled, his brief confidence ebbing as surely as Agatone's patience, as he caught a glimpse of Zartath's exposed fangs beneath the ex-Black Dragon's hood. He started babbling.

'We patched up a big one, as big as you he was. And a stranger too. We sent him…' He pointed, and his hand was shaking. 'That way.'

Agatone stepped in. It was do that or allow Zartath to kill them all.

'You have a medicus then?' asked Agatone.

The old man nodded.

'Show me to him,' said Agatone. 'Now.'

'And if we don't?' said one of the crowd behind the leader, a youth with more bravura than sense.

Agatone pulled his cloak aside to afford the human dregs a glance at his armour and bolt pistol.

'That would be unwise,' he counselled. 'Now,' he said, 'your medicus. My friend is injured and in need of aid.'

'You are far from the stars, adept,' a strong, but veteran voice uttered from the shadows.

The surgery was a grim and poorly lit facility, although the word 'facility' did it overdue credit. It huddled between two other structures, stubby tenements rammed with more of the human waste that dwelled in the underhive settlement. A wrought iron staircase, indicated by the leader of the men who had first stopped them, led to this hovel and now he had found it, Agatone was beginning to regret his decision to seek aid here.

'You know of the Adeptus Astartes, do you, medicus?' Agatone stepped forwards into the dull lamplight of a hanging phosphor globe. It was the room's only illumination, and flickered intermittently.

'Some,' he admitted. 'I once fought beside them as part of His Eternal Majesty's Ecclesiarchy. And my name is Issak,' said the man, he too then moving into the light. 'Though I'd suggest we get acquainted later so I can see to your friend.'

Whilst he reconnoitred the surgery, making sure it was not a foolish attempt at an ambush, Agatone had given Exor up to Zartath. Judging by the ex-Black Dragon's mood, he was not confident Zartath could stay his killing mood and, in error, gut the one man who might be able to restore Exor should he in fact prove to be genuine.

As he regarded the weathered features but bright ruby-coloured eyes of the one who had introduced himself as Issak, Agatone was glad of that decision.

'I saw you,' said Issak, tapping a gnarled finger against a cracked pict screen which showed the area immediately outside of the surgery's door, 'and heard the booming thunder of your voices all the way down in the square.' His eyes narrowed. 'I wonder what three adepts of the stars are doing here in Kabullah.'

'Kabullah?'

'This settlement's name, or as was,' said the medicus. 'Few live now that remember it, or care. Many call it "the sink". I'm sure you can appreciate why.'

The nomenclature was an appropriate one – this place was a hole, a sink in all respects.

Issak gestured to the door behind Agatone with his chin. 'You had better bring him in.'

Agatone watched Issak keenly as he worked. Together, he and Zartath had managed to get Exor inside the surgery and onto the operating table. Despite its roughshod appearance, Agatone discovered the place was clean and sanitised; the tools at Issak's disposal were simply beyond their best and patchwork as a result.

The air was acerbic with counterseptic chemicals and Issak performed his ministrations behind a half-mask rebreather. He also wore a dark tan medical smock over functional leggings, a crumpled shirt and padded flak vest. Agatone noted, even though it was tight, Issak did not remove the armour to perform surgery. The room was cramped with equipment, various philtres, vials and bespoke medical machinery all hinted at and half shrouded in shadow.

With Agatone's help, Issak had removed Exor's armour, surprisingly not reacting to the Techmarine's bionic augmentations. As to the extent and nature of Exor's injuries, the medicus had merely said, 'You need to climb when the klaxons wail. That's vermin tide and is best avoided even for warriors such as you.'

'Had we known that...'

'You would not be here now. I understand.'

Issak worked quickly and diligently, first cleaning the wounds, careful not to get any of Exor's blood on his skin directly, though he could not have known of the true origin of its poison, and then sealing them where necessary. He used an adhesive gel rather than thread, trusting to the meagre medical provisions available to him.

Agatone had only ever seen an Apothecary work with greater skill at patching up an Adeptus Astartes.

'You said you fought with us, before?' asked Agatone.

'Not you, precisely, another Chapter,' Issak replied. His attention was mostly absorbed by his ministrations, so he only glanced at Agatone when he added, 'Nor your other friend's Chapter either.'

Zartath waited outside as ordered. There was little room in the surgery and the reek of blood was having an undesirable effect on him. It affected Agatone too, and made the keening seem louder. Perhaps, though, it was just the tight confines of the surgery.

Agatone ran a hand through his crest of hair, and found his forehead was lathered with sweat.

Issak glanced up, 'Should I examine you next?'

'It's nothing,' Agatone replied, then asked, 'You know something of our order?'

Issak had tended the physical wounds as well as he could. It had taken time, and the medicus was obviously not a young man, but went about his task with vigour and purpose. Agatone suspected it had been a while since Issak had found genuine fulfilment in his work.

'I am Nocturnean, I should.'

The deep red pupils, the leathern skin darkened by the sun, Agatone saw it at once.

'Vulkan's name, you are aren't you?'

'Epimethus. Like so few of my fellow Nocturneans, I sought a different path to that of ore-miner or black-smiter. I boarded a ship, part of a human auxilia and, after a few years of war, I found a different calling on a nearby shrine world. I became a missionary, entrusted with teaching the Emperor's glory to the heathen and the ill-educated,' said Issak as he scrubbed his hands clean for the next stage of Exor's ministrations. 'Molior seemed as foul a place as any to begin.'

'How long have you been here, medicus?'

'Over thirty years. I ventured down into the underhives when I heard of the squalor and depravity there. I took the role of medicus because I used to be a field surgeon. If at the same time as healing broken bones, I could heal the crack in a man's faith, then I would consider that a blessing and a good day.'

'And have you had many? Good days, I mean.'

'Fewer than I would like,' Issak admitted, 'but I try to keep faith.'

'And what does your faith tell you about my friend's chances of recovery?'

'His blood is tainted, but you already knew that.' Issak put on fresh surgical gloves and went to retrieve a device from a locked cabinet he had close to hand.

Agatone considered just how worldly-wise this medicus was. As a missionary in the Ecclesiarchy he would be privy to some knowledge, but clearly he had experience of the Chaotic. To Agatone's mind, it was wasted here and he wondered what must have driven Issak to seek out this life, this place. Perhaps it was penance? Perhaps that's why Tsu'gan had fled here too? It was the closest thing they could find to hell, a fitting place for sinners Agatone supposed. It mattered little. He needed Exor and so he needed Issak. The Ecclesiarchy's loss would be Agatone's gain. He could live with that, but he still had questions.

'You saw another of my kind recently?'

'Is that really a question?' Issak worked as he talked, preparing his tools for the patient.

'No,' admitted Agatone. 'How bad were his injuries? The alderman said you'd patched him up.'

'The alderman's name is Garvat, and your quarry left here half conscious but alive. You are hunting this man, I assume?' Agatone nodded, seeing no value in obfuscation at this point. Issak continued. 'The sawbones at Seven Points would see to the rest of his treatment.'

'And his blood, was it tainted like my brother's here? Is that why he nearly succumbed to his injuries?'

'No, it wasn't,' Issak answered flatly. 'I assume he climbed.'

The crash had obviously hurt Tsu'gan badly enough that he had been forced to seek aid in Kabullah. Despite the medicus's efforts, it had left him weakened enough that a group of human slavers had been able to take him prisoner. What happened after they got him to the arena... that, Agatone did not know.

'You expected to learn more?' asked Issak, seeing the Space Marine lost in thought.

'Honestly, I don't know. I hoped...' Agatone's gaze strayed from the shadows around them back to Exor lying supine on the medicus's slab. 'How could you tell?' he asked.

'About the blood? A warning in my gut. A disquiet I have learned to recognise. It's hard to explain.'

'None is needed. Just tell me, can you cure him?'

'Yes, but it's not a matter of faith, brother…?'

'Agatone.'

'Agatone. Yes, he needs blood. Your blood, to be precise, as it's a close genetic match.'

'A transfusion?'

'Exactly.' Issak set the device up on a bench and Agatone saw that its purpose was the exsanguination of a patient or donor.

Agatone frowned.

'Will that work? It seems… simplistic.'

'I believe so. The blood carries a pathogen that is currently inhibiting your friend's ability to regenerate. We remove enough of that pathogen by transfusing your blood for his, we restore his natural regenerative ability.'

'How long?'

'A few hours. It might take five or six transfusions. Perhaps, during the wait, you can tell me why you are here and not upon some battlefield somewhere.'

Agatone turned from the machine to look the medicus in the eye.

'What makes you think we're not on a battlefield?'

Issak nodded, as Agatone began to remove his greave for the first transfusion. He clicked on the comm-bead.

'Zartath, maintain watch on our perimeter,' Agatone said. 'Exor can be healed but it's going to take a few hours.'

A grunted affirmative returned on the other end of the feed before the link was cut.

Agatone had given the hound his leash – now he would find out just how tame the ex-Black Dragon was.

CHAPTER TEN

Nova-class frigate, *Forge Hammer*

As the atmospheric craft touched down in one of the *Forge Hammer*'s hangars, Urgaresh felt his battle-brothers strain at the leash. Thorast was the exception perhaps – in him there was nobility still. But then, he had always possessed the most outwardly balanced mien of the zorn or 'wrath' as it was known on Gauntlet. Urgaresh told himself they could come back from the edge, but only once they were whole again. They needed leadership. It had wounded them to lose him like that, and then be cruelly denied by a quirk of fate. He wondered what of their fates once this was done. Would they rise? Could they? Human blood slaked Urgaresh's claws. It stank of damnation. A necessary evil, he told himself. Committed by a necessary monster.

And we are, all of us, monsters.

Unlike the bone-cold Apothecary, Haakem and Skarh snarled and spat every moment they were airborne, gnashing their incisors until their gums bled. Both warriors clenched and unclenched their fists at the void of not having a weapon to hand. They felt it as keenly as a missing limb. Urgaresh knew this with certainty, because he felt it too.

Ghaan was the last of them. The old vexilliary was akin to a brooding storm, sullen and adapting to the pain of his injuries with all the civility of a sabre-wolf. He had once carried their standard, and considered it an honourable duty. His banner had long since been lost to ruin, burned by a dark lance. In its absence, Urgaresh found it hard to remember what

105

they were fighting for. He supposed it was for each other and when that was no longer a tenable belief, he would fight for a good death instead.

Yes, they had risked much in braving the slave pits of Volgorrah. Four caskets in the old *Fist of Kraedor's* mortuarium attested to that more poignantly than any ragged banner ever could. The bodies were lost to them now. Jerrak, Skellig, Neroth and Bhar'thak. All gone, their legacy in Thorast's care now.

None had escaped wounding. Urgaresh carried a limp, a hand span of xenos steel still embedded in his right thigh. Both Haakem and Skarh bore head injuries, the mounting pressure of which had made them increasingly volatile. Urgaresh had to keep the leash tight on those two, and maintained a vigilant watch aided by Thorast. The Apothecary had lost an eye, but it did not spoil his already brutish face. The loss of depth perception meant his scalpel was less reliable but his blade arm was still strong and that was all that really mattered. Ghaan had been untouched, but now had extensive burns from the Thallax's lightning gun.

They had lost their ship, gutted during their escape and with only enough strength left in her weary bones to get them within sight of their goal. The *Kraedor's* crew all dead. The four corpses of their brothers. There was little left but the mission. It would have to be enough.

They would have to be enough, but they were dangling by the thinnest of threads.

Urgaresh knew these warriors, like he knew his own blood. The zorn needed a victory. They had fought and died together in a search that began in Commorragh and would end here above this dirt-ball world in the corridors of some insignificant frigate. Their journey had begun in anger and a desire for retribution, so it would end the same. Urgaresh liked the symmetry of that, though his soul was far from poetic. Before their first steps, they had been monsters. With everything that had happened, Urgaresh had no word that could describe them now.

'What will you do with us now?'

The voice intruded on Urgaresh's black mood. His mind's eye was awash with revenge scenarios. He saw now only in two hues, both well matched to his humours. Red and black.

Fire and bone.

As if waking from a dark dream, Urgaresh looked down at the diminutive mortal who had showed such defiance in the cryo-vault. Urgaresh wanted to smack the pride right out of him, but stayed his hand. It would achieve nothing but to satisfy a savage urge.

He was the necessary monster, he knew, but would not let it be his keeper. I choose when you are unleashed. I. Choose.

'Leave this vessel,' Urgaresh rasped, as a low growl began to build in the hold from the others.

The mortal looked perplexed. Wary.

'You are releasing us?'

Urgaresh leaned in close, and let the rank odour of his charnel breath wash over the man.

'Flee now, maggot. I won't offer again.'

He rose back to his full height and the mortals left the ship, casting wary glances behind at the black-armoured warriors, and carrying their wounded survivor between them.

'He will raise alarum, brother-sergeant,' said Thorast. 'More will come.'

Urgaresh bared his teeth. So did Haakem and Skarh.

'Let them,' he declared, snarling as the bone blades pierced his flesh.

Ghaan came to his sergeant's side, his movements awkward and pained. The burning had reached deep. The old vexilliary felt it gnawing with every step.

'What are your orders, brother-sergeant?'

'First, we three take the armourium.' His gaze encompassed Ghaan and Thorast. Our weapons were lost aboard the *Kraedor*. We need replacements.'

Ghaan nodded.

'They'll expect us to strike for the bridge immediately,' Urgaresh went on, 'and will make their defences accordingly.'

'And us, brother-sergeant?'

Urgaresh turned to Haakem and Skarh.

'You will unpick those defences before we get there, brothers.'

Haakem bared his teeth a little further as he anticipated the hunt to come. Skarh unsheathed his bone claws and began striking them against one another to sharpen their edge.

'A warning,' said Urgaresh before they moved out, satisfied he had given the mortals enough of a head start, 'no killing unless we must. We are cursed, but we are not damned. Not yet.'

Descending the ramp of the Arvus lighter, they entered the darkness of the frigate's landing deck. The hunt began.

CHAPTER ELEVEN

Heletine, on the border between Escadan and Canticus

Smoke collides and the last vestiges of light die with the phosphor flare.

Ash is clouding my vision, choking me despite the enhancements of my transhuman body. The transformation is only partial. I am without black carapace, and the last few muscle and organ inducements to make me truly fire-born.

I am dying, encumbered by a weight on my back I can't remember bearing.

So close…

I thought I could see fire, just the edges of it, lapping like a burning sea at the end of the fire chasm. I need only reach for it, like a beacon. But even that is lost to me.

Pain, rage, anguish. They fall upon my shoulders, adding to my burden.

Ash, smoke, the resonance of heat like a throbbing invisible wall. If I reach out I can touch it with my fingers and feel it burn.

No direction left. No flare to guide me. No firelight from the edge of this chasm. I am lost.

I cry out a name. It is defiance, not a hail for aid or me beseeching for divine providence. We are taught not to believe in such things, and even if I did I am undeserving of any favours.

I was a fool to come here into the darkness and shadow. I wanted to be a hero. I wanted to save them, just as I had been saved. But I am not of Nocturne. I am a Scorian and the weakness of that has left me undone in this place of hell. How arrogant of me to believe I could tame it. None could tame this fiery wilderness, certainly not one such as I.

The name I cried rips from my dry lips one last time. It is like breathing in a furnace and the act leaves my throat raw. I imagine my flesh burning, all of it ending, my bones as ash. I will rejoin the earth and the Circle of Fire shall turn again. There is no coming back. No one can do that. Not even…

A light…

I see a light. A flame is kindled within that echoes the one I can see without. The spark of it ignites. Now it is a beacon I can follow. A figure is outlined in the smoke. He is carrying the firebrand and urging me and the two I carry to safety. The steps are hard. I am exhausted, but hope gives me purpose. My captain has forged me to be strong, so I am determined to reward his faith with effort.

The edge of the fire chasm comes into view and the smoke begins to thin at last.

Half delirious, my vision fading, I look up to see a figure standing over me.

It is not Ba'ken as I first thought.

'Rest…' he says. I swear I know him. But it can't be possible, for this man is dead.

Va'lin came around with a sudden start. He had been meditating, trying to restore some of his vigour from the earlier battle. He had scarcely got his bearings when he heard a voice he recognised.

'You make a poor sentry, brother.' Naeb's gentle laughter turned it from a rebuke into mild cajoling.

Va'lin had been perched on the edge of a jagged promontory of a former scriptorium at the edge of Escadan. Everything within the archive had been destroyed, set to the flame or simply obliterated during the initial bombardment. The vista did not change very much below either. A sea of destruction stretched into the distance where Imperial-held Escadan gave way to the viciously contested streets of Canticus. For even here, at the edge of the Imperium's strongest bastion on Heletine, the war was rudely felt and its works laid bare for all to see.

Va'lin eyed his brother shrewdly. 'I am surprised to see you alive, let alone upright and with strength enough for mockery.'

Naeb opened his arms. The mark from the split in his armour remained, though the blood had been cleaned away and the damage to the war-plate fused by a Techmarine.

'Sepelius might be a grim and unpleasant snakr'ah, but he knows his craft.'

Naeb used an old Nocturnean word to denigrate the Apothecary. It loosely meant 'snake-skinner' but more broadly referred to 'one of ophidian nature, with a lowness of bearing and character'. To Epimethians like Naeb, most other Nocturneans were snakr'ah, except the regal born of Hesiod. And they had other names for the nobles of that Sanctuary City.

Va'lin noticed Dersius looming behind his friend and nodded to the burly Themian. Though he doubted Dersius would admit to it, Va'lin suspected he was keeping a watchful eye on their wounded brother. Naeb's easy humour could not hide the fact he was in pain. Va'lin read it in the slight grimace when Naeb had showed off his injury and thought his brother was not looking. The fluid movement that made Naeb such a fierce sparring partner in the battle-cages seemed unrefined and halting.

Dersius nodded. 'Va'lin,' he said, taciturn as ever. Naeb thumbed over his shoulder at the massive warrior. 'My keeper,' he explained, with only a little wounded pride to add to his physical injuries. Va'lin saw clearly that Dersius had appointed himself Naeb's shadow until he was restored to his former strength. Self-reliance was a tenet of the Promethean Creed but so too was self-sacrifice, a virtue in which Dersius had excelled often.

Both fire-born carried their battle-helms and something of their faces was revealed in the flickering firelight from below. Naeb had the cultured features of a rogue trader, albeit bulked out and hardened by his transhuman physique. He wore his salt-white hair in three short rows that cut his scalp into four equal black segments. He was also handsome for a warrior, which suited his sanguine demeanour well.

A Themian tribal tattoo painted Dersius's flat and uncompromising face. The pigment used to ink the warrior was deep blue, so the icon of a leo'nid rampant was difficult to make out unless observed in the proper light. Like most from the City of Warrior Kings, he was bald and had features more in kind to rock than flesh. In many ways Dersius reminded Va'lin of his old captain, Ba'ken.

'Have you come to summon me then, brothers?' asked Va'lin.

Come the dawn, which was still an hour or two off, the Imperial forces and their Ecclesiarchy allies would muster for a massive offensive. Word had reached all officers, and through them their warriors, of a huge push into Canticus to reclaim the city in its entirety and drive the heretics out. Many had died in the last failed offensive. Many must therefore be mourned before commencement of the next. Fires littered the ubiquitous ruins on the border between cities in recognition of that fact as the Salamanders war host about to descend on it observed their rituals of flame and ash.

Power-armoured figures were gathering below, forming circles around distant blazes. Each was a pyre, the burning of a brother in arms.

Naeb's expression grew serious.

'Iaptus wants us to remember Sor'ad.'

Va'lin nodded, needing to say nothing further.

All three donned their battle-helms. A slew of situational data appeared in crisp glowing green across Va'lin's retinal lens display: trajectories, wind speed, ground distance. Fuel levels and engine temperature for his jump pack were reading optimum.

'See you when we hit earth,' he said to the others over the vox-feed, and cast a glance in his brothers' direction as they lined up on the ruined promontory alongside him.

'Shall we wager on who lands first?'

Va'lin smiled behind his faceplate. Naeb's spirit was beyond dampening it seemed.

'Agreed,' Va'lin replied, 'name the stakes.'

'The honour of leading the combat squad when Iaptus splits us again.'

Va'lin bent his knees slightly, descending into a crouch and saw the stance echoed by his brothers.

'How can you be sure he will?'

'He will.'

'Making bets when we are about to mourn our brother?' Dersius's tone smacked of disapproval as his deep voice came over the vox-feed.

Naeb had to crane his neck a little to regard him eye to eye.

'Do you want to lead or not? Sor'ad would have approved.'

Dersius nodded, and it was as if the snarling drake teeth on his battle-helm had cracked a rare smile.

'Just say when we leap.'

'On a count of five,' said Naeb, and a chrono flared into life on Va'lin's and, he knew, his brothers' retinal displays.

'Was it Dak'ir?' Naeb asked.

Va'lin turned his head towards him.

'What?'

'Your dream.'

'I...'

'Mark!'

The chrono hit zero the same second Naeb announced it. Two ignition flares lit up the ruined scriptorium, spilling gouts of flame across the promontory. Va'lin was a fraction behind, gunning his jump pack in the wake of the others, but he was too late. Naeb's jump arc, superior to Dersius's, would carry him earthward first. The honour of leadership would be his.

Iaptus was waiting for them around the fire with the rest of the squad. A shrine devoted to Saint Hafetus had stood here once, a known smith according to Xerus. Near to the Canticus border, it had suffered during the war and was now little more than a ruin. Despite that, it was deemed a fitting place of commemoration.

Arrok, Vo'sha, Illus and Xerus were already crouched by the pyre, their bare faces swathed in flickering shadows. Half glimpsed through tendrils of smoke, Va'lin saw Ky'dak sat a little distant from the others. Even in this solemn act, he was a man apart. Va'lin was at odds whether to despise or pity him.

Xerus nodded, and bade the three latecomers sit down. He was the other specialist in the squad, but preferred a broad-barrelled plasma pistol to the flamer Va'lin carried. Iaptus approved, of course. He said it gave the squad balance. Xerus was a veteran, and possessed of a generous spirit that had seen him become something of a mentor for the younger special-ist. Proficient in many weapons, since his earliest days in the Devastators and then Tactical before joining Captain Dac'tyr's Wyverns, Xerus was an exceptional teacher. Through his guidance Va'lin had thrived, despite his relative inexperience.

Flames of burned orange and vermillion flowed over a silhouette of scorched black plate. The last of their number, late of the corporeal realm dominated the gathering. Here was Sor'ad's final rest, his armoured corpse in repose upon the pyre with its progenoids since excised by Sepelius to preserve the dead warrior's legacy. Dark smoke rose in a great column from the smouldering body, driven upwards by the heat of the blaze and blighting the sky, as the mood of all present was blighted by their loss.

'We gather to remember...' said Iaptus, his face framed by firelight which heightened every noble groove and peak. Honour scars branded in linked chains of Nocturnean sigil were etched upon his cheeks and forehead. An arrowhead of short wiry hair that was the colour of black volcanic ash covered his chin and jaw. His scalp likewise. In the old language, the sigil-dialect of the first Nocturnean earth-shamans, Iaptus meant 'Piercer'. On first impression it was an ill-fitting honorific for one who carried a thunder hammer and fairly bludgeoned his opponents, but as leader of Squad Iaptus he was every shred the lance Dac'tyr used to core his enemies, heart and all.

Like the others, Iaptus had removed his battle-helm out of respect and his ornate jump pack was unclasped and leant against the remains of the walled enclosure that surrounded the squad. In the middle of the ruin, encircled by a ring of stones, the pyre had grown into a conflagration and reached up into the night.

The other three took their places by the fire, Va'lin sparing only the brief-est glance for Naeb who had the audacity to wink at his battle-brother.

'We gather to set a flame...' Iaptus continued once the rest of his squad was gathered and crouched.

Through the fire, Va'lin noticed two others attending the rite. Zan-tho and Sepelius, without squads of their own, stood at the fringes and looked on. Though he was not Sor'ad's brother-in-arms or from Squad

Iaptus, Zantho still mouthed the other sergeant's ritual benediction. He inclined his head to Va'lin when he saw him watching and the younger warrior looked away.

'And let it burn,' the squad uttered as one, each removing a gauntlet.

'Let us remember So'kan Sor'ad,' said Iaptus.

Together, they thrust their bare hands into Sor'ad's flames. During the ritual burning, Dersius cried out as he sang a Themian war-lament. Va'lin did not know the words, but he knew their meaning for Dersius had explained it to him the first time it was sung. It recounted the tale of a hunter of the old tribes who stalked a great leo'nid across the Arridian Plain. The beast had slain his wife and child, taken them down to the hot earth where it had devoured their flesh. Only by finding and killing the beast in turn could the hunter give his loved ones peace and also lay his own grief to rest.

It was a melancholy tale, made all the more so because it had no ending. The hunt went on after Dersius had finished and would do forever. Through the verse, Va'lin noticed Ky'dak's usually severe expression darken further. Ky'dak was Themian just like Dersius and Va'lin wondered what it meant, if anything, beyond the fraternal grief they were all experiencing.

The lament concluded and Squad Iaptus removed their hands from the flame. The blaze would burn long into the night, rendering metal and bone to ash and returning Sor'ad to the earth.

'Vulkan's fire beats in my breast…' Iaptus intoned, striking his burned fist against his breastplate.

'With it, I shall smite the foes of the Emperor,' uttered the rest, saluting as their sergeant had done.

'A few words, brother,' said Iaptus to the figure behind him.

Zantho stepped into the light. The tank commander had a broad, expressive face forked and sculpted by rendered sauroch fat. It was framed by a red beard that extended into a mane of rugged hair and jutted from his scalp in spikes. Made room for in the circle by Arrok and Vo'sha, he knelt down to give them all his wisdom.

'Ours is a violent calling, but as adherents of the Promethean Creed we believe in the Circle of Fire.' Zantho put the tips of his fingers together to make an 'O' shape and held it out in front of him. The others did the same as he went on. 'None can come back as they once were, but in death we are returned to the ash from whence we came to be born anew, our blood and bone bonded with the earth. Through fire are our remains made protean, through fire and the reunion with earth do we experience rebirth. After death, after our duty is ended, we give ourselves to these elements and in so doing become a part of them. This is the nature of the Circle of Fire.'

Many amongst the gathering were nodding. Xerus even reached over to clap Zantho on the shoulder. Va'lin knew the words, he knew the teachings. They had been Vulkan's and thus did every Salamander learn them, but he wondered about the first part, about not coming back. One amongst the gathering had an even more sceptical reaction.

'Death is death,' uttered Sepelius, cowled by a drake-skin hood, his face akin to a cadaverous rendering of the fabled reaper itself in the firelight.

'Don't you believe in rebirth, Kratus?' Zantho asked without turning around. 'Are you so morbid that your beliefs don't allow for the possibility?'

'I am a realist, brother, that is all. I don't have the luxury of indulging such existential notions.'

'You are a cynic,' Zantho challenged.

'Yes, that too,' Kratus Sepelius agreed, utterly unfazed.

'Then why attend the ritual at all, Apothecary?' asked Arrok, a little too wounded, a little too headstrong. Xerus laid a hand on the younger warrior's shoulder to remind him where he was and who he was addressing.

'To see it was properly observed. I might not believe in rebirth but that doesn't mean I want our traditions to be mishandled.' He smiled, though it might as well have been a scowl at Arrok. 'My duty is to the living, and keeping them that way. Legacy is maintained by science,' he tapped the progenoid flask of his reductor with a gauntleted finger, 'not through fire and ash. Such archaic concepts are anachronisms of the "old ways", but none here have ears for my thoughts, so I shall bid you all a good burning and be on my way.'

Sepelius gave an ironic bow before stepping back into the shadows. A few seconds later he was gone.

'Are they all like that?' asked Arrok.

'All?' Iaptus queried, his gaze on the void left in the darkness by Sepelius's exit.

'Apothecaries.'

Iaptus frowned as if the question was a facile one.

'Indeed, Brother Arrok. How did you think they were chosen for the apothecarion in the first place?'

A moment of stunned silence followed before Xerus glanced at Zantho who both then erupted into laughter.

Arrok looked appalled at first, that such experienced veterans would dishonour the solemnity of the ritual, until he realised this was the ritual.

'Aye,' said Naeb to Va'lin, as Arrok found his humour at last, 'I think Sor'ad would have approved.'

But Va'lin's gaze was on the pyre, and he barely heard Naeb. He watched transfixed as the body burned and recalled again what he had witnessed in the fire canyons, occluded by smoke.

Rest, the figure had said.

None can come back. Those were Zantho's words, echoing the Promethean belief in the Circle of Fire. None can come back.

But someone had.

A winged figure watched from its perch on the rock, an angel armour-clad in black. Her pinions were fluted steel, her aspect that of a preying rook.

Sister Stephina could be sure she went unobserved by those below, hidden as she was by shadow. Lurking like this offended her martial spirit but Stephina reminded herself she was not in combat. Not yet. She had seen everything from her lofty vantage, the ritual of fire in its entirety. She witnessed them burning their flesh, and heard their savage plainsong cried out across the ruins.

Eyes of tempered fire. Coal-black skin. Diabolic in every aspect. There could be no denying the physical aberrations, but her secret vigil had revealed something of the Salamanders' spirit. It was tribal, almost shamanistic.

Seeing everything she needed to, Stephina unfurled her ebon wings and took to the sky.

CHAPTER TWELVE

Heletine, on the border between Escadan and Canticus

After the ritual had ended, Squad Iaptus broke up and went their separate ways. The time of battle was drawing near and with it the need for the swearing of oaths and the marking of brands in flesh. Most of the Salamanders were returning to the barracks houses in central Escadan except, notably, half of Sixth Company's Devastators led by Venerable Kor'ad. The Dreadnought had maintained heavy bombardment throughout the night in conjunction with armoured elements from the Cadian 81st under Colonel Redgage. Military intelligence could not ascertain whether the punitive barrage was achieving much beyond the slow depletion of ammunition but Kor'ad had assured Captain Drakgaard it was the only way to safeguard the sections of the city they still held and so such attrition had been deemed worthwhile.

Va'lin had not gone back with the others, despite Naeb's vocal protests. He craved solitude, wanting to return to his reverie begun in the eaves of the shattered scriptorium before Sor'ad's ritual cremation. So he took to patrolling the Escadan/Canticus border in an effort to still his racing mind. He went armed and armoured, flamer in hand but with the igniter for its promethium reserve still cold. Canticus was still contested and designated 'safe' regions could change quickly in such a fluid theatre of war. Several enemy spies and would-be saboteurs had already been discovered and neutralised since nightfall. They added to the clutches of deserters who also presented a problem to Drakgaard's officially sanctioned patrols but who had lessened in number since the Ecclesiarchy's arrival. Despite the ostensible distrust between the other Imperials and the Battle Sisters, Va'lin considered that their presence on Heletine might be of some benefit.

Not long after leaving the others, Va'lin felt the hackles rise on the back of his neck. This was despite the heat and heft of his hulking armour with its low humming generator a constant presence. He reached out with his auto-senses. Someone was following him, but not bothering to hide the fact. Their identity did not remain mysterious for long. Va'lin knew of only one candidate.

'Why are you following me, Sepelius?'

Va'lin heard the Apothecary step out into the open as the weight of his armoured form crushed rubble underfoot.

'What gave me away?' Sepelius asked sardonically, gesturing to his bone-white battleplate.

Va'lin turned his back on him. 'I came out here for solitude, not further cross-examination.'

'Through the fire,' said Sepelius just as Va'lin started walking. 'I saw it.'

Va'lin stopped, but did not turn around. 'Saw what?'

'That look in your eyes. You have been dreaming again.'

Va'lin stayed rigid, but felt his irritation giving way to curiosity. He longed to understand everything he had seen in the fire canyons and what it portended, if anything.

'He dreamed, you know,' said Sepelius.

'Who did?'

'Dak'ir.'

Now Va'lin turned, his eyes burning with anger. 'Don't insinuate, brother. I am tired of hearing your lips do it.'

Sepelius held up his hands plaintively. 'I merely point out the correlation. Curious, how history can echo through the ages. How prophecies can align more than once in a given generation.' He paused for a beat. 'Rebirth.'

Va'lin said nothing. His eyes spoke for him, making the Apothecary's narrow in turn.

Sepelius smiled incredulously. 'You think he's alive.'

A sudden tightening in Va'lin's jaw cascaded across his features until his entire face had hardened. He did not bother to veil the threat – the warning in his tone was obvious.

'Leave me alone.'

Sepelius bowed, then backed away obeisantly.

'Dak'ir almost destroyed Nocturne. Are you worried you might be like him, Va'lin? A vessel through which he might return?'

'He was our saviour...' Va'lin wanted to put more conviction into his reply but it came out half-hearted.

'He was both and none, or so the prophecy of the ferro ignis portended.'

'You don't believe in prophecy. Empirical truth is all you care about.'

Even to Va'lin, it sounded weak as a retort.

Sepelius saw it at once. He gently shook his head.

'Now you're just reaching, brother. Think on what I've said, Va'lin. We can talk again, you and I,' he said, and disappeared off into the ruins.

Va'lin let him go. He had moved off again when he heard the faint crunch of stone once more.

'Sepelius, I told you to–'

Another stood before him, clad in deep green. It looked almost black in the darkness as if a shadow lay across the figure.

'Ky'dak?'

'Follow me,' said Ky'dak and went off into the ruins.

Va'lin saw he was heading deeper into Canticus, and followed.

In the darkness of the night, the ruin resembled even more of a hollowed-out shell, shrouded in abject black. Sor'ad had died here, his duty ended by the teeth of a Chaos warrior's chainblade. His blood still painted the wall from where it had jetted free of his body in a crimson arterial spray. A pall of death and regret lay heavy on the site of their skirmish with the Black Legion Terminator. The warrior's blood also tainted the place but in a different way. Both bodies had been removed, the traitor's dragged out with chains and then incinerated without ceremony, so only the echoes of their passing remained.

Working their way silently through Canticus's shattered streets and buildings, the two Salamanders got as far as the breach Va'lin and Naeb had made in the outer wall when Ky'dak raised his gauntleted hand for caution.

'Why are we here, Ky'dak?' Va'lin hissed.

Ky'dak gestured into the gloomy hollow of the building.

With his enhanced vision Va'lin could see in the darkness, but when he followed Ky'dak's pointing finger the meaning of what he saw was still unclear.

They retreated to either side of the breach. Va'lin called across it, careful to keep his voice quiet.

'Who is she?'

One of the Adepta Sororitas was inside the ruin, her back to them and currently unaware of the Salamanders' presence.

'I tracked her after the ritual. Thought she was the enemy,' Ky'dak hissed back.

Va'lin was considering whether they should just announce their presence and call the Sister out then and there, but when he looked inside again she was gone.

He mouthed to Ky'dak, 'Where?'

Ky'dak gave him the facial equivalent of a shrug, but then nodded as the Sister reappeared. She had emerged as if from the shadows, seemingly out of nowhere. Her route took her deeper into the ruins and away from the breach in the wall, so she remained ignorant of being watched.

Va'lin waited with Ky'dak until she was gone before moving inside. Donning his helmet, he cycled through the visual spectrum afforded by his retinal lenses until he found what he was seeking. A small sub-chamber existed below the floor, hard to see in the rubble and half hidden by the dark. Exchanging a glance with Ky'dak that prompted both to ready their weapons, Va'lin descended a set of shallow steps and went inside.

More darkness within, but Va'lin saw everything in variegated hues of night-vision green. Bones lay smashed all over the floor, disturbed from within alcoves. Some had been snapped, others crushed underfoot. Were he seeing it in daylight, Va'lin believed he would have found scorch marks too, for the faded stench of burning smothered everything.

They were standing in a reliquary chamber, one of the holy sites the canoness had described during her volatile first meeting with the Chapter.

'Place looks ransacked,' said Ky'dak.

'Doesn't look like a search,' Va'lin replied.

Ky'dak knelt down to run his hand through the shattered bone fragments.

'He was here,' he muttered, 'the traitor that killed Sor'ad.'

'How do you know?' asked Va'lin.

'His taint is pervasive. There is blood mixed in with this grave dust. He didn't just want to destroy,' said Ky'dak, standing.

'He wanted to profane,' Va'lin concluded. 'Why?'

'To weaken it.'

Va'lin turned his head.

'The spiritual hold of the Throne on this city,' Ky'dak explained.

'To what end?'

'To let whichever master he served do whatever it is he cannot do while that hold is still strong.'

'And the Sister?'

Ky'dak slowly shook his head.

'I don't know yet.'

More questions lurked in the shadows of Heletine before any answers would be forthcoming. Va'lin had one he could ask immediately.

'You could've done this alone. Why involve me?'

'I couldn't be sure what I would be facing. Two stand a better chance of someone making it back. As it is, I don't know what to make of any of this.'

Va'lin nodded, deeming it reasonable justification.

'We do nothing for now,' he said. 'Not until we know more.'

'Agreed.'

Va'lin held out his hand. 'I may have misjudged you, Ky'dak.'

Ky'dak ignored the offer and headed back up the stairs.

'No you didn't,' he said.

Klerik watched the two drakes. He liked to watch, a murderous voyeur crouched atop a perch of crumbling stone. He was relatively close, close enough to tell they had no idea what the female fanatics were really here on Heletine to do. It amused Klerik to linger proximally to his foes, to revel in the knowledge of their ignorance of his presence.

I could kill them easily from this distance...

So still and quiet, deep in shadow, a casual passerby would have mistaken him for a statue.

The drakes disappeared into the ruin, but they would be back.

Nothing for you there, little drakes.

Klerik only broke his silence when the Salamanders had gone and he realised he was not alone.

'Good evening, brother.'

Someone had tried to creep up on him, sleekly wending their way up the shattered ridge to his rocky vantage point. No one surprised Klerik – he had a... way about him, a means of simply knowing when others were present and what their intentions towards him were. Not precisely – he wasn't that gifted – merely a vague sense of their humours at a given moment.

An armoured warrior stepped more heavily from the shadows, resorting to his usual gait now his subterfuge had been uncovered so expertly. 'I thought I had you that time.'

'I know you did, Juadek. I read your sanguinity as easily as Preest reads the vagaries of the warp. So, beyond your feeble attempts to catch me lurking, what is it exactly that you want?'

'You are requested, brother,' Juadek replied, quietly settling down to crouch alongside Klerik. 'Everyone is being recalled.'

Klerik raised an eyebrow, wrinkling the skin across his handsome face. Like so many of the Emperor's Children, he aspired to be perfect. And, like so many of his brothers, that desire had become twisted over the millennia. Klerik's skin was porcelain-white, his features strong and chiselled as if they were hewn from marble. His eyes were black, shiny like opals, his hair silver-white. Daggers were his favoured weapon, and he carried two sheathed at each hip. A short cape of cured human leather trailed below the power generator of his armour, which was pristine in heliotrope purple.

'Interesting,' Klerik replied. 'And what does he say about the others – any news from the warp?'

'They made planetfall, but nothing further beyond that. He thinks the mission may have gone awry. Blames fate.'

'Fortunate then that we have a further opportunity here.'

'Indeed, brother...'

Juadek went quiet, but lingered on the rock with Klerik.

His armour was the same heliotrope purple as his comrade's, only not as well tended. It was battle-worthy but festooned with fetishes, strings of severed hands, ears and other appendages. Juadek also liked spikes and had hammered them into his pauldrons, greaves and boots – any plate that would take them. They even protruded from his cheeks and close-shorn scalp. For a servant of Slaanesh, he was an ugly brute.

'You deliver your message, and yet you are still here forcing me to breathe the same air,' said Klerik. 'Evidently, you have a question.'

'Do you believe what is said about him?'

'About whom, Juadek?'

'The captain. That he killed all of his old comrades and took their flesh for his own?'

'I don't know.'

'That he's not a man at all, but an amalgam of several?'

'I don't care.'

'You should, Klerik. What if he has designs on killing us, we, his inner circle?'

'You say that so proudly.'

'I have no desire to be a part of his shared flesh.'

'Nor I,' Klerik agreed, 'but there are others who would certainly like to kill us.' Klerik gestured to the street rubble below and the warrior sifting through it. He offered Juadek his scope. He didn't need it to see, but he enjoyed the enhanced detail it provided. Detail was important.

'She is searching for something,' said Juadek, adjusting the focus on the scope.

'No, she has what she seeks. It just isn't what she wanted to find.'

'Hmm...'

'That's where they killed Vaug,' Klerik uttered solemnly.

Juadek sniffed his contempt. 'Vaug was a bastard.'

'He was also a Cruciator, and they do not die easily or well.'

'His slayers entered from the north,' Juadek replied, returning the scope to Klerik who took a good look.

'I have already seen them.'

Klerik shook his head, nonplussed and unimpressed at the same time. 'How did they kill him?'

'That remains a mystery,' said Juadek.

Klerik put the scope away and started to back down the ridgeline, careful not to raise too much noise lest they be discovered.

'Tell me something, brother,' he said to Juadek as they dipped out of sight together. 'If Lufurion killed them all, who lived to tell this tale?'

'Preest claims a daemon told him.'

'My brother should take more care about who he shares his secrets with.' Juadek laughed as if suddenly understanding a joke.

'Heh. Preest. Klerik.'

'Say nothing further, unless you aren't attached to that fool's tongue sitting in your mouth.'

'You have to admit, it is amusing.'

'You find everything amusing, Juadek.'

'Especially this… and death.'

'Would you find your own death so funny, I wonder?'

Juadek answered with silence.

'Thought not,' Klerik replied as they reached the bottom of the ridge and made their way back through the ruins to their dark masters.

CHAPTER THIRTEEN

Heletine, on the border between Escadan and Canticus

Canoness Angerer, not Laevenius, was waiting for Stephina when she returned to the Order's encampment. Drop ships and armoured transports marked the confines of Ecclesiarchy territory. Shrines and chapels in the lee of the vehicles, their votive candles sheltered from the katabatic wind blowing off the mountains, threw a lambent glow across the laager. Censer smoke spiralled from the iron cradles of braziers, their cloying aromas leavened by the same southward breeze. Figures huddled in the shadows on penitent knee, alone and in groups. Some wept, others flagellated as the crack of punitive whips sounded on the night air.

To Stephina's eyes, looking from on high as she descended on her Seraphim's wings, it seemed an overly defensive position to uptake when surrounded by allies. But then, she supposed that was why the canoness had given this sacred duty – to ascertain if the non-Ecclesiarchy on Heletine could be trusted.

In addition to the vehicles, the Order of the Ebon Chalice and its attendant congregation had been afforded the use of several barracks houses and minor templum during their occupation of Escadan. It was in one such billet Stephina had hoped to find Laevenius. The Celestian had been her mentor, then her trainer after the drill abbots had exhausted their martial teachings and, so Stephina believed, the closest thing to an actual sister in the Order.

Angerer was alone in the barracks house, her charges dismissed to their duties or in many cases prayer and supplication before the Throne and He on Holy Terra. Her ornate armour with its string of white rosary pearls and one black opal hung upon a metal frame. Her weapons likewise hung on a steel rack in one corner of the room. In place of her armour, Angerer wore her simple white chasuble. Her feet were bare and her silver hair was fastened in a tight scalp lock and trailed down the nape of her neck.

In the opposite corner a small votive candle burned before a holy triptych of Saint Alicia Dominica. Its small flame flickered over a stained-glass vista of the saint vanquishing hordes of Unbelief, at prayer before an effigy of the Golden Throne and giving holy benediction to her sacred charges, the Sisters of the Ebon Chalice. Even seeing a glass simulacrum of these events stirred Stephina's blood, reminding her of everything Saint Dominica had sacrificed and her own path towards martyrdom. Briefly her thoughts turned, as they often did, towards why she had never been blessed by a vision of the saint, as Stephina knew Angerer and Laevenius had, but she dismissed her concerns as selfish and unworthy.

Angerer had neither seen nor heard the Seraphim approach, lost as she was in her fighting katas and holy effusions. Despite the obfuscating censer smoke, Stephina marvelled at her canoness's martial skill. As a figurehead of the Ecclesiarchy, a gifted orator and spiritual lodestone, it was all too easy to forget that Angerer was, first and foremost, a holy warrior. Amongst the Order of the Ebon Chalice, there was none finer.

Fighting in such voluminous holy vestments was not easy, but Angerer performed her combat patterns expertly and without profligacy of motion. She was fluid, powerful. Her every thrust with the fingers, every cut with the blade of the hand, every punch with palm and clenched fist was precise and explosive.

'Step into my sight, Sister,' she said, a little breathless from exertion but maintaining her patterns without pause or loss of efficacy.

Stephina obeyed, the canoness seeing more than the Seraphim realised.

Angerer spared her a glance as she moved through a series of punishing elbow jabs.

'Have you come seeking Sister Laevenius or myself? For I can tell you, I am the only one here.'

Stephina lowered her gaze in contrition as Angerer concluded her training cycle.

'It's all right, Stephina,' she said, shrugging off her chasuble to stand naked before the Seraphim. 'It is to be expected you would seek out Laevenius. She was your original mentor, after all. I assume this means you have something of import to tell me.' Angerer's body was lean and taut, despite her age. Rejuvenat, a strict regimen of physical exertion and bodily purity had kept her in peak condition.

As her vestments touched the floor, a male frateris swept in from the shadows to pick them up. A second serf, also male, then appeared and began anointing the canoness's sweat-dappled skin with holy unguents and water blessed by a cardinal of Convent Prioris. These ablutions lasted several minutes before Angerer was provided with another, lighter robe. Dismissing her serfs, she beckoned Stephina to follow her into a small antechamber.

'Apologies, canoness,' said Stephina once she and Angerer were alone. 'I assumed you would still be in tactical discussions with our allies.'

The canoness had taken a seat at a small writing desk in what appeared to be her private library. Scrolls and prayer books, canticles of faith and catechisms warding against the unholy, were stacked in a pair of cases lining two of the walls. A lantern mounted on an antigravitic platform hung in the air just above Angerer's head, its oil plate flame flickering in a slight crosswind that skirled through the barracks.

'Those concluded some time ago,' Angerer replied, the weaker lamp light casting long shadows across her face. 'Prayer and martial discipline are firm allies to my mind. Both require precision, purity of thought and determination of purpose.' Angerer looked up from the scroll detailing the various relics that were at risk amongst the Canticus ruins. Stephina was surprised Laevenius was not in possession of it and directing efforts to find the holy treasures described. If anything, the weather-beaten parchment appeared almost as if it had been discarded.

'Do you not think so, Sister?'

'My canoness?'

'Purpose, both martial and religious,' explained Angerer mistaking Stephina's response for confusion when she had actually been distracted by the anomaly of the discarded scroll, 'have much in common, their sum greater than each individual part.'

'Yes, my canoness. A pure and pious mind leads to a sure and deadly sword arm,' said Stephina, remembering herself.

Angerer nodded, satisfied her wisdom had been heeded.

'So tell me then, what else have you learned?'

Stephina spared no detail, and by the end of her account Angerer's face was a mask of righteous indignation.

'It has thus ever been, since the Adepts of the Stars were allowed to roam so far from Terra's holy light.'

Stephina frowned, prompting Angerer to elucidate.

'Unlike our Holy Ordos, which are pure and free of taint, the Space Marines are at best... inconsistent. None could doubt their prowess. To do so is to invite destruction. But as to their purpose, their devotion... What kind of creed preaches the anointing of flesh with fire? What savage culture proselytises with tribal wailing?' Angerer's brow furrowed, her internal consternation manifesting physically. 'This is deeply concerning, Sister Stephina.'

Stephina said nothing, waiting for her canoness's instruction which she knew would be forthcoming.

'Tomorrow, at dawn, we fight alongside these devil-skinned monsters. I would not have my Order so close to potential calamity.' Taking up a fresh sheet of vellum parchment, Angerer began to scribe furiously with a quill. 'Have a cherub transcribe this and deliver a copy to each Sister Superior. Let none of the other Imperial officers see it.'

'These are dispositions, canoness,' said Stephina who could clearly tell, with the barest glance, the nature of the document Angerer was writing.

Angerer nodded, only half listening as she focused on finishing her task.

'It does not look like an allied deployment,' Stephina ventured.

'Because it is not. Our purpose is not their purpose, Sister. We have our sacred duty. We shall attend to it ourselves.'

'If the other Imperial forces are expecting us to occupy certain battlefield positions, that will leave them exposed if we are absent those positions.'

Angerer stopped writing and placed the flat of both hands against the desk as she stood. She kept her eyes down, fixed on the slowly drying ink on the parchment.

'You know I have little time for dissemblers, Sister. Out with it.'

'Are we going to betray the Salamanders?'

Now Angerer lifted her gaze. It was hard as Fenrisian ice and froze Stephina where she stood.

'We are going to do what the Throne requires of us and liberate this world of its Ecclesiarchy relics. That task will be made much easier with the heretics engaged with our allies.'

Stephina did not need to hear the callousness in her canoness's tone to realise she was being lied to. The relics were not Angerer's main concern. She also realised that Angerer had planned this duplicity from the moment they had arrived on Heletine and needed only the thinnest of excuses to justify it to herself.

Wrath was her first reaction, anger at being used, but Stephina buried it behind a false face of dutiful adherence, hoping the canoness would not notice her clenched fists.

For months, Stephina had laboured under a feeling of unease. She had believed it was out of doubt in her faith, the fact she had not been visited by the saint. But now it was as if a veil had been lifted from her eyes. Whatever Angerer's true motives for coming to Heletine, they had begun all those months ago and were now slowly emerging.

We are blind, thought Stephina as Angerer returned to her treacherous scribing, orders that would surely condemn many to death. Utter devotion and conviction to their canoness's will had blinded the Order to the truth of whatever personal agenda was being served here. Certainly, it was not the will of the Emperor.

With all her strength, her martial prowess, Stephina was still powerless to intervene.

Angerer finished her scribing and handed Stephina the piece of vellum. It looked so innocuous in the canoness's outstretched hand. The Seraphim saw it for what it was – the death warrant of countless souls.

CHAPTER FOURTEEN

Sturndrang, the underhive of Molior

Ever since he had been a prisoner on the Volgorrah Reef, Zartath had preferred his own company to that of others. He valued the bonds of brotherhood and had missed being a part of a Chapter, hence his decision to adopt a new one, but his mind was most at peace when he was alone.

Agatone had asked him to maintain a watchful eye but he could not do that surrounded by the unwashed masses of this hole they had found themselves in. He needed distance; he craved silence.

But silence was not so easy to come by these days…

The keening had begun as soon as the klaxons had ended, he later realised. With the clangour still ringing in his ears, he had not been able to differentiate the echo of that from the tinnitus now gnawing at his reason. It hurt – moreover it encouraged certain feral instincts, and Zartath hoped that some solitude would prevent him doing something regrettable. Slipping from his perch outside the surgery, he had gone back out into the square and walked until he was beyond the settlement's borders.

He ignored the fearful glances, the half-muttered threats. Blooding his claws on such wretches would be dishonourable. Sometimes his martial honour was all that Zartath believed he had left, so he clung to it in the vain hope it would save his soul. Aboard the *Vulkan's Wrath* and the *Forge Hammer* after that, he had affirmed this belief staring into the eyes of his cracked and broken battle-helm, its coal black surface dented and scraped just as he was.

Sleep came rarely and for short spates only. Were he not transhuman,

Zartath would have died from chronic insomnia by now. As it was, he clung on, sustained by unspoken grief and a barely caged anger he did not fully understand. Something had snapped inside him on the reef, he knew that now, and there was no way to tether the disparate halves. He had forgotten so much, entire annals of his previous life. Little of it remained, scraped away as it had been by the dark eldar. So he sought solitude when he could – not for contemplation, like his adopted brothers, but to try to be still, just for a moment.

Even at the edge of the derelict shanty, where the clutter of humanity was not so strangled by the overcrowding at its core, life still gasped and scratched for air and light. 'Warren' would describe it adequately, the people like cattle in their murky tenements. A hive was a collective, but it was also a hub of industry and labour. Upon reaching the extremity of the settlement and the limits of his own imagined rope, the vista that unfurled before the ex-Black Dragon as he looked back was one of squalor: a stinking fetor, a pit of spiritual apathy, its inhabitants left to scrape an existence from rock.

Fear clung to this place in a filthy shroud, curling Zartath's lip into a snarl as he felt the apathy and despair as palpably as furnace heat. The captain would chastise him for such disparaging thoughts, but compassion and empathy were not amongst Zartath's virtues.

Zartath gave a bitter smile, 'Captain...' he murmured. More like whelpmaster. He was under no illusions about his role, and his leash. 'I am a savage beast.' The smile became genuine. Still a prisoner then, albeit one with roaming privileges.

Putting distance between himself and the loathsome dregs of humanity had not eased his agitated mien. Zartath's teeth were still on edge with the keening and he wondered if it was something to do with his mutation, if he was somehow made differently to other Adeptus Astartes. With his comrades all dead on the reef, he had no frame of reference anymore, but was vaguely aware of a change manifesting in him that had begun with the first of those torturous days at the hands of the dark eldar.

Crouched at the briny water's edge of a sump pond, Zartath tried to still his mind. It was vast and dark as the pond, like a rotten canvass, and stretched for some distance into the shadows. A child dressed in rags scurried at the pond's fringes but was careful to maintain a safe distance from the hulking, cloaked figure at the bank.

Zartath drew deeper into his hood, abruptly self-conscious of the horned nubs upon his pate and the fangs that crowded his bestial mouth.

I am a monster.

'Bless the curse...' he muttered to ward off a sudden pang of melancholy. The words were part of an old Black Dragon mantra, one in which they celebrated their physical aberration and embraced it. He remembered so little of his old life, but knew that at least. Zartath felt a fresh curse affecting him now, a malady of the mind and possibly even the spirit, not the body. He tensed his forearm and the bone claw sheathed beneath the skin tore out, a thin line of his blood limning the razor edge of the distended radius.

He looked up, but the child had gone. The sump pond burbled and spat as something moved beneath its viscous depths but was wise enough to stay hidden. An outflow pipe feeding the sump pond trickled thick, foetid ooze. Doubtless other things travelled its ironclad concourse and with that thought, Zartath belatedly realised the child had borne a spear. It was hunting.

Zartath stood up, jerking the bone blade back into his arm with a minute muscle movement. As he turned his head to the pipe's mouth, the throbbing in his skull intensified the way the auditory of a vox-caster did when angled directly at the receiver.

He drew closer, only half aware that he was ankle deep in the sump pond. Behind him, Zartath heard a voice. It was a warning, but the keening grew louder with its siren call and he was powerless to ignore it. Creeping closer still, the foul water up to his shins and beginning to corrode his armour, Zartath tried to discern the nature of the sound. Part static, part plaintive wail, it was impossible to identify. He needed to get closer...

Something seized his leg, a clamping of jaws not so dissimilar from a vice. Zartath was turning, the throbbing in his skull reaching a crescendo. His blood pulsed with it, a deeper refrain. And just before he felt his head was going to explode, he passed out.

The coppery tang of blood filled his mouth, and as soon as Zartath tasted it he knew it did not belong to him. Head throbbing, he tried to stand but staggered and collapsed before he had even managed to get to one knee.

Stay down, snarled an angry voice inside his head. Even Zartath's subconscious was belligerent. Find your bearings...

He did not need to open his eyes to know he was indoors. It felt like a small chamber he occupied. The floor was hard and cold, but metal rather than stone. Slick too – the rough fabric of his cloak was adhering to it. A viscous liquid pulled lightly at his finger tips as he moved them. They felt something else too, something sharp against the haptic nerves... Zartath's bone blades. He could not remember unsheathing them, but then everything had gone black after the edge of the sump pond. The keening, he recalled that. It had diminished to a dull ache, just audible above the faint patter of rain against the roof.

No... not rain. The dripping sound was emanating from inside.

The smell hit Zartath last of all but near overwhelmed his olfactory senses. It was everywhere, as pervasive as the reek of filth that clung to the underhive like a miasma.

At last, Zartath opened his eyes and left sleep behind.

With waking came horror.

The room was dark, but the walls and floor and even ceiling shone wetly in the ambient light. Black against black, Zartath knew the shade well. He had painted with it, though scarcely regarded what he did as art. And in all the blood that coated every surface, that stank with charnel acerbity, that dripped down from ceilings and door frames and the slats of half-broken windows, were two bodies.

Or the remains of such.

A butcher's leavings had more definition than the offal trailing steam in the chill underhive air.

The same blood discoloured Zartath's claws, clothing them in a glistening dark sheen.

The boy at the sump pond... The memory was not a pleasant one for it led Zartath towards an unpleasant conclusion. He had been hunting... because this was where he lived.

Past tense.

Horrifying clarity crashed in on Zartath and he fled as he felt a sudden claustrophobia threaten to choke him. He ran outside and emerged into a place he did not recognise. He was still in the underhive of Molior, no longer on the same bank of the sump pond. A vast lake of effluence did stretch out before him though, and it took him a moment to realise he had traversed the pond or been ferried across it.

Through the mist of pollutants rising from the surface of the sump, Zartath saw the settlement. As his bearings slowly returned, other things became apparent too. Rain was falling, or some approximation of what passed for rain in the underhive of Molior. The run-off from an atmosphere condenser, a malfunctioning hydration compressor. It fell in heavy sheets, but was laced with chemicals: acidic and alkaline agents that would scorch flesh.

Zartath willed it to burn, but his enhanced physiology would not oblige him. It cascaded down his face, his chest and arms, washing away the dark blood but not purifying. He watched it spill in black runnels from his exposed bone claws and pool at his feet. In his mind's eye, the blood remained and though he had no memory of it, he knew what he must have done to earn this stain.

The rain hammered him, but Zartath knew as he threw back his head to howl at the imagined gods of a false storm that it could not cleanse the darkness in his soul, or the darkness of whatever he had wrought with it.

When his throat grew hoarse from screaming, he slumped down again, down into the filth where he belonged and cradled his head. The keening, always the keening. It spoke to him in octaves of pain. And it was getting worse.

CHAPTER FIFTEEN

Nova-class frigate, *Forge Hammer*

Shutting off the bulkheads would achieve nothing. By now, they were already aboard and infiltrating the ship. It was dark on board with most of the systems powered down, aside from life support and the barest sensorium. Emergency lumens fed the companionways with dull, amber light, a little brighter over the junctions. Tiny vibrations still ran through the ship's hull, felt through the bones of its super-structural skeleton, but they were minimal. With the hunters still at large on the world below, they needed to stay hidden. Communication limited, engines cold, weapons and shields nullified – anything that might show up on an atmospheric monitor or deep space augur probe.

Standing in the corridor of the *Forge Hammer*'s aft-section, Makato considered their limited options.

'We can't just attack them head on. I'm not even sure it's us they want to fight.'

Navaar was lying on his back unconscious, Jedda crouched by his side keeping an eye on his vitals. He looked up at the lieutenant. 'So what do they want, sir?'

'He said revenge, but Throne only knows for what. Our lords have accrued enemies over the decades and centuries, but something seems a little off about this one. We need to find out soon, though. We are far from help out here and no one will be coming to find us. Not yet. Not soon enough.'

With the vessel on silent running, all longer-range communications were down this far from the bridge. All three had since shed their atmosphere suits, so at least they could move faster, but just under a kilometre trek from the embarkation deck through corridors and access tunnels stood between them and the nearest available help. An alarm could be raised a little closer than that, but there was no guarantee how soon it would get picked up. Besides, Makato doubted the frigate's armsmen would trouble the enemies he had been forced to let aboard.

Not a living soul had met them since their recent arrival. Even their landing had been automated. Dull-eyed servitors had met them on the landing strip. Their doctrina-wafers slaved them to maintenance tasks only. They had no capacity for defence or even the raising of the alarm. For now, at least, he and Jedda were alone.

'Why do you think they spared us?' asked Jedda, watching over Navaar. The supine armsman was barely breathing.

Makato shook his head, glancing up at the gloomy corridor space they had just left behind and tried not to imagine the black-armoured warriors stalking them down it.

'Honour, I suppose.'

Jedda turned sharply from his vigil to look hard at the lieutenant.

'What honour? They killed Bharius and Halder. The enginseer and his watchdog too.'

The man was fraught with stress, close to losing his cool. Makato let the minor insubordination go but warned, 'Remember who you're addressing, sergeant.'

Even in as bleak a situation as this, chain of command had to be observed. Order and a calm head would be vital to their survival now.

Bowing his head, Jedda showed he knew that too.

'Apologies, sir. I am simply...' Words failed.

'We all are, sergeant. But we fired on them first, remember?'

'After they laid an ambush, sir.' He paused for a beat. 'And they are mutants. The blades in their arms were made of bone. Their bones.'

Makato nodded, pensive.

He needed Lord Xarko, but before that he needed a way to reach the Librarian.

'How far to medical?' he asked.

Jedda didn't answer straight away, prompting Makato to look at him. He was bent over Navaar, ear pressed close to the wounded armsman's mouth and then pressing his fingers to his neck to check for a pulse. Jedda sat up, sighing his contempt at the fates that had brought them to this.

'He's dead.'

Jedda got to his feet, the weariness bleeding out of him making room for a different emotion. Makato recognised it in the hardness of the man-at-arms's eyes, because it gave him purpose too.

'We need weapons,' said Jedda, 'and more men. A lot more.' When they had been taken prisoner, the black-armoured warriors had disarmed them. They even took the plasma-cutters. Everything else was back on the Arvus.

'So do they,' said Makato. His gaze met Jedda's. 'That's where they are headed, to the armoury. Not the bridge. Not yet. That gives us a little time.'

'There's another one deeper into the ship.'

'Deck three?'

Jedda nodded.

'That's where we keep the track mounts.'

Jedda smiled. 'Yes it is, sir.'

Makato smiled too. He took off his cloak and laid it over poor Nav-aar's body. They had tried to save this man, or at least give him a fighting chance. They had also let him and Jedda go relatively unharmed. That did not strike Makato as the action of traitors, but they were on his ship and he would do everything in his power to defend it.

Gripping Hiroshimo Makato's silver braid, he told Jedda, 'Currently we are all that stands in their way. Come on.'

Xarko swam the fire tides. He had no intention of defying the will of Agatone, but something in the hot depths had called to him. Instinct had ever been the Librarian's guiding force and right now it was telling him to ply the waves deep. And as the fire folded him within its embrace, Xarko's concerns beyond his sanctum faded as did his awareness of the *Forge Hammer*. The void was quiet, he had told himself and the voices were calling. So he opened up his mind and plunged, ignorant of the corporeal world and everything in it.

CHAPTER SIXTEEN

Heletine, at the outskirts of Canticus

A second dawn lit the sky over Canticus as the heavy guns of the Cadian 81st erupted with fire and thunder. Colonel Redgage commenced the heavy bombardment from the cupola of his command vehicle.

The earthshakers spoke first, the remnants of Eighth Squadron releasing several tonnes of heavy munitions into the uncharted northern district of Canticus. They lived up to their name – Redgage felt the micro-tremors all the way back to his Chimera.

The intention was to deliver a punitive barrage into the heart of the enemy stronghold and then assault in force, which was problematic as that stronghold tended to move. No sighting had yet been made of the enemy commander, though what scant intelligence the Imperials did have suggested it was a high ranking Traitor Space Marine officer. Three other battle groups, supported by elements from the Ecclesiarchy, launched simultaneous attacks in an effort to bring the heretics to open battle and destroy them.

Dust still clearing from the initial punitive barrage, Redgage ordered a second salvo. Held at the back of the line with the Basilisks that began the shelling, Griffons and Bombards launched ordnance. Three troops of siege engines fired in unison, the weak dawn light briefly obscured as a heavy rain of shells soared overhead. The violence of the combined mortar launch rocked the ground, shaking Redgage's Chimera but he was too busy watching the parabola of their lethal payloads through his magnoculars to notice.

The strike was good – a long chain of explosions spewed earth and rock skyward some three kilometres away. In the short aftermath several taller buildings, their previous form and function long since eradicated, collapsed. They tumbled slowly like felled trees, releasing huge clouds of dust and grit when they hit the ground.

Redgage slipped one cup of his ear defenders over his helmet and turned to the war machine.

Venerable Kor'ad remained still and faced forwards his squads of heavies likewise. The Salamanders wore scorch marks on their armour like it was war paint. Their armour was patched in places too, evidence of the hard graft of their armourers trying to maintain a decent level of combat efficacy. The retreat had hurt them, and not just physically. The Dreadnought had refused Zantho's aid after that, preferring Redgage's armoured company instead.

This was the first time they had met, officer to officer; one of flesh and blood, the other a walking battle engine. Two other war machines stood behind him, but were subservient to this ancient warrior. Translation issues were to be expected. Redgage guessed the meaning behind Kor'ad's silence.

'Hit them again,' he voxed to his crews, turning back towards the city as he put the sound-deadening cup back in place.

First the Basilisks then the heavy mortars. Plumes of earth rocketed into the air again, fires broke out in some quarters, more buildings buckled under the weight of the Imperial hammer of war. Redgage observed everything through the magnoculars. Finally, the backwash of heat and seismic disturbance hit him from the initial bombardment, tickling his moustaches and inducing a cough with all the displaced dust. Even at distance, the destructive fury of the heavy tanks was impressive but the Imperials had no way of knowing if it was also being effective.

Their answer came after the third round of shelling.

A cacophony of shrieking presaged a flock of Heldrakes, darting from some unseen silo and spreading their wings as soon as they had pulled clear of their hidden nest.

Behind the colonel and overhead, a flight of Stormtalons and the patched up remnants of his own fleet of Vulture gunships roared across the sky to intercept. Engines burning, bleeding cloud contrails and heat vapour, they cut through the air like daggers. The approaching dawn light shone brightly against their wing tips and angular nose cones. It was, briefly, a magnificent sight.

'Throne protect you, lads,' muttered the colonel, stroking the aquila pendant he wore around his neck.

Punisher Gatling cannons opened up in the lead Vultures, stitching the air with darting flashes of tracer fire. One of the Heldrakes took a burst across its left wing. A second burst raked its fuselage and it dipped, trailing fire and something reminiscent of blood and oil but far less earthly.

Rocket expulsion bloomed in vapour clouds under the wings of the second wave of Vultures as the air was choked with missiles. An ululating screech tore from a Heldrake as it tried to pull away from the salvo. Three hunter-killers impacted against its open span, tearing off one wing and blowing it out of the sky. Secondary explosions erupted moments later as a third monster went down, its neck streaming flames and gore.

Then the Chaos flyers were amongst them and the killing began in earnest. Redgage saw a Vulture ripped in two as it was seized in iron claws. A second went down burning after it was enveloped in daemon-fire.

Piloted by Space Marines, the Stormtalons were fairing a little better, their assault cannons racking up an impressive tally of enemy kills, but the sky was still hotly contested.

'Hydras move up, firing solutions at these coordinates,' barked Redgage, conveying the data from his spotter aboard the Chimera to all flak tank commanders. On the right flank, two troops of anti-aircraft platforms rolled into position on grimy tracks. A few seconds later their autocannons were chugging high-calibre rounds into the dogfight above. The artillery quads on each tank thumped back and forth alternatively like pistons, spitting out an incredible rate of shells. Two more enemy flyers were torn apart, dismantled by chasing autocannon fire.

Retaliation was swift. A Heldrake broke off from the interception sweep, diving in low to unleash its nose-mounted cannon. Hell-hot rounds whined in like hail and sawed one of the Hydras in half. A stray round hit the fuel tanks and the whole engine went up in a fiery plume. Exploding shrapnel shredded the exposed crew of the tank alongside it but mercifully its armour prevented a chain of destruction.

Turrets swivelling, the other Hydras tried to track the monster amongst them but it was flying too close and too low.

Strapping into the Chimera's pintle mount, Redgage tried to distract it with a burst of heavy stubber. He needed to keep it away from the siege tanks. Solid shot chased the monster through the air before peppering its armoured hide.

Redgage roared down the vox as the Heldrake came for him. 'Vulture Six, peel back and engage!' And in that moment the battle shrank to just he and it, witnessed down the myopic ironsights of a heavy stubber. Impervious to his cannon, Redgage had just made it angry.

'Vulture Si–'

Vulture Six went down, its pilot shouting in the colonel's ear until his screams were eclipsed by static. The rest of the air group were already engaged. A low dive from the Heldrake became a strafing run.

'In the Emperor's grace I trust,' said Redgage, his fingers clenched on the heavy stubber's triggers. Brass casings cascaded down at his feet, sparks cracked across the Heldrake's armoured face. 'Let it be a light in dark places...'

Balefire ignited within the monster, its eyes already aflame, mouth trailing smoke.

'Let it be my shield,' whispered Redgage, and began to shut his eyes.

A flare of actinic energy slammed into its neck, wrenching it off course. The balefire went wild, streaming wide and burning up the ground. Kor'ad brought the Heldrake down with a second burst, coring a hole right through its fuselage with his plasma cannon. It limped on in defiance of the mortal injury before crashing a half-kilometre away, towards the western district of the city.

Still a little shaken, Redgage nodded his thanks but got nothing from the Dreadnought who had already turned away.

Though the Emperor's Angels had begun as men, in the broader sense, they were far removed from that biological paradigm after their genhanced apotheosis. Redgage admired them, was in awe of their prowess and fortitude, but found he could not understand or relate to them. And allegedly, the Salamanders were the most human of all the Chapter Adeptus Astartes. Some of the men were afraid of them. None had admitted as much, but Redgage saw it in their eyes as they looked on the green-armoured monsters. Still, they fought like black-skinned devils and that was good enough for the Cadian colonel.

The skies were clearing over war-torn Canticus at last. After receiving enough punishment, the Chaos flyers had broken off and the wings of Stormtalons and Vultures were ordered back. Several did not make the recall.

'A good fight,' murmured Kor'ad, surveying the devastation through his sensors. With the grind of leg pistons, the Dreadnought faced the colonel. 'You honour them.'

Redgage wasn't sure that he was the one being addressed at first.

'My lord?'

Kor'ad's impassive vision slit regarded him. For Redgage it was like staring back into an unfeeling abyss.

'You stood, willing to sacrifice your life. You honour them,' Kor'ad repeated.

Was the Dreadnought giving him praise? Redgage was unfamiliar with any Adeptus Astartes offering praise to lowly men, especially a warrior as ancient as Kor'ad.

'I am the one who is honoured,' said Redgage, mustering enough resolve to converse with the massive war machine. Even sat up in his cupola, the Dreadnought stood eye to eye with the colonel. 'By their bravery. I vouch for every one of these men, tankers and flyers both.'

'I see now why the mettle of Cadia is mentioned in such high regard,' said Kor'ad. 'Your courage and magnanimity do you credit, colonel. Refer to me as brother from now on – you are my warrior-equal, not my serf.'

Redgage had no reply, genuinely aghast and humbled. He did not need one – Kor'ad had already turned away to address the battle group.

'Skies are ours,' he uttered thunderously through his vox-emitters. 'Advance into the city.' With ground-quaking purpose, the Dreadnought led his squads out. It was a half kilometre march to the next bombardment point, and from there into Canticus proper.

Redgage consulted his tactical slate, fighting down the swell of pride in his breast at the Dreadnought's words. Artillery was staying behind, at the first line. Two troops of Demolishers and a pair of Thunderers moved forward with his Chimera. Once they hit beyond Canticus's outer borders, an infantry battalion from the Adepta Sororitas that was coming up from the blockaded eastern road would link up with them. Just before they rolled out, Redgage ducked his head back inside the tank.

'Any word from the Ecclesiarchy?' he asked his comms-operator.

'Nothing yet, sir.'

Redgage took another look at the slate. In order to make an incursion into Canticus, they needed that infantry support. At distance his tanks were lethal. They had already turned much of the outer reaches into rubble and debris. But at close range, in that warren of streets, they would be vulnerable. Best defence against infantry was infantry, and Redgage had heard the Battle Sisters excelled in that role. He got back on the vox to his commanders.

'We are heading into the belly of the beast, officers,' he announced with full-blooded conviction. 'Keep a tight formation. Roll out.'

Subtle vibrations from the turbofans trembled the Thunderhawk's interior but it was background noise to those seated within. Amber strip lighting just below the ceiling glowed but shed little light in the gloomy hold. Despite the ostensible calm, the mood in the gunship bordered on tense.

The Wyverns of Fourth Company were anxious. One of their own lay dead: a tax in enemy lives was demanded in payment.

Va'lin had been with Sor'ad when he died and so had the warrior sitting across from him. Not since their foray into the Canticus ruins had the two of them spoken. Ky'dak kept his feelings guarded as if like Va'lin he did not know what to make of the reliquary or its meaning to the enemy or the Ecclesiarchy. Voicing concern prior to deployment would serve no useful purpose, so Va'lin had kept quiet. His eyes met Ky'dak's, trying to read him but saw nothing but a granite wall. In the end it was Va'lin who looked away. His averted gaze arrived at another difficult sight.

Sor'ad's empty harness was like an open wound. Xerus sat alongside the vacant spot at the end of the row, muttering to himself, or perhaps it was with his slain brother that he exchanged conversation. Except for Xerus, a solemn mood persisted, the others preoccupied with grim thoughts. Dersius leant his head against the hull, eyes closed in meditation. Vo'sha and Illus bowed their heads, murmuring final oaths of moment. Arrok filled his mind with routine, mechanically thumbing brass-shelled mass-reactives into spare clips, oiling and sharpening the teeth of his chainblade. Naeb was quiet. Sepelius had declared him combat-ready but Va'lin suspected his injury was paining him.

'Silence suits you, brother.'

Naeb returned a weak smile.

'I do not plan on making it habit.'

'A pity. You would make more friends that way.'

'I need none. I have one, a long-suffering ally.'

Va'lin laughed, letting his relief show at Naeb's good humour.

'Indeed, I am.'

For a moment, Naeb grew serious. 'I meant Dersius, brother.' He held Va'lin's gaze a moment longer before laughing loudly.

Dersius's eyes remained closed but he said, 'If you are disparaging me, Naeb, I will see you in the cages once battle is done.'

'I think you upset him,' said Va'lin, thumbing in the burly Themian's direction, one eyebrow raised. His eye fell on Iaptus, and he felt their levity bleed away before the sergeant's intense stare. Iaptus rarely smiled, seeing little value in humour. He was a stark, serious man but a warrior they all aspired to emulate.

Mastery of thunder hammer and storm shield in combat was not easy. Harder still was wielding them proficiently whilst aloft on the screaming fire-jets of a jump pack. Iaptus had mag-locked his shield to a weapons rack inside the hold, but his thunder hammer was to hand, sitting across his lap. His stare was penetrating, searching, as if he knew everything Va'lin and Naeb were thinking, as if every fault and flaw were laid bare to him. He nodded to give them reassurance. His one intention for them all was victory, and retribution for a brother lost.

'Blood for blood, brothers,' he said aloud, looking directly at Va'lin, 'We go to avenge Sor'ad.'

Nine Salamanders thumped their fists against their breastplates.

So it was said, so it would be done. Iaptus had just given them his word, and that was more unbreakable than his storm shield.

The hold's vox crackled, admitting the voice of Brother Orcas.

'Prepare for imminent disembarkation, brothers,' said the pilot. A lumen glowing next to the Thunderhawk's rear access ramp changed from amber to green. Gusting pressure release filled the area around the point of egress with pneumatic gas before a crack appeared delineating the ramp and began to let in daylight.

'Helmets on,' said Iaptus, disengaging his restraint harness so he could stand.

The crack of daylight became a yawning chasm as the ramp slowly unfurled. Iaptus was framed in the light, his armour rimmed in a rising umber dawn. He shouldered his storm shield, thunder hammer gripped in his right hand.

'Let this be a day for vengeance!' he shouted over the wind buffeting inside the hold.

The ramp distended fully, eight armoured silhouettes standing behind Iaptus who waited patiently for their target to present itself in the conflict below.

A vast bridge, wide enough to accommodate entire armies stretched below. Well fortified, its arches and buttresses were thronged with razor-wire. Forked tank traps, huge crosses of barbed and rusted metal, littered the roadway. Sand-bagged gun emplacements, sniper nests, minefields and barricades fashioned from the burned wrecks of freight loaders and ground cars turned Salvation Bridge from a major artery into the city into a death trap.

Squad Iaptus were about to dive right into it. Gladly.

Orcas brought the gunship in low. Firefights on the ground were keeping most of the insurgent heretics busy, so they attracted little in the way of flak. Even so, the hull shook with close impacts and the smoke from explosions swept in through the open hatch.

'Confirmed visual on Zantho's line-breakers...' Iaptus voxed.

Orcas did not reply, preoccupied with keeping them aloft, but the turbofans burned harder in response and Iaptus saw the drop point through the blur of smoke and fire swilling across the hatch.

Four Predators armoured up with dozer blades were trying to push through the wreckage. Zantho rode up in the cupola of the one in the middle, Annihilator-class, preferred to his Redeemer. After the grubby fight in the Canticus ruins, the commander had ordered the Land Raiders kept in reserve. It was the knock-out blow and the cleansing fire that would rid them of the enemy once they had brought them to battle. Predators were lighter, more manoeuvrable, and equipped with dozer blades they made shovelling through debris look easy. As well as his own, Zantho led four other similar Destructor-class battle tanks and three siege-breaking Vindicators.

This was the armoured fist that would punch through the heretic defences, reach in and crush its throat. The Wyverns just had to help breach the 'gate'. It was code for the mass of wreckage blocking the bridge. Its opening was their primary mission and would be effected by incendiaries, melta charges, but there was work to do beforehand. Cleanse and purge were the secondary missions. Heretic infantry armed with all manner of improvised bombs, explosives and even crude rocket tubes colonised the debris below. Before Zantho's tanks could properly advance, they needed excising. Squad Iaptus was the ideal scalpel for such an operation.

Iaptus smacked the flat of his thunder hammer against his shield, sending a minor charge through both. Heat vapour was already eking from the exhaust vents of his jump pack as he sank to a crouching position from which to launch.

'On my mark...' he said, 'now fly!' and leapt from the hold.

Va'lin was third out behind Xerus, body angled down like a spear and accelerating fast. Wind shear hit him like a mailed fist and he corrected with small bursts from his turbine engines. Nine armoured forms knifed through clouds of smoke and rising ash, their eyes ablaze. Iaptus drew them into a wedge, himself as the spear-tip.

'Give them tooth and claw,' said the sergeant. 'Show them how drakes fight and kill.'

Va'lin clenched his teeth as his combat reflexes began to kick in, but felt his body shaking as the rapid descent hammered his armour systems. A counter in his left lens cycled down the metres as he hit terminal velocity. Smudged shapes began to resolve into fighters clad in rags and crude armour. Detail increased. Some of the fighters were shouting, gesturing wildly at the sky and aiming their weapons.

An explosion blossomed on the right, but Naeb ploughed through unharmed. Whining solid rounds were thickening the air, pranging armour plate. Va'lin felt a lucky shot smack his pauldron and ricochet.

'Eye to eye, brother,' Naeb's voice came over Va'lin's personal vox-feed. He was laughing all the way down. Va'lin could not prevent a feral smile.

They were close. Distance diminished as the crater-strewn roadway rushed up to meet them and Iaptus angled his body so he went down feet first.

'Ready to engage,' he uttered over the vox, taking a slew of hits against his storm shield.

Eight affirmatives responded in near-perfect unison as Squad Iaptus mirrored its sergeant.

Va'lin could not suppress a snarl as he gunned the engines of his jump pack, violently arresting his ascent on twin cones of fire.

A conflagration spread out below, cooking the drop zone and everything in it in successive waves of flame. Flesh and rockcrete blistered equally, and Squad Iaptus landed amidst a score of blackened corpses.

Iaptus touched down at the epicentre of a ring of fire, cracks webbing the rockcrete at the impact point, his warriors radiating out from it. He launched again seconds later, a small burst that took him just beyond the scorched perimeter of the drop zone and into a warren of burned out maglev carriages.

Heretics infested it like lice. Armoured in a mismatch of heavy carapace, flak and improvised plate metal ripped from various transports, the
enemy had neither cohesion nor tactics. Men, their faces daubed in crude
violet tattoos, threw themselves down on the Salamanders. Their minds
were lost, for no sane man would commit to such a suicidal charge.

The killing was intense but no more than a conditioned reflex.

Va'lin's flamer was still mag-locked to his jump pack as he favoured his
sidearm and gladius for close quarters. An elbow strike broke an arm, a
left swing carved open a clavicle, the return swing took a head. Another
three seconds passed and the same rote repeated. Two bolt-rounds from
Naeb accounted for a team attempting to set up a heavy cannon at the
end of a corridor bracketed by a pair of carriages. More deranged heretics scurried from the carriages' shattered windows. Dersius gave them
a bloody welcome.

Naturally splitting into their combat squads, Xerus went with Iaptus
on the opposite side of the makeshift enemy barricades. He cored the
plate shield of a tripod-mounted autocannon that was being set up on
a carriage roof. The plasma bolt burned through metal, skin and bone.
Arrok and Vo'sha raced on ahead, gaining a little loft from their jump
packs before hitting two groups of dirty-looking soldiers that had finally
scattered from the Salamanders' irresistible onslaught.

A thick knot of warriors, armed with various solid-shot weapons and
blades tried to bulrush Dersius down a flanking avenue. The hulking
Salamander launched into them, breaking the pack before laying about
them with chainblade and bolt pistol. Va'lin was right on his heels, Naeb
just behind him, when he saw a second mob piling over a barricade on
the opposite side.

'Douse them, brother,' said Naeb through his mouth grille, 'I'll reinforce
Brother Dersius.'

Va'lin nodded, and came to a halt so he could level his flamer. Prome-
thium-fire bathed the onrushing horde, rendering them down to charred
and steaming bone. Va'lin moved on.

'Brothers,' Iaptus's voice came over the vox-feed, 'cleanse this nest then
break for high ground.'

The secondary objective was all but achieved – now for the primary, the
opening of the 'gate'.

Dersius and Naeb finished the first mob just as the last of the heretic
dregs were thinning out. More were positioned further down the bridge,
but were bedded in and would need digging out. Dersius voiced their
collective frustration.

'We're wasting our time with this rabble. Where are the real warriors?'

'They are here, Dersius,' said Naeb. 'They're just afraid to fight you,
brother.'

Laughter echoed loudly across Salvation Bridge, incongruous when heard over the carnage.

Va'lin was scouring the vehicular warren and barely noticed.

'Where is Ky'dak?'

Naeb scowled, 'Probably waging a one-man war, as always.'

In the fierce melee, Va'lin had lost sight of the Themian, but found him again in his peripheral vision boosting to the roof of a flamed freight loader.

'I see him...'

A quick burst from his jump pack put Va'lin on the same level. He heard his two brothers land heavily behind him.

Ky'dak was gutting a half-armoured heretic with his chainblade. Tech-marines had tried to repair it, but the weapon was only partially functional and it made a grisly, flesh-chewed mess of the mortal. Ky'dak appeared to relish the gory baptism and, upon seeing his brothers, waved them on.

'He is mad,' said Naeb.

'Have you never seen an angry Themian, brother?' asked Dersius.

'Every time you grace me with your brave countenance, brother.'

Va'lin barely heard them. For the first time since the drop, he had a decent view above the swamp of wreckage of Salvation Bridge as it stretched away into the middle distance. At the far end, Zantho's line-breakers were pushing against the deluge of rubble and debris trammelling their route across the roadway. Pockets of heretics dotted these ruins and barricades like cancerous growths. Unlike the chaff Squad Iaptus had just destroyed, these warriors were not only dug in, they were more disciplined. Only fire would burn them out. Likely, they were military trained, possibly comprising a large number of native former-Imperials and even some Cadians.

Redgage, if he had been present, would likely have disputed that, but the evidence of Va'lin's eyes suggested the contrary.

'Nine hundred and eighty-eight metres,' said Dersius, gauging the distance from their current position to the slow moving line-breakers through his helmet's auto-senses.

'Then let us run the gauntlet,' replied Naeb with a hint of teeth bared. Battle was an unequalled panacea it seemed, for the Salamander's injury did not look to trouble him now.

'Lead on as earned, brother,' said Va'lin with wry amusement, 'or we'll miss the war.'

Naeb gestured to the mounds of corpses they were leaving behind.

'What do you call this, brother?'

'Distraction.'

Iaptus, Xerus and the rest of the squad barring Ky'dak were already advancing, bounding across the sundered vehicle wrecks on pillars of flame.

Two massive stone arches loomed ahead and above them. The veteran sergeant's voice came over the vox-feed.

'Those arches are crawling with heretics. Gut them. Burn everything. I've marked your targets on retinal displays.' The link cut off.

Ky'dak abruptly joined them on the freight loader's roof. He was bloodied, but every drop of it was an enemy's.

'Stay in formation, brother,' snapped Va'lin, stomping over to confront him. 'You risk more than yourself by giving in to these reckless urges.'

Ky'dak looked about to bite back but Dersius's looming presence seemed to dissuade him. He gave a brief nod of contrition instead.

'Far archway is ours,' he said unnecessarily. Everyone had the same view through their lens display, the farthest structure outlined in mission-critical red.

Iaptus and the other half of the Wyverns were taking the first arch already.

'On your order, brother,' invited Va'lin, giving a last warning glance to Ky'dak. Something volatile ran through the Themian's veins, hotter than the blood of Mount Deathfire. The truth behind it was hidden in whatever Ky'dak had seen in those flames at Sor'ad's burning, but there was no time to address that now.

Naeb slammed a fist against his breastplate in salute.

'Advance on my lead. We cleanse the nest of vermin then move on to the barricade. We'll make that breach,' said Naeb, feeding power to his turbine engines, 'and open the way for Zantho's line-breakers.'

CHAPTER SEVENTEEN

Nova-class frigate, *Forge Hammer*

The cell was empty, apart from one crucial detail.

'This is no holding cell…' said Urgaresh, his voice a rasp. He was crouching on one knee, surrounded by the 'wrath', a piece of broken metal clenched in his gauntleted hand. The rest of the armour was lying on the floor, discarded. It was almost identical to the armour worn by Urgaresh. Shell shrapnel peppered the outer ceramite, burns scorched its cuirass and greaves a deeper black. The clasps were broken, forcibly removed. Urgaresh held a face. It glared back at him through shattered eye lenses, a ragged scar across the scalp and cheek. Light blazed through this cleft from a brazier of coals glowing beneath. Urgaresh felt its heat next to him as he turned to his brothers. They were all armed, and not just with their bone blades. The armoury had been unguarded and provided bolters, sidearms and a chainsword the sergeant had taken for himself.

'It's a torture chamber,' said Urgaresh and held up the ruined faceplate to the others, the separated battle-helm still lying at his feet. 'This is his armour.'

Thorast held out a gauntleted hand. 'Let me see it.'

Urgaresh handed the faceplate over to the Apothecary who examined it carefully, whilst Haakem and Skarh tried to marshal their anger at the discovery. Ghaan stood apart from the others, leaning heavily against the cell wall, half in light and half in shade from the open doorway.

They had met no resistance so far. No klaxons sounded. No boarder repulse-teams tramped down the corridors to meet them. After letting the mortals go, the Black Dragons had expected transhuman intervention. It was why they were here, after all. This latest discovery changed everything, though. Urgaresh felt the leash binding them all, the one he alone grasped, slipping. A growing part of him wanted to let it go.

'Too quiet,' Ghaan slurred, still feeling the effects of the Thallax's lightning gun. As well as the wall, he leaned heavier on the only boarding shield they had found amongst the cache of weapons. His brothers would have disparaged him for claiming it, but everyone in the 'wrath' knew he was dying – so did Ghaan.

'Where are they, brothers?' snapped Haakem, fingers twitching. Despite the fact the armoury had been well-stocked, Haakem had refused any weapons. He was a silent killer, best deployed from the shadows. Bone blades were all he needed, or so he had declared with obvious disgust at the others, even though it was tactically sound to arm up.

'Hiding behind their serfs,' snarled Skarh. 'Honourless dogs.'

'Be calm, brother,' Urgaresh told him, though he felt anything but himself. He turned to Thorast. 'Well, Apothecary? Am I right?'

Thorast gently put the faceplate down. For a moment he stared into the broken lenses as if regarding the lifeless eyes of an old friend for the last time.

'Yes,' he breathed, voice choking with emotion. 'It is definitely his. The wound patterns are grievous...'

Urgaresh arose, and stood next to the Apothecary.

'Is he dead, Thorast?' he demanded. 'Can we be sure of that at least?'

Thorast bowed his head and all eyes from the 'wrath' went to him. Haakem and Skarh calmed their violent energy. Ghaan stood just a little straighter and with only the shield for support. Eyes wide, Urgaresh seized the Apothecary by the shoulder.

'Brother, an answer!'

Thorast only had the strength to murmur. 'Yes... he is dead.' He raised his head and there was something in his eyes burning away the grief. Urgaresh chose to interpret it as anger and spoke to the 'wrath' himself.

'Zartath is slain.'

He looked each of them in the eye, finding their rage enough to drown worlds.

'Spare no one,' he rasped. 'Everyone on this ship dies.'

Makato could hear them coming. By some miracle, he and Jedda had reached not only the deck three armoury but also a comms-station through which the lieutenant was able to gather reinforcements. Makato had cleared all noncombatants from the areas aft of deck three and assembled his armsmen at key points across the *Forge Hammer*. One hundred and thirty-two men and women stood ready, over fifty in this section alone. Makato would have preferred double that.

After the visit to the armoury, the lieutenant was wearing heavy-duty combat carapace. It came with a helmet and a bandolier of blinders. He still had his grandfather's sword and father's braid. The latter was wrapped around his fist in some vain attempt to curry the favour of the dead.

We that are soon to join them, he thought as he turned to Jedda and said, 'Bring up that cannon.'

It ground noisily across the deck on thick, metal tracks. The weapon mount had a colourful designation, or so Makato thought: Rapier. Quad-heavy bolters cycled ammunition as the track-mount moved, arming up in preparation for whatever was coming down the corridor.

'Save that idiot grin for when the ship is safe and we're still alive,' Makato warned his man-at-arms, prompting Jedda to adopt a more stoic demeanour. Like his lieutenant, Jedda was armoured in carapace. Whilst he carried the Rapier's control unit, his combat shotgun was slung over his back. The corridor was long and narrow – he had the perfect arc of fire. It was dark, however. Despite being able to access most of the *Forge Hammer*'s on-board systems, shutting off bulkheads and conduits to force the aggressors into this bottleneck, the available power with the ship on silent running still only afforded limited illumination. Only Xarko had the authority and ability to change that, but currently the Salamanders Librarian was unreachable. His sanctum was impregnable to any means of breaching it Makato had at his disposal, and despite numerous attempts at contact, silence persisted between it and the rest of the ship. The lieutenant's armsmen were all there was to defend the ship. They would just have to be enough.

Makato turned to the man behind him, but his words were intended for all fifty-something armsmen cramped in the small junction, backs pressed against walls, into alcoves and behind what little cover they had.

'These warriors are not like ordinary boarders. We still do not know what they want, either. Be ready, for they'll move quickly and savagely. Stay together, hold position and listen to my orders and you will have a much better chance of staying alive.'

Satisfied his speech had done all it could, Makato turned back to face the corridor.

'Keep it close, Jedda,' he said, referring to the track-mount and making sure only the man-at-arms could hear him. 'I want every inch this corridor can offer. We stop them here or we don't stop them at all.'

'There are just five of them, sir.'

'Five angry Renegade Astartes,' Makato replied. 'Even one would worry me, Jedda.'

'You know this location is not secure,' Jedda murmured.

'Even so, I am staying here.'

'There are too many maintenance ducts, tunnels, companionways... I cannot guarantee they haven't infiltrated one or more of them.'

'I have eyes watching every possible access. Even if we can't lock them down, we will see them coming.'

'I just wanted to make you aware, sir. No one would misjudge you if–'

Makato held up his hand. 'You're a fine soldier – none finer serve on this ship and I can say that even surrounded by all of these brave souls because they know it too, but don't lessen my respect for you by saying what I think you were going to. They are on my ship. I will be here, at this line, until that is no longer the case.'

Jedda nodded, and that was an end to it.

When the talking ceased, the sounds of the ship and its circadian rhythms took over as deafening as silence. Air-recyc hummed, the hull groaned, engine drone kept at its lowest impulse throbbed like a migraine. Surprising then that no one heard the dull clank of heavy boots against the deck, or even saw the bulky shadow of black-armoured warriors bearing down upon them until they were already halfway down the corridor.

The armsmen behind Makato spotted the danger first.

'There!' he cried just before a shell whined through the dark and blew his head apart like an egg. Bone, brain and blood were still raining down as Jedda triggered the heavy bolters. Four cannons lit up at once, muzzle flashes throwing harsh light down the corridor. Sparks cracked against a solid mass, as if the darkness itself was moving on them. And it was getting closer. A heavy boarding shield, a massive Adeptus Astartes-sized thing. It was almost broad enough to fill the width of the corridor. Without better firing angles, the armsmen would be forced to shoot right at it. What had started out as a sound tactical position had turned into a weak and predictable one. Rather than a quintet of armoured figures advancing upon them, it was a single mass.

Makato saw the danger and bellowed to shock his men into action.

'Take out that bloody shield!'

A fusillade of shotgun bursts and lasgun cracks filled the air, adding to the Rapier's louder boom. Aim was poor with barely half the armsmen managing to hit the target, in spite of its size and singular nature. For many, this was the first time they had fought against Space Marines. Makato knew Jedda had drilled them hard, but no amount of training could have prepared them. Hands were shaking, hearts failing.

Frustrated, Jedda pushed the control panel into the hands of a rookie armsman and hefted his combat shotgun.

'Aim and fire,' he roared, showing how by example. Burn scars and pellet marks cratered the boarding shield but it was made to withstand sterner punishment and the warriors behind it to weather fiercer opposition – it just kept on coming.

Ghaan was feeling the pressure. Two thirds of the way down the corridor, and he slipped. Thorast was there to hold him up.

'Almost there, vexilliary,' the Apothecary told him.

'Need… a moment,' he said, gasping for air smack in the middle of the fire storm as the others took snap shots from behind the boarding shield. Ghaan grasped the side of his battle-helm, struggling to release the clasps. 'Help me get this off.'

'We need to move,' said Thorast, but Ghaan's hand upon his arm cooled his urgency. There was something about the way he did it, the manner of his grip.

'Brother…' Ghaan insisted, 'I can barely breathe.'

Hunkered down, Thorast released the locking clamps to help Ghaan take his battle-helm off. It clanged loudly as it hit the floor, the sound all but drowned out by the fusillade hitting the shield.

'Better?' asked the Apothecary. 'Now can we move forward?'

'Do I look better, brother?'

'Like death, Ghaan.'

Ghaan chuckled ruefully. 'Good.' He licked his lips – there was blood on them. His armour glistened with it. 'A pity we have no banner…'

'Don't you know yet, vexilliary,' said Thorast. 'It was you, not the banner, that we followed.'

Ghaan laughed again, but the Apothecary was not finished.

'We owe a debt of blood,' he said, grimacing at the blistering fire just above his head. 'We cannot stop.'

Ghaan nodded wearily, pushing the shield with the Apothecary's help, grinding it against the deck for a few feet until the vexilliary had lifted it again.

'Then I rest,' Ghaan breathed, coughing up frothy, blood-flecked sputum.

'Then you rest,' echoed Thorast, knowing exactly what the vexilliary meant.

It wasn't working. The shield was too robust, their weapons ineffective. Armsmen were intended for the security of a ship, its internal security principally. Against deck ratings, unruly overseers and bondsmen, they were the very best. Even in a limited boarder repulsion role, they could be extremely useful, but this was the *Forge Hammer* – its complement of Adeptus Astartes was supposed to defend it. The one that had been left behind was absent. As a result, Makato felt distinctly outgunned. He considered falling back. There were junctions and chambers deeper into the ship that would afford better arcs of fire, and present an enfilading position to reduce the effectiveness of the boarding shield. Slow the advance of the renegades might be but, against small-arms fire and even the track-mount, it was inexorable.

Close up, even behind their mobile barricade, Makato got a better look at the Black Dragons. He recognised their leader, the one with the excessive bone growths. They had shown mercy earlier, expressing a desire to fight with the Chapter warriors aboard this ship. Makato had sensed some honour in them. What had happened to drive them into such a berserk rage?

'Hold fast,' he shouted to the others, having drawn a bolt pistol and firing it single-handed like a naval officer of old. 'We can break them. We can break them.'

'Munitions are running low, sir,' said the rookie who was manning the Rapier.

Jedda had advanced to the forward line, just to the side of the chugging track-mount, a grimace etched onto his face from the retort of the heavy bolters.

'Stop and reload,' replied Makato, reaching for his bandolier. 'I'll buy you some time.'

The rookie went to it, getting help from the nearest armsmen who had overheard the lieutenant, just as Makato primed a blind grenade.

'Blinders out!' he bellowed, prompting the men to turn and shield their eyes as he lobbed the flashbang in the renegade's midst. It lit up the corridor in a flare of magnesium, so bright it seemed for a moment to bleach the walls white. Their shadows still receding along with the sudden light burst, Makato got a good look at the enemy.

Four warriors still stood. The shield still stood. It had hurt them, though. He heard curses and–

Four warriors…

The thought struck Makato like a blast of chill wind. There had been five on the ship initially and with no casualties that meant one was unaccounted for.

'Jedda!' cried Makato, just as the fusillade started up again, but he was already too late.

CHAPTER EIGHTEEN

Nova-class frigate, *Forge Hammer*

Though it was tight, Haakem slipped through the maintenance shaft with the stealth of a viper. Using his bone-clawed elbows, he quickly dragged his armoured body across the floor of the tiny duct. Never stopping, he remained intent on his point of egress as dictated by Urgaresh. It was hard to think without his brother-sergeant's instruction, the throbbing inside his cracked skull a constant distraction. It made him… wrathful.

Ahead, a light burned. It hurt his eyes – he much preferred the dark – but knew it meant the execution of the next phase of his mission was at hand. Execution was just what Urgaresh had charged him with. Encouraging the bone blades to slip a fraction from the flesh sleeves in his forearms then through the gaps in his armour, Haakem let the savagery that was ever at the edge of his thoughts take over.

Preceded by the clatter of a hatch hitting the deck as it was stripped off its hinges, something large and black burst from the maintenance duct and into the armsmen.

Makato was already turning as a solid armoured mass hit his men like a wrecking ball. Demolition did not accurately sum up what happened in the seconds that followed, however. Massacre did. Blood arced in fountains from suddenly screaming armsmen – so did their limbs and heads as the monster's bone blades began to carve.

'Take him down!' Makato screamed, trying to bully his way through the press of bodies that were understandably retreating from the murderous whirlwind that had sprung up amongst them. A panicked scrum developed, between those men within reach of the monster and those trapping them. Makato had packed the corridor tight. He wanted overlapping fields of fire, a cannonade that would bring even Space Marines down. They were positioned at a junction with three exits, guns pointing towards aft, one exit to the side and the rest of the corridor behind. Death clad in black came from this direction, and unlike the slow inexorable force often recited in bleak poems and soliloquies, here death was swift and bloody.

Order was lost. Even if they could stop this one monster, they were utterly undone.

Ahead of the armsmen watching the corridor, the boarding shield moved aside and admitted a fresh band of deadly warriors. With the Rapier's ammo-mags still half in, half out, Makato's men were reduced to small arms fire. Shotgun bursts and lasgun beams smacked and ricocheted off the renegades' armour, but the Black Dragons were undaunted. They came on like a tide, bolters crashing like the thunder of waves.

Makato froze, trapped in an island of indecision. One way, the monster threshing his men like crops on an agri-farm; the other, a rushing force tired of hiding and committed to the charge. For the first time since Yugeti Makato had given him his inaugural sword-fighting lesson, Kensai did not know what to do. Strike or fade?

Strong hands seized him by the shoulders, almost hauling Makato off his feet. Decision made, but not by him. Jedda rushed in front of him, taking charge and waving the two men who grabbed Makato away.

'You can shoot me for insubordination later, lieutenant,' he said to the thrashing form of Makato as he disappeared down the side corridor. 'This is your ship. You have to live if you're going to defend it, sir.'

'Jedda!' Makato screamed, remembering how he had screamed as Yugeti had dragged him away from his father's body, Hiroshimo dead to a pirate's blade. Though the household guard, the Bushiko, had repulsed the xenos raiders, Kensai Makato had become a man that day. He had made his first vow, to join the Imperial Navy and honour the legacy of Hiroshimo and Yugeti Makato. This was how it was supposed to end for him, embattled with weapon in hand. He railed against it, his cheated fate, but was powerless to stop it as Jedda vanished into the shadows.

'I will hold them as long as I can,' he called, wading in with the others as the bulkhead door slammed down, cutting him off from view and silencing the screams.

Urgaresh saw the officer dragged off by his own men and knew the fight was theirs. It had been the moment Haakem had emerged amongst them, but with them now trying to save their leader it meant the mortals had all but accepted their fate.

By his side were Thorast and Skarh, the latter firing off quick bursts from his purloined bolter to try to break up the wall of solid shot and las peppering the Black Dragons. There was no sign of Ghaan, but Urgaresh could not worry about that now. He had tossed his own bolt pistol when the mag ran dry and wielded the chainsword two-handed, leading into the charge with his shoulder. He was hurting. His eyes still burned from the blind grenade, despite the optical compensators in his battle-helm. Urgaresh knew Thorast and Skarh had felt it too. Both were seized by a feral rage.

With Haakem at their backs, cutting flesh as he was born to, and Thorast, Skarh and Urgaresh pushing from the front, the fight was mercifully short. For what they had done to Zartath, Urgaresh wanted to punish the mortals more but was cogent enough to realise these wretched souls were not the true focus of his ire. He wanted the Salamanders.

'Where are they?' snarled Skarh, battering a man to death with the stock of his bolter. Ammunition was short, and now they were amongst the armsmen it made sense to try to conserve it. Urgaresh was surprised at Skarh's restraint. Perhaps they were not as lost as the sergeant believed. 'They should come. We slaughter their men.' Skarh lifted a man by the throat, crushing the mortal's larynx with a savage twist before dropping him and breaking another. 'They should come.'

Haakem met his brothers from the other side of the melee. Anointed with blood, there was something monstrous and unpredictable about him even to Urgaresh.

'Well met, brother,' rasped the sergeant, using the flat of his chainblade to swat a figure into the wall. Its face was crushed on impact, the armsman's helmet splitting across the middle of the crown. Urgaresh barely registered it – the burring chainteeth of his sword were already cutting into more meat. In the carnage his enemies had ceased to be people anymore – they were just obstacles in his way, laid waste to by his wrath. The slaughter became mechanistic, almost perfunctory. A momentary flash of pain in his cheek brought him out of this murderous torpor, and belatedly Urgaresh realised he had been shot almost point blank in the face. He staggered, and felt the hot knives of the shotgun pellets where they had penetrated his helm and embedded into flesh. The vox-grille was wrecked, so he ripped it away with his free hand, warding off his attacker with his chainsword in the other.

He was a skilled fighter, this mortal. Urgaresh recognised him from the *Fist of Kraedor*. Still fending off his attacker, Urgaresh tore off his battle-helm completely and swung. The blow came unexpectedly and struck the man across the torso and neck. He snapped back, disarmed. Urgaresh spared him no words and thrust the chainblade into the mortal's prone body.

It was over. The rest either died or fled. Urgaresh did not bother to give chase, nor did any of the 'wrath'. They would get to them all soon enough. This had been the defenders' best attempt to stop them, and it had failed.

'Is this it?' snapped Skarh, glaring at the spread of bodies lying beneath him in rapidly expanding pools of their own blood. He turned to Urgaresh, a savage look in his eye visible where one of his retinal lenses had been smashed during the fight. 'My fury is not yet slaked, brother-sergeant.'

'We aren't done,' said Urgaresh, largely ignoring Skarh's minor tantrum while he inspected the chainsword. Some of the teeth were broken and its motor hardly purred anymore. Perhaps he had gone at the mortals harder than he first thought. In his peripheral vision, Urgaresh noticed Haakem. Drenched in blood and sweat, he released a cascade of mortal fluids as he shook his head. The act was not unlike that of a dog, and Urgaresh wondered again at where this road was taking them all.

'I would have Salamanders blood for Zartath,' hissed Skarh, gripping the edge of Urgaresh's plastron.

Urgaresh glared at him. 'So would I,' he calmly replied. 'Now, release me.'

Skarh obeyed, bowing his head in swift compliance as he realised his overstep.

'Skarh is right, brother-sergeant,' said Haakem. 'This is barely worth the effort. I joined a rescue mission that turned into one demanding vengeance instead. With that I have no issue, but slaughtering these dregs...' he gestured to the bodies. 'It's butcher's work, not worthy of us. We're unscathed and yet they–'

'No, brother,' uttered the solemn voice of Thorast. The Apothecary was kneeling next to Ghaan, his reductor already unsheathed. 'Not unscathed.'

Ghaan was dead, his body slumped against the boarding shield but still more or less upright. He had died on his feet, which was little more than they could all ask. The shield had taken some grievous hits after all. There were gaps in the armour, gaps that Ghaan had stopped with his own body.

'"Do not fail your brothers. Though their bodies die, their spirit must return to the Chapter. That is your charge."'

'So it was said,' murmured Thorast, nodding at Urgaresh's recitation of the Credo of Apothecaries.

'So too shall be done,' the sergeant concluded.

All watched as Thorast took Ghaan's gene-seed and added it to the rest from the *Fist of Kraedor*.

'It's done,' said Thorast, turning to his sergeant. 'What now?'

'Are we monsters, brothers?' asked Urgaresh.

'We are what our masters on Terra made us to be,' said Skarh.

'Then we head to the bridge. If there are Salamanders here on this ship, that is where we will find them. I want to look them in the eye before we kill them, and ask why.'

'What kind of answer do you want?' asked Thorast.

'It hardly matters, I suppose. I just want them to know what this has all been for, what they have forced us to do, to become... and what we must do next.'

Without transhuman reinforcements, the ship was at the mercy of the Black Dragons. For what the Salamanders had done, Urgaresh would see it crashed on the dirty world below.

CHAPTER NINETEEN

Sturndrang, the underhive of Molior

Agatone found Zartath wandering alone at the edge of Kabullah's border. The ex-Black Dragon looked punch-drunk as if he had just had a bout with Ba'ken in the practice cages and the hefty captain of Seventh Company had given him some brutal 'instruction'. He almost staggered in Agatone's direction when he saw him. Recognition was not instantaneous, either.

'Are you all right?' asked Agatone, wary, and kept his hand within reach of his holstered bolt pistol. There was something about the way Zartath moved, the blankness in his eyes, that gave the captain pause.

Blinking once, Zartath nodded. He did it slowly, wearily.

'Did something happen, brother?' Agatone asked, approaching him but still alert. His eyes narrowed when he saw the blood stains only half washed off Zartath's armour. 'Where have you been?'

'It's nothing,' Zartath replied, and seemed to regain some of his senses.

'Where, brother?'

'I am my own man, brother-captain,' said Zartath, only now understanding the level of caution Agatone was showing towards him.

'Where have you been?' Agatone pressed, and touched his fingers to the grip of his sidearm. He had known this day might come, that he might have to take Zartath to hand, the way a master deals with a feral dog. Agatone knew he might have to put the ex-Black Dragon down.

Zartath raised his hands in a gesture of surrender, and stopped.

'Needed time alone,' he admitted, 'away from the roar.'

'You were supposed to maintain watch, brother. Were this a conventional mission–'

'But it isn't, brother-captain. Nothing about it is,' Zartath replied, and lowered his hands. 'Tell me something, though. Have you heard it too?'

'Heard what?'

'You know what I'm talking about.'

The drone, that strange keening that had persisted ever since the klaxons had first sounded for the so-called 'vermin tide'.

Agatone eased off a little but still kept his guard up. He gave one, slow nod.

'So have I. It drums in my skull even now.' Zartath took a step but no more than that. 'I heard it at the sump pond, pounding through a waste pipe, coming up from below somewhere. There is something rotten here, brother-captain. It has tainted this place beyond the corruption of the flesh. It is tainting us, even now, as we hear it. Our helms, would that we wore them, would be no protection, either. It is within us.'

Agatone had suspected as much, but to hear his suspicions spoken aloud by Zartath gave them form and palpability. It also clarified them. He saw the truth of it now. The vermin that had attacked them were incubators for some pathogen, and the blood, their tainted blood had been a carrier that unlocked some deeper evil at large in Molior's underhive. And they were hearing its siren call in the droning. For now, there was nothing Agatone could do about that. For the second time he wondered if Tsu'gan had run afoul of this 'evil', and tried to vanquish it. He hoped they were hunting for a living fire-born and not merely a corpse. Either way, none of it explained the blood on Zartath's armour.

'I need to know what you did, Zartath.'

Zartath showed Agatone his palms again.

'Would that I knew what that was. Something… attacked me, I think.'

Agatone scowled. 'You think?'

'I ventured into the waters of the sump, drawn by the siren call in my head. I felt something wrap its jaws around my leg. The next moment, I awoke covered in blood.'

'So you killed it, whatever it was?'

'I would not be alive otherwise.'

'A reflex then?'

Zartath nodded mutely.

Something was missing from Zartath's testimony, Agatone was certain. What he could not be sure of was whether the ex-Black Dragon was deliberately hiding the truth of that, or whether the savage warrior simply did not know. Part of the reason Agatone had once stringently opposed his inclusion into the Chapter was on account of such murderous blackouts.

Elysius had convinced him it was a worthwhile risk – the hunt for Tsu'gan demanded it – and for his part Zartath had performed well, proving a valuable asset, but frequently Agatone questioned his suitability. He did so again now.

He scrutinised Zartath for a few seconds, hoping the silence might reveal something his questions had failed to, but found nothing new. In the end, Agatone beckoned him to follow.

'Come on. Exor is awake, and we need to move out.' He turned and led Zartath back, the ex-Black Dragon a few paces behind. 'You need not walk at the back of me,' Agatone called to him, tramping back to the muddy lights of the settlement.

'It is my place,' said Zartath, and the words gave Agatone renewed pause. The captain was wise enough to realise something had happened during the three hours he had been transfusing his blood to save Exor – it had left him a little weakened, but the effects would wear off quickly, a Space Marine's Larraman cells more advanced than mortal blood cells. Regeneration and replenishment would be swift but he had neither the time nor means to interrogate Zartath further. Exor and, he hoped, Tsu'gan, were waiting.

Issak was the one waiting for them when they returned to the settlement. He was standing at the bottom of the staircase to his surgery, armed and armoured with a pack on his back. Some of the natives, including the ageing but relatively well-attired alderman, lurked nearby, looking concerned.

Agatone read their fear and anxiety immediately.

'Going on a trip, medicus?' he asked, and looked upwards in the direction of the surgery.

Issak was wearing light flak armour with a mesh underweave. It looked old, but serviceable, clearly Militarum-grade. His pack most likely contained his med-kit, spare ammo and whatever provisions he needed. It too was Guard-issue. His boots were dark, functional, with visible metal toe-caps and he had a leather skullcap too. A combat shotgun and stubby autopistol on a leather strap across his back and hip holster respectively were the extent of his arsenal, barring any knives. A storm cloak completed the image of underhive gun for hire.

'Your comrade has recovered to an extent,' Issak replied, following Agatone's gaze all the way up to the surgery. 'He is upright and mobile, at least.'

Agatone gave a slight bow of the head. 'And for that you have our gratitude, but you didn't answer my question.'

'I suspect you already know the answer, along with my destination.'

Agatone turned to Zartath who had just caught up to him. 'See to Exor,' he said. When Zartath was tramping noisily up the staircase, Agatone resumed his conversation with the medicus.

'Craving the glory days, are we?'

'Not exactly. I told you once I was a religious man. In coming here, I served the Throne and ministered to the faithless, preaching the Imperial Creed. I found the very worst hole of existence I could, and made it better. For the Imperium. For these people. I knew it would not be forever.'

'I don't need another gun – I have two already and others in the hive city I can call upon.'

'With respect, lord, I believe the former but not the latter. You needed me to patch up your Techmarine because he's the only one you've got. Vox-comms don't work so cleanly in the underhive and where you're going they will cease to function at all. The feral one and your wounded brother currently in my surgery are all the manpower you have at your immediate disposal.'

'And your gun arm will tip the odds back in my favour, will it?'

'I don't offer it... at least, I don't offer it alone. Finding Seven Points is easy if you know your way around. It's also a lot safer if you're familiar with our hazards.'

It made sense. Issak had decided he had been given a sign from the Emperor, that the Salamanders coming presaged a calling of sorts. A guide would make the journey to Seven Points easier, but Agatone struggled with the morality of putting the human's life in danger, especially as he had just, in all likelihood, saved Exor's.

'I can't guarantee your safety,' Agatone told him.

Issak laughed. It was a warm, genuine sound that smacked of his natural beneficence.

'Had I not walked these treacherous roads for years before your arrival, and not ventured from Sturndrang's surface to this sub-strata, I might find a warning note of caution in those words, Agatone. Alas...' he concluded, and opened his arms wide as to suggest the decision was already made.

'Well then,' said Agatone, first seeing Exor then Zartath emerge at the summit of the stairway, but his eyes falling on Issak last of all. 'Seems your duty to the Throne is not yet done. Take us to Seven Points.'

Seven Points, or the 'cross' at it was sometimes known on account of the seven interlocking and divergent paths that led to this nexus point, was in ruins. Granted, most of Molior's underhive had a broken down, dilapidated appearance but even for an arena this was a war zone.

'A battle was fought here...' hissed Zartath. He stated the obvious, not with the intention of drawing his companion's attention to it but rather as part of his internal process of deconstruction. The four of them, three Adeptus Astartes and one missionary-turned-medicus, approached the battlefield along one of the seven paths. Stretching out in front of them was a scene of carnage, but of a battle already fought and ended. Judging by the amount of bodies, it was a conflict with few victors.

Zartath went on ahead, weaving amongst the corpse-strewn wreckage and still-smoking fires. He kept low, even though there were no obvious signs of life. More than once, a careless scout had toured the aftermath of a battle believing all threat ended, only to find enemies alive with their blades still sharp, their desire for vengeance even sharper.

'Five distinct groups fought here…' Zartath went on, beckoning the others as he stopped at intervals to examine any sign or spoor.

Smoke hugged the ground in a thick veil. Broken limbs and weapons stuck out from it, breaching the surface like flotsam on a beach exposed by retreating surf. Heat haze still wavered the air from conflagrations that had diminished into mere blazes since their ignition. The shells of burned-out buildings hung open like old, blackened wounds yet to heal.

'I see only four,' Exor replied. He moved tentatively, without the confidence of full fitness, but was as battle-ready as Issak could make him. To Agatone's mind, it would have to do.

'As do I, Zartath,' the captain agreed with his Techmarine.

Exor had said little during the journey from Kabullah to Seven Points, which had been made mercifully short thanks to Issak's knowledge of these depths. The Techmarine had kept a wary eye on his auspex at all times, which Agatone deemed as normal behaviour for one schooled by the Martian adepts, so left him alone. Exor's anvil would come later when he was pressed into the fires of battle again. Then Agatone would see the true measure of his readiness. But as of right now, all they had was the hunt and that was Zartath's area of expertise.

The ex-Black Dragon scurried through the ruins, amongst the bodies. Some he stooped to examine, others he left alone. His level of scout-craft was, admittedly, a mystery to Agatone.

'Where is the fifth, brother?' Agatone called, eyeing the high gantries above where the smoke was rising with suspicion. Below, the dead were all underhivers, variously gang affiliated.

'Close and few in number,' Zartath answered cryptically. 'There are many signs.'

Some of the bodies had the trappings of gladiators, escapees from the arena or perhaps even unleashed by their masters. If what the alderman had told Agatone was true, then two gang lords ruled this quarter. Their men would be amongst the dead.

With Zartath so engrossed in his task, Agatone turned to Issak. 'You know the markings of the local gang lords here?'

Issak nodded, pointing to a corpse wearing thick factorum overalls and a grey bandana tied around his neck.

'Junkers,' he said pointing to another, this one thickly muscled and squeezed in dark fetish leather. 'Hel-kytes.'

There was a third gang, Agatone noticed. These wore red hoods with heavy smocks, almost akin to robes. Cultists.

'Them I don't know,' Issak admitted, having followed Agatone's gaze.

'Can't see him amongst the dead,' said Exor. He was kneeling by the body of a gladiator, a chrono-slave who had been gutted by a heavy blade. Nearby was an abhuman, classification ogryn, its head separate from its body and a heavy cannon, still fully loaded, in its rigor-mortised grip. 'This one was evidently for security,' offered Exor, before running a scan with his auspex.

'Seven Points looks far from secure,' murmured Agatone, as he delved further into the carnage with the others. 'Any sign at all of Tsu'gan?' he called out to Exor.

'Nothing from the bio-scan, but we might have better luck deeper into Seven Points.'

Agatone nodded, and they pressed on. 'Stay by me,' he growled at Issak. Wisely, the missionary obeyed.

By the time they reached the middle of Seven Points and its infamous arena, Agatone had counted more than a hundred dead and that was just at the periphery. Many bore the trappings of the Junkers and the Hel-kytes but there were red hoods too. Amongst the slain, they found the gang lords, Silas Krebb and Otmar the Brute. Issak seemed genuinely disturbed to see both men killed so casually, not because he carried any regard for them but on account of the fact that their power had seemed absolute in this quarter. He remarked as much to Agatone.

'A sudden break in their alliance, perhaps?' asked the captain.

Exor shook his head. 'Judging by the position of their bodies, they were fighting side by side against a common enemy. Releasing their slaves suggests they were desperate too.'

'You know of anyone who wanted their territory, medicus?' Agatone asked Issak. 'For if my errant brother is not with either of these men's organisations, then he might well be with the victors.'

'I've never seen these red hoods before, nor heard any talk about them. If someone was planning on muscling in on either Silas's or Otmar's territory then I would have heard something. This doesn't look like a turf war, though…'

'That's because it's not,' rasped Zartath, having appeared silently at Issak's side who started at the hunter's sudden return. 'It's a sacrifice. This is a place of Ruin.'

The arena was close, the nexus of where the crosses intersected – the heart of Seven Points. Sunken into a deep manmade depression, the floor of the arena itself had been excavated, potentially even after the battle as the bodies inside had been dragged to its periphery. Underneath the dirt and grime and blood were the archaeological remains of the paths from which Seven Points had derived its name. Only there weren't seven, not originally. Exposed by the excavations of the victors was an eighth.

'An eight-fold path…' said Exor, his voice low and resonant with mechanised reverb.

Issak muttered a quiet benediction to the Throne as Zartath and Exor descended into the arena. Six bodies had been cut up and laid upon the eight divergent paths, blood, limbs and entrails. The naked flesh was etched with arcane symbology, carved there indelibly.

'Search this entire arena,' said Agatone, his face a mask of grim discomfort. 'Make it fast. You stay with me, medicus, and tell me what you can about this atrocity.'

Issak slowly shook his head as Zartath and Exor went to their duties. Peripherally, Agatone noticed they did not make eye contact and went to opposite ends of the arena. They might have just been intent on their duty, or there might be some residual distemper between them. Like much of what had happened in Molior, there was little Agatone could do about it now but he resolved to confront it later. When Tsu'gan was in his custody.

'I am of the Ecclesiarchy not the Inquisition,' Issak confessed. 'I have little knowledge about the rituals of Chaos, let alone what any of this means.'

'Just tell me what you see.'

Issak half turned and for the first time since Agatone had met him looked unsure of himself. Many mortals had such a reaction when confronted by the evidence of Chaos desecration up close.

'But how does this help you find your quarry?' he asked, wiping sweat off his brow, even though the air around Seven Points was chill as hoarfrost and Issak's breath ghosted from his mouth.

'He either fought and killed them or was killed in turn. Since I can see neither a body, nor evidence of this cult's destruction since the ritual site is intact, I have to assume he fought, killed and then escaped or was captured,' said Agatone. 'We find the cult, we find our quarry.'

Issak nodded, still obviously uncomfortable, but examined the bodies more closely.

'It's a blood ritual, that much is clear,' he said, careful not to actually touch anything but getting close enough so he could scrutinise the individual elements. 'The cuts are precise, measured. I've seen surgeons with inferior blade-craft to this, good ones.' He skirted around the ring of sundered flesh. 'Each piece was arranged meticulously, and with purpose.'

'To what end?' asked Agatone, watching the medicus keenly.

'I have absolutely no idea, but I see no evidence of summoning. I cannot see any taint, detect it through my olfactory senses or otherwise.' He looked back at Agatone. 'Perhaps an attempt at some form of communion?'

'They were sending a message?'

'Yes, possibly, but I don't know. Like I told you, I am a missionary, a medicus before that, not a daemon-hunter. Please...' Issak added, 'I would like to leave this place now.'

Agatone nodded. The others were returning anyway.

Exor brought news.

'He was definitely here,' said the Techmarine. 'There is a lower level, cells by the look of them, a sort of barracks to house the gladiators between bouts. I found markings carved into the wall. Agatone, it was Nocturnean sigil-dialect, akin to the symbols we use to brand our flesh.'

'What did he carve, brother?'

'The anvil and the hammer, over and over again,' said Exor. 'He is punishing himself. Tsu'gan wants to suffer.'

Agatone knew that Tsu'gan had always had a masochistic streak. He supposed all Salamanders did to an extent, the Promethean Creed demanded it of them, but there were rumours about Tsu'gan's addiction to pain that had never been proven one way or the other. His disappearance after the rescue mission into the Volgorrah Reef that had yielded Zartath as well as its intended targets, Chaplain Elysius and Sol Ba'ken, had prevented any meaningful enquiry. The fact was, no one had spoken to Tsu'gan since that moment except for Dak'ir, and he was dead or presumed so.

'One of us fought here,' Zartath confirmed. 'I found transhuman blood, whether from this battle or another in the arena...' He shook his head, scowling. 'Impossible to determine. There are tracks, footprints that radiate from the ritual site. Their gait is uneven, drunken.'

'Perhaps they fell into some kind of torpor after whatever they did here?' suggested Agatone.

'It's likely,' said Zartath, appearing to be more lucid and focused than before, the hunt seeming to have done him some good. He offered something to Agatone in his open hand, a small silver dagger. 'I doubt they would have left this, otherwise.'

Agatone regarded it but did not touch it. Issak made the sign of the aquila.

'It's not the weapon they used to cut up these sacrifices.'

'No,' Issak agreed, finding his voice again at last. 'They'd need a saw or at least something with a serrated edge to get through bone. The athame was probably used to cut the sigils into their flesh, a spiritual icon more than a weapon. I am surprised they didn't come back–'

Zartath's raised fist interrupted Issak.

'Who says they haven't?' he hissed.

Zartath hurried away from the ritual site to the arena wall and pressed flat against it, prompting Agatone and Exor to do the same. Issak belatedly followed their example.

'That fifth group,' Zartath muttered to Agatone. 'They are here.'

'Auspex reads nothing' said Exor.

Zartath faced him savagely. 'They will not appear on any scanner, brother. But I can smell their scent.' His lips drew back into a snarl. 'And I hear them. Listen!'

Exor had to bite back his anger, but did as he was told.

'Four of them?' guessed Agatone, frowning as he strained to pinpoint the enemy's exact numerical strength.

'Five,' Exor confirmed, his augmetic hearing surpassing even that of Zartath's, though the ex-Black Dragon did nod to confirm.

'Tread's heavy,' Agatone whispered, then addressed Issak. 'You stay here, medicus. Keep your head down whilst we engage.'

Issak nodded. Though he could not hear as well as the Space Marines, he paled with fear. 'No arguments here.'

Zartath was already scaling the arena wall, driving his bone blades into patches of exposed earth. His upper torso rippled with effort, describing the muscles in his lithe frame. Saliva drooled from his open mouth, fangs glistening with it, as one of those above drew close to strike.

'Get ready...' he hissed to the others, and lunged.

It began with a wet *slurrch* of flesh and ended in a low grunt of pain. Zartath roared, and heaved a body almost as large as he was over his head. Initially impaled in its heart, the bone blade slipped out, tearing flesh and cartilage as Zartath brought the body down into the pit.

Issak barely had enough time to take in the monster's grotesque appearance – its swollen musculature and physical mutation, the blood-stained robes and battered armour underneath, its array of bizarre weaponry, the strange tubes attached to its back and neck – before Exor had launched something into the air, a spherical object, dark in colour and blunt of design. Issak saw it winking, three second-long pulses, and caught the warning from the Techmarine just in time.

'Hide your eyes!'

The flare from the blind grenade was intensely bright. Even turned away, hands clamped over his face, Issak still found his vision was impaired afterwards. He heard a scream, though, and knew it had surprised the ones above.

Agatone was climbing from the pit, bolt pistol in hand. Exor lingered a fraction behind him, but was soon lost beyond the captain's peripheral vision. Zartath had already engaged, using the momentum of his earlier

kill to spring up and out onto the battlefield. Three sharp booms echoed
from Agatone's sidearm as the mass-reactives found purchase in living
tissue and subsequently detonated. He had made a mess of the creature's
left arm, but it had two of them on that side alone so its combat efficacy
was barely diminished.

It was brutish, heavily gene-bulked and mutated. Something pumped
into its carotid vein, some kind of adrenal philtre or chem-shunt.
Hunched, still mewling from the sting administered by the Techmarine,
the monster was only a little shorter than Agatone. Raised to full height it
would dwarf the Salamander. A glaive had been surgically grafted to one
of its remaining arms and the blood spouting from the region Agatone
had ruptured with his three-round burst was rapid-healing, which meant
it had some kind of regenerative cocktail in its system. Nerve pain had
been shut down too. It should have been in shock from a wound like that,
but instead it came for him with the glaive.

Though it might once have been human, now it was an aberration bent
on murder. And even with the one Zartath had gutted and thrown into
the pit, it was one of four. Gritting his teeth, Agatone drew his gladius
and fired his pistol as he moved to engage.

Exor struggled over the lip of the arena wall, slowed by his injury. Pain
knifed into his side, his back, anywhere the machine did not touch him.
He was cursing his flesh-weakness when he noticed he was in the crosshairs of a mutant's bow-caster. It looked crude, almost rudimentary, but
the barbs on its ammunition were sharp. The crossbow jerked and Exor
screamed as the bolt quarrel thunked into his upper torso.

The medicus went to move to his aid, until Exor shouted him back.
Then he was moving, dragged up and over the lip of the pit wall and
across the ground as the firer retracted its harpoon bolt on a length of
high-tensile cable.

Agony spreading through his chest and back, Exor fumbled for a plasma-
torch, even his knife, but he was being thrown around too fiercely and
could not reach them. Glimpsing a blade in the mutant's meaty hand,
he let out a frustrated roar of pain. It had staved the bow-caster into the
ground and was reeling in the Techmarine remotely.

Forgetting the knife or the plasma-torch, Exor went for his sidearm. That
too, he struggled to reach. His hands slipped against the holster clasp,
his fingers trembling as his body fought the intense strain it was under
to prevent him from passing out again.

Then the cord went slack, cut abruptly at the source. Exor rolled on his
back in time to wrench the barbed hook out and see a welter of blood
shoot up from his assailant's slit throat.

* * *

Zartath hunted without pause. Every cut, every feint and counter was chained together. From the first to the last motion, he fought with utter kinaesthetic awareness and acuity. Out of the death of the first opponent, he blended into his attack on the second. It was fluid, deadly. Like art, only bloody. In a skirmish at close quarters, momentum was everything. Keep your enemy off balance, hit him where he's unprotected and unprepared. Make him react to you. Zartath epitomised this credo. He was born to it. Experience had honed him to become this. On the Volgorrah Reef, in the xenos death-labyrinth, it was a way of life.

Two more remained. Zartath had already discounted the one against Agatone, confident the captain would despatch it.

The first opponent jabbed at him with a spear. A heavy, powerful thrust but one Zartath easily dodged. He cut open the warrior's shoulder, severing a vital nerve cluster in its deltoid region that made the arm go limp. With his enemy debilitated, Zartath proceeded to weave aside from another wild retaliatory strike and cleave through its neck. The blow wasn't clean, just as Zartath had intended, and the head hung back as the neck opened in a grotesque yawn of ruddy flesh.

A bellow to his left. Close. He could smell its breath, feel the transformative heat of its body as the chem-shunts went to work rapidly fuelling its metabolism. Anger would make it clumsy. Zartath smiled, already moving, always moving. Slipping aside to avoid its opening attack, Zartath knew the fight was over.

Something stirred in the pit, and Issak realised it was the body of the dead mutant. Only it wasn't dead. Brackish, foul-smelling liquids pulsed into it as it drank greedily. The blood had stopped flowing, now clotting completely, and the wound in its chest was closing.

Muttering a prayer to the Emperor to gird his soul against contamination, Issak ran over to the corpse with shotgun in hand. He racked the slide to chamber a round. Did it one-handed. It was a gorgon-class variant with a short barrel and broad muzzle. The range dipped on account of the modifications, but the trade-off was stopping power. Pressing the shotgun's mouth to the monster's forehead, he had time to see its eyes blink open once before he declared, 'Try and come back from this,' and pulled the trigger.

Then he ran back to the wall and climbed.

Three more rounds put the creature down, evacuating the contents of its torso in the process. Agatone kicked the body over and saw Zartath decapitate the fourth and final mutant. Then he went to Exor and helped the Techmarine to his feet.

Once he was back up, Exor bowed his head. 'I'm sorry, brother-captain. My wounds are…'

'Still fresh,' Agatone replied. He lightly examined the goring of Exor's chest caused by the harpoon. 'With fresher still to join them.'

'I can fight,' he assured Agatone.

'You will have to regardless of your readiness for it, brother.' He looked to Zartath who was approaching slowly, his armour painted in arterial sprays of crimson. 'Why decapitation, brother?' Agatone asked him.

'To be sure of death.' His savage eyes briefly went to Exor, and there was a mocking smile within them. Weak. A liability always in need of rescue, they said. 'I've not met an enemy yet who can come back from having no head.'

'Best be certain,' said Issak's voice behind them. He was walking towards them, having just clambered from the pit, his robes also flecked in dark blood.

'You injured, medicus?' asked Agatone, with a hint of concern.

'Not mine,' he replied. 'I had to put my shotgun to the head of the one in the pit.' He looked at Zartath. 'It was rising.'

'I cored its heart. That's a sure killing stroke,' snarled the ex-Black Dragon.

Agatone looked around them. The mutants had been reduced to meat chunks but their limbs yet quivered. At first he had thought it nerve endings catching up to the fact that the body was dead, but now he really scrutinised the dead he saw eyelids flickering, lips trying to form words even when the heads upon which they featured were severed.

He glanced around quickly.

Zartath's bone blades slid from their flesh sheaths as he went to finish what he thought he had done already.

'Wait…' Agatone held up his hand, and gestured to a cluster of nearby drums, the kind used to house fires that kept out the underhive chill. 'Bring them to the pit,' he told Exor. 'Zartath and I will get the bodies.'

'To what end?' Zartath asked.

Agatone met his feral gaze with stern resolution.

'To torch them. We burn everything. It's the only way to be sure.'

They dragged the dead into the pit, wary of potential and sudden resurrection. With Issak's help, Exor dropped in the barrels, oil spilling across the arena floor. At Agatone's order, the Techmarine took out his hand flamer.

'Is there anything you don't have on that rig?' said Zartath, jutting his chin in the direction of the small mechanical frame attached to Exor's back. Much smaller than a servo-harness, the rig's array of tools was limited but small enough to be hidden under the Techmarine's cloak.

'I believe in preparation. Not a philosophy you're familiar with, I'd suspect.'

Zartath opened his arms wide. 'Everything I need, I already have.'

'And how would you have ignited the accelerant? By spitting on it?'

A roar of flame crowded out Zartath's response as Exor put the barrels and the bodies to the torch. They watched the fire burn, the four of them, letting it warm their faces. Shadows were flickering across Agatone's, the conflagration's glow reflecting in his onyx-black skin.

'He came looking for hell, and he found it,' he whispered. 'Tsu'gan is here. And he's not looking for punishment, not any more. He wants redemption, not death. Against this cult, whoever or whatever they are, he may find both.'

'Something changed those men into monsters,' uttered Exor. 'It wasn't just will that drove them to damnation. The method by which they regenerated, the way their blood clotted and skin knitted back together... I have only seen that on one other life form.'

Agatone nodded, as Zartath stared into the flames.

They had come hunting for Tsu'gan and discovered he was engaged in a hunt of his own. And it was a particular quarry he was after.

Traitor Space Marines. The legionaries of Chaos had come to Molior.

CHAPTER TWENTY

Heletine, Canticus, Salvation Bridge

Dozer blades attached to the front of Zantho's Predators shouldered aside the minor wreckage but not the heavier land-freighters and hauler-trams the heretics had used to block the road. Using their turret weapons would not clear them, either. If they managed anything more than a dent, they would only create more trammelling wreckage. Zantho was not accustomed to relying on others, no fire-born was, so he decided they would try to barge their way through.

'Roll back,' the tank commander ordered. 'Push again.' He was starting to regret holding the larger Redeemers in reserve, but nothing could help that now.

Small-arms fire from scattered pockets of enemy fighters was peppering Zantho's position, but it was no more irritating than a persistent hail against his power armour. The various cannon nests dug in across the bridge and shored up in alcoves and on ledges high up on its Victory Arch were less easily dismissed.

Salvation Bridge was the single largest span leading into Canticus. It was almost four thousand metres long with six major arches and twelve minor arches stretching over its fifty-metre width. Heretics occupied the first third of that. Victory Arch was but the initial major arch across the bridge. That left at least one more major, and up to four minor arches, a total of over one thousand metres of hard, dug-in fighters. Tough did not begin to describe the task before Zantho.

And he needed to get through it. In the north, Kor'ad led a force that was moving into Canticus through its templum district and then on to its slums. A large disposition of heretic armour had been sighted moving through that region and an attack from the angle of the slums to the north and Salvation Bridge to the south would not only bracket the enemy armour, but also see it destroyed as a result. Any other outcome would leave one or the other force outgunned, outmatched and likely defeated. Smashing this armoured convoy was the key to gaining a foothold in the city, above and beyond the scraps of territory the Imperial alliance had so far achieved. And from that staging ground with the Adepta Sororitas as reinforcement, they could begin a meaningful invasion.

A major step was opening the 'gate' and releasing Zantho's armour onto the bridge.

He winced when a las-beam came close, searing the side of his face with its passage of heat. High-calibre solid shot and heavy bolt-rounds followed it in withering storm, but the same wreckage that was impeding the armour group's progress absorbed most of the impact. It was the lascannons that gave Zantho the greatest concern.

As soon as the beam flashed past, he opened up the vox-feed.

'Storm bolters on that nest. Hose the whole damn thing down.'

The arches were riddled with alcoves and crawlspaces. Ledges, suspension wires and gantries clung to every surface. There was room enough for an entire army to bed in, if they so desired.

The pintle mounts on the Predators were already firing, and aimed up simultaneously to put pressure on the lascannon nest. It was firmly entrenched in the arch's plascrete, surrounded by sandbags and wire-threaded crates. The brief salvo forced the gunners into retreat but failed to neutralise the threat.

Most of the Predators' heavier cannon, the turret and sponson weapons, were ineffective until they could get beyond the barricades and effect some decent lines of fire. Zantho had forbidden the use of their more powerful turret weapons against the arches and the Vindicators did not have the range or potential missile trajectory. Salvation Bridge must stand if they were to cross and support Kor'ad's push across the northern templum district. If even one of the four arches fell, the bridge would likely collapse with it. Stalled, boxed in, the greatest strengths of Zantho's tanks were mitigated, their weaknesses enhanced.

It was an unenviable position outlined by the *Nocturnean* taking a solid hit to its front armour. A second split it open and struck the fuel tanks. The tank went up moments later, throwing shrapnel across the width of the bridge. Zantho ducked below the cupola, throwing the hatch closed as the resulting fire storm rolled over the remaining tanks.

'As Vulkan bears witness,' he roared down the vox. 'Get this damn barricade down!'

They rolled forwards, engines growling in protest and were met by the sound of slamming steel and the continued frustration of not going anywhere fast.

More las-beams stabbed down from the nests. On the Victory Arch they looked like incandescent threads of light. One unstitched another of Zantho's Predators. It took off the tank's left tread leaving it floundering and useless trapped behind the barricade.

Back above the hatch, the fires were still burning. Strength of Xavier and Immortal Anvil had been next in the line to the sundered Nocturnean and bore the brunt of the frag and fire. Both were black as soot ash, their hulls jutting with pieces of shrapnel. Zantho had three lines left. Four Predator Annihilators and three Destructor-class in the first two lines, with two Vindicators at the back. As he appeared back above the cupola hatch, Zantho had a pair of magnoculars in hand and brought them up to his eyes. Scanning through the billowing smoke, he caught sight of one of Fourth's Wyvern squads. They were fighting their way across the bridge.

Zantho smiled. 'Vulkan be praised.'

Then he saw the shadow flash overhead, and made out through his scopes the underside of a Thunderhawk. The smile faded as he recognised the icon scored into the metal. A brazen eight-pointed star with an unblinking eye at its core. So far they had fought heretic insurgency fighters, mainly dregs with some Militarum-trained defectors. Well-armed, but more irritating than genuinely troubling. That all changed with sighting the gunship. It meant a different calibre of enemy had just entered the battlefield.

The Black Legion.

Iaptus and his combat squad were climbing all over Triumphal Arch, bursting into the traitor gun nests and digging them out by force. It was slow and painstaking, but the first half of the Wyverns went about their task methodically. The arch would be cleansed. Ahead of it was Victory Arch and the point closest to the Salamanders tank armour. That too would need to be cleared out before a breach on the gate could be attempted with any strong chance of success.

Though much of Salvation Bridge's aesthetic beauty had been destroyed by the war, the bold arches still retained some of their artistry. Huge frescoes of prelates, cardinals and other ecclesiarchs stood alongside palatines and lord-commanders, one on either arm of the arch, soaring into the sky. Heletine was a world that could trace its lineage back to the Great Crusade. The men and women sculpted on these arches were its founders and leaders in ages past. It had weathered the Great War of Heresy, and endured. It was tragic then that with the invasion of the Arch-Traitor's sons, that legacy could be nearing its end – unless the descendants of another primarch could prevent it.

Naeb craned his neck to take in the monolithic spectacle of the Victory Arch.

'Vulkan's blood…'

'Afraid of heights now, little drake?' asked Dersius.

'No, brother. Only wary of you falling and hitting me on the way down,' Naeb replied, and focused on the mission. 'Two-man teams,' he said. 'We cover more ground. Who knows how many nests and lurkers are up there.' He glanced at Va'lin. 'Dersius and I. Va'lin and Ky'dak. East and west, respectively. Stop when you reach the summit.'

'It's dirty work,' said Dersius.

'Tell me when war is anything other,' Va'lin replied, and Dersius nodded in agreement.

Ky'dak snorted his impatience, 'Moving to engage,' then boosted his engines. Va'lin had to hurry to keep pace. They veered to the west side of the arch as ordered, whilst Naeb and Dersius went east.

'Try to keep up,' Ky'dak said through the vox-feed. 'Fall behind, I'll leave you behind, brother.'

'Look to your own part in this mission,' Va'lin replied, gaining one of the lower ledges, 'and I'll look to mine.' It was unoccupied, and he boosted his engines again quickly to stay on Ky'dak's heels who was already soaring for the arch's higher echelons.

'I intend to.'

They hit the first nest together, surprising a four-man crew with a pair of autocannons. Upon forcing his way inside, Va'lin crushed one with his sheer bulk. Ky'dak despatched the other three with short stabs of his gladius.

Above them a second battery of gunners had spotted the incursion and were rapidly trying to uncouple a heavy bolter from its mountings so they could aim it at the Salamanders. Va'lin sent a six-metre jet of flame into their alcove and three fire-blackened figures plummeted from the nest screaming.

'Burn little heretics,' Ky'dak laughed.

Va'lin ignored him, focusing instead on the other gun nests.

'I count fourteen.'

'Agreed,' Ky'dak replied. 'Four are harbouring snipers.' He pointed so Va'lin could also pick out the grainy light haze from their targeters.

The second nest went down bloody with Ky'dak going in aggressively again. By the time they had reached the third, any advantage surprise had given them was over as the gunners split their fire between the tanks held up at the barricade and the warriors assaulting them from below.

'Need to move,' said Va'lin, boosting ahead of Ky'dak who had paused to finish off the last group of gunners. As he crested the next sunken nest, Va'lin heard the sharp whine of sniper shot whistle by his head. He caught a round in the leg, but his armour took off any sting. It slowed him incrementally, though, and he was still readjusting when he entered the fourth nest. It was larger than the others so far, a host of five heavy cannon present, and well-defended. As he moved on the first, he noticed one of the heretics come barrelling over a low wall of sandbags. Va'lin turned his flamer on him – he could take out all five cannons with a single burst – when he saw the grenade in the man's clenched fist. He never got a chance to throw it, but the grenade went off anyway as did the bandolier of frags around his chest.

The explosion smashed into Va'lin's chest, so hard it kicked him back and took him over the edge of the nest. For a few seconds he was falling, until Ky'dak grabbed his wrist and hauled him back.

'Up, brother,' he said, and there was a hint of a smile in his voice.

The gunners in the nest were all dead, burned to death by Va'lin's flamer or blown apart when the grenades had cooked off.

'Let's waste no further time then,' Va'lin snapped, locking a firing ledge in his sights and surging for it.

As he was about to hit the ledge, he caught sight of Naeb on the far side of the arch. He was clinging to a buttress jutting from an ornate column fashioned into the arch, and activating the vox.

'Black Legion!'

Va'lin followed his gaze to the sky where, through roiling clouds of smoke, he saw the outline of two gunships emblazoned with the eye of Horus.

'Ky'dak...' Va'lin began, about to engage until he found the firing ledge empty.

The other Salamander joined him.

'Strafing run?' asked Ky'dak staring upwards at the passing ships.

'Too high,' said Va'lin. 'And looks too slow for–' he stopped when he saw something fall from one of the gunship's cargo doors. Too large to be a missile, too anthropomorphic for something so lifeless. A form spiralled in freefall from the gaping hatch. To be precise, there were three forms. Three from each gunship.

They plummeted. Six dark shapes in total that resolved into warriors, their arms outstretched.

'Not a strafe,' Va'lin confirmed, watching the two enemy gunships peel off into the upper atmosphere before they attracted the attention of the nimbler Salamanders Stormtalons. 'Reinforcements.'

'They'll die,' said Ky'dak, but reloaded his bolt pistol and took aim at one anyway.

'Save your ammunition, you'll never hit it from this range.' Va'lin shook his head, 'No they won't. That's Tactical Dreadnought Armour.'

Terminators. Of the self-same creed and kin as the monster who had butchered Sor'ad and almost killed Va'lin and Ky'dak. Other than its champions, the Black Legion had no deadlier warriors and six of them were hurtling towards Salvation Bridge.

Va'lin turned his attention back to the barricade and Zantho. 'We need those tanks out here now. They're about the only thing that'll cut through those warriors.' He opened the vox-feed to Iaptus. 'Brother-sergeant, are you seeing what we are?'

'Heretics falling from the sky, brother. Yes, we see it. Disengage and head for Zantho. The gate opens now or not at all. Regroup on my marker.'

Iaptus cut the feed, leaving Va'lin to inform his brothers.

'Naeb...' he began, but was too late. Naeb and Dersius were almost at the summit of Victory Arch when two of the heavily armoured forms slammed down right in their midst.

The Terminators used their claws and fingers to grip the arch, tearing deep drag marks in the stone. Using the furrows like handholds, they proceeded to climb.

'I see them, Va'lin.' Naeb sounded pained, feeling his injury again.

'Disengage, brother,' Va'lin urged. 'We can face them together on the ground.'

'We're pinned, Va'lin. Between the nests and these two, we would never make it down in one piece. You and Ky'dak have to take the gate with Iaptus as ordered.' He cut the feed.

Another Terminator landed on the bridge after clambering down one of the minor arches. He was already priming a cannon slung under one arm. Two more hit the opposite side of Victory. The sixth missed its target and smashed straight into the road, splitting a freight-loader in half and carving a large crater into the rockcrete with the impact.

Va'lin was about to launch, when Ky'dak gripped his wrist.

'What are you doing?' Va'lin asked sharply.

'What are you doing, brother? Naeb and Dersius are good as dead facing off against those things alone.'

'I won't disobey a direct order.'

'I won't leave two of our squad to die.'

'What do you care about the squad, Themian? You fight as if you're alone, heedless of squad cohesion and regard for others.'

'We avenged Sor'ad. I don't want to have to avenge Naeb and Dersius as well.'

Va'lin swore, before re-opening the feed.

'Sergeant Iaptus. We cannot join you on the ground.'

'Cannot? It's an order, Va'lin. I am not giving you a choice.'

'I can't leave the rest of my squad, sergeant.'

'We are also your squad, brother.'

'That said, I cannot abandon Naeb and Dersius. Vulkan be with you, brother-sergeant.' The link died and so did any standing Va'lin might have had with Iaptus. 'I never wanted advancement, anyway.'

Ky'dak shook his head. 'Neither did I.'

Together, they boosted for the east side of Victory Arch.

From his vantage point of his cupola hatch, Zantho saw one half of the Wyverns break off, headed for the barricade, whilst the other remained to take on the recently deployed Black Legion. The heretics infesting the two major arches were far from neutralised. It was a gauntlet from Victory to the edge of the barricade, threaded with solid shot and las-fire. As soon as the enemy saw what the Wyverns were attempting, they would be the focus of every cannon that had range and line of fire.

Zantho saw it for what it was: a suicide run. His fellow sergeant knew it and wanted to improve the odds of getting enough bodies to the barricade to make a difference. With half his squad cut out, selling their lives cheaply against the Terminators, those odds had just been slashed drastically.

'Iaptus, you fool...'

Zantho ordered all secondary weapons on the arch to strafe and suppress, but even with twice the number of guns he knew it would not be enough.

CHAPTER TWENTY-ONE

Heletine, Canticus, Salvation Bridge

Iaptus was furious. He boosted beneath the towering Victory Arch with all haste, intent on reaching the barricade and fully aware of the storm that was about to come down on them. It began ahead of schedule as the Terminator on the ground opened up with his reaper.

'Evade and into cover!' he bellowed, as the distant muzzle flare roared.

The combat squad slammed down roughly fifty metres beyond the arch, hunkered down behind a clutch of drums and a wrecked loader. Solid shot stitched the metal, threatening to bore a hole right through it, as the Terminator fired and advanced.

From above, las-beams cracked against the road behind them. An errant missile from a hand-held rocket tube spun away to the left and exploded, its firer blown apart by a bolt round.

Arrok switched targets and released another burst. Vo'sha and Illus had joined him at rearguard as the five Salamanders formed a loose, protective circle.

'We can't sit here for long, brother-sergeant,' Xerus reminded Iaptus unnecessarily.

'I don't plan to, brother.' Peeking through a gap in the wreckage, Iaptus caught sight of the Terminator. He was advancing up the road, his sustained barrage on pause whilst he slammed a fresh clip in the reaper's stock. Barely visible through the smoke, a second Terminator was slowly dragging itself out of a crater a few metres behind the first.

'Outflank and engage,' Iaptus told Xerus. He held up two fingers, indicating the number of targets.

Xerus nodded and peeled away, prompting the autocannon to start up again as soon as he was airborne. Iaptus did not wait. He boosted straight forwards, clearing the wreckage with a single bound and landing a few metres away from the reaper-armed Terminator. Caught between two potential targets, the Terminator started to back up, spreading his arc of fire as he moved.

His companion was on his feet, advancing rather than retreating, and swinging a crackling power axe. Xerus hit him with a bolt from his plasma pistol but took a few rounds in the chest from the autocannon in return. The soaring Wyvern veteran was unceremoniously plucked from the sky and sent earthward where he rolled and scraped across the ground.

Illus was at Iaptus's back; he saw the battle-brother's icon on his retinal display. Arrok and Vo'sha were on Xerus.

This was an ambitious plan, Iaptus realised, attempting to run a gauntlet of heavy guns whilst simultaneously taking on two Black Legion elite. But he was committed now, and so would see it through to whatever end.

Iaptus led with his shield, taking a desultory salvo from the reaper before his enemy was forced to disengage so his close combat-armed comrade could wade in. Iaptus tried to barge him, using the momentum of his jump, but the massive warrior just shrugged it off and threw him across the roadway.

Illus took over, landing just in front of the Terminator as Iaptus skittered half on his knees, digging the head of his thunder hammer into the rockcrete to slow himself down. The other Wyvern managed two swings before the Terminator severed his left arm and then took his head. Illus was falling back, neck gouting blood, as Iaptus squeezed a little thrust from his jump pack to smash into the Terminator from the side. This time his enemy was distracted, and staggered against the blow. Iaptus took the warrior's return swipe against his shield, and saw the power axe's blade chip the edge. Pressure building, Iaptus punched with the thunder hammer's head and broke the Terminator's armoured hip. As he sagged with the loss of support on one side, Iaptus hit the warrior again, this time across the shoulder. A burst of energy was unleashed with the blow, and the Terminator roared in agony as his face and torso were fried. He had enough time for one final wild swing, before Iaptus caved in his helm and skull.

Sparing no thought for Illus, Iaptus reengaged his turbine engines. Fire spewed from the twin jets, the dragon mouths venting their fury and carrying the sergeant across the open ground to the overhang of broken vehicles where the rest of his squad took cover.

Xerus was alive but so was the other Terminator, though it had been forced back and wide by the sudden assault, and resumed hammering against their meagre shelter with the reaper.

'We should advance. Can't stay pinned here,' said Xerus. His armour was pitted and scored from where the autocannon shells had hit him.

'Agreed,' said Arrok.

Iaptus had his eyes on the road ahead. A hail of gunfire was chewing it to pieces. It would chew them to pieces as well. They had scarcely progressed a hundred metres. Surprise was no longer an asset at the Wyverns' disposal, and now the enemy knew where they were, the threat they posed and that they were pinned down by one of their dark lords.

'We aren't getting through that.'

Xerus sounded grim. 'What are your orders, brother-sergeant?'

'Fall back to the arch and regroup.' Iaptus opened the vox. He had to tell Zantho. 'Brother,' he began, his voice heavy with the sound of bitter defeat and grief for Illus, 'we won't be able to breach that vehicle blockade.'

'Armour is moving,' Zantho returned, and Iaptus could hear the grind of tanks and the dull report of their turret weapons behind the other sergeant's words.

'What?'

From their vantage point, pinned down beneath the overhang of wrecked vehicles, Iaptus and the others could not see the barricade but according to Zantho it was open.

'Our angelic Sisters obliged us.'

And now Iaptus saw it… saw them.

They were like angels, rising on wings of fluted steel, their black armour shining with reflected firelight. Seraphim.

They brought fire of their own. It burned down heretics in swathes. The black armoured angels landed amongst them like a flock of murderous ravens, hacking and cleaving with their blades. Death screams, even the crash of bolt weapons and chainblades was rapidly eclipsed by a growing swell of bellowed prayer.

Behind him, Iaptus heard two distinct heavy impacts as a pair of Terminators hit the ground.

'Eye to eye, brother-sergeant,' said Xerus.

Iaptus nodded, 'Use your speed and manoeuvrability. Do not get pinned down and do not try to take these warriors on alone. They'll kill you. It's that simple.'

Message delivered and understood, Iaptus led them out. They would engage the Black Legion and then join up with the chorus of Seraphim sweeping across Salvation Bridge. Never before had it seemed so aptly named as in that moment. Behind the Seraphim, Zantho's tanks crushed the lesser barricades underfoot. The vehicles were all ablaze, the lurkers within who had been carrying incendiary devices and other explosive armaments burning with them. A mass crematoria of the damned, a fitting end for traitors.

Dersius and Ky'dak held off the Terminator's chainblade as the traitor tried to force it into Dersius's face. Clinging to the arch with one gauntleted hand, the Terminator fought both Salamanders to a stand-still. His strength and brutality were almost overwhelming. Chainteeth ground against one another, releasing fits of sparks. Already damaged, Ky'dak's weapon was proving unequal to the task and as the Terminator pushed hard, the rotating belt snapped and the teeth exploded from the Salamander's weapon. Several embedded in the armour of all three combatants. One struck Ky'dak near the eye, shattering his left retinal lens. The helmet had only recently been repaired but the gouge was deep enough that it would require major work to restore again. That only mattered, of course, if Ky'dak still had a head to put it on. The impact threw him back, almost off the arch itself, and crucially left Dersius to fight alone.

Ky'dak had been right. Their brothers would be dead if not for his and Va'lin's intervention. Despite their disadvantage, the Black Legion warriors had enclosed the exposed Assault Marines quickly, lurching hand over hand across the face of Victory Arch and making fresh handholds with their immense fists. They practically simmered with corruption, both warriors exuding a dark aura as palpable and real as the squalls of smoke rising up into the air around them.

The first was armoured head to toe. Curling tusks protruded from his faceplate and helm, which was shaped in the aspect of a ram. A soaring crest of lurid pink hair, its provenance likely human, arced from his brow to the nape of his neck. The other one was bareheaded with the broad, oddly symmetrical features common to most transhumans. His expression was almost obscenely benign in a face that exceeded the usual conventions that would regard it as 'handsome'. The warrior was, in many ways, beautiful but it was a physical perfection born of Chaos and therefore wholly repellent. Disparate in appearance, both Black Legionnaires were united in their cause of destroying the Salamanders within their reach.

Chased by weapons fire, tracked by the tracer rounds of the deeply embedded snipers, Naeb and Dersius had found themselves back to back in one of the alcoves they had cleared, effectively pinned. Ky'dak had gone in hard, surging upwards from below on thick bursts of flame from his jump pack. His initial impact and impetus had staggered the 'handsome' Terminator, allowing Va'lin to find an opening. The Salamanders, however, were still boxed in, trapped in the empty gun nest and on the defensive.

Va'lin ducked a savage blow that would have taken off his head had he been any slower, and shot back with his bolt pistol. At such extreme close range, the flamer would do more damage to the Salamanders than the traitors, so he had switched to his sidearm. So far, the effect of his rounds had been negligible. In tandem, Naeb landed a solid hit with his chainsword against the monstrous Terminator's breastplate but only managed to chew metal and further blunt the teeth of his weapon.

Behind him, Dersius roared with effort. The Themian was big, almost as big as Ba'ken, and clutched his chainsword two-handed, but the ram-headed warrior was incredibly strong and the battle was a losing one for the Salamander. Ky'dak was dazed, blinking the blood out of his eye and thanking the Throne he was not blind in it. He struggled to his feet, lurching unsteadily on the ledge on which they duelled. The heretic had managed to get one of his massive armoured feet onto the ledge and was using the extra purchase to lever more pressure onto Dersius.

'Brothers...' Dersius was in trouble. He had been forced down onto one knee, his enemy now bearing down on him.

'Glory...' whispered the handsome killer. His voice was like music, but the symphony was cloying and strangely discordant. Ky'dak struck him like a bullet, full-blooded and impelled by his jump pack on maximum burn. The backwash of heat and fire flooded the already scoured nest. It spilled over Va'lin and Naeb too. Rockcrete split apart at the point of attachment between Victory Arch and the traitor's clenched fist. He still held a chunk of it as Ky'dak barged him off the structure and was borne down with him to the roadway below.

Va'lin clenched his teeth as the blazing promethium fire coursed over him. Ceramite was primarily designed to be flame-retardant and his power armour offered some protection, but he was not of Nocturnean blood like Naeb, so it still burned. It burned through the joints and the minute fissures. It burned with the sting of rapidly heated metal and seared mesh against his skin. He would have screamed but he did not want to give his enemy the satisfaction of knowing he was hurt.

Naeb recovered fastest from the flames. He aimed a thrust that skidded off the ram-headed warrior's chestplate but bit through where two sections of his armour joined and released a thin gout of blood.

Now, the Terminator screamed or rather, roared. He smashed Naeb onto his back, opening up the Salamander's wound but also overextending his reach. For a moment he poised to cleave down on Va'lin until the Wyvern shot the rockcrete he clung to and sent him flailing. Ram-head clawed as he fell, trying to find fresh purchase. Dersius had recovered and launched from the nest, small-arms fire from the lesser heretics cracking all around him.

'Naeb,' said Va'lin. He turned around, trying to see if his brother was badly hurt.

Naeb struggled back up and waved him on. 'Go after him. I'll follow Ky'dak. If we land through this sket storm and still have all our limbs, it will be a miracle, brother. If we die, I would rather go out on jets of flame as a Wyvern.'

Va'lin was only half listening. He stared towards the entrance of Salvation Bridge, where Zantho's tanks had floundered. Only now they were moving, and in force. The streamers of gunfire hailing up at them had lessened considerably.

'Miracle, you said?' said Va'lin as dozens of glorious Seraphim soared like black angels out of the sky.

Stephina led forty of her Sisters, soaring at the head of a Seraphim chorus. The bridge was thick with smoke from weapons discharge and rampant fires, but her battle-helm filtered out the worst of it and improved target acquisition.

Hordes of traitors were scurrying across the bridge, a ragged force of cultists and Imperial deserters. The sight of them sickened Stephina to her stomach. How easily man turned from the light of the Throne when the dark gods made promise. She wanted to personally smite every heretical one of them but had to satisfy her desire for righteous punishment vicariously through Sister Helia and her squad of 'Exculpators'. It was an ironic cognomen. There was no forgiveness for these wretches, only death.

Helia's warriors went about their duty with hand flamers, sending bright bursts of purging fire through the heretic ranks. As their growing conflagration soared, so too did Helia's and the Exculpator's voices, prayer and punishment as one.

'Sister Avensi, Helia's flock have cleansed the path,' uttered Stephina across the vox-link. 'Show our heathen brothers to the light.' At her order, a second squad of Seraphim broke off from the chorus and landed on the roadway at the edge of the heretics' barricade.

Stephina lost sight of Avensi and her 'Shrivers' soon after that, but knew her orders would be carried out to the fullest. She had to spearhead the remaining twenty Seraphim, Cassia's 'Sanctifiers' and her own 'Archangels', and reinforce the stricken Adeptus Astartes fighting on the bridge.

Despite their obvious tribalism, their rough and brutal nature, Stephina found she admired the Salamanders in that moment. From the ritual she had witnessed out on the ridge overlooking the ruins, she had supposed theirs to be a base culture, one with little in common to the Imperial Creed but they fought with courage. She wondered then, as she drew blade and plasma pistol, if the Order had perhaps misjudged them. Simultaneously, she experienced a wellspring of guilt fount up within her.

'My Sister,' came Avensi's voice across the vox-link, 'the breach is made. We have begun a flood of wrath to wash away these traitors!'

The 'Shrivers' melta bombs had done their work. Now the Salamanders fighting on the bridge had tanks as well as avenging angels in support. Even with her Seraphim's intervention but a few minutes old, Stephina could see the fight was over. There were just a handful of warriors left who would not die without a struggle.

'Return your flock to the chorus, Sister. There is yet more corruption to be purged.'

The targeting reticule in the retinal lens of Stephina's helmet focused and locked on one of the hulking, black-armoured warriors on the bridge. It was slaved to her plasma pistol. Building up a full charge, she fired off a bolt just as she was coming in to land.

Va'lin watched the ram-headed Terminator force his way through a wall of flame. Most warriors would have withered under the super-heated burst, but the heretic strode against it as if it were merely a strong gust of wind.

'Dersius!' Va'lin cried, and saw the Themian in his peripheral vision begin to rise from where the Terminator's first blow had sent him sprawling.

'We can't kill him this way, Va'lin.' Dersius used the vox, the intensity of the battle too loud to converse without it now.

'We don't have to,' Va'lin replied.

The Seraphim came to earth in a vast, heavenly host. Their leader hit the ground first, firing off an incandescent bolt of energy moments before landing. Ionised plasma tore a scorched rent in the Terminator's war-helm, ripping off a tusk and exposing his snarling face beneath. On fire, he advanced on the Seraphim but she was already darting away from the warrior's enraged charge and unleashing another bolt. This one struck the gorget, and blew out part of the Terminator's neck. Ram-head did not waste time trying to staunch the bleeding – instead he fired off a stream of rounds with his combi-bolter, spitting fury at his enemies in an old, dark language.

Va'lin's flamer had run empty. Without time to reload a fresh canister, he drew his gladius and ran at the Terminator. Now, while the traitor was still reeling, there was only this chance. Pulling his sustained salvo in a wider arc, the ram-headed warrior tried to hit both the Salamander and the Seraphim at once. Va'lin took a round on his shoulder guard. It staggered him, but he kept on moving. His gladius locked with the sarissa bayonet on the Terminator's gun. He fired twice with his bolt pistol, both point-blank bursts that raked the warrior's chest and face, but the traitor turned the damaged aspect of his war-helm aside to weather the bolt storm against his near-inviolable armour. He was about to bring his chainblade around when Dersius rushed in and slammed his own weapon up against it. Even two against one, the Salamanders strained against the massive warrior. Servos grinding like screams, the traitor slowly bore his opponents down and forced them onto their knees. He was gloating, his laughter half heard through his vox-grille and the tear in his helm. His breath was sickly like overripe fruit.

Seeing her opening, the Seraphim leapt forwards in close quarters having dodged the earlier bolter salvo and slashed her powerblade straight through the Terminator's broken gorget, taking neck, head and all. The wound cauterised instantly, though the traitor did stagger for a few seconds before his body realised it was dead and collapsed.

It was over: the traitor Terminators were done. Seeing her Sisters had no need of her, the Seraphim bowed to one knee as she murmured a prayer to the Emperor.

'Vulkan's blood...' Dersius swore, an eye on the angelic Sister as he caught his breath.

Va'lin nodded, glad to be alive. 'You sound tired, old man.'

Dersius glared at him. 'Older drakes are the most dangerous.'

'And disagreeable.'

'Aye, that too.'

Freed from the prospect of imminent death, Va'lin was able to take in his surroundings beyond the duel with the now dead ram-headed warrior. An entire squad of Seraphim were gunning another of the Black Legionnaires down. Several of the angelic warriors lay dead, but it only served to enhance the fervour of those still standing. Ky'dak and Naeb lived, the Themian holding the Epimethian up whilst the Seraphim harassed the other enemy warrior to the edge of the bridge and eventually over it. A traitor gunship returned to evacuate what was left. By now, Zantho's battle tanks had smashed their way through the smaller debris littering Salvation Bridge and were in range with their turret weapons. It took a few hits, but the gunship managed to take off and speared up into the covering smoke, battered but airborne.

Much like the earlier battle in Canticus, the lesser heretic dregs were hounded and destroyed. Some pitched off the bridge after their Black Legion master but would not survive the fall. Others tried to fight, as would a feral beast when dying and cornered. None surrendered.

When they heard the rumble of battle tanks behind them, Va'lin and Dersius moved aside, one to either flank. Zantho was up in the cupola hatch and saluted down at them both as he rode past, now headed for Canticus north and the link up with Kor'ad.

Split from his battle-brothers while the armour column drove by, Va'lin found himself on the same side of the bridge as the Seraphim. When she had finished praying, he offered his open hand to her.

'Your intervention was timely, Sister. You have mine and my brothers' thanks.'

She at first looked at Va'lin's gauntleted hand like it was a viper poised to bite her.

'I have no diseases,' said Va'lin, but it appeared his attempt at humour was misplaced for the Seraphim did not even smile. 'Not that I know of, at least.'

After a few more seconds she simply stared.

When he realised the Sister had no idea what she was supposed to do, Va'lin gripped his own forearm by way of demonstration.

'Like this,' he told her.

Understanding, she reciprocated and they greeted one another in the way of warriors.

'This is the old way,' Va'lin explained. 'We are taught it is from the days of the Legion.'

'By whom?' asked the Sister, her manner still a little prickly and over-stern. She was genuinely curious, though.

'Our Chaplains, the keepers of our Chapter's history and ancient lore.'

'Do they teach you to burn your bodies in supplication to the dead, also?'

Va'lin cocked his head to the side a fraction and saw the Sister had revealed more of what she knew than she had intended. She had wit-nessed Sor'ad's cremation, the Circle of Fire ritual, so must have been watching them in secret. Seeing no benefit in calling her out, Va'lin decided to let it go.

'You do not trust easily, do you?' he asked, releasing his grip so he could remove his helmet. 'I am Brother Va'lin.'

Still unsure of the protocol, the Seraphim removed her own battle-helm.

She was younger than he had expected, and more beautiful. A compas-sion in her eyes undercut her more obvious zealotry and in that moment Va'lin believed a genuine accord between the Order and the Chapter could be possible.

'Sister Stephina,' she told him.

'You were at the council, one of the canoness's officers.'

'I am Preceptor Angerer's devoted disciple, yes.' An awkward silence descended, and Stephina looked around at the carnage. The end of the armoured column was in sight and soon they would be back with their respective warriors again.

'So few of you,' she said. 'To take this bridge – you needed more war-riors. Only nine...'

'And now we are eight,' interrupted another voice.

Va'lin saluted Iaptus immediately. The brother-sergeant approached in an open manner but gave nothing away of his true feelings, despite the fact he too had removed his helm.

'You have the gratitude of the Wyverns and our Chapter, Sister.' He did spare a sideways glance in Va'lin's direction, which promised a reckoning later.

'Your… brother has already given it,' Stephina replied. 'To attempt such a task with so few. I do not know if it is reckless bravery or simple stupidity that drives you.'

The tanks had passed; Stephina's Seraphim were waiting. She nodded, without needing an answer and boosted up and across the bridge to rejoin her forces, leaving Va'lin and Iaptus alone.

'Illus is dead,' Iaptus began before Va'lin could speak.

'Brother-sergeant, I–'

Iaptus held up his hand to stop Va'lin short. 'He was slain by Black Legion, enemy warriors we owe a great debt of blood.' He looked over at the distant form of Sister Stephina. She was gathering her flock, doubtless calling in for extraction. 'She is right. We are too few, and have been for several weeks. But we also have our duty, the one given to us by Captain Drakgaard. He is not Dac'tyr, he is not Fourth, but he is our general in this war and so we will heed his orders as if they were Vulkan's himself. And you will heed my orders, Va'lin. Two of our brothers live. One does not. I don't have the prescience of Librarian Xarko, so I cannot say if the outcome would have been different had you not defied me, but I do know it will not happen a second time.' He leaned in closer, enhancing his threat and presence. 'Were we not on the frontline and needed elsewhere, every one of our few, I would have submitted you to Chaplain Elysius for punishment. Some say he has grown soft since he returned from capture, but believe me when I tell you his wrath is undiminished.'

Va'lin bowed his head, 'Yes, brother-sergeant.'

The heat of Iaptus's barely contained anger lingered and was slow to fade.

'Don't make me brand you with the penitent's mark, Va'lin. Show me again why you are part of the Wyverns, why Captain Ba'ken and Sergeant Lok recommended you so highly.'

'I will, brother-sergeant.'

Iaptus held his gaze a moment longer. For Va'lin it was like staring into the mouth of a furnace.

'I know you will, brother.'

Exfiltration would be momentary. Stephina had called in their transport and was informed it was en route to them at Salvation Bridge. The Seraphim would not join the Salamanders at the heart of Canticus north – they were to redeploy with their Order. According to the plan discussed during the council, they would act as a reserve force for an Adeptus Astartes and an allied Imperial spearhead. The memory of Canoness Angerer's redeployments returned and for a fleeting second Stephina wondered at their sagacity. She remonstrated herself for her doubt almost instantly, forcing her attention to the present and her Throne-given duty.

Helia, Avensi and Cassia all lived. Several of the chorus did not, having given their lives in service of the Emperor. Would that all Adepta Sororitas could be martyred in such glorious cause. It was that Stephina ever hoped for, that and a holy vision of their saint.

'Four dead,' announced Cassia gruffly. Her right eye had a patch over it that concealed the empty socket beneath but not the grievous scarring around it she had carried since the war against the tyranid on Gethseda. Her black armour was flecked with blood, her chainsword bearing the grim evidence of her kills.

'They are at His side now,' said Avensi, and muttered a quiet prayer for her Sisters' souls. Avensi was a zealot, and wore her hair shaved almost to the scalp with votive tattoos inked onto her pate. Whilst she and Cassia offered up their thoughts to the dead, Helia approached Stephina with something else on her mind.

'What were they like, Sister?' she asked. Unlike the others, Helia was without scarification or devotional mutilation. Her hair was almost pure white, cropped to her shoulders. It reminded Stephina of chiselled alabaster, for like Helia's face, it was edged and cut like stone.

'Who?' asked Stephina, her eyes searching the horizon for the gunships that would ferry them from the battlefield and back to the Order.

'The heathens,' answered Helia, and gestured to the Salamanders. 'I hear they call themselves fire-born?'

All four Sister Superiors turned to regard the Adeptus Astartes.

'Unexpected,' said Stephina, looking back.

Cassia nodded, as if catching on to Stephina's meaning. 'They fight hard and with courage. Any warrior who will shed his or her blood alongside me and stand, I regard as an ally.'

'Their practices, though, are… barbaric,' said Avensi.

'What did he say to you, Sister?' asked Helia.

'He told me he had no diseases before greeting me in the old way of his Legion.' Confused silence followed her remarks, so Stephina continued. 'He also said we do not trust easily, and in that he was right at least.'

'Well they have earned my allegiance, Sisters,' declared Cassia. 'Such brave warriors.'

'But so few,' said Stephina, donning her helmet as she looked to the sky where the sound of approaching gunships could be heard.

CHAPTER TWENTY-TWO

Heletine, Canticus southern district, 'the Cairns'

So named for the immense stone pillars beneath which were the burial mounds of saints, ecclesiarchs and palatines, the Cairns had ever been a place of solemnity in Canticus. That sense of reverence had been shattered with the arrival of war, and the Cairns was no longer a place of peace anymore. It was a vast area, deep into the southern district and far beyond the fragile territory the Imperials had established with their previous victory.

Surrounded by his honour guard, the Serpentia, and standing amidst these ruins, Drakgaard regarded a holo-map of the region.

'What do you see, Elysius?' he asked his Chaplain.

The grey image rotated slowly, hazing in and out of focus as it completed each revolution. It showed contours, structures, even a degree of geological depth. The various reliquaries, tombs and votive shrines Canoness Angerer had described were visible as darker areas on the map, representing fissures and subterranean undercrofts. Some were very deep, and the trail of relic sites went for long periods without interruption.

'I see a world beneath a world, brother-captain,' said the Chaplain. 'Hidden from our sight.'

Word had come back from several of the other battle groups operating within Canticus. The assault on Salvation Bridge had been successful, thanks in no small part to some of Angerer's Seraphim. In the templum district and adjacent slums, Kor'ad had conducted a successful bombing campaign to link up with Sergeant Zantho's armoured column. Enemy resistance was staunch but ultimately overcome. Combined, it was the single largest territorial gain the Salamanders had made since arriving on Heletine.

'Here, though?' asked Drakgaard. 'The war rests on this city alone. Victory in Canticus means victory on all of Heletine. I need to understand why that is.'

'Perhaps the canoness is right,' offered Elysius. 'Some ritual significance has drawn the warlord of the Black Legion to the city. By thwarting these plans and killing him, we break his warband and free Heletine of this tyranny. It matters not, brother-captain. All that matters is we prosecute this duty to its bitter conclusion and make the lives lost in payment of it worth something.'

By turning his wrist, Drakgaard altered the bare topographical view and brought up a tactical overlay displaying the current disposition of his forces throughout the Cairns. Such a large region demanded a wide dispersal and Drakgaard had split what remained of his troops and the Cadian survivors into two distinct battle groups. Eighteen pillars, or 'Cairns', soared into the smoke-choked air above Canticus. Occasionally, when a strong wind briefly swept away this red-grey miasma, the summits were visible without need of spectral magnification. Seven of the eighteen still had the statues of the pious individuals whose bones were allegedly buried beneath them, along with a swathe of lesser faithful, too numerous and unimportant to mention beyond an engraving on a votive plaque at the base of the pillar.

According to its now scattered population, the pillars were believed to 'uphold the roof of heaven' and should they ever fall, the very firmament above Heletine would collapse. Drakgaard wondered if there was any truth to that. Were the heretics attempting to sunder the pillars? Was there a weakening of the veil between reality and the warp in this place, and would this act of destruction bring about a rift between them? Drakgaard was no psyker. His knowledge of such metaphysics, while far superior to the average citizen of the Imperium, was crude compared to the likes of a Chapter Librarian. He knew the pillars were immense in size and despite the war all had endured so far. Perhaps the heretics sought to use other, non-corporeal means to collapse them? Certainly, he had heard of great temples that had stood for millennia crumbling inexplicably when their spiritual link to the Emperor was severed. It would explain the targeted destruction of the relic sites as well as the Adepta Sororitas's presence on Heletine.

All of the eighteen adhered to a pattern, forming an octakaidecagon with nine pillars each on either side of the Sanctium Vius, or 'holy road', a long and expansive processional avenue that ran all the way from the Cairns to the Veloth desert in the east.

Drakgaard's two battle groups, led by himself and Veteran Sergeant Kadoran, were arrayed either side of this processional, deep into the labyrinthine avenues and sprawling habitation towers that riddled the area. It was tight, fraught with dead ends, choke points and blind zones. In short, it was dangerous territory and likely occupied in some force. Unfortunately that enemy was also currently in hiding. Fortunately, Drakgaard had the means to seek them out, from whatever rock they had crawled under.

'Targons,' he addressed a squad of five fire-born clad in hulking Centurion armour. The Targons were borrowed from Fourth Company, nominally the heavier class of Assault Marine compared to the lighter and faster Wyverns. Each armature or rig was equipped with siege drills on both arms, and underslung heavy flamers. Unlike his men, Sergeant Bar'dak's rig was equipped with meltas instead. All five Targons were armed with hurricane bolters, fitted to the torso. Essentially individual warsuits, the Centurions were effectively worn by the Assault Marines who simply stepped into the up-armoured rig in full battleplate.

At the sound of Captain Drakgaard's voice, Brother-Sergeant Bar'dak turned. He was slow to do so, the warsuit pilot sacrificing speed and manoeuvrability for superior offensive and defensive capabilities.

'You are the vanguard, brother-sergeant,' said Drakgaard, clenching his fist to shut off the hololith. 'Take us in.'

Bar'dak led the line of warsuits out. Within minutes, their armoured forms were lost amidst smoke and dust. Only the sound of their heavy footfalls as they stomped through the rubble gave away the fact of their existence.

Drakgaard had his Serpentia honour guard and a tactical squad moving up in support. He switched his retinal lens display to tactical view and saw a truncated schematic of the terrain and his units advancing through it rendered as icons over his left eye. He opened up the vox-link.

'Captain Helfer, you are to stay behind us with the Devastators until we breach this area proper.'

'Understood, my lord,' came the swift reply. Helfer was the leader of four squads of elite Kasrkins. They wore heavier armour than Colonel Redgage's regular troopers and carried rebreather masks along with an array of specialist assault weaponry and hellguns, an enhanced version of the lasgun. Hellguns enjoyed improved armour penetration capability over their standard-issue counterpart, but even with this augmentation they were no match for power armour. Ordinarily cast as storm troopers, the Kasrkins were reduced to a support role until the Targons could establish the level of enemy resistance and root it out. Drakgaard had assured Redgage he would not use his men as bait, or treat their lives cheaply. Against Traitor Space Marines, the Kasrkin were at a disadvantage. Drakgaard wanted to mitigate that first before deploying into the Canticus war zone.

An icon associated with the second battle group flashed up on Drakgaard's right lens display, rendered in luminous crimson over a transparent background tinged the same only lighter. Veteran Sergeant Kadoran had just given notification of simultaneous deployment of his own troops. As of yet, there was no word from Canoness Angerer. Drakgaard was about to try to raise her on the vox when a final marker blinked up on his display below the first.

'Sisters are moving in behind us,' he voxed to Elysius alone. 'Angerer left it late for confirmation.'

The Chaplain had joined the Serpentia as part of Drakgaard's command squad.

'She is still unhappy that you insisted on us going in first.'

'It is our right,' Drakgaard replied. 'I won't have the glory of this victory stolen from under us by the Ecclesiarchy.'

'Glory? Is that why we are here, brother-captain?'

'Now is not the time to try and peer into my immortal soul, Chaplain.'

'Just so long as you are clear why we are fighting this war.'

'It is our duty, Elysius.'

'That is our purpose, to do our duty, not the reason why we came to Heletine.'

The pain of his injuries was making him irascible, so Drakgaard cut the conversation short before he said something to the Chaplain he would later regret. There was one thing he wished he had voiced aloud, though. A question.

Can we trust them, brother?

Angerer fed the string of rosary pearls between her gauntleted fingers. She paused when she reached the black opal. All those souls she had saved and just this one eluded her. Sensing she was being watched, Angerer glanced up. Laevenius was staring at her.

'How can you know where?' asked the scarred warrior. Her Celestians were nearby, waiting patiently for their Sister Superior and canoness outside of the ship. It was one of several corralled together and brimming with Adepta Sororitas. They had touched down at a landing strip at the edge of Canticus, ostensibly to redeploy once the Salamanders and Cadians had made sufficient ingress into the city and engaged the enemy.

'With faith,' Angerer replied, letting go of the rosary, 'and with this.' She produced a small, brass artefact. When flat it resembled a teardrop, but unfolded across its fragile hinges it was more like a compass. In fact, that is exactly what it was. Setting the brass compass down, Angerer then took a phial of clear liquid from her trappings.

'Precious little sorrow left,' she murmured.

Laevenius remained still and stared at the glass bottle as Angerer decanted the last few drops onto the arrow of the compass. Then she waited. The seconds seemed to lengthen, both warriors waiting in silence for the compass to move. It trembled at first then the arrow spun around to settle in one direction. Angerer removed one of her gauntlets, and held her bare hand over the compass so she could feel its emanations against her skin.

'Not far…' she said. When she put her gauntlet back on, Laevenius saw a reddening of Angerer's skin from where the compass had lightly blistered it. Gently, Angerer picked up the compass and handed it to Laevenius. 'Give this to only your most trusted warrior then get everyone on board. We are leaving immediately.'

'And the others, my canoness?' asked Laevenius, taking the compass reverently and being careful not to spill a drop of the liquid.

Angerer was already moving to the front of the transport where she would take up position in the cockpit alongside the pilot and gunner. She only half turned.

'Have them hold position for now. I want to be absolutely sure before we commit to this. I want to see her with my own eyes, Sister.'

There were catacombs beneath Canticus, and they stretched beyond the bounds of the city. Some reached as far as Escadan, others went all the way to Solist. They were old, and largely forgotten. It was where the Heletines had once buried their relics and their dead. It was a place of saints that had now become a lair for sinners. No one ventured into the catacombs anymore – they were dark and uncharted places. None save for those with longer memories and the reason to do so. None save for the unholy and the blasphemous.

The anteroom was carved from the very bedrock of the world, and festooned with skulls like the rest of the underground ossuary. Sigils had been cut into the walls, signifying the proto-Imperial Creed that had since spread to become the dominant form of religion in the galaxy. Smashed, befouled, these sigils had no power here now. Pillars raised the ceiling. In places it was high enough to house a Titan, stretching up into gloomy vaults speared with stalactites. There were deeps. Great wells that fell into black oblivion. A core of Heletine's raw elements had existed here once, a fossil fuel used to synthesise promethium production. Miners and riggers had denuded this wealth, sacked it for their profit and prosperity. Men now long dead, their skeletons had joined the masses already entombed but with unmarked graves and forgotten lives.

In their wake came the Ecclesiarchy, the great Adeptus Ministorum. In vast ships, they crossed the ocean of stars and braved the empyrean itself to bring a lost world back into the fold. Some said it was the Crusade reborn, but they were foolish men, given over to vainglory. It was but one world, yet no less significant for that fact. The Ecclesiarchy reclaimed this land from the industrial tyrants who had yoked from it Heletine's blood and marrow. Tombs thought lost for millennia were rediscovered. New relics were interred in the earth. Shrines were raised. Reliquaries formed. For the cardinals and the palatines knew this world's legacy as well as its spiritual significance, and sought to gird it. But holy men are not the only beings privy to secrets, those locked away in ancient librariums or contained in the rasped whispers of the damned – daemons know things too.

Two warriors knelt before an immense statue. It was dark in the chamber, the only light cast by flickering torches, and in the shadows the statue loomed over them, powerful and oppressive. So still that, despite its anger, anyone entering the chamber without prior knowledge could otherwise be forgiven for not realising it had anima and was flesh, not stone.

Kneeling was not easy for these warriors, and not just because the hulking armour plate they were wearing had not been fashioned with the need for penitence in mind. Pride had compelled them to remain standing, but against the will of the towering statue figure they fell awkwardly in supplication.

'We have lost the bridge, my lord…' rasped one. His armour was festooned with skulls, several impaled on spikes with others hanging from loops of dark chain and wire. A war-helm was clasped under his arm, a blood-red topknot rising from the crown in a plume. His face was patchwork, a raft of knitted-together skin each taken from a different provider. None of the flesh-givers had been willing participants in Kargol's art, however.

The statue spoke, though in the darkness it was hard to tell if his lips actually moved. His voice was unmistakable, and though akin to human was most definitely unkind to any mortal being.

'There were six of you that went out. Where are your brothers?'

There was genuine concern in the question and it was obvious then that the statue figure's anger was directed at his enemies for the slaying of his men and not for the apparent failure of those self-same warriors.

Now the other spoke up. A long barrelled reaper cannon rested on his knee. He too was helmed, but left it on. It was part of him, fused to his flesh and could not be removed. Jade embers blazed behind his eye slits as if beneath the irremovable helm his face was perpetually on fire. For all his brothers now knew, perhaps it was. Ever since the 'changing', Kaid had been this way. Unlike some, he embraced the gifts and willed his gods to bestow further boons. He wanted glory, so he had gladly bended the knee and joined the rest of the Children of Torment when the Warmaster had made his offer.

Here, in this dusty catacomb of piled skulls and other forgotten bones, he did so again but not in the same cause. Conquest, a chance to fight at the head of a Black Crusade, that was Kaid's desire. Glory. Down in the dirt with the long dead, he felt far indeed from such a promise. For how could his gods see him here in this pit, searching and scrabbling in the dirt?

'Arvan and Helux are dead. Socred we lost to the river. Only the Eye knows where he now resides.' There was bitterness in Kaid's voice that he failed to hide. Despite the helm, his ambition was etched plainly on his brute, metal 'face'.

'Should I ask it?' said the statue figure, affecting an air of menace with the coldness of his tone to the two veterans knelt before him. 'Or would you like to, Kaid? Your desire for advancement is as palpable to me as the blade sheathed at my hip.' He did not move to the weapon, which was immense and forged of warp-bonded black iron. He did not need to enhance the threat he had just made. 'But know this, brother,' the statue added, 'there are many ways to ascend, some more inglorious than others. You are in service to the Warmaster's Black Legion. On Heletine, I am Warmaster. If I choose to have you scrabbling in the dirt then that is what you will do.'

Kaid suppressed a shiver. It was as if the words had been plucked from his mind.

'Or, the alternative is I bury you under it. For a brother...' he paused, and there was emotion straining his voice, 'a true brother never questions the orders of his captain. How I long for such days again...'

Kaid bowed his head, as the towering figure seemed to lose himself in remembrance. He knew he had gone too far and was quick to show contrition.

'That will not be necessary, my lord. I can track Socred. Either bring back him or his body.'

'Socred will find his own way back to us, if he lives,' said the figure, dismissing Kaid's offer with the slightest shake of his head. 'I suspect he will attempt to "amuse" himself along the way.' As he moved, the weak underground light inside the cavern caught the edge of his face. It glistened, and did not resemble skin at all, though that is what it was supposed to represent. It was more like porcelain or glass, the kind of material used to create a doll or the facsimile of a man.

'And our enemies,' he asked, 'they move?'

Kargol silenced his brother by speaking first. 'They move, my lord. In armoured column with outriders wearing jump packs.'

'Then we have nothing to concern us. Arvan and Helux will be remembered. Socred too, if he is also dead. Rise,' said the lord, turning to face the figure in the background who was regarding them. 'Return to your brothers. Our other enemies will be here soon. We must be ready for them.'

Kargol and Kaid got to their feet with the snarl of servos, and took their leave. Down the long tunnel behind them and in the larger cavern beyond, the sound of the muster could be heard. Warriors were preparing for battle. With over half their number dead or missing, the two brothers would divide the warbands evenly.

'You see, Kaid,' uttered the lord to the warrior's back as he was walking away, 'your fortunes in the eye of the gods improve already.'

Kaid paused, 'Yes, my Lord Faustus,' before moving on.

Faustus paid him no further heed and approached the watcher, stepping into the light as he did so.

Apart from his head, which was bare and oddly the most artificial part of him, Faustus wore full war-plate. Coal-black, it wrapped his muscular form like a second skin, the epitome of his legion. It was also of a size and magnitude greater than the warrior in front of him, Faustus half again larger in every aspect.

The other warrior bowed, but without the trepidation of the two Terminators.

'Why do you insist on them calling you that?' he asked.

Faustus was nonplussed. 'It is my name. Heklion Faustus.'

'It was your name.'

'And what is your name, brother?' Faustus asked, though he knew it full well and was crafting a lesson for his favourite underling. The other had received this particular teaching before.

'Lufurion, as it has ever been.'

'But you are not he, not entirely.' Viperously fast, Faustus seized Lufurion by the edge of his gorget and dragged him forwards. The light from a brazier's flame flickered over them both, casting deepening shadow. It made the ridges of their armour shine and burn with reflected fire. More importantly, it exposed Lufurion's surgeries. Beneath his armour, every major limb and joint bore the marks of amputation followed by attachment. Only the neck and arms, which were bare of armour plate, bore them obviously. Lufurion's face was not his own. That had been a fire-ravaged ruin. He had taken his new visage from an old friend, one who had betrayed him and who he betrayed in turn. He smiled, revealing an over-wide jaw. Pointed teeth ran all the way across his face, up to his ears, and there was an acid burn etched into an inverted 'v' shape on his chin.

'True,' Lufurion replied, seemingly unconcerned. One of his lackeys devised to draw a weapon but a savage glance from Lufurion stayed the foolish warrior's hand. Fortunately, Faustus was too lost in his own theatre to see it. 'I have made myself flawless again. But you,' Lufurion said, smiling thinly and nodding at the monster holding him in its grasp, 'are not Faustus.'

'I am a true Cthonian,' Faustus sneered proudly.

'That you are.'

Faustus wasn't ready to let him go just yet. He glared, pain and hate warring for dominance in his eyes. They were strange, eldritch things, simultaneously ageless and yet also weary.

'You and I are not familiar enough. You are not Klaed or Ahenobarbus, or Narthius. They were true brothers...' Faustus drifted into the past again, and Lufurion took advantage of the warrior's momentary lapse in purpose.

'I came to tell you we are ready.'

Faustus blinked, as if revived from a dream. He let him go.

'Show me.' The genuine longing in Faustus's voice was in stark contrast to the practiced indifference of Lufurion's.

'Of course. This way, my lord. I'll be with you momentarily.'

Faustus deigned not to answer.

Lufurion met Klerik's gaze. He was Incarnadine, one of Lufurion's sworn warriors, now allied to the Children of Torment. Like the rest of the warband, and its warlord, the Incarnadine Host wore armour of heliotrope purple. Fashioned over the plate metal were leathern strips of cured flesh, baked and hardened. To this grisly apparel was added studs, spikes of bone and bloody daubing. Blades were favoured. Every man was scarred, imperfect in some way to better emphasise their warlord's own flawlessness. Lufurion knew it was vain, but he did not care.

All except for Klerik. As Lufurion's bloody right hand, Klerik was permitted to be flawless too. Aside from a short cape of flesh, his armour went without the fetishistic trappings of his brothers.

'Marshal the men, Klerik. It will not be long now. They'll be coming for her.'

Klerik nodded, eyeing Faustus as he left the room, then asked, 'Who is dealing with our other pressing concern?'

'Vorshkar.'

Klerik gave a quiet, ironic laugh. 'That maniac. Hopefully he'll end up dead.'

'Hopefully.' Lufurion's tone suggested he didn't think that was going to happen.

'I heard our errant brothers met with ill fortune, captain,' Klerik whispered, though Faustus was already gone and had paid the warrior's furtiveness no heed.

Lufurion clapped him on the shoulder.

'This makes our endeavours here even more important.'

Klerik nodded again and went to his duty as Lufurion went after Faustus into another subterranean cavern. It was deeper than the previous one and they had to descend a long ramp of earth to reach it. In ages past, some effort had been made to pave the area with stone but much of it had been worn away by entropy. Stepping through a wide arch, high enough for Faustus to pass under without stooping, was a vaulted chamber that ran on for several metres. A silver casket lay on a plinth at the end of it. Three of Lufurion's warriors surrounded the casket, the igniters on their flamers burning a dormant blue.

'Within, the sacred bones of Lucrezzia Absetia,' said Lufurion, his words barbed enough to pierce flesh.

'She is one of their saints? Another false idol?'

'Just a mouldering corpse, one this false empire likes to revere,' Lufurion replied, nodding to his men.

Tongues of fire spewed from the mouths of their weapons, lapping at the casket eagerly. For a moment, the venerable tomb of Saint Absetia seemed impervious but after a few seconds it ran with flowing silver tears. Quickly turning molten, the casket bled all over the plinth and then the floor, oozing like wax.

Like many of his kind, Lufurion was a child of the warp. Though not a true neverborn, he could nonetheless feel the veil between reality and the ether thin with the destruction of the casket. He shuddered, chilled and excited at the same time. A ripple passed through Faustus too. Lufurion saw it reflected in the mirror sheen of the silver before it curdled and blackened. In it Faustus was revealed as a monster, a daemon-spawn trapped in the shell of a man. The Luna Wolf was screaming, a proud warrior of Cthonia no longer.

Lufurion did not witness what Faustus saw: a warrior of the old war, the first great war, clad in legionary battleplate. He saw the ideal, the lie. Slipping from the present for a moment, his gaze seemed to wander as he outstretched his gauntleted hand.

'They are close...' he whispered. 'I can hear their voices, calling out to me. Ahenobarbus... Narthius... Klaed... all of them.' Faustus lowered his hand, withdrew from the warp and the past life it held in thrall. He turned his attention to Lufurion. 'Bring forth the witch.'

At Faustus's command, a tall enrobed figure emerged from the shadows into the dying light of the fire. His violet armour marked him out as one of the Incarnadine. Lufurion gave Preest a subtle nod as their eyes met across the lake of molten silver that had spilled from the casket like blood.

Faustus stepped through it, largely heedless of the sorcerer and intent on whom he clasped in his gauntleted hands.

She was little more than a girl, weak and blind, a gossamer-thin chasuble clinging to her frail frame like a pair of flaccid, diaphanous wings. She was, in many respects, an insect but a useful one. At least for the present. She was flanked by another pair of mortals, a male and female, their features hidden behind their robes but all too visible to the daemonic sight of Faustus. He noted the chains that were locked to the iron collars around their necks, and was careful to keep his distance.

Preest bowed in supplication.

'Master…' he hissed.

Faustus ignored him, stooping to seize the girl by her bony jaw. She was weeping, for her plight or the desecration of Saint Absetia's tomb, it did not matter. All that concerned Faustus were her tears.

'Cry, little witch. Tell me where my brothers are to be found.'

CHAPTER TWENTY-THREE

Sturndrang, the underhive of Molior

'He lives,' said Zartath, standing amidst the carnage of the arena battle, 'and walked away from the fight.'

After burning the mutant cultists, Agatone had set the ex-Black Dragon loose. They had reached Seven Points, found it to be a haven for the depraved and debased worshippers of Slaanesh, but their quarry was gone. With no other lead, they needed to find Tsu'gan's trail, and soon, before it went cold.

Zartath had done just that and was crouching over a spoor he and he alone could discern.

Agatone joined him, leaving Exor to watch over Issak and act as sentry. Though most were no match for Adeptus Astartes, the underhive was fraught with many hazards Agatone was keen to avoid. A delay now could destroy any remaining chance they had of finding Tsu'gan, and he was determined to bring the wayward fire-born back. Third's reputation was damaged, the confidence of its Chapter Master in it tarnished. They needed this. Agatone needed this. It would be done, one way or the other.

'Which way?'

Zartath gestured vaguely east.

Even to Agatone's enhanced senses, it was just more industrial gloom. The pipes, gantries and striated sub-levels seemed to extend endlessly.

'How long ago?' he asked.

'Few hours.'

Keen to get moving again, Agatone was about to rise and summon the others when Zartath grabbed his wrist.

'He did not leave alone,' said the ex-Black Dragon.

'An ally?'

'Perhaps,' said Zartath, 'or a prisoner,' he snarled, not liking that word for all the memories it raised of his own incarceration, and let Agatone go.

Agatone got to his feet and hailed Exor.

'Techmarine, we leave now.'

Exor turned. He looked battered, his carapace armour shredded by the rat swarm, but at least his wounds were healing.

'Zartath has his trail,' Agatone concluded.

'Still no word from the others,' said Exor as he joined them. The Techmarine had been checking the vox-bands, trying to locate the frequencies of the other hunting parties and make contact. All of his attempts had proven fruitless so far, however. 'Some sort of deep subterranean interference. Perhaps if we could get higher, above some of this metal and compacted industry...' He sounded irritated, and Agatone wondered how much his injury was bothering him or whether he could still hear the keening. It lingered at the edge of Agatone's hearing, like a barely audible sub-tone, grating but still present. His system had been purged of tainted blood, but some of its effects clung on tenaciously.

'Lok and Clovius's warriors would be very useful right now, but we go where Zartath leads us,' he said. 'Keep trying, brother.'

Exor nodded.

Agatone turned his attention to Issak.

'You kept your word, medicus. You've honoured us with your service, but I won't ask anything further of you. Here is where we part ways.'

Issak smiled, as a man does when he realises a fundamental truth and takes pleasure in his own enlightenment.

'I was wrong, Brother Agatone.'

Agatone frowned, restive and eager to be moving on.

'Speak your mind, medicus.'

'My calling is not in Kabullah. It is here, with you and your warriors. Let me come with you, and see this through. You have already said you cannot vouch for my safety. I accept that and will join you anyway.'

'He will slow us down,' said Exor.

Issak gave the Techmarine a sideways glance.

'With respect, in this terrain, in the underhive, you would slow me down.'

'He has a point...' said Agatone, considering. 'The medicus comes with us, but we go now,' he decided, brooking no further protest and turning to his huntsman. 'Zartath...'

The ex-Black Dragon was staring into the shadows. His gaze followed the distant figure of a blood-stained boy carrying a spear. But there was no water and no fish for him to catch.

'I can see…' Zartath began, half rising before he realised it was an apparition, some manifestation of his subconscious, and not a boy at all. A second figure stood behind it, looking on grimly. So, both father and son had returned. Though he could not yet fill the lacuna in his memory, Zartath knew he had done this to them. He felt their revenant malice, their cold, dead eyes glaring and–

'Brother!'

–was brought back from the edge of the nightmare by Agatone's voice.

'Are you still with us?' asked the captain.

Zartath nodded, obeyed. He led them away from Seven Points, following Tsu'gan's trail. And the keening inside his head thrummed ever louder.

As the others followed, Agatone slowed to grab Exor's shoulder.

'Keep a watchful eye.'

The Techmarine nodded.

Despite his familiarity with the underhive, Issak struggled to keep pace. Zartath moved quickly through the wreckage. Sometimes stooped, occasionally on all fours, it was hard not to think of him as a beast. But he traversed the low ceilings, access pipes and crawl spaces like he was born to it. To his brothers, he seemed driven. To Issak, the transhuman warrior looked possessed. Something had invested him with purpose, a bloodhound with the scent of its prey pungent in its nostrils. A singular imperative drove him, one the others had no knowledge of. It rang loudly inside his skull, a promise and a curse combined.

For several hours they gave chase, following Zartath into the underhive, not really knowing how far or how deep they had plumbed in search of Tsu'gan. Occasionally, Zartath would stop, pausing to examine some detail or re-check their route. They had only doubled back once before he had Tsu'gan's spoor again.

They were getting closer.

No one challenged them. There were no more gangs, no more monsters, just darkness and metal, the toxic agglomeration of centuries' worth of neglect and industrial entropy. Agatone was uncertain what the silence presaged, but he assumed and prepared for the worst.

When Zartath finally came to a halt, he did so standing at the precipice of a wide, circular abyss. It was vast, large enough to accommodate a small starship and its ragged edge suggested it had either fallen to ruin or something had punched through it.

'Another false trail?' asked Exor as he watched the shadows around them for any sign of disturbance.

Agatone slowly shook his head, his eyes on Zartath's unmoving form.

'I don't think so. Not this time.'

The ex-Black Dragon had his back to them but it was obvious from the angle of his neck that he was staring down in the chasmal darkness in front of him.

'I have heard of this place,' said Issak. He was walking in between the two Salamanders, protected on either flank. Agatone might have acceded to his joining them, but was not about to leave the medicus undefended.

Agatone stopped, prompting Issak and Exor to do the same. He kneeled down like a father might to a son, so his eyes and those of the medicus were at roughly the same height.

'Tell me what you know.'

'It's called the Well, and has been here for as long as I can remember.' He spared a glance towards the chasm and Zartath loitering over it, who appeared to be transfixed, before averting his gaze back to Agatone. 'You have to understand, Molior is old. Its roots go deep. Much of its vastness is uncharted. Unknown. What the Imperium does not need anymore,' here he gestured to their immediate surroundings, 'it forgets, and leaves it to decay. Do you know what this place was before it became a hive?'

Agatone shook his head. He also gestured to Exor to go and keep an eye on Zartath.

Issak went on. 'It was an Administratum archivium, a place of secure knowledge about the Imperium and its history. Over the centuries, millennia even, it was neglected. Forgotten.'

'What is your point, medicus? And how can you know all this?'

'You hear things. Learn things… My point, Brother Agatone? The knowledge kept safe… it is still here.'

Agatone saw Exor in his peripheral vision. The Techmarine was waving them over.

'Whatever lies here, it is no concern of ours. I want Tsu'gan. Zartath says he's close. That means we're almost done. I won't linger.'

Zartath looked down into the abyss, as still as a statue. Exor was standing beside him surreptitiously running a bio-scan.

Agatone stalled the Techmarine's report with his upraised palm. He had known something was wrong with Zartath since Kabullah. It didn't matter now. He had to hope the ex-Black Dragon would perform his duty long enough so that they could achieve the mission.

'What do you see?' Agatone said to Zartath, no louder than a murmur.

'Darkness… something is alive down there.'

The so-called 'Well' reminded Agatone of a long gullet, fanged with spiky and uneven teeth. It was not so much of a stretch to imagine it having sentience, to being a microcosmical glimpse of something larger and more terrible. In truth, the gullet was a wide and broken shaft, rough at the edges, and the teeth were jutting rebars and large splints of twisted metal. He looked up to the ceiling, and saw the pattern repeated. Rather than at the bottom, Agatone gauged they were actually somewhere in the middle of the shaft.

'I can see a trajectory,' said Exor.

Agatone nodded. 'Something crash-landed here, hot and violent enough to bore through the surface and several layers of sub-hive beneath.'

'I hear it...' uttered Zartath, and made the others turn.

He was still staring.

'The keening?' suggested Agatone, at which Zartath nodded.

'It's much louder below.'

Agatone turned to Exor. 'What did that scan tell you?'

'Nothing. Physically, he is fine. Better than I am, for certain. Whatever's wrong with him is not in his body, brother-captain. But I am no Apothecary.' He looked to Issak, and the medicus shrugged.

'Without conducting a more thorough examination, from what I can tell he is right. Zartath's illness is psychological.'

Agatone scowled. He still needed the huntsman, but Zartath was verging on the catatonic. He tried to get what he needed.

'Is Tsu'gan down there? Did he follow the keening too?'

'No. He climbed...' For the first time since he had reached the Well, Zartath looked up and pointed, 'up there.'

He gestured to a gantry leading to a stairwell, which rose up and over the edge of the shaft that had been cored through Molior and into a higher level.

Moving away from the shaft seemed to help Zartath's cogency, so Agatone gently pulled him back from the edge. Zartath looked him in the eye.

'It doesn't matter what you do, captain. I must go to it. End it.'

Agatone seized Zartath's shoulders, trying to stay the focus of his attention, but the ex-Black Dragon's eyes wandered.

'We are close, brother. I need you here with me if we're to finish this.'

'This is as far as I can go by your side, captain,' Zartath replied, shrugging out of Agatone's grasp.

Engaging his retinal augmentations, Exor scanned the point Zartath had indicated.

'I have faint heat traces, some blood.'

Hope kindled briefly as Agatone turned to the Techmarine and asked, 'Recent?'

'Very.'

As if drawn to it by the siren-like keening, Zartath was moving towards the edge of the shaft again. When Agatone reached out to hold him back, the ex-Black Dragon snarled.

'Stand down,' Agatone warned, but didn't let him go.

'Release me,' Zartath growled.

'You are not yourself, brother.'

Exor drew his bolt pistol, firmly pushing Issak behind him, but Agatone waved him off.

'I am handling this.'

'I am a warrior,' said Zartath, his tone almost pleading, 'I am not to be handled like some beast.'

'You are not a beast,' Agatone replied, but heard the lie in his words. 'At least… I know you can be more than that.'

For a moment Zartath almost looked like he believed him and the hollow opals that were his eyes softened in a fleeting impression of remembered brotherhood, before it was swallowed behind something darker and more feral.

Breaking free of Agatone's hold, Zartath roared and the bone blades slid from his forearms.

Not waiting for a command, Exor fired. The shot was high and deliberately wide, glancing Zartath's shoulder. The impact spun him and he staggered backwards. It was enough to send him over the edge of the shaft and into the darkness below.

Agatone leapt to grab his flailing hand, but missed.

'No!'

He was left on his stomach, facing the abyss and watching Zartath's slowly shrinking form as it descended, until the darkness claimed and he was lost from sight.

'Captain.' Exor came rushing over. 'I had no choice. I had to–'

Agatone got up without the Techmarine's help.

'At that range, you could have killed him. I thought you would have. What stopped you?'

'I saw the man grow larger than the beast,' Exor replied. 'I believed, as you did, that he could be saved.'

'Do you still believe that?'

'I do, brother-captain.'

'Can you track him?'

'Yes, I can follow his biological trail easily enough,' he tapped his bionic eye as if that explained how, 'but what about Tsu'gan?'

'Go after Zartath. Find whatever is driving him to the brink of insanity and bring him back. I won't lose one in order to find another. I'll continue after Tsu'gan.'

'Take the auspex then,' said Exor. 'It's inloaded with Tsu'gan's biological signatures. Not foolproof but it'll help you find him.'

'Won't you need it?'

'I can find him in that hole without it. If he's alive, I'll bring him back, captain.'

Agatone nodded his thanks, attaching the scanner to his belt. 'When did you do all that? The data inload, I mean?' he asked.

'A few seconds ago when I blinked.'

Agatone laughed out loud. 'Secrets of the Martian brotherhood, eh?'

'There is only one brotherhood that has my allegiance.'

Agatone smiled, finding a soul tempered by the anvil.

Exor seemed not to notice and gestured to Issak, who was looking in the direction of the shaft where he had just seen, or thought he had seen, Zartath plummet to his death.

'What about him?'

'The medicus comes with me. I'll need him.' Agatone held out his hand, and Exor seized it in the warrior's grip.

'You do realise it's madness to split up our party,' said Exor.

Agatone nodded. 'Sometimes you have to risk everything in order to succeed at something.'

'Vulkan's fire beats in my breast,' Exor said to his captain.

'With it I shall smite the foes of the Emperor,' Agatone concluded. 'Move quickly.'

As part of his trappings, Exor had a high-tensile strength wire and grapnel gun. Stepping back, he fired the launcher into the Well where it snagged on one of the many outcrops of metal debris. He then attached several disc-shaped objects to his belt.

'Suspensors,' he explained. 'They'll slow me down enough that so I don't break my neck or get impaled on a rebar.' Then he leapt over the edge and let gravity take him.

Agatone didn't need to watch him land and make the slow traverse. Exor was on his own now. Entering Molior as little more than a neophyte, he had grown into a battle-brother with similar skill and judgement to a veteran. Agatone wanted fiercely to have him as a member of Third Company. He would need warriors like that to help rebuild it, and forge its reputation anew. First, he had another fire-born to bring to heel.

Issak looked up from the Well. 'How could he have survived that fall?'

'We Adeptus Astartes are hard to kill, especially fire-born. Takes more than a long drop to finish us.'

'But Zartath isn't a fire-born,' Issak replied.

'Ah medicus, but he is. And I would see all my brothers returned to Nocturne's forge.'

Urging Issak to move, Agatone eventually reached the other side of the chasm, where Exor had indicated Tsu'gan had gone. Clambering up to the precise spot, Agatone reached down to help the medicus and easily hauled him onto the ledge where he was crouching.

Standing, Agatone looked out into the deeper underhive, trying to imagine Tsu'gan's route and what he could have been doing. All he saw was further wreckage: a sloping ceiling, shattered pipework, trails of viperous

but inert electrical wire… and an icon. It was half-buried in all the detritus, begrimed and otherwise obscured by filth. But Agatone's keen eyes
discerned its symbol as well as its meaning.

It was an Imperial eagle split down the middle, one head and wing lost
to decay.

Agatone checked the auspex. The trail led to the broken eagle. Beneath
it there was a gap in the rubble just large enough for a transhuman body
to crawl through.

'The archivium you mentioned,' said Agatone, pointing, 'could that be
it?'

Without a Space Marine's genhanced vision, Issak didn't see it at first,
but after a few seconds he made out the eagle.

'It must be.'

'Tsu'gan went inside,' said Agatone, without a trace of doubt.

Issak frowned, unable to make the connection. 'To what end?'

'I'm not sure it was his idea,' said Agatone. 'Either way, that's where we
are going.'

Exor hit the ledge hard and felt the impact throughout his body. His
wounds were healing but more slowly than he'd like and they flared angrily.
He winced, taking a moment to marshal the pain and catch his breath.

The suspensors were lightening his weight, but not enough. As a
means of lessening the encumbrance of a lascannon or heavy bolter,
their intended purpose, they performed well. Utilised as an improvised
anti-gravitic, less so. In his current condition, without them he might
already be crippled so he bit down, retracted the grapnel and prepared
for the next jump.

Launching the cable into the darkness, focusing on a point where he
could snare the grapnel hook, Exor tried to gauge the distance to the
ground but couldn't. Depth was impossible to speculate as was Zartath's
eventual position. He could be dead. If that was the case, then Exor would
still have to locate him and haul his body back to the surface then wait
for Agatone's return.

He leapt out into the unknown.

Heat from a venting pipe seared his face as Exor passed through a grimy
cloud of steam and gritty particulate. He landed awkwardly, jarring his
knee and wondered if he had over-estimated his fitness for duty. Rolling onto his back, he looked up through the now-dissipating miasma
jettisoned from the pipe and estimated he had descended almost eight
hundred metres by variously rappelling down and leaping from ledge to
ledge.

As the mist cleared fully, he saw something else. A claw mark, just two
or three metres above him.

The inner side of the shaft led to the various sub-levels of the underhive. Whatever object had cored through each level had exposed them to each other, like layers of diseased flesh. Ordinarily accessed through myriad tunnels, lifters or stairways, the Well made reaching Molior's sub-strata much easier. Zartath had chosen this place to make ingress, hunting down an enemy only he could perceive. Exor would have to follow him and hope they could overcome that enemy together.

As a Techmarine, and a relatively inexperienced one at that, he knew little of battle psychology. But it didn't take an expert to know that Zartath, whilst loyal, was damaged. He had heard about the ex-Black Dragon's imprisonment in the alien realm and his subsequent rescue by the Firedrakes. He had also heard about his heroism during the dragon-strife when all of Nocturne was at war, but Zartath was still an enigma. If he found him, alive, sane, Exor was not sure what to expect or how to approach him. Logic would dictate he formulate a plan, but that was of no use here. Instinct was all he'd have to go on.

Noting the position of the claw marks and Zartath's likely entry point, Exor lifted himself up using a strut of broken rebar for support. As he did so he felt a tiny vibration, like a minor seismic tremor, ripple through the metal. At first he thought he had got up heavily, moving awkwardly because of his injuries, but then realised the vibrational resonance persisted even when he was still and the ledge had settled under his weight.

Tiny flakes of metal peppered his armour and exposed skin. So focused on the descent through the Well, Exor hadn't noticed until he had stopped and taken stock of his situation. Now he looked up and saw the glinting, metal drifts fogging the air. Larger pieces of debris accompanied them and as he analysed the scene in more detail, noting the massive chunks of wreckage on the verge of plunging down into the shaft, Exor was put in mind of a slowly eroding cliff face. Only in this instance, the cliff was a steadily widening hole suffering under the effect of sustained seismic resonance. He realised that the Well had been much smaller originally. It must have taken decades for it to reach its current size. Whatever initially came through was likely much smaller than he had first estimated but its arrival had triggered an effect that was slowly shaking the entire area apart.

Using the haptic implants in his bionic hand to analyse the vibrations, Exor estimated that the source was coming from deeper into the hive, exactly where Zartath was headed.

Securing his gear, the Techmarine climbed the short distance up the shaft to where the claw marks mapped his path. There he found a large vent, the inside recently scratched as someone had crawled through it. First drawing his bolt pistol so he could crawl with it in front of him, Exor entered the vent. It led to a narrow access tunnel, tight enough that he dragged himself slowly on his elbows.

Exor emerged onto another ledge into a flickering halogen glow. A cluster of overhanging lamps fizzled with their weak electrical connections, casting the scene in front of him in murky grey monochrome.

A capacious chamber opened out in front of him helping to banish the claustrophobic sense of containment engendered by the rest of the underhive. It had a vaulted ceiling and the outward appearance of a wrecker's yard, for a few metres below the ledge was a steep slope of accumulated industrial detritus. Rather than the slow degeneration of neglect and disrepair Exor had seen so far, this wreckage had been piled here deliberately. In the weak light he discerned girders, roofing plates, blast doors, gantries, several tonnes of mesh grating – all the debris that had come down on top of whatever had crashed through the hive levels in the first place and ended up here in Molior's underhive.

There were bodies as well, most too emaciated and skeletal to have been recent. Victims of the collapse? It was certainly possible – some of the half-mangled structures looked like tenement habs. If Kabullah was any gauge then the collapsed structures would have been vastly overpopulated when the sky fell down on them. Tens of thousands could be rotting amongst the rubble, and Exor realised with a rare spike of compassion that he was looking at a mass grave. Wasted limbs jutted from the industrial morass. Skulls, skin stretched thin as parchment across the bone, leered at him through the lattice of collapsed metal.

'Vulkan's mercy…' he breathed.

There were no heat traces, nothing in close proximity. Whoever had piled the wreckage had since moved on. Nothing had been scavenged either, which seemed at odds with the philosophy of the underhive he had come to understand. There was only a path wide enough for a small cargo loader or four-track freight hauler to traverse that led deeper into the level. Whatever was waiting at the end of that road was obscured by the subterranean gloom and the peaks of wreckage. It had to have taken a small, dedicated army of workers to shift that much metal.

Exor tried to contact Agatone but the vox return was too weak. Signal interference from the depth, he assumed. About to move out, he stopped when he felt the blade against his neck and silently cursed for allowing himself to be caught off-guard so easily.

'You whisper too loudly,' said a rasping voice, redolent with the stink of raw meat. 'Should I kill you now? Is that why he sent you?'

Exor holstered the bolt pistol, raising both hands so that his assailant could see he was unarmed.

'I came to find you, brother.'

'Am I your brother now then?'

'Petulance doesn't suit you, Zartath.' Exor tried to break away but the bone blade sank deeper, nicking the skin around his neck. 'Why save me back then, only to kill me now?'

'A slave to logic, trying to reason with an animal. You amuse me.'

He gave a throaty laugh, causing spittle to fleck across Exor's cheek but the Techmarine didn't flinch.

'You are still a man, brother. Agatone would not have–'

'Agatone! I am our captain's faithful dog, brother. He keeps me leashed, or have you not noticed? I am the necessary monster he needs to achieve his mission.'

'Then why send me after you? To put you down like the rabid dog you think you are?' Exor laughed too, mustering as much derision as he could. Since Mars and his induction into the secrets of the Mechanicus, emotion had become increasingly difficult. 'Leaving you down here to rot would have been much more logical.'

Silence lingered in the wake of Exor's voice, broken only by the ex-Black Dragon's feral breathing. Slowly, the pressure against his neck eased and Exor turned to face Zartath's cold staring eyes.

He snorted. 'How did you ever advance beyond the rank of Scout?'

'I had help.' It wasn't a lie. Va'lin had been at his side throughout. It had not been easy to leave him – their bond had been forged in blood, but their paths diverged. Brother-Captain Ba'ken had told them it was Vulkan's will. Exor wondered if his battle-brother yet lived.

'And are you here to help me or stop me?' asked Zartath, shaking his head. 'The latter will not go well for you, I think.'

Exor knew he was in no condition to fight. Even fully fit and armed, he would struggle and likely die going up against the ex-Black Dragon.

'I've seen you fight,' he said, holding up his hands in surrender.

Zartath regarded him for a moment, gauging the Techmarine's veracity before giving him a draconic smile that revealed both rows of his fangs.

'Your instincts are better than I thought, Martian.'

'I am not a Martian,' Exor replied. 'I am fire-born.'

'That is what they tell me also,' said Zartath, leaping silently over the ledge and scaling the wreckage below.

Exor went after him, slower because of his injuries. When they reunited at the bottom, Zartath concluded, 'But we know differently, don't we, brother?'

Exor chose not to answer. Zartath was in a capricious mood – it made him more unpredictable than usual. As a Techmarine, Exor based his interactions with others on logic. The ex-Black Dragon adhered to no such principal, he was a creature of pure instinct. Perhaps that was the source of Exor's distemper towards him and the reason why negative emotion was easier to illicit in his presence. He chose to be direct instead.

'What's down here? What made you leap into the pit?'

Zartath's face darkened and all his humour bled away, replaced by haunting neutrality.

'The keening.'

'That's not an answer.'

'There is no answer. It just is!' he snapped, allowing the briefest chink of weariness to show. 'It's like a passenger I cannot release,' he pointed to his skull, 'inside my head. Calling. Always.'

Exor had felt it too, but not to this degree. A drone lingered at the edge of his hearing, but so faint he dismissed it as imagined or a part of his subconscious. Zartath's exposure to the taint running through the blood of Molior's vermin had been much less, yet his affliction appeared magnitudes worse. It had to be something else. Zartath's mutant physiology had made him more attuned, exposed him because of his greater sensitivity.

Exor knew something of xeno-biology, that there were several known species that could emulate a 'siren-call'. Such abilities were psychic in origin, but perhaps in this case there was a physical factor also. However there was another explanation.

Chaos. It was the moral corruption of the soul. Mutation was its physical expression. Some mutation was tolerated, even essential. Navigators, astropaths, even the Adeptus Astartes Librarius – the Imperium would cease to function without them. They were also the individuals at greatest risk from contamination by the warp. Such men and women were conduits that, if improperly channelled, became doorways for unnatural creatures. It was logical to assume that mutants, those bearing the physical stigmata of Ruin, could also be susceptible in some way.

Whether on account of his mutation or some, as yet, unrevealed taint within him, Zartath's psychosis was pulling him to this place. Like a piece of driftwood caught in the maelstrom's inexorable gravity, he could do nothing to prevent it. Exor merely feared the reaction when Zartath was finally forced to confront that which had almost driven him insane.

'And when you find whatever is causing this... keening, what will you do?'

The coldness returned, Zartath's eyes like chips of carved jet.

'Kill it.'

He moved off, low and fast into the flickering half-light. He seemed different, edgier and feral.

Exor had no choice but to go after him.

CHAPTER TWENTY-FOUR

Heletine, Canticus southern district, 'the Cairns'

Demolition of over half the city during the bitter fighting made the deployment of heavy armour almost impossible. This deep into Canticus, the streets were choked with debris. Barricades, tank traps and other improvised defences only made the going even harder for track-mounted vehicles. Razorwire threaded every avenue. Chunks of fallen masonry were riddled with mines and live grenades. Shells of tanks still smouldered in hidden trench lines and pits, their crews silently decomposing within.

None of this offered any impediment to the Targons.

Bar'dak's warriors advanced doggedly through the corpse of the once proud city, their Centurion armour more than equal to its hazards. As vanguard troops, they were almost unrivalled, and ranged several hundred metres ahead of the main force which included the overall Imperial commander, Captain Ur'zan Drakgaard.

Where the Wyverns ruled the sky, the Targons dominated the ground. All things in balance, or so Vulkan's teachings went, and Bar'dak believed vehemently in this Promethean creed. Like all fire-born, he was a warrior ascetic but to the greatest extreme. Bar'dak forever needed to test himself, to know the limits of his endurance and determination.

During his early years of initiation, he had walked the length of the Scorian Plain and swam the straits of the Gey'sarr. He did so alone and without fanfare or audience. For it was not out of a desire for adulation that Goran Bar'dak performed these feats – he did so because he had to know if he could.

According to Chaplain Elysius, pride was a sin to be wary of, one Bar'dak knew himself to be guilty of. Not selfish pride but esteem for his Targons, an indulgence of ego he found he was unable to temper. Live long enough unscathed and any man, however humble, will start to believe he is immortal. Not the Chaplain's words, but part of Zen'de's philosophy. Bar'dak knew it well, and recognised the truth of it in his own hubris. No battlefield had bested the Targons yet, and no recruits had joined their ranks since the current squad was formed almost a century ago. None had been needed. As records went, even the lauded sons of Ultramar would struggle to name an equal.

'Sergeant,' Ush'ban's voice crackled over Bar'dak's vox.

One of the tower-templum that sprang up around the Cairns like fungus in shadow had collapsed across the street, effectively blocking it off. Its foundations jutted from the earth like nubs of broken bone, the tower the limb from which they had been severed.

Civilians, mainly pilgrims and minor Ecclesiarchy functionaries, lived and prayed in these templums. The city had been evacuated weeks ago, but encounters with the human populace of Canticus were not unheard of. No matter how dire things became, mankind would always strive to cling to what it has and what it knows. The majority of these desperate, lingering few had been swept up by the heretic army and pushed into service as conscripts, indentured slaves or worse. Most clutched crude stubbers or shotguns, improvised cudgels or blades and had been fighting against the Salamanders since they had arrived on Heletine several weeks ago.

They were not the men and women they might once have been. Scarification marked their naked flesh, the burned brand of their Chaos potentate whose favour they now sought. Self-mutilated, armed and armoured with whatever they could scavenge, foreswearing Throne and Emperor, their souls were lost, their bodies grist for the ever-grinding war machine of the old enemy. Madness and desperation were inevitable.

Ush'ban's war-plate still carried the burns and gouges of an improvised explosive wielded by one crazed devotee. In sacrificing himself, the cultist had levelled half a city district. Ush'ban's warsuit had protected him, but Colonel Redgage had lost a lot of men in the blast. Captain Drakgaard had insisted the fire-born bear the brunt of the fighting after that incident, only utilising Guard armour in a vanguard role and the dwindling Cadian 81st as support. The decision was met with resistance by a conflicted colonel, who had no wish to throw away the lives of his men but at the same time had felt his honour besmirched. The matter had only just been resolved when the arrival of the Adepta Sororitas complicated everything again.

'Bore through,' Bar'dak replied, his expression hard as stone behind his battle-helm. With no time to search, if any civilians were hiding like vermin in the ruins they would likely be killed. Momentum was everything. On Drakgaard's order, Bar'dak would ensure it was maintained. He relayed as much to the captain through the vox, and the rest of the battle group hunkered down several hundred metres distant until the impediment could be removed.

Siege drills engaged, Ush'ban and Nerad tore through the collapsed tower. The three-headed, triple-bladed boring tools were attached to their armoured fists as a concomitant part of the warsuit's armature and hungrily ate up the rock. Both Centurions punched and moved stolidly with unceasing momentum. As Ush'ban and Nerad made the initial breach, the other two in the squad stomped in their wake amidst squalls of heavy dust to widen the gap. Bar'dak followed on as rearguard, liquifying any jutting chunks of debris the siege drills had missed with his melta.

'It is desultory work, brother-sergeant,' Brother Amadu remarked, igniting his heavy flamer and dousing what remained of the tower. Caution was necessary, even at the risk of harming or killing anyone taking shelter within. Canticus was riddled with insurgents. Like an infestation of maggots, they lurked everywhere. Ush'ban had been fortunate. Others were not so. To die in such an ignominious fashion, Bar'dak could scarcely think of a worse fate for the warriors in his charge. He had vowed they would maintain vigilance.

'It is also necessary, brother,' Bar'dak replied, emerging through the slowly diminishing flames and onto the other side of the ruin. The way ahead looked no less restricted as a string of choked streets and rubble-thick buildings dominated the vista in every direction.

'Such destruction...' breathed Ramadus. 'How could any civilisation ever recover?'

'None could,' Bar'dak answered, 'but that is not our charge here, brother.'

Ramadus bowed his head slightly after the mild rebuke from his sergeant.

'Hold here,' Bar'dak ordered the squad, who responded by forming a defensive line that faced all directions ahead of them.

It was dark over Canticus. The day was dying fast and smoke still occluded what little light shone over the benighted city. Utilising his omniscope, Bar'dak searched the ruins for any sign of the enemy. After a few seconds, he hailed Drakgaard on the command channel.

'Report, brother-sergeant,' declared the weathered voice of the captain.

'Negative contact. Advancing. Maintain distance.'

'Understood. On your order, sergeant. You are our eyes.'

With the all clear announced, Drakgaard would lead the others out. Bar'dak watched them form up and deploy in the tactical display shown on his right retinal lens. If desired, he could widen the scope and see Sergeant Kadoran's troops effecting a similar manoeuvre. All Salamanders and Cadian forces were making deep ingress into the city, bolstered by their allies in the Adepta Sororitas who were acting as relief. Though Bar'dak could not see the Sisters on the tactical feed.

The Centurions reached another fifty metres further in when Bar'dak was forced to retract his earlier remarks. Ush'ban, Nerad and the others saw why at the same time as Bar'dak, so were quick to come to a halt and form up.

'Is that...?' Amadu began. The Targons were arranged in a dispersed formation and still relied on the vox to communicate.

'Two civilians,' Bar'dak saw them clearly and closely through the omniscope as he answered for Amadu. 'They're scavengers.'

'I was under the impression all the city's non-combatants had been evacuated,' said Ush'ban.

'They were, but some stayed,' Bar'dak replied.

'We cannot leave them to die,' said Nerad, the grittiness of his voice at odds with his ostensible compassion.

'If I ordered it so, then it shall be done,' Bar'dak asserted, not needing to see Nerad to know he had been understood.

'Then what should we do, sir?' asked Ush'ban.

Bar'dak blink-clicked and two identicons flashed up on his retinal lens display. They represented Amadu and Nerad.

'You two will secure the civilians immediately and send them back to our lines. The Kasrkin can escort them out of the city, whilst we continue to advance. Make it fast, but know the eyes of your brothers are watching out for you.'

Both Centurions gave signal affirmation then stomped over in the direction of the civilians, roughly a hundred metres away.

Bar'dak watched them very carefully through the omniscope, moving from his warriors to the scavengers and back again.

'Didn't see them,' Bar'dak murmured, forgetting to close the vox-link.

'Sir?' asked Ush'ban.

With Amadu and Nerad leaving formation, the remaining two Centurions had moved up to create a wedge of three with their sergeant at the tip.

'Before, when I surveyed the area. They weren't there.'

'Who, brother-sergeant?'

'The scavengers. It's as if they just... appeared out of the air.'

The tactical overlay displayed on Bar'dak's right retinal lens showed Drakgaard and the others had passed through the breach and were moving up behind the Targons. He was about to vox their discovery when he noticed something across his auto-senses.

Movement.

A moment of terrible premonition dawned on Bar'dak with the realisation his martial pride was about to suffer a wound from which he could not recover. In that instant, the truth of his own self-deluded ego was revealed to him along with the arrogance of the belief that the Targons were indestructible.

'Centurions!' Bar'dak roared, voice distorting through the vox.

The warsuit was not built for speed, but Bar'dak forced it into a desperate half-run. Ush'ban and Ramadus followed close behind their sergeant but were equally encumbered.

For all the razorwire, the trench-pits and the minefields, the Targons had neglected the most obvious trap. A baited snare: two wretched human scavengers acting as the draw. As it was sprung, several power-armoured forms emerged into the diminishing light to confront Amadu and Nerad.

The edges of their dark armour shone, the dull brass catching the last shafts from a fading sun above. Seconds later, cloud obscured it and threw the streets into shadow so that only the warriors' weapons glowed with malefic light. A beam shot from the gaping maw of one. It struck Nerad in the shoulder who screamed in pain as his defensives were pierced, his skin and bone seared black.

Black was the hue of these warriors, darker than sackcloth, their armour studded with bone and bestial horns. Their helmets of deformed metal were stretched into the image of the neverborn. Hell writhed within these flesh hosts, Chosen of the Warmaster's own Legion.

Bare-headed, an eight-pointed star branded into his ivory white pate, the leader of the Chosen made himself known.

'Vorshkar!' he declared, then spat a stream of invective in an old language Bar'dak didn't understand. The meaning was clear, though.

Crackling jags of blood-crimson light were already stabbing towards the Targons as Bar'dak summoned his hate.

'Targons! Death to the traitors!'

Seconds separated Bar'dak and the rest of his squad, but crucially they were split and thus their formation weaker against an experienced enemy.

Shuddering hurricane-bolters mounted in the torso plates of the Centurions kicked out a frenetic storm of return fire as the air between Chosen and Targon was threaded with beams and shells, so thick that every obstacle between them was destroyed almost instantly.

Ush'ban staggered, clipped by a burst of mass-reactive shells and needing a few seconds for his armour to compensate. Ramadus went ahead of him, releasing a long stream of intense, white fire from his heavy flamers. It caught one of the Chosen who was engulfed instantly and fell to his knees. Blinding shrapnel erupted around Ramadus as a missile exploded against his shoulder guard, knocking him off balance.

With the pressure relieved, the burning Chosen hauled himself up and recommenced firing. Ramadus ignored the shells and kept on, trying to locate the heavy. He saw the launcher a fraction too late, swinging around his flamers as a second missile spat from the rocket tube. It detonated square in the Centurion's chest, cracking the ceramite and rendering one half of the hurricane bolter array useless. Ramadus put the other to use, raking the traitor's armour. The bolter fire on his flank was intensifying, the warning runes flashing up on his battle-helm's display too insistent to ignore. He half turned, expecting to see his enemy braced and firing but was instead confronted by a third Chosen, charging at him with a power fist.

Ramadus desperately geared up his siege drills, bringing them around into a defensive posture. The horned-headed traitor punched straight through them, shattering four out of six drill heads with sheer strength augmented by his power fist's energy field.

Staggering, Ramadus tasted blood. Some of it had sprayed against his face plate. He could smell it, copper-sharp and indicative of internal bleeding. His suit concurred, but he shut down the trauma alerts so he could focus on surviving. One arm of his Centurion warsuit dangled uselessly by his side, whilst the rest of his armour was studded with drill shrapnel. Ramadus tried to fire his bolters. They were torn from his chest by power-gloved fingers, most of the breastplate ripped out with them and cast onto the ground. Knowing he wouldn't survive a third blow, he went to turn and use his bulk to overwhelm the smaller Chosen. A glancing missile burst impacting against his shoulder showered both combatants with frag and slowed Ramadus just enough that his chest was exposed when the traitor thrust for his heart…

Ush'ban saw his brother die with his chest torn out. For a few seconds he stood upright, cold as a statue as his killer exulted in the death. Then the missile struck and Ramadus, his Centurion armour and the belief that the Targons were invincible was violently blown apart.

As Ramadus died, Ush'ban was already moving and advanced into a storm of hurled metal: chunks of plate that used to be armour. Bone and blood came with it, a grisly shower of viscera that clung to Ush'ban like guilt. He had fallen behind, and let Ramadus die alone.

Plunging through expulsion smoke from the landed missile, retribution was Ush'ban's only salve as he met the one with the power fist who had just slain his brother.

'Engaging!' Nerad shouted down the vox, and moved to shield the civilians from a torrent of gunfire roaring from the Chosen. Through the tactical feed in his retinal lens, he was aware of Bar'dak and the others trying to bridge the gap between them and him, but right now he and

Amadu were on their own. Nerad was hurting, the wound in his shoulder serious but he cut out the pain and triggered his chest-mounted bolters. He counted six Chosen in his eye line, but his auto-senses were picking up three more. Ramadus was dead – the odds against the Targons were worsening.

'Two squads,' he voxed to Amadu.

Amadu nodded, reaching down to grab one of the civilians.

'Female,' he said to her, though she still had her back to him, 'we must get you to safety.'

Bar'dak had the one called Vorshkar in his sights, less wary of the flanged mace he wielded in both hands than the trail of ethereal mist it was exuding. He only saw Amadu briefly, approaching the female, and saw her look up at her saviour while at the same time unclasping the collar she wore around her withered neck...

Amadu felt the danger before he saw it in the rising of the hackles on the back of his neck and the acid taste on his tongue, despite his battle-helm's rebreather.

Psyker...

The thought came too late. Amadu had less than a second to regret his decision as the collar was breached and a flood of power unleashed. Magnesium-bright, searing hot pain overloaded the Centurion's auto-senses. His indomitable warsuit cracked. Smoke issued from the frame as it partly sloughed away, merging with the slurry of his deliquesced flesh, bone and organs.

A bolt of arc lightning had struck Amadu, spat from the mouth of the female, impaling him through the chest like a crackling, fulminating skewer. His entire body transfixed, he shook with such violence that he cracked the retinal lenses in his battle-helm. Smoke issued from the joints of his armour, which had begun to scar and blacken, then melted before Ush'ban's eyes.

Ush'ban had fought alongside Amadu for ninety-six years. They trained together. The ceremonial gladius Ush'ban wore at Chapter gatherings had been forged by him, a gift reciprocated by the bolt pistol Amadu had once carried as his sidearm. His death was a physical blow to Ush'ban but the mental upheaval it caused was far more debilitating and he almost missed the Chosen as the traitor sought to add to its kill tally.

The first swing caught Ush'ban a glancing blow on his hip and sent painful shockwaves through his leg and abdomen. He blocked the second with the outside of his siege drill but lost the armature in the process.

It freed him up to use his armoured glove as something more than just to trigger the drill, and when the third blow came in Ush'ban seized the Chosen's arm then hoisted him off his feet. Powered servos grinding and shrieking as he exerted them, Ush'ban threw the traitor across the rubble and into the facade of a partially collapsed temple ruin. Falling masonry buried the Chosen, silencing his roared curses.

Amadu's demise happened quickly, the rest of his life measured in no more than a few seconds of excruciating agony. His death flame was like a photon-flare going off, only magnitudes greater. His silhouetted afterimage was ingrained on Bar'dak's cornea, as his battle-helm tried desperately to compensate for the intense flash of light. It blinded him, and Bar'dak's last sight was the Chosen advancing on him with that warp-touched mace. He had little time to worry about it. The psyker-witches who had killed Amadu weren't finished. Emaciated, skeletal, the male wretch staggered unevenly to his feet and unclasped his own collar to begin the crescendo of what the female had unleashed.

Crackling lightning coruscated around the male, his body transfixed like a cruciform banner pole. Particulates in the air around him slowed until suspended as gravity was undone. The effect spread outwards, levitating grit, dust and debris. Amadu's ruined body lifted with it. Bar'dak was caught in the wave along with the others and felt himself grow lighter as a sliver of air slipped between his boots and the ground.

Reaching its apex in a few seconds that seemingly stretched to minutes, the wave drew back like a tide recoiling from land. Like a long inhaled breath, reverse katabatic winds recalled it to its origin point, the male psyker-witch on the verge of going supernova.

Bar'dak realised this creature was a weapon, a human bomb no different to the ones that had killed so many of Colonel Redgage's men and scarred Ush'ban's armour. Only the technological aegis of the Mechanicus would not protect him this time – it would not protect any of them, not from this.

Gravity returned and in the same instant the inhaled breath was released in a terrifying storm.

CHAPTER TWENTY-FIVE

Heletine, Canticus southern district, 'the Cairns'

'What just hit us?' asked Drakgaard, staggered by the sudden blast wave but on his feet.

Elysius was about to shake his head when he sniffed the air.

'You smell that?'

'Soiled meat? Old blood?' suggested Drakgaard, his gaze flitting between the Chaplain and their surroundings.

'More like sour milk,' said Elysius. 'Warpcraft.'

Captain Helfer was being helped up by one of his troopers. 'Feels like a damn bomb just went off,' he groaned. Blood was trickling down his face from a cut sustained across the forehead, and his closely cropped moustache and beard were powdered with a fine layer of dust.

Most of the Kasrkin were down, some of them not moving.

Elysius regarded the mortal, his tone ominous.

'I believe it just did, captain.'

Like their officers, the fire-born weathered the blast better and stayed standing, though had to check their advance mid-march. Dust was still rolling across the street in swathes as Her'us of the Serpentia broke formation and went to reconnoitre.

Rubble, indistinct and ubiquitous, lay everywhere but offered no answers. The tactical display was down, whatever had struck them taking out their short-range comms and helm visuals. Based on their previous

229

position, Drakgaard knew the Centurions could not be more than two or three hundred metres away.

'Did you hear gunfire prior to the blast?' Drakgaard asked Elysius.

The Chaplain nodded. 'We should move.'

A slow advance became a run, Drakgaard to the fore with the Serpentia his vigilant shadows. With Her'us back in their ranks, they surrounded the captain like a cloak of drake scale and moved in concert.

Caution was discarded in the wake of whatever had hit them. Gunfire scarcely heard before the blast resumed loudly on the air.

Close on the heels of the Serpentia were Squad Vah'gan. Led by Captain Helfer, the Kasrkin followed on as rearguard and left the slower Devastators behind.

After a few minutes, they found Bar'dak. The sergeant was lying on his back at the edge of a circle of scorched earth, his armour blackened just the same. Smoke clouded the area, seeping through the ruins. Fires crackled in the open, creating flickering shadows.

Warriors moved in the gloom, too indistinct to know exact numbers and disposition, their weapons fire succinctly revealing their allegiance.

'Serpentia, engage!' shouted Drakgaard, advancing steadily with the honour guard as Sergeant Vah'gan and the Kasrkin swiftly moved up in support.

Return fire erupted across the Imperial line, a collimated mix of bolter shells and hellgun las-rounds.

A missile exploded nearby as the Salamanders briefly overloaded armour systems came back online. Targeting reticules lit up the retinal lens displays of twenty fire-born, who unleashed a fearsome salvo against their hidden enemies.

Then silence.

As quickly as it had manifested, all enemy resistance died away to nothing. The last few echoes of Squad Vah'gan's bolter fire were fading as Drakgaard held up his hand for them to cease.

'Hold here,' he said, allowing the Serpentia to reach the stricken form of Sergeant Bar'dak. 'Apothecary...'

Sepelius broke ranks to kneel by Bar'dak's side. Taking out his bio-scanner, he assessed the damage whilst the rest of the squad shielded him and the injured Centurion.

'Life signs are weak,' he told his captain, noting the arrival of the Devastators through the press of bodies.

Drakgaard nodded grimly before turning to Elysius, who pre-empted him.

'I'll see to the others.'

There were three other Centurion war frames lying prone in the dirt. The fifth and final squad member was scattered around the battle site in pieces.

As Elysius went to check vital signs and provide final rites if needed, Drakgaard surveyed the ruins. They were quiet, but that didn't mean anything. He ordered both Devastator squads to bombard the next city block to be sure of no further surprises. As a massive firestorm engulfed the distant ruins, Sergeant Vah'gan approached.

'Sir, we've just received word from Sergeant Zantho.'

Drakgaard bade him to continue.

'His armoured column has joined up with Venerable Kor'ad and the Cadians, and awaits further orders.'

'Tell him to push up. Head east.' In his mind's eye, Drakgaard imagined a wave of purifying flame sweeping across Canticus, burning all heretics to ash and finally ridding Heletine of the Black Legion's consumptive presence. He bristled with fury at the thought, his grip tightening on the haft of his kaskara. 'We are become two mailed fists, which, when they meet, will crush the heretics utterly.' Drakgaard allowed himself a vicious smile, which more resembled a snarl on his scarred face. 'Have Sergeant Kadoran converge on our location. Tell him we're consolidating our forces before advancing further into the ruins.'

'And the Sororitas, brother-captain?'

He had almost forgotten about them. Their knowledge of the relic sites had stopped the fire-born from chasing shadows and let them finally engage the enemy. In the wake of current events, these facts seemed somehow less significant.

'Relay to them to move up in support, but not to get ahead of our lines. This is our victory, sergeant, one for the fire-born not the Ecclesiarchy. They may have whatever relics remain at the end, but I want the honour of breaking these traitors to go to none but us. Am I understood?'

Vah'gan saluted firmly, his eyes blazing with fierce pride.

'Aye, sir.'

In his wake, Elysius returned. Judging by his body language his mood was less choleric.

'Bar'dak was the only survivor,' said Elysius gravely. 'The rest of the Targons are slain.'

A tremor of anger rippled through Drakgaard at this news, and he felt his old wounds flare in painful sympathy. He had always believed pain was useful if it could be honed into anger and that anger then put to use. His retinal lenses shone in the bright incendiary flare of the concentrated barrage from the Devastators.

'Sepelius and a squad of Kasrkin will stand guard until a transport is scrambled from Escadan to provide extraction.'

'It is a great loss to the Chapter.'

'It will be greater still if we do not march again soon. The Targons will rise again, brother.'

'You're more sanguine than I expected, Ur'zan. Bar'dak was a Centurion in more than just rank as his service studs will attest.'

'I am not sanguine, Elysius, I am wrathful.'

'And when put to proper purpose, wrath can be useful...'

Drakgaard smiled, though he knew the Chaplain could not see it.

'Are you reading my mind, brother?'

'But,' Elysius continued, 'if prompted to act rashly, it can be a severe detriment.'

Now Drakgaard faced him, seeing the sermon for what it was.

'Speak what's on your mind, Chaplain.'

'We should tread warily.'

'We will, but with purpose,' Drakgaard countered, and Elysius saw how the long weeks had taken their toll on an already injured warrior. He was old, and worn like drake hide. Such treatment makes the scale hardy and unyielding, but beat it too much and even the toughest hide will crack.

'I know you are eager for this, Ur'zan, but we should not overreach ourselves. There is much we don't know, such as what killed Bar'dak and his squad.'

'Bar'dak lives.'

'By a thread! His part in this war is over.'

'I will take any and all precautions. I am not Adrax Agatone, charging off half-cocked. A pity he did not heed your council as I have.'

'Would you hear it now?' Elysius asked.

'Only a fool would ignore the wisdom of his Chaplain.'

Elysius laughed mirthlessly at the politick answer. Whilst there was respect, a gulf of mistrust existed between them. Where Drakgaard believed Elysius to be suspect because of his former association with Third Company, Elysius was convinced Drakgaard was so desperate for glory that he might neglect his own good sense. None of this could be said aloud, for it would undermine command and it was not the way of Adeptus Astartes to voice such open dissent, but it was the truth.

'Hold here. Fortify and defend what we have won, and send in scouts to see what lies before us,' Elysius said.

'Why would I do that when our enemy retreats?'

Elysius tried not to sound exasperated. 'It's a dozen warriors, perhaps fewer.'

'They are on the run, for the first time since this war began.'

'We have been afforded a glimpse and know nothing of our foes' disposition or strength. Look to the evidence of your eyes and see the peril of underestimating what is out there.'

'Are you a military tactician, Chaplain, or do you in fact advise on the spiritual wellbeing of your brothers?'

Heeding his better judgement, Elysius did not give in to pettiness.

'I am a servant of the Emperor, as are you, whose solemn duty is to preserve the rituals of the Chapter and guard against false pride.'

Drakgaard was stubborn. He bit back a sharp reply and instead answered, 'As soon as Sergeant Kadoran arrives, we advance, and nothing shall dissuade me from that course. We have been made fools of by a dwindling warband of heretics who used the terrain to their advantage. That ends. Now.'

It availed them nothing to be at odds now – for good or ill. Drakgaard would receive his full support.

'In Vulkan's name then,' Elysius replied, but the words rang hollow.

Eighteen armour kills littered the field, their shells still burning. Another seven were scattered throughout the connecting streets. Most were light vehicles, with only a few actual battle tanks amongst their number. No Renegade Astartes armour, no foul engines of the Dark Mechanicus. This was a distraction force, thrown together with the express purpose of dragging Zantho's company deeper into the ruins. The tank commander was beginning to wonder if a real army still existed on Heletine, or if in fact they had been chasing shadows for the past weeks. Such a warren as Canticus made it difficult to know.

Ever since they had cleared and crossed Salvation Bridge, the route had become ever more crowded with scrap and wreckage. It had taken two hours to destroy the heretic armour. Zantho had been forced to reduce much of the district to rubble in the process. Fortunately, the arrival of Kor'ad and the Guard battle tanks had made bracketing the enemy easier. It was then a simple matter of tenaciously advancing down every road and street that could accommodate a battle tank until nothing remained.

In the end, they had pinned the last recalcitrant enemy armour in an expansive public square. The rare allowance of space did little to improve manoeuvrability, such was the overcrowding of vehicles. Victory came swiftly to the fire-born but felt almost profligate.

'We should aim south, break through here,' Redgage indicated a point on the hololith with his gloved finger where a wide road circumvented the city outskirts, 'and then reroute east as ordered.'

Zantho stroked his beard. It was part of the great red mane of spiked hair that framed his face which, presently, was wrinkled with consternation.

'A long diversion, colonel.'

'True, but faster than slogging our way through these streets where we're at risk of being ambushed. Concealed infantry should be our main concern.'

'My main concern is following my commander's orders,' Zantho replied, looking up from the grainy map image to see the Vindicators had almost cleared the enemy wrecks with their attached dozer blades. Embarkation was imminent. 'But you're right,' he conceded, looking back at Colonel

Redgage. They had only lost four vehicles during the battle, and all of those to hidden demolitions teams. 'I'll give the order to head south.'

'Right you are, sir,' said Redgage, smoothing his grey moustaches. 'My lord,' he added, looking up nervously to Zantho's left before saluting crisply and returning to his tank with his men.

The three commanders had met in the square in the shadow of Zantho's Predator. Redgage had come with his entourage. Zantho was alone, so too the third officer of this gathering.

'You cannot bear me a grudge for following orders, brother.' Zantho kept his eyes level, and didn't look up. 'Had I not acted as I did, further lives may have been lost.'

'Lives were lost,' a deep, mechanised voice replied, conveyed through a vox-emitter.

'It is war. That is its currency,' said Zantho, finally gazing up at the towering form of Venerable Kor'ad.

'One which I have long accepted, since before you were even an initiate.' The Dreadnought turned a fraction, easing his sarcophagus over the sergeant to glower through his vision slit at him.

'For an ancient, you are petty, Kor'ad.'

'For an ancient, I am temperate!' roared the Dreadnought, stomping towards Zantho so he had to back away or be crushed. 'But do not think me blind, either,' he said more calmly. 'I know what Drakgaard ordered you to do, as I know my own orders. He is frustrated and believes he can lose this war. To compensate he throws himself into the crucible without proper caution.'

Only an ancient such as Kor'ad would ever openly criticise his commanding officer in this way. Such things, whilst incredibly uncommon, were not without precedent. Yet the fact of hearing it still rankled with Zantho.

'Defeat is always possible. Though, I never took you for cautious, brother.'

'Not for the victors. And I am mindful. There is a stark difference.' Kor'ad paused, letting the harsh grind of servos articulate his mood. 'If you are so certain of our captain, why are your largest war engines languishing in Escadan?'

'To reinforce us. I am being prudent.'

Zantho didn't feel it, though, and Kor'ad was wise enough to see that.

'Grind down a blade enough,' uttered the Dreadnought, 'and soon even the sharpest sword will lose its edge.'

'Zen'de, but what has philosophy got to do with any of this?'

'Our captain functions with blunted purpose.'

'Then it is our duty to help restore it. I say again: what is your meaning, Kor'ad?'

'Be mindful, that is all. As we speak, Ur'zan Drakgaard is dangerously close to being reckless,' said Kor'ad, turning and stomping away.

The last words of the ancient troubled Zantho, for he too had noticed the strain Drakgaard was under. His old wounds had made him bitter, the fact of his being sidelined to the reserve companies even more so. This was a great opportunity for him to show his mettle and, in his opinion at least, restore the Chapter's reputation. Drakgaard had needed a war of his own; he just didn't need this one.

Climbing back aboard his Predator, Zantho took up position in the cupola hatch and stared out into the dark horizon. The way ahead was occluded but he felt a cold wind against his face and wondered what it might portend.

Naeb landed with a minor ignition flare from his jump pack, burning the earth around him and searing the short grass underfoot. This part of Canticus had once been its ornamental gardens and vineyard, but the war had made it a dirty brown mess of felled trees, broken statues and fire-blackened vegetation. The grass was churned to dark earth from the tramp of booted feet, the fountains were broken or choked with chemicals. A single tree stood alone in the midst of this destruction, the fruit on its branches withering and rotting in the actinic air.

'A world has lost its innocence, brother,' Va'lin remarked as Naeb killed his turbine engines.

'I'm not sure if Heletine was ever innocent, but it has certainly lost much.'

An explosion detonated fifty metres away, turning a fallen ornamental arch into rubble but neither fire-born reacted beyond a glance.

Redgage's engineers were demolishing the gardens, clearing a path for the tanks to traverse unimpeded. Until they were needed elsewhere, the Wyverns had been tasked with ensuring the sappers' safety.

Va'lin stared into the darkness, willing the enemy to appear. Since Salvation Bridge, he had seen little in the way of combat and now the silence of that was becoming deafening. Instead of foes, though, he saw the squad widely dispersed over the expansive area, patrolling in loose pairs. His mood darkened further. With the deaths of Sor'ad and Illus, they had been reduced to eight.

'You saved Dersius and I,' said Naeb softly, as if guessing Va'lin's dark thoughts. 'Illus died a Wyvern, fighting hard and on his feet. None of us can ask for more.'

'Then why does it bother me still?'

'Because they are dead, and we would wish them not to be. It's not so hard to understand, brother.'

'You have an over simple view of the world, Naeb.'

'And you think too much.' Naeb gestured to Dersius as he landed nearby and within earshot. 'Try being more like the Themian. An anvil feels nothing.'

Dersius did not rise to the bait as Iaptus and the rest of the squad landed a few seconds later. In the distance, a Chimera had arrived to ferry the engineers. Evidently, their work was complete.

'We push north,' Iaptus told them, 'acting as escort for the armour. Brother Orcas will provide infiltration momentarily.'

'Do we have eyes on the enemy, brother-sergeant?' asked Va'lin.

'The Black Legion? Not yet. Nothing since the bridge, but apparently Captain Drakgaard is confident we are close.'

Above, they could all hear the heavy whip of a gunship's turbo fans as it came in to land.

'Even the skies fall quiet...' muttered Ky'dak as the vague outline of the Thunderhawk appeared overhead.

'They will be aflame soon enough,' said Iaptus, flatly.

Arrok ventured a question, 'Brother-sergeant, what of the Sororitas? Have we received word of their movements?'

Iaptus looked up at the descending gunship, which was close and right above them.

'Nothing beyond their pledged support.'

'I, for one, am grateful of it,' said Xerus, the veteran having nothing but praise for the Seraphim who had fought beside them on Salvation Bridge.

Iaptus nodded, but kept his own counsel.

Ky'dak exchanged a glance with Va'lin, their discovery of the Sororitas scavenger in the ruins still fresh in the mind.

'Tell me, brother,' said Naeb, his words lost to the others in the down wash of heat and noise as Orcas brought the gunship down to land, 'I neglected to ask, what did she say to you on the bridge?'

'She said we were too few,' Va'lin replied as the ruckus from the engine was diminishing.

Everyone heard him – their silence provided the same answer.

They were too few, and alone could not win the war.

CHAPTER TWENTY-SIX

Heletine, Solist

In the early days of the war for Heletine, Solist had suffered in the punitive bombardments of the local militia. Its name had once meant 'sanctuary' in native Heletian, but had become a thing of bitter and chilling irony. For days, falsely believing it to be the heretics' muster point, macro cannon bursts and ceaseless missile salvoes had pummelled the city into a desert of grey rock and partially irradiated dust. The desperate actions of the now-dead planetary governor achieved little except the wholesale destruction of one of Heletine's major cities, together with its unwillingly sacrificed populace.

Only bones inhabited Solist now.

Picked clean by the carrion that roamed the wastes, a skeletal hand reached up out of the sand trying to grasp the sun. The clawed stanchion of a black gunship crushed its bleached fingers, its turbine engines kicking up dust in savage, twisting squalls. The embarkation ramp was descending before the ship had touched down, Angerer's silhouette framed just inside it by the hold's internal illumination.

'Laevenius…' said the canoness, summoning her second-in-command, and allowing the ship to land before she stepped out.

The Sister Superior followed, twenty Celestians looming behind but waiting aboard the transport. As she walked down the ramp, Laevenius's armoured grip tightened around the leather book, her gauntleted fingers digging in. Though to a casual glance it would appear nondescript, the

237

book was far from ordinary. It described the identities of traitors, those believed shown to Dominica by the Emperor before she was sainted.

It was a list of prey, of those meant for death or incarceration. In Angerer's mind that was currently a list of one... the Order's great shame, the black opal on her rosary chain. Many knew of her existence, but few knew of her provenance.

A wretched creature crawled over to the canoness on its belly, emaciated by radiation poisoning. It had once been a man, a soldier judging by his tattered uniform. A sigil of Chaos marked his blighted skin, doubtless an act of desperation when the pain had become too much to bear. Many of those in Solist were afflicted thusly, a shambling and half dead host, the dead governor's dark legacy.

Angerer stalled the wretch's progress with her armoured boot, and looked down at him through cold retinal lenses. All the Sisters had donned their helms. Only low-level radiation permeated the city now, and Angerer was sure their faith would protect them, but a layer of hermetically sealed adamantium and ceramite were also adjudged prudent.

'The Dark Gods don't grant succour for the weak... nor does the Throne,' said Angerer, levelling her fusion pistol and ending the wretch's suffering. 'The brass compass, sister,' she added, staring macabrely at the cauterised stump of neck where the man's head used to be. 'His soul will burn as do the souls of all traitors.'

By the time she looked up again at Laevenius, the Sister Superior was holding out the compass.

Twenty Celestians had marched from the gunship's hold, filing out in ivory ranks, their chasubles the hue of sanctified blood. Bolters locked across their bodies, they loosely encircled their leader. Angerer had barely noticed, her attention instead on the compass and the teardrop still balanced precipitously on it. Even wearing her gauntlets, she could feel the heat of divination. It told what she believed to be true in her heart.

'She is here,' she breathed, her hand straying subconsciously to the rosary pearls and the single black opal that spoiled the perfect chain. 'What did I tell you about belief, Sister Laevenius?'

Whilst Angerer was establishing the proximity of their quarry, two more ships had landed on the barren wastes and were disgorging the rest of the canoness's forces. Two further squads of Battle Sisters and a squad each of Retributors and Dominions. The latter half of the force was heavily armed, equipped with flamer and melta weaponry.

Angerer was taking no chances, not with this prey. Not with this particular traitor. Over sixty armoured Sororitas waited silently on the sand, standing at the ready outside their transports, and it was still not enough.

'Signal the rest of the Preceptory. Give them the code command, Angelicus.'

'All of them, my canoness?' asked Laevenius.

Angerer turned sharply, her glare like a chastening fire even through the icy blue of her retinal lenses. 'Bring everything to this city. Have them hold position at the border. Nothing must prevent us from getting off Heletine with our prisoner. Do it quickly. As soon as our troops move, the barbarian drakes will suspect they have been betrayed.'

'Have they not, my canoness?' asked Laevenius again.

Angerer scowled, unaccustomed to being questioned by anyone, let alone her trusted right hand. 'For good cause. Our ends justify the means – never forget that. Is your faith wavering, Sister? I thought we were of one mind and soul on this matter, its consequences and its cost…'

'We are, canoness,' Laevenius replied, lowering her head and touching the book. She remembered the scar on her face and looked up. 'By the Emperor's will, by Throne it shall be done.'

Satisfied, Angerer gave the order to move. Only Laevenius and her trusted Celestians would accompany her. The rest would stay with the gunships to protect their egress. A rise up ahead of the landing zone shielded what she knew was a valley where they would find Sister Revina and redemption for the Order. She could not wait for further reinforcement. She had waited too long already.

It was hard to make out at first. A hot wind blew through the valley, creating a veil of dust that occluded whatever was lurking at its basin in murky grey.

Something was down there, Angerer was certain. And as she and her entourage drew closer, it began to resolve. First an indistinct smudge against the grey, then a roughly humanoid shape, finally a woman dressed in a ragged robe.

She was staked down in the sand, wrists and ankles, and left to bake in the sun.

Angerer's wrath warred between those who had subjected her sister to this degradation and Revina herself. Of the former, there was no sign. Tracking auspex and bio-scanners revealed nothing, too fouled by latent radiation to provide an accurate reading. Trusting to caution, Angerer approached slowly and sent Laevenius with one squad of Celestians out into flanking positions that encircled the torture site.

She eyed the ridgeline – so did Laevenius from the left flank. Nothing manifested. No surprise attack, no trap was sprung – Angerer merely got closer. As she closed, she saw the caked blood around Revina's mouth: her cracked and bone-dry lips, the patches of exposed skin where the sun had burned her.

It took a good deal of Angerer's composure not to rush over and free her, to roar her defiance at the slow torture visited upon Revina. She wondered how long she had been here, if the heretics realised who and what she was. It felt like a goad, Revina trussed up like this. It felt like she was bait.

'Sister…' Angerer uttered across the vox-link, afraid to speak too loudly and disturb the silence of the desert into action. So quiet, so eerily still in spite of the eddying dust clouds and even they had begun to subside in the last few seconds.

'No movement,' answered Laevenius, knowing precisely what was going through her canoness's mind.

'Do not be fooled,' Angerer replied, casting her gaze across the opposite ridgeline again. 'We are not alone out here.'

Sister Revina was only a few metres away now, and Angerer could see she was aware of her Sisters' presence around her. She did not struggle or cry out. Her throat was so parched she would not likely speak again, or soon anyway.

Angerer stopped, staring at Revina who stared back through seared and bloodshot eyes. Angerer detected no fear, no pleading, just a solemn kind of acceptance she found altogether more unsettling, as if Revina knew this would happen and knew what was about to happen too.

Signalling the Celestians in her bodyguard to halt, Angerer went the last few metres alone. Revina was her mess to deal with, her dirty secret. She would meet her without the others, one sister to another.

'Revina,' she said, surprised at how faint her voice had become. 'Revina,' she repeated more loudly, displaying the confidence she wanted to feel. 'Sister…'

Revina blinked, once. It must have taken great pain and effort to do so. Her lips began to move but she could not utter a word, even if she wanted to.

'I confess I questioned whether or not we would find you, but your tears showed me what I wanted to know.' Casting aside the compass, Angerer drew her mace and crept forwards another step.

'And here you are… witch.'

Now Revina's eyes registered some emotion. Pity. For a sister who cleaved to duty over blood and who feared the uncertainty of her own future. She glanced to one side, trying to find her other sibling, trying to find Laevenius.

'Your sister reviles you as much as I,' spat Angerer. 'Perhaps more so,' she added, then gestured to the Celestians, 'but I have brought an entire war host to track you down and bring you back. I should have killed you, but death is too good for you now. I won't let you escape your fate that easily.'

Again, Revina gave her that pitying look.

Angerer wanted to crush her skull for it, for it was a mirror into the canoness's own soul and the reflection did not paint her in a favourable light.

Time was wasting. Angerer felt it like the irradiated sands of Solist moving inexorably beneath her feet.

She was about to order her Celestians to release Revina and make her their prisoner again when she realised the sand was moving. It was feeding slowly towards some at first unseen aperture that was rapidly expanding into a broad fissure. The fissure became a chasm, huge swathes of sand pouring inside it and, like a swimmer ensnared by the tide, Angerer was dragged along with it.

Seeing the canoness's peril, the Celestians rushed forwards but that only made it worse and several were caught up in the swell. Revina disappeared with it too, the sand draining away and in its wake revealing armoured forms that had been concealed until that moment.

Laevenius was the first to react and gave the order to open fire, but the traitors were already firing. At first there were ten, then twenty, then thirty, until forty armoured Black Legion warriors emerged from beneath the desolation of Solist to add more corpses to the tally of thousands that already rotted there.

The Celestians closest to Angerer were the first to die. One jerked backwards, the perfect sheen of her ivory power armour broken apart by an explosive shell and painted a darker crimson than the blood-red of her robes.

Another half turned, raising her bolter at the enemies suddenly in her midst, before her arm was vaporised from her body.

A third cried out some canticle of hatred against the traitor as her right eye lens was shot out and her helm, skull and the matter within erupted outwards a few seconds later.

Eight Celestians lay dead before those that were left made any sort of reply. The two survivors joined Angerer in the pit – a steep-sided, six-metre trap with a grated sand sluice at the bottom – but were not to last long. Something else besides Revina was down there with them, something massive and powerful. It crafted itself to look like a man, a transhuman warrior of some bygone era but was anything but. Its sheer size and menace, the empyreal nature of its form, suggested otherwise.

Angerer put a word to it, spoken in a half rasp of barely contained terror and righteous fury.

'Hellspawn!'

As the daemon closed on her, the pair of Celestians rushed forwards with the name of Saint Dominica on their lips. It was a brave, reckless display but one that ended in both being dashed against the steel walls of the trap with their skulls crushed.

Angerer brandished her mace, knowing it to be a more effective weapon against daemonkind than her fusion pistol. Unlike her charges, she knew firsthand how dangerous such creatures could be.

'Get back,' she warned, mustering her hate to try to ward off the terror that was threatening to paralyse her.

The daemon laughed, as ungodly a sound as it was possible for a thing to make, an exhalation of derision redolent of sulphur and decomposing flesh. Angerer's censers, their votive incense, did nothing to repel it. Like their mistress, they capitulated before this horror, shrinking back until the daemon eclipsed them in its unearthly shadow.

CHAPTER TWENTY-SEVEN

Heletine, Canticus southern district, 'the Cairns'

Ever since he had become captain of Sixth, Ur'zan Drakgaard had felt overshadowed. Though he was a campaign veteran, a warrior of esteemed and lengthy service, his banner had never been as lofty or lauded as the battle company captains. Amongst the reserves, a warrior learned his place was by the sidelines or reinforcing his Chapter brothers as support.

Few were the opportunities to step into the light of war's ever-present flame and be recognised. It had never bothered Ur'zan Drakgaard. He knew, amongst the fire-born, he was not remarkable. He did not possess the charisma Ko'tan Kadai had before his death or the martial prowess of Pellas Mir'san. Adrax Agatone was a superior tactician, Dac'tyr was unrivalled in naval warfare. Even Sol Ba'ken of Seventh had a better rapport with his battle-brothers. His best traits were his determination, singularity of purpose and utter refusal to capitulate under any circumstances. His wounds, a vast and spreading colony across his body, testified to that.

But here, now, Ur'zan Drakgaard had a rare chance to step into the light. He told himself he was just doing his duty, that personal glory didn't matter. It was for the honour of the Chapter he fought and would one day die.

Ur'zan Drakgaard told himself this lie as he led out the line, a feral smile twisting the corners of his scarred mouth.

Reunited with Sergeant Kadoran's troops, the Salamanders storming across the Canticus ruins represented almost the entire Sixth Company's martial strength. They were further reinforced by a cadre of elite Kasrkin.

The mortal soldiers were showing their mettle by maintaining pace with the faster, hardier Space Marines. Helfer had trained them well and such warriors did him credit, but Drakgaard knew the true test would come when they engaged the enemy proper.

The heretics could not be much farther now. This was the deepest Imperial troops had ever ventured. Beyond the snap fire from the shadows when they had first discovered the defeated Centurions, resistance was non-existent. Privately, Drakgaard did wonder what manner of weapon had dispatched one of Fourth Company's most elite units so comprehensively. Perhaps they had managed to destroy it during the fighting. Bar'dak was in no position to refute or deny that, by now on the way back to Escadan aboard a Thunderhawk with Apothecary Sepelius.

No resistance meant only one of two things: either Drakgaard was right and the heretics had been so diminished by attrition they no longer possessed the military strength to stand and fight, or the fire-born at his command were being drawn into a trap. In a way, it didn't matter. Root them out, burn their bones, it was all Ur'zan Drakgaard knew how to do; it was all he had ever done.

Every few moments, he checked the tactical display. The Salamanders and their Cadian allies were making steady progress, despite the heavy terrain. Sentinel walkers had been tasked with flanking the advancing force, acting as scouts and outriders, their design uniquely disposed to the urban environs. Between them were Drakgaard's infantry, an alliance of Tactical and Devastator squads, and the Kasrkin. The Serpentia held the centre under the overall commander's leadership with his Chaplain.

From the south, two companies of Imperial armour under Commander Zantho and Redgage picked their way through the rubble and would link up with the troops on foot soon. Ingress into the heart of the city via armoured tank tread was far from easy. Wide-scale devastation had rendered most of Canticus a ruin barely traversable by foot, let alone battle tank, but a road that adjoined the Sanctium Vius from the south provided the means for both battle groups to reunite. Once alloyed, Drakgaard believed it didn't matter what level of martial strength the heretics still had; it would be crushed between hammer and anvil.

'Even with a hundred charges, it would take hours to shatter it,' said Naeb.

Although all of the Wyverns knew how to break into a defended position or destroy a wall or bunker, Naeb had the greatest expertise in demolition. He surveyed the collapsed column of stone through his bionic eye, searching it for weaknesses but finding none.

'I doubt even our brother's lumpen head,' he said, looking at Dersius, 'thick as it undoubtedly is, could split it.'

The Themian took a step forwards. 'Shall we wager if it would break your faceplate instead, Naeb?'

Va'lin intervened to halt their banter.

'Naeb's silence suggests declination, brother.'

Dersius laughed loudly.

Naeb gave Va'lin a short bow, 'Astute as always,' he said, as his gaze strayed to a lone figure standing at the edge of the rubble. 'A pity our other Themian does not possess Dersius's good humour.'

If Ky'dak heard him, he didn't react. His was staring into the shell of a distant building, the fires within it guttering but still bright.

Va'lin murmured, 'What does he see when he stares into the flames?'

'Whatever it is,' Naeb replied softly, 'it does not improve his demeanour.'

'Wyverns!' Sergeant Iaptus called from the opposite side of the column. 'Gather.'

To call it a column was like referring to Mount Deathfire on Nocturne as a hill. It was immense, one of the so-called 'Cairns', inexplicably felled across their route of march, effectively shearing it in half.

Divided by the Sanctium Vius, the armoured force under the overall command of Venerable Kor'ad had occupied and was traversing the southern fringe of the octakaidecahedral region when the great column had fallen. Advancing in file, several battle tanks had been crushed during this calamity, at first trapped and then unable to get out of the way in time. In the process, a wedge had been driven between the recently joined companies.

Sent ahead to assess the damage, the Wyverns were standing atop the fallen edifice like conquerors over the corpse of a world but found no reason to be triumphant. Nearby their gunship piloted by Brother Orcas idled on a patch of scrub that served as a rare landing zone.

'Inconvenient how it splits us in two even halves,' said Arrok, as the Wyverns came together.

'Not so even...' Ky'dak muttered.

On one side of the monolithic column were the Cadians, on the other side Zantho and his tank company.

Va'lin heard him and was quick to remonstrate. 'Don't dishonour them, Ky'dak. They have fought bravely so far.'

'And yet,' answered Ky'dak, 'they are still just mortals.' He leapt down from the flat-sided column to join Xerus below.

'It stretches credulity to think this was mere happenstance,' said Xerus. Unlike the others, the veteran had been standing at ground level, investigating the column's rupture point. 'There are powder marks here from blasting charges. Some of the stone also bears evidence of las-cutting. It was worn down over several days of demolition before the final push was applied to collapse it.'

'So the enemy armour drew us here deliberately,' Iaptus was furthest forward of the squad and peered into the distance, 'is that what you're saying, brother?'

'It is, brother-sergeant.'

None of this was improving Iaptus's already irascible mood.

Vo'sha was just behind the sergeant, looking ahead through a pair of magnoculars.

'The route diverges,' he said. 'No way to link our two forces – we'll be pushed farther south before we can head east again.'

Zantho's voice came through the vox.

'How far, brother-sergeant?'

'Difficult to judge...' said Iaptus.

Vo'sha adjusted the magnification through the scopes. 'A detour of several hours at least.'

Zantho heard and cursed quietly in Nocturnean. Exhaling a frustrated breath he said, 'Join up with Kor'ad. I'll inform the ancient he's going to be lighter by several battle tanks but that at least the Wyverns will be watching his flank.'

Iaptus sent Zantho his affirmation sigil and opened a link to the waiting Thunderhawk.

'Brother Orcas, prepare for departure. We're joining Kor'ad and the Cadians.'

Ignoring the thrumming engines, Sister Stephina bowed her head in prayer. In the darkness of the transport's hold, she shut her eyes to the outside world and beseeched Saint Dominica's aid.

For years, Canoness Angerer had been her lodestone and a constant reminder of her faith and duty to the Throne. In all that time the latter had never wavered, but knelt in the dark before the votive shrine, Stephina confessed to doubts about her preceptor.

'Our teachings are the words of the Emperor, His Throne we serve in perpetuity and in so doing sacrifice all mortal concerns and desires,' she whispered. 'Our Order so does pledge, by our Ebon Chalice, sigil of Our Martyred Saint Dominica.'

The canticles of faith passed quickly across her lips, Stephina afraid that in doing anything other she would be exposed for her lack of faith and forever diminished in the eyes of the Emperor and the saint.

'Grant me faith, oh Dominica – let me see how my canoness serves the Throne. Her will is the will of the Order, she who represents you on earth. And yet...' she paused, breath catching in her throat. To believe her canoness acted out of some selfish agenda was one thing, to speak it invited actual condemnation if she was wrong, 'I cannot see the Emperor's hand in her works.'

'Sister…'

Stephina's heart trembled in her chest, so engrossed in prayer was she that for a moment she believed it was the voice of Alicia Dominica and not her fellow Seraphim that had addressed her.

'Casiopia,' she said, managing to sound calm as she opened her eyes serenely.

'Orders have been received from the Canoness-Preceptor.' Sister Casiopia clutched a leaf of parchment in her hand, reverently bowing her head so her superior could rise from prayer and accept it.

Stephina read the wax-sealed parchment, knowing already what it contained.

'What was the signal word, Sister?' she asked, her face darkening as she took in Angerer's written orders. Despite her prayers, she could not help but see the treachery in them.

'Angelicus, my Sister.'

Stephina nodded, dismissing Casiopia.

Twenty Seraphim occupied the hold of the transport; another almost equally burdened gunship flew alongside it not twenty metres away.

'We are to Solist then,' said a voice she knew.

Sister Helia, her white hair and alabaster complexion marking her out as angelic in more than honorific alone, approached from the other side of the hold. It was not spacious but neither was it at capacity, so there was room enough to move and seek solitude if needed.

'I had no wish to interrupt,' she added, clutching the same parchment orders as Stephina did. 'You seemed… troubled, Sister.'

Of the entire Order, there was no one Stephina trusted more than Helia. Except perhaps Laevenius, but Stephina believed she was somehow allied to whatever scheme Angerer was fulfilling.

They were blood sisters, after all.

Even so, she had to consider what she said to Helia next.

'Troubled to what end, I cannot fathom.'

'Is that why you were so deep in prayer, Sister? It is not so shameful to admit you have doubts.'

'I see only bloodshed on this parchment,' Stephina confessed, trusting enough in Helia to speak her mind.

'You worry for the savages?'

'What is in Solist that we must abandon our allies to obtain?'

Helia frowned as if she'd just been asked a facile question. 'We obey our preceptor, Sister. Her faith is our guide, her will the will of the Throne.'

'We are leaving them to die, Sister.'

'They are capable warriors.'

'Who believe they are reinforced by a holy Order of the Adepta Sororitas. Tell me this does not sit ill with you.'

'We follow the decrees of Canoness Angerer. Our duty is to the Ecclesiarchy, above all else.'

'And what if the preceptor is not serving the Ecclesiarchy in this?' Stephina lowered her voice, glancing sidelong to see if anyone else was listening but fortunately the drone of the engines was masking the conversation. 'What if she serves her own ends?'

'Do you have proof?'

'I have the inexplicable nature of these orders,' said Stephina. 'I have my faith.'

For a moment Helia succumbed to doubt. It was written plainly on her face, her look of angelic serenity marred by sudden confusion.

For a moment, Stephina hoped it had not been such a stretch to implicate their canoness so boldly. It did not last.

'I have never seen you like this before, Stephina.'

'Because I have never been told to abandon my post and allies of the Imperium for a clandestine mission. Let the Inquisition be ruled by such subterfuge – we Battle Sisters are of higher morality.'

'Sister...' Helia reached out to hold Stephina's hands. They shook with anger. 'Be calm. You are weary, that is all. Rest, pray. There is a little time before we reach Solist.'

It was like shouting into a storm. Helia would not hear her, and Stephina was yet unsure what she could do. Appearing to heed her Sister, she gently released herself, bowed her head in gratitude and returned to the shrine.

'Answer me this, Sister,' she said whilst her back was turned, just about to kneel down again. 'When did we become betrayers?'

Helia could not.

CHAPTER TWENTY-EIGHT

Sturndrang, the underhive of Molior

The din of machinery and clattering metal resolved on the warm air, suggesting the excavation was still ongoing.

And close.

A heady scent pervaded, cloying and noxiously saccharine. It dulled the otherwise industrial and actinic scent of the underhive Exor had come to know but overlaid a much more unsettling odour that felt incongruous in the sweating, metal confines.

Somewhere close was the nexus of whatever foulness had crept into the heart of Molior and taken root. It was the source of Zartath's disquiet and the reason why the vermin were so grossly mutated. Facts interleaved, coincidence became causality and all the disparate threads they had been following suddenly conjoined at this point, in this moment.

Logic and instinct had reached the same conclusion in the same instant and so its two agents in Molior found themselves at the precipice of a great and dark discovery.

Slowing naturally as instinctive caution took over, Zartath signalled for Exor to take the opposite flank of the wreckage. The path they had been travelling, shouldered by peaks of discarded metal, had widened, the summits either side shrinking as the debris flattened out in a rusted plain.

Exor nodded, understanding, and as the warriors diverged they crouched low and moved quietly between scraps of cover.

As well as the noise from the machines, there was light now too. As

Exor crept closer, he tried to keep Zartath in his field of vision. Agatone had sent Exor after the hunter to bring him back and now the Techmarine found himself in league with him, facing some terror of the subterranean world below Sturndrang. Even with his mission parameters changed in the face of empirical evidence, Exor knew he needed to keep Zartath in his sights, watch him as his captain had ordered. It was impossible. The hunter moved too swiftly, Exor a lumpen clod in comparison. He had to settle for knowing he was close by and that, for now at least, their objectives were in alignment.

The light was coming from a string of phosphor lamps, rigged above a deep pit from which the scattered and piled wreckage had been excised. More light emanated from drum fires and the metal shells of vehicles and structures that had been turned into massive burning braziers. They reminded Exor of ribcages and he briefly wondered if their design had been deliberate.

Figures huddled in the light. Men and women, not so dissimilar to the dregs he had seen in Kabullah. The differences between them were subtle, but immediately alarming. A nervous vitality affected the ones now before him. It drove their weary bodies back to the pit where half a dozen vehicles were crowding. Three of the vehicles were industrial-grade excavators, drilling and digging. Two others were cargo haulers, brimming with scrap from the pit. The last vehicle was a freight loader, a four-track. On the back of the truck a tall figure in purple robes murmured sibilant imprecations.

The men and women were not slaves; they were supplicants. Through his visual implants, Exor discerned sigils scratched into their flesh. Self-inflicted wounds. Scarification marred faces already withered by malnutrition. None of this disfigurement or wretchedness appeared to dampen their spirits, though it was difficult to tell if they laboured in thralls of rapture or melancholy. The mood of the supplicants seemed to wax and wane according to their proximity to the pit. Exor estimated almost forty at the dig site, including the robed demagogue who he assumed was the leader. As his imprecations grew louder, chanting began in the cultists' ranks too and a realisation was quick to form.

This was who they had fought at Seven Points, who Tsu'gan had fought too. A cult of Chaos was at large and growing in Molior's deep underhive. Unchecked, it would be the end of this world.

About to creep closer and try to find Zartath, Exor saw the first sentry. Unlike the diggers, it moved languidly as if affected by some torpor. Disguised beneath its robes and afflicted by some kind of physical mutant action, gender was hard to determine. He did make out the strange arrangement of tubes in kind to the creatures they had dispatched at Seven Points. Seeing it for a second time, Exor was reminded of the amulet the underhiver wore when they had first delved into Molior. Tainted blood had corrupted these men and women, turned its vermin into monsters.

Pipes fed down into the pit, extracting, exsanguinating. Whatever lurked within was being siphoned and turned into a narcotic that altered its takers in initially subtle but ultimately ruinous ways, like the one that had affected the ganger called Karve.

The taint: this place in the darkness was the epicentre and the radial fractures of its corruption were slowly spreading. Like hacking down a dead tree to expose the insects burrowing under its seemingly healthy bark, the fire-born had uncovered an infestation. Only one course of action remained to them – exterminate it at the source.

Exor edged forwards, low and to the shadows, careful to avoid the sentries' patrols. Techmarines were not adept at stealth but the sentries seemed so entranced that sneaking amongst them was not much of a challenge. The sudden and painful throbbing in Exor's skull was. The closer he got to the pit, the louder and more agonising it became. The supplicants' rapture was his torture. It could only be worse for Zartath.

The keening, that's what he had called it. In mythic ages, it was a siren's call dragging sailors to their doom. Only this siren was embedded in the deep earth of the underhive, not an ocean, and the sailors were the two fire-born who had tracked it to its lair.

There was no tuning it out, and no solace from the call. It was inside, a hollow drone that rattled around within the skull like a broken chip of bone, the damage being caused by its existence unknown until it was too late.

An ordinary man would have been driven mad by it, or driven to it, foreswearing all oaths and friendships in order to be in service to the keening. But Space Marines were not men, and did not give in to Chaos easily. A duty lay before Exor now, one he had sworn to uphold when he became fire-born, to defend mankind from threats without and within to his dying breath.

As part of the Chapter or alone here in the dark of the underhive, it did not matter.

'Vulkan's fire beats in my breast…' he began, affirming his purpose and planning a route through the sentries that would get him to the demagogue. Then all thoughts of duty and tactics deserted him.

He had found Zartath. The ex-Black Dragon was on his feet, charging down the nearest sentry and roaring like a beast unhinged.

Horrified and agape, Exor watched as Zartath bore the sentry down with bone blades embedded in its chest. Shattering its blood-vials, Zartath was back on his feet and running again before the creature expired with a strange whimper of pleasure-pain. He moved low but with long, loping strides like a hound on the hunt. Blood sprayed across his muzzle, the sense-shattering keening coring out his skull – Zartath was as close to truly feral as he had ever been. So singular of purpose, so maddened, he was heedless of almost everything except the keening.

All thoughts of stealth now abandoned, Exor rose up and opened fire on the mutant closing on Zartath's blindside. It cradled a strange-looking fusil, the stock and trigger clutched by long, bony fingers, the barrel steadied with a coiling tentacle. Truly, they had unearthed a den of ruin in Molior.

It had to burn.

Exor fired again on the move, taking the mutant somewhere in its midriff. The shot knocked it off its feet, torso and legs sheared apart in the resulting explosive crescendo. Heads turned. Faces with too many eyes regarded the second interloper in their midst. With a clawed hand outstretched, his own face occluded by the folds of his hood, the demagogue marshalled his disciples.

As one and with eerie synchronicity, the supplicants dropped what they were carrying and ran like wolves at the fire-born.

A solid shot whipped past Exor's ear; he felt the heat and heard the speed of its passage. Another clipped his slim shoulder guard and he was reminded how perilously unprotected he was without his power armour. He broke into a run, loosing off three more shots in quick succession, aiming for the sentries as they were armed and already firing.

Two more went down, broken into chunks of smouldering meat by a bolt-shell's explosive impact. He thought he had missed the third, but the round had actually bounced off the mutant whose hide was like a sheath of impervious armour plate.

A head shot overcame the problem and decapitated the sentry. There was no time to be subtle – only brute aggression would prevail. Exor knew he had to get to the pit, then confront and kill whatever was in it. He would have to go through the demagogue and his flock to reach it, unless Zartath got there ahead of him.

The ex-Black Dragon was eating up the ground between himself and the pit with long, determined strides. Reacting instinctively, he switched between evasion and sheer power. Anything in his way was cut down. Three mutant sentries so far, their spilled and noisome innards steaming on the collated trash they seemed to worship. Resistance had been fleeting, suicidal even, but as Zartath closed on the pit the ranks of defenders thickened.

It was all Exor could do to maintain a steady pace. Loosing three more bursts, his clip began to run dry. He finished it off and ejected the clip, reaching for another, but there were none so he drew his combat blade. Cursing, he realised he must have lost the spare during his descent.

Fortunately, not only had Zartath thinned the herd, his insane dash

towards the pit had drawn everything to him. A morass of bodies, supplicants and sentries both, enveloped the hunter. Excited and terrified
at the prospect of his own imminent death, the demagogue grew more
animated. His sermons devolved to ranting. He was baying now, baying
for the transgressor's blood with all the fervour of a frothing lunatic.

A greater madness had been unleashed against him, though. Zartath
had survived the labyrinthine prison of the Volgorrah Reef and killed
Renegade Astartes – no enrobed zealot was going to resist him for long,
even with a host to protect him.

Exor arrived to find Zartath cutting the last of the disciples down, a
butcher cleaving meat. He ended the slaughter with the demagogue, who
finally fled but stumbled when his robes snagged on a piece of twisted
metal and fell onto his face. Crawling on his stomach, he reached the edge
of the crevice his followers had been digging.

Even from a little distance away, Exor could see the shallow but widening gyre they had made in the wreckage. A speartip of metal jutted just
high enough for the Techmarine to see from where he was standing. It
looked like the cone of a drop pod…

A predator sensing wounded prey, Zartath sprang on the mewling demagogue who was desperately trying to claw his way into the pit. Part of
his trappings had torn loose, revealing the corruption beneath. Twisted
flesh, an over-wide maw in place of a natural mouth, his eyes small slits
of flesh, surrendered for this other mutation. As always with Chaos, one
must give in order to receive.

As he was thrown onto his back by the rough hands of the ex-Black
Dragon, the demagogue uttered a single arcane word. His oratory was his
gift, a boon from his dark patrons that had helped him enslave the citi-
zens to his will. It was meant to stop his assailant dead, a single, chiming
utterance of power. Zartath was singularly unmoved.

Mad with rage, Zartath rammed his bone blade through the side of the
demagogue's skull, silencing him, but failed to quieten the daemons in
his own head.

Battle over, the cult vanquished, Exor went to join him at the edge of
the pit.

When he was a sword length away, Zartath whirled around.

'Broth–' The Techmarine stopped short as the searing fire of the bone
blade coursed through his chest and out of his back in radiating tremors
of agony. He cried out in pain, but his voice was half-strangled and came
out as a gasp. Reaching up, Exor grabbed Zartath's shoulder in support,
in trembling accusation and tried to meet his gaze.

Wild, dark eyes of pure fury looked back. There was no recognition in
them, no guilt or remorse. Whatever was gnawing at Zartath's mind was
still there, embedded in his psyche. Exor staggered, the heat of the wound

dulling and turning to ice as he contemplated how close to death he was again. The ice floes he felt in his blood spread to Exor's back then his limbs, until every part of him that was meat and bone became as cold as the metal of his bionics.

This must be how the world feels to give yourself fully to the Omnissiah, he thought, imagining the cybernetic tutors of his Martian training but seeing the snorting, snarling image of the monstrous warrior he called brother in front of him instead, staring with unrestrained hate. Exor realised it wasn't meant for him. It was fuelled by something else.

In Exor's head, the keening was fading but in Zartath's it had reached a deafening fever pitch he could no longer resist.

As the bone blade withdrew, a spurt of dark blood jetted from the wound. Internal bleeding. Organ damage. He didn't need his power armour's biological data stream to know he was in trouble. Exor was released but found his legs could no longer support him. He collapsed, the culmination of his injuries felling him.

Awareness dimming as his body began trying to shut itself down, Exor fought to stay conscious but slipped into such delirium he could not be sure of what he saw next. Memory, reality and fiction began to blend. Something emerged from the pit, hauling itself over the edge from a cocoon of metal. Striated by age, withered by entropy, the drop pod must have shifted to this place over time, moving in vermicular fashion through the slowly disintegrating layers of the underhive.

Its siren call was weak, and needed time to infect its followers and make them fanatical. Even then, releasing it from its prison would have taken years. It was the blood, leaking into the pit from its prison, siphoned by its desperate acolytes and fashioned into an elixir that promoted strength, resilience, even escape from death. Exor could think of few species whose blood was capable of such wonders.

From out of the pit emerged a figure armoured in heliotrope purple. Whether it was the presence of such august enemies that drew it forth, or some other incredulous coincidence, Exor would never know. They simply had to kill it.

Flayed skin hung in ragged strips from its war-plate. Fetish chains strung with shrivelled ears and fingers looped around shoulder guards and greaves. Its face was scarred like the men and women who had freed it and its eyes were dense chasms of fresh-remembered hate. No pupils, just two orbs of incarnadine red. There could be no mistaking a warrior of the old Legions.

A Traitor Space Marine, trapped in Molior for years.

It rose up to its full height, flakes of debris breaking off from its body and cascading downwards like shed skin. Years of accumulated dust and grit spilled from the joints of its armour. Wrenching free transfusion pipes it had attached to its exposed skin, it drew an old and scarred sword from a dusty scabbard.

The challenge it uttered was in a language Exor didn't know, but used words and sounds that set his teeth on edge.

Zartath faced the warrior, lathered in a feverish sweat, his chest and shoulders rising and falling with heavy breaths.

A few strides separated them.

Bone-blades against tainted steel – who knew what curses were bound up in that traitor's sword?

Spitting back a guttural retort in his native tongue, Zartath lunged at the pallid-skinned warrior.

It was then his enemy spoke, truly used its voice…

A nerve-shredding discord sawed through Exor, forcing back alertness such was its strength and amplification, so loud it almost transcended sound and turned it physical.

Zartath opened his mouth to scream but his voice was swallowed by the terrible clangour resonating through his skin, flesh and bones. He sank to one knee, clutching his fractured eardrums as the true power of the keening was unleashed. The traitor's siren call, that which drew the weak-minded and the easily influenced to the traitor's service and bent them towards its emancipation, had become a weapon. It was killing Zartath.

Slowly dying, but defying his enhanced biology's attempts to put him into a regenerative coma, Exor struggled back to his feet. Fellowship to the Martian Priesthood came with the acceptance of a simple rubric – flesh will ultimately be surrendered to the machine; the machine is perfection. Exor arrived on the red world a being of flesh and blood and left partly cyborganic. His hand was a bionic; both his eyes were augmented, the corneas replaced with synthetics incorporating targeting matrices and enhanced magnification; part of his left side, his shoulder and hip were also mostly machine. Last of all was his auditory cortex – both ears and the minuscule bones inside, drum and ear canal too, had been manufactured in the forge temples of Mars.

The drumming in his skull, the latent power of the keening, had abated in preference to a more direct attack: one Exor could filter out. As he disengaged his hearing, a momentary deafness overcame him. The pain in his vibrating bones still hurt, but the paralysis from the auditory overload lifted.

Out of ammunition, his knife lost when he had first fallen, Exor used the only weapon he had left. Himself.

Scrambling, lurching bodily with every ungainly step, he threw all of his considerable mass at the Traitor who turned, seemingly dumbstruck at the insanity of the reckless attack.

The old sword swung around, hefted with less speed than it might once have been, the warrior's muscles stiff and mildly atrophied from his long confinement. Instead of spearing the Techmarine through the sternum, it cut into his clavicle and sheared against the edge of the bone.

Agony of a thousand white-hot needles impaling his raw nerve endings shot through Exor but not enough to stop him. He careened into the warrior, hearing armour split, bone crack as it yielded to his machine-borne strength.

The discord abated and Exor hit the ground as his eyesight began to darken. But through an ever-dwindling corridor of shadow, he saw the hunter take his prey at last. As the traitor tried to rise and reassert his dominance a shaft of yellowed bone, the bloodstains on it dark like oil, impaled his gullet. A second pierced his eye socket. For three seconds he trembled and then was still.

Like a flood rushing to fill a crater, darkness swamped Exor's sight. His hearing came back briefly, restored by some instinctive physical signal. Nothing at first, but the ambient rhythms of the underhive. It stayed like that for minutes, Exor clinging on.

Breathing, initially heavy but eventually more even, drifted through the mental fog of unconsciousness. It touched Exor's face, wet and foetid with the stench of raw meat.

An untamed beast will be a slave to its instincts. It cannot think, it cannot reason, it can only react, survive.

'Get up...'

The words were so distant, like whispers from the summit of a well, they seemed imagined.

'Get up and let me carry you...'

A man decides, makes choices – he lets his conscience guide him and the fact he has a higher nature. His own survival is secondary to those he would consider as kin.

'Let me carry you, brother...'

CHAPTER TWENTY-NINE

Nova-class frigate, *Forge Hammer*

Amongst the fire tides, time was fluid. It flowed as easily as the burning waves Xarko swam against.

Unmoored from reality, slipping free of temporal concerns was all too simple. The tides were aligned to the aetheric plane, a place not so easily bent to mortal geography and chronology. Time here flowed differently. Diurnal and nocturnal, these cycles had no bearing in such an uncertain realm. Enter at the nascent dawning of the universe and a moment later emerge to find it inert, surrendered to the inevitable rigours of entropy. But to the contrary, enter in the twilight years of creation and find yourself returning to worlds in youthful bloom only seconds later. Life, matter, existence, all of it could be altered in course by the pervasive nature of the warp.

The fire tides were the warp, and the warp the fire tides.

As an accomplished student of the arcane, Xarko knew of the tacit relationship that existed between the two sides of the veil – the real and the unreal – and the metaphysical implications of that relationship. Geography mattered, timing and context mattered. What to the uninitiated and the ignorant might appear random was a scheme of near-incomprehensible complexity to those with enough esoteric knowledge to discern it. To behold the entire tapestry was to invite certain madness and dissolution, but to perceive a strand, a thread or two of the weave… That came as close as anything not unborn could do to navigating the vagaries of the tide.

257

Xarko sought such a thread, and swam in pursuit of it. He had been afforded but a glimpse, a narrow aperture through which he could perceive past, future and present colliding together in a fateful continuum. Life. Death. Rebirth. Over and over again. He knew that in attempting to locate what he had seen before in the tides he risked great danger. Only a psyker of considerable ability and confidence would ever trawl this incorporeal sea. Looking had a habit of resulting in finding, except not always the thing you wanted to unearth. Not only life, but the soul was also at stake. Things… creatures with old names, and hunger that was older still, hunted eagerly for the warmth of souls.

Amongst the fire tides, these creatures were the black slivers. As Xarko swam, his body locked safely away in his sanctum aboard the *Forge Hammer*, he felt the predators lurking at the edge of perception, threatening his mind and soul.

Wary after the last time, the predators did not attack immediately, as if waiting for a better opening or a vulnerability to present itself. Xarko was determined to show them neither, so he swam on. He had passed beyond the chamber, penetrated the first wall and had emerged into the twilight fire sea that so closely resembled the Gey'sarr or the Acerbian from back on Nocturne. It varied with every fresh tide.

For a time there was nothing beyond the usual susurrus of voices, the chronology of the universe laid out for him to listen to and observe. Faces, images wrought from fire, materialised in the deeps but were not the one Xarko was seeking.

He went further, pushing his body even though rationally he knew it was his will he exerted. Physical strength meant nothing here, but manifested anyway as a way for the mind to make sense of what it was experiencing. To an untrained mind, it would appear terrifying, even impossible. The fire would seem to burn and the mind would close in on itself. Some who chose to swim the tides had not returned. Their faces were mirrored in the waves now, stretched taut in expressions of agony and despair. Their bodies were long gone, rendered to ash in the true mountain. Some lived on in a catatonic state, watched over by the brander-priests and shackled in Prometheus's deepest cells.

Still the resonance of what he had experienced before eluded him. He went deeper and the black predators began to converge as they sensed Xarko's mental reserves draining. Strong currents tugged at his body as Xarko went further and further. One sharp pull threatened to drag him into an unseen well, the tendrils of a maelstrom that had begun to swell out in the distance. Pouring more effort into his strokes, Xarko managed to get free of it but was badly shaken and needed a moment to recover.

The predators chose their moment, striking fast and stabbing barbed hooks into Xarko's flesh. He screamed, pain knifing into his skull as the hooks dragged. He thrashed, kicking out with his legs and managing to dislodge one of the fiends. He kicked again, the equivalent of a mental push, and thrust away from his twin assailants.

Arm over arm, breath sawing in and out of his lungs.

The tides heaved and pounded at his bones. Xarko was nearly at the end of his resilience but he fought on, knowing the black predators were behind him. Strong tendrils of current pulled at his limbs, and he realised the maelstrom could be his escape. He let the currents take him, surrendering to their will. As he was flung past his pursuers, taking cuts from their blades, he saw a face appear in the fiery spume. Half its skin was ravaged by scars, not the branding marks of the solitorium but a wound that had changed its complexion. Here was the thread Xarko wanted, fleeing from his grasp as he was pulled away by fate and his own weary mind.

No.

The word echoed in Xarko's mindspace, calmly delivered but powerfully resonant. It shook the dark sky above the ocean, and tore strips into it with arcing jags of crimson. Pulled under, Xarko felt the bite of the preda-tors once more and as he turned in the maelstrom's ferocious undersea spiral, the face dissolved and was replaced by the insistent drumming of his heart…

Thud.

Thud.

The beat became a rap of knuckles, hard against metal. Despite his nausea and disorientation, he could hear the desperation in the sound. Sensation was slow to fade. Psychic echoes clung to the corporeal realm and Xarko struggled to detach them. Visions bled into reality, of the fire, the dark predators. He could smell their spoiled flesh, hear their sibilant whispering grating against the metal of the chamber. With a singular effort, he closed his mind to it, denying a foothold to the voracious deni-zens of the fire tides. The sanctum resolved, a fire-black circle surrounding him. Steam and smoke rose from his bare flesh.

It took a few seconds to marshal his disorientation and remember exactly when and where he was.

Alive, awake and restored to the physical plane, Xarko tried to stand. He collapsed, grimacing in pain at fresh wounds on his back and torso, souvenirs from his encounter on the other side.

Someone was hammering on the door to his sanctum. Even weakened, he managed to reach out with his mind, touch the surface thoughts of those closest to him and know something aboard the *Forge Hammer* was terribly wrong.

On instinct, he activated a distress beacon to their forces on Sturndrang, hoping they would hear it.

'I've swum too long…' Xarko hissed, reaching for his armour with shaking hands.

Makato would not have the deaths of these brave men and women on his conscience. The weight of guilt he bore was already heavy, and he had no desire to add to it.

'Jedda, Halder, Navaar, Bharius.' He said each name aloud to honour the promise he had made. They were just the ones he knew. Many others had died to protect this ship, to protect him. Makato hoped someone would remember them and their noble sacrifice.

'I go to join you soon…' he murmured to the walls of the empty corridor.

Makato was standing alone outside the blast doors to the bridge. Behind him, on the other side of two metre-thick reinforced ceramite and adamantium, were twenty-eight armsmen and fourteen bridge crew. No captain sat upon the command throne, but consoles were manned and the ship was still in the hands of its crew. Never in all his years of service had it been otherwise.

Swearing on the souls of his father and grandfather, Makato vowed that would not change this day, this hour, this moment.

He knew though that the moment had run out.

Every effort had been made to slow the Renegade Astartes but they had advanced through the ship inexorably, their path bringing them to this nexus where Makato was now standing.

He saw the first of them, their sergeant, appear in the low light at the end of the corridor. Scarcely twenty-four metres separated them but Makato felt no fear.

Instead, he slowly stripped off his uniform, removing the jacket and vest beneath until he was standing naked from the waist up in boots and breeches.

'Shang'ji Hiroshimo!' he said and drew his ancestral sword to cut a shallow wound across his chest, honouring his father.

The black-armoured warrior was approaching with three others when Makato drew a second cut.

'Shang'ji Yugeti!'

Again the blade sliced his chest, bisecting the first wound, honouring his grandfather.

He stepped forwards, entering a fighting stance with his sword held up and behind him. With the words of his native lands echoing into silence, Makato saluted the leader of the renegades.

He stood no chance, but if he was fated to die, to rejoin his ancestors then he would do it his way, on his terms.

Feeling the rough cord of his father's old braid between the fingers of his off-hand, Makato muttered a prayer to the Throne, and prepared to meet his death with honour.

Snarling at the sudden scent of fresh blood, Urgaresh signalled a halt.

'What are we waiting for?' snapped Skarh. 'Cut him down and be done with this.'

'No,' murmured Urgaresh. 'We are not animals, not yet.'

He alone advanced, dropping the bolter he had scavenged, uncoupling the clamps that bound the cuirass of his armour to his body. Greaves and vambraces hit the deck with a loud clatter, obscuring the dense thud of Urgaresh's purposeful footfalls. Gauntlets next, they clattered with the many plates used to form their fingers as they hit the floor.

'I see you, warrior,' said Urgaresh, coming to a stop and standing a few metres from the mortal. 'And accept your challenge. Never let it be said,' he snarled, revealing sharp incisors, 'that the Black Dragons are without honour.'

With the sound of tearing skin and the light patter of blood hitting metal, Urgaresh slid his bone blade from its fleshy sheath.

The man raised his chin arrogantly, or perhaps it was defiance. The subtlety of mortal gestures was often lost on the Black Dragon.

'I am Kensai Makato, grandson of Yugeti, son of Hiroshimo,' he declared without fear or hesitation.

Urgaresh smiled ugly, a shark's smile that never reached his cold, dead eyes.

'Good,' he hissed, 'I shall carve it on my sword when you are dead, so none will forget your bravery.'

He gave a stiff nod in the mortal's direction by way of salute, and attacked.

During the years he had with his father and grandfather, Makato had been well trained. Even before his tutelage in the art of Shogu was complete, he could best all of the household guard. There was not a man among the Bushiko who did not treat Makato's sword arm with respect.

Countless drills in the training yards had prepared him, under the shadow of Mount Kiamat where the Tahken Dynasts dwelled upon the mist-shrouded peaks, jealously guarding the secrets of their kaisen blades.

Makato's training could have afforded him a position in many august professions: Astra Militarum, Adeptus Arbites, Protectorate Nobilis, but in the end he chose to serve the Imperial Navy as an armsman, to maintain the generational thread.

But no training, no will of tempered iron could have prepared him for a one-on-one duel with a warrior of the renegade's calibre.

* * *

Urgaresh went in hard, spitting a curse as he lunged at the mortal. Inexplicably, the blow failed to land but he felt a hot line trace his pectoral muscle instead. The Black Dragon turned, chasing his elusive prey and crafting a slash that went high to low.

Again, the mortal avoided the blow, stepping back with the speed of a well-trained swordsman.

Urgaresh snarled, wondering if his muscles had been irrevocably atrophied from their time in cryo-stasis aboard the *Fist of Kraedor*.

'Don't worry about them,' he said, as he noticed the mortal looking over his shoulder at the three Black Dragons now standing behind him. 'You're fighting me. Don't insult my honour by suggesting treachery.'

Urgaresh attacked again, filling the corridor with his bulk and favouring an overhead cut he knew the mortal would have to block. Bone scraped against well-honed metal, drawing sparks and filling the corridor with the stink of burned ulna. The mortal avoided the swift counter, a low punch designed to cave his ribs and leave him spitting blood as his organs ruptured. Instead, he rolled aside, allowing the Black Dragon's bone blade to slide off his sword and embed itself into the deck with the force of its own momentum. Urgaresh drove into the mortal as he tried to slip past again, crushing him into the corridor wall with his shoulder even as his bone blade stuck fast.

The air was driven hard from Makato's lungs. Winded, he felt a bone fracture somewhere in his side, possibly two ribs. Despite his martial discipline, he let out a yelp of pain but managed to get past the hulking warrior whose weapon was lodged in the deck plate.

Turning on his heels, ignoring the scything agony in his side, Makato thrust two-handed and impaled the warrior's back. The blade went straight through and punched out of the warrior's chest in a welter of blood. He tried to withdraw, intending to back off and wait for another chance to counter but the warrior turned too quickly and too violently. Eighteen years of his grandfather telling him never to lose his grip on his sword was rendered meaningless as the weapon was wrenched from Makato's hands.

Fury was lending Urgaresh strength and speed now. Shutting down the pain of breaking his bone blade so he could face his opponent, ignoring the sword sticking out of his chest, he aimed a savage kick that caught the mortal off-guard and sent him sprawling down the corridor.

Dazed, chest throbbing, nerves screaming, Makato looked up at the dull lume-strips above and realised he had landed on his back. Too badly injured to get to his feet, he reached for his father's braid that had been flung from his grasp and apologised to the spirit of his grandfather for losing his sword.

Makato hoped, despite his defeat and his death, he had made them proud. He smiled at their memory, imagining the monsoon clouds over Mount Kiamat, training with his patriarchs in the brooding shadow of a storm. It had made him feel so alive, so vital.

The heavy, approaching footfalls of his opponent brought Makato back to his senses.

'Yugeti…' he croaked, 'Hiroshimo…'

Briefly mastering his warrior-rage, Urgaresh gave the mortal a second nod as he stood over him grasping a sword. It was a ceremonial piece, beautifully crafted although more like a short sword in Urgaresh's massive fist.

'Whoever those men were,' he said in a rasp, 'you honoured them.'

Raising the ceremonial sword, intending to drive it through the mortal's heart, he added, 'I hope it is fitting I use this blade to return you to them.'

The tip of the blade stopped a hand span from Makato's bloody chest.

He looked up, craning his neck to do so, trying to understand his sudden stay of execution. The renegade was locked fast, though his face showed signs of exertion. He wanted to kill Makato, but couldn't. Ice rimmed the blade in a thin veil of hoarfrost. Tiny particles of it dappled the renegade's brow and caused his breath to ghost the air in clouds of vapour.

Unable to crane his neck any longer, Makato collapsed back, closed his eyes and surrendered to unconsciousness.

Urgaresh was furious.

'Where is your honour!'

Though his eyelids were heavy with accumulated frost, he was able to look up at his enemy.

Standing in the open doorway that led to the bridge was a warrior clad in a deep green, though one arm of his battleplate was painted blue. A high metal collar rose up from his gorget around the back of his neck, where thin crackles of lighting could be seen coursing between its psycho-conductive nodes.

Two eyes blazing with cerulean blue regarded Urgaresh from a face as black as onyx. A white arrow-point beard masked the chin. Three corn-rows of close shorn hair bisected the scalp in straits of black and white.

Urgaresh felt his anger renewed as he looked up at the witch.

'Salamander…' he growled, fuelled with enough rage to break the bonds foisted upon him.

* * *

Xarko held out his upraised palm as if brandishing it could stop the Black Dragon.

It could, and did.

The warrior had broken the psychic bindings causing his initial paralysis but now faced an invisible kine-shield that sealed off the entire corridor. Only when the warrior's aggregated blows struck against it did the impacts bloom like tiny star flashes in midair.

'You'll find no passage through here...' said Xarko, but he was already beginning to show the sounds of strain in his voice.

Three more warriors joined the first, spitting curses and expletives between blows, though the psychic barrier occluded the sound of their guttural voices.

'Take him,' Xarko rasped. He was far from at full strength when he emerged from the sanctum. It was the only reason he hadn't already incinerated the infiltrators and cleansed the *Forge Hammer* of their presence.

As a pair of armsmen rushed forwards to drag Lieutenant Makato's prone form back onto the bridge, Xarko felt the absence of souls aboard the ship of the men and women slain by the Black Dragons. It made him angry, but he was also confused as to what could have brought about such an act of aggression from a Chapter the Salamanders considered as allies.

Admittedly, he had never fought alongside them personally and he had heard about the instability of their gene-seed that manifested in their bizarre osseous mutation. The monsters aboard the *Forge Hammer* bore all the hallmarks, their leader the worst afflicted.

+What do you want?+ Xarko managed to send, shocked at the pure animal rage of the leader as he brushed against the Black Dragon's thoughts. Red, an ocean of red, washed over every instinct, every emotion. Red wrath, black hate – psychically, it was like battering against a fortress gate inlaid with spikes. It hurt.

+GET OUT OF MY HEAD, WITCH!+

Another blow. The warrior's rejection of Xarko's telepathy was so violent it actually staggered the Librarian. For a moment, he feared the kine-shield would breach but marshalled enough strength to restore it.

Reason was out then. It left little other recourse.

Xarko wanted to crush them, to unleash the full potency of his gifts and rescue the ship but his earlier exertions in the fire tides had severely weakened him. With a growing sense of impotence, he realized he could hold them off but that was all. Every blow was a smack to his already bruised psyche. He didn't know how long he could last like this. The distress signal had been sent. No doubt the bridge crew were also trying to raise assistance now Xarko had broken their silence. He only hoped it would reach Agatone soon enough to matter and that a weary crew, not a massacre, would await his overdue return.

CHAPTER THIRTY

Sturndrang, the underhive of Molior

To Agatone, it felt as if they had been searching for hours for any piece of evidence that would unlock why Tsu'gan had gone this way and who had gone with him.

The archivium was vast, an immense sprawling space, a catacomb that stretched into the subterranean shadows and went on further still. According to Issak, it was an ancient Imperial repository, an information storage facility. Data within the archive appeared to go back millennia to the time of the first Great Crusade, yet the majority of it was so old that it had fallen into ruin and decrepitude. Much was also so heavily encrypted as to be almost useless.

Not long after he and Issak had entered the place, Agatone had given up trying to glean anything of import from the scribed mess strewn throughout the chamber.

'Looks relatively undisturbed,' he had muttered, only partly to himself, as he had regarded the hundreds of stacks replete with books, scrolls, slates and countless other methods of storage. Theodolites sat in dusty alcoves alongside incunabula. Oraculums and divinifiers abutted stone tablets of prognostication. Reams of parchment, trapped in humming stasis fields, ranked up next to scriptora rendered on the flensed skulls of martyrs. It stretched for what appeared to be countless metres, a cornucopia of informational data requiring an army of lex-mechanics, auto-scribes and scriveners to decode and collate.

'This will make it harder to track them,' Agatone had concluded when faced with the gargantuan repository.

Once inside the archivium, the readings from the auspex had grown patchy. It got them beyond the threshold of the labyrinth but Agatone soon attached it to his belt, settling for passively scanning the ancient chamber.

Everything was old and carried a heavy veneer of dust. Motes clung to the air, caught in slow motion free fall in the thin shafts of light that penetrated the chamber's fractured roof. Such scant light did little to lift the gloom, nor did the meagre ventilation help alleviate the choking clouds of dust they had inevitably disturbed.

Without the gifts of his transhuman ally, Issak had to blunder around in the shadows until Agatone had realised he was struggling and snapped on a lume-strip.

'Here,' he had said, passing the illuminated stick to the medicus.

In its magnesium-bright flare more details were revealed.

Entire volumes had been colonised by mildew. Mould corroded leather and wood. Data-slates were rusted, their glass screens cracked and useless. Some of the parchments and book bindings had even been gnawed upon. For though the archive was ostensibly sealed within the massive vault, the pervasive vermin of the underhive had still managed to find a nook or cranny through which to gain entry.

Judging by the crack in its main door they had seen earlier, the breach in the archivium's passive security was recent. Agatone had no doubt Tsu'gan or his companion had perpetrated it.

For long minutes he and Issak had negotiated the musty confines of the archivium in silence, the air so still and thick it subconsciously demanded a certain solemn observance. It was after a particularly lengthy stretch that Agatone finally broke this quietude.

'Watch your step, medicus.' He put out a warning hand, the other one currently occupied by his bolt pistol.

Part of the floor had fallen away, revealing a gaping dark hole into the all-consuming and ever-hungry sink of the underhive. Everything was drawn to it, or so Agatone had come to feel, its gravity impossible to resist. And the only way to stay beyond its reach was to climb, build higher and higher, new atop old and layer upon layer. Those who did not, or could not, would be dragged to this pit never to return.

Having protected the medicus this far, Agatone had no desire to lose his charge to mishap.

Issak nodded in gratitude and, as he raised the lume-strip to get a better sense of his surroundings and footing, saw something in the congested route ahead.

'Does that look fresh to you?' he asked.

Agatone followed his gaze.

One of the stacks was damaged, hacked apart to make a passage through it. Clean and raw blade marks were visible in the hard wood.

'They went this way.'

As he reached the shattered wood, Agatone paused to inspect it. He ran a hand across the split, trying to gauge what kind of weapon could have made it.

'Single hit...' he muttered, again only partially to himself. 'Bladed weapon... very wide.'

A blunted chainaxe sprang to mind. Blunted or simply exhausted of power.

Definitely Adeptus Astartes, Agatone was certain.

'Recent...' he said, concluding the analysis. He looked over his shoulder at Issak. 'We must hurry.'

Issak seemed not to hear him and was panning his lume-strip around the stacks, picking through scraps of displaced parchment.

Agatone barked at him, impatient to be moving on. 'What is it?'

'Everything looks...' Issak met the Salamander's irritated gaze, his face faintly lit in the glow of the lume-strip, 'familiar.'

'I thought you said you'd only heard of this place, not been here?' asked Agatone, frowning in consternation.

'I haven't, but I still recognise it. As if I have memories of this place, but no idea where they're from or to whom they belong.'

Agatone sniffed the air.

'Atmosphere in here is addling your mind, medicus.' The auspex began to chime softly but insistently. Agatone unclipped it and checked the screen. Then he looked up. 'Shine the strip over there,' he said to Issak, pointing to where he wanted the light.

Issak obeyed, revealing a sweeping stairway cluttered with debris but still passable.

'No more delays,' Agatone growled, sensing his prey was close, and made for the stairs.

He emerged well ahead of the medicus into an upper level. Several of the archivium's sealed stacks here had been broken open, their locks cast aside in haste.

'Here,' Agatone called down as he sighted an old lifter at the back of the room, its activation panel glowing with life. 'We rise, medicus.'

A long, metal shaft was bored down into the roof of the archivium surrounded by a lattice of reinforced plasteel. Agatone realised they must have been exploring the basement levels of the repository, where its oldest records were kept. He assumed the upper levels were no more, consumed by war, disaster or time. Only this fragment of the archivium had endured but so too had its entry shaft and the lifter that would convey them to the surface.

Breathless, Issak reached the summit of the stairway and saw what had captured the Salamander's attention.

'You want me to ride in that? It's probably at least hundreds of years old!'

Agatone smiled darkly. 'Someone has revivified it, medicus. We will follow them.'

Scowling, Issak approached Agatone who was already throwing back the lifter's security gate.

'Why do I get the impression you're enjoying this?'

'Because we are close. For good or ill, Tsu'gan is coming back with me. That's all that matters now.'

He wrenched the gate aside with a loud clatter and ushered the medicus within. When Issak was standing on the boarding plate, hands firmly gripping the guide rails, Agatone followed and closed the gate after.

'Up?' Issak hazarded, standing next to the operation panel.

Agatone nodded, craning his neck so he could look to the summit of the shaft where a faint scrap of light beckoned. 'Up, medicus.'

Issak hit the activation stud and the lifter started to rise.

CHAPTER THIRTY-ONE

Sturndrang, the underhive of Molior

They were moving. It was all Exor could tell with any degree of certainty. Consciousness was fleeting, flickering in and out like a lamp pack struggling for power.

He saw the tunnel he had crawled through, though this time he had the vague sensation of being dragged.

Then the Well and him rising, the hard breaths and grunted curses of his saviour accompanying him every metre they climbed.

It was a long climb, though Exor only experienced it in fragments.

'Where…?' he managed to croak, before blacking out.

A hard smack and hot lances of pain in his cheek brought Exor back around. His head was throbbing and it was hard to breathe. His skin burned like it was on fire. Sweat lathered his back, face and chest as his enhanced biology reacted to the severe wound he had been dealt.

'Wake up!' snapped a guttural voice.

A second blow – it hurt just as much as the first.

'Rest is for the dead,' declared the voice, 'and the weak.'

A third blow was threatened that Exor stopped.

'Cease,' he croaked, dizzy and faintly aware he was lying with his back against a wall.

Despite his ocular augmentations, the image that eventually resolved in front of him was indistinct, but he immediately recognised Zartath's snarling visage.

'The thing that caused the keening is dead. I am free of it,' he growled. 'We are going back. Our original mission is still unfinished. Agatone charged us with tracking his quarry, so that is what we are going to do.'

'I can barely stand, let alone track,' said Exor.

'You need do neither,' Zartath replied. 'You came after me when you could have left me for dead. That's twice I owe you fire-born a debt.'

'You fire-born?' Exor queried.

Zartath nodded. 'We, us. I am fire-born now.'

Though it was but a brief glimpse, Exor saw the face of the savage give way to that of the man Zartath wanted to be but which his nature would not yet allow.

'Get up,' he snarled, the beast rumbling up to the surface again.

Zartath heaved the Techmarine onto his back, grunting at the strain.

'Leave no one behind,' he said and followed the trail left by Agatone.

CHAPTER THIRTY-TWO

Sturndrang, the underhive of Molior

The scrap of light became an iris then an oval, getting wider and wider until it was a portal that led close to the surface of Sturndrang.

Agatone closed his eyes as moist, relatively fresh air from the world above washed over his face and body, cooling the underhive heat. He blind-loaded his pistol, hoping he wouldn't have to use it, then secured his combat-blade and spare clips.

'Are we going into battle again, Brother Agatone?'

'Yes, we are,' Agatone replied, opening his eyes but keeping them fixed on the portal of light.

'I thought you knew him, this…' he recalled the name, 'Tsu'gan.'

'It's because I know him that I'm preparing for a fight.' Agatone glanced down at the medicus to convey the seriousness of his next words. 'Tsu'gan won't go down easy.'

The light enveloped them and a bracing wind whipped around the lifter's carriage as its two passengers were exposed to the elements. They had emerged into an expansive shipyard, one lost to decay and neglect but still usable for embarkation.

Ostensibly still very much a part of the underhive, the shipyard was situated at the bottom of an immense and long shaft that fed all the way to the surface of Sturndrang and the void beyond.

Wrecks of old vessels, their fuselages ripped open and gutted like animal carcasses, littered a flat rockcrete plain studded with snapped

271

communication spikes and relay towers. Hangars and warehouses, their gates broken open and contents scavenged, colonised one small area of the yard and there were workshops and a freight depot. It wasn't hard to imagine this place as once being inhabited but only ghosts lingered now and the echoes of old lives.

There were bodies, not of men but some indigenous prey-creature as far as Agatone could tell. Several corpses had been left out in the open to rot. What he first believed was metal reflecting off the ambient light above were actually eyes, blinking in the shadows. More of the prey-creatures, too afraid to venture closer with the bullet-holed bodies of their kin stinking in plain view. Agatone counted eight, most of which had been split by a heavy blade not unlike the one used in the archivium. Some had simply been blasted apart by some immense and unsubtle weapon.

'Stay close to me,' Agatone murmured, eyes scanning for threats.

'Is he here?' whispered Issak.

Agatone nodded.

'How can you be–' Issak began.

The dull throb of a turbine rotor cycling up interrupted him.

Agatone snarled, and spoke between clenched teeth. 'No, not again…'

He ran, leaving Issak behind to fend for himself. He didn't call back or tell the medicus what he should do. He just ran.

Bursting from behind a hangar and through a knot of ships, Agatone emerged into a sparsely occupied area of the shipping yard to see a gun-cutter rising in the distance. Comms traffic had started crackling in his ear and he assumed some of the towers retained some small level of function. He ignored it for now, intent on the figure waiting below the rising vessel. It was muscular, broad-shouldered and wearing strange armour. It was also bald with onyx-black skin.

Agatone ran harder, pumping his arms and urging his legs to greater effort. A large chasm split off the part of the shipping yard he was on and the spur currently occupied by the figure. He realised they must have scaled it. Glancing up, Agatone saw it was the only place that offered a clear run up the shaft. He could make the leap. If the figure could do it, then so could he.

A side hatch in the ship opened, sliding left to right, and another figure appeared. Smaller, human, male. Agatone locked the details away in his memory for later use. A line was lowered and the waiting figure grasped it as it came down. It still had its back to Agatone, heedless of his rapid approach.

'I can make it…' Agatone hissed between his teeth, psychologically preparing for the jump. It was at least twenty metres. The crackling in his earbead resolved into words. A distress beacon that was coming from the *Forge Hammer*. Agatone listened, scowled.

Ahead, the figure had wrapped the line around its wrist and was signalling for the vessel to take off.

Agatone could still reach it. The chasm loomed. One solid leap and he would be on him.

The message continued – Agatone began to slow, fists clenched in slow frustration. He skidded to a halt at the edge of the abyss and could only watch as his prey was pulled into the air and away from his grasp.

The *Forge Hammer* was under attack. He had no choice but to return. Agatone activated the locator signal that would summon the waiting ships to come and retrieve him. He set off another beacon for both Lok and Clovius so they would know the hunt was over. Comms might be patchy but the beacon would get through.

'Tsu'gan...' he uttered breathlessly.

The other vessel rose, the figure disappearing within, the turbine engines carrying it far away.

Agatone found his voice, and his fury.

'TSU'GAN!'

CHAPTER THIRTY-THREE

Heletine, Canticus southern district, 'the Cairns'

Drakgaard watched his troops on the tactical display as they delved further and further into uncharted Canticus. For almost an hour, since the Targons' fateful encounter, there had been no sign of the enemy and no word from the Adepta Sororitas, either. It was as if the heretics had retreated so far into their own lines that they had emerged out of the other side of the city and into the desert. Unopposed, Drakgaard felt increasingly like he was walking into a trap but his desire to grasp what he saw as a chance at a final victory overrode his better judgement.

Little was left in reserve, only a few Cadian infantry platoons, some light vehicles, any Stormtalons that could be spared: Drakgaard was betting almost everything he had on a single, decisive attack. Sergeant V'reth's squad was too distant to recall, likewise the other Cadian regiments. Their engagements were skirmishes now, insignificant to this. The relics forgotten, Drakgaard had a taste of the enemy and was storming through a once unconquerable city in a belligerent mood. It didn't occur to him that the ragged line of his formation was brutally vulnerable, that in a single, knockout blow his enemies could destroy him and his army.

That possibility didn't occur to Drakgaard until he remembered something he had heard about Canticus, about the old districts where his enemy hid from sight, about the old tunnels, the world beneath a world, the city concealed as a bed of leaves would a huntsman's trap.

Ahead, a ridge of high ground emerged through the darkness, the edges

of its lofty buildings picked out by the Sentinels' search lamps. They had
strayed into an urban valley, a basin of land before the city rose up higher
and more dominant.

Drakgaard was turning, his Chaplain reaching the same conclusion as
his commander, their eyes meeting as a sense of impotent urgency filled
them. The order to fall back was barely formed on Drakgaard's snarling
lips before a low rumble filled the valley, swelling to a bellowing crescendo and the world beneath the world rose up to engulf them.

Zantho felt the quake before he heard or saw anything. It rumbled up
through the chassis of his Predator tank in subtle tremors that rocked his
pintle mount and told him something terrible had just happened.

As he called down for the vox to try to establish contact with Colonel
Redgage, he noticed the plumes of smoke and dust occluding part of the
city. They came from the direction of the second armour column, the
one accompanied by Kor'ad and his troops. The Dreadnought had been
en route to link up with Captain Drakgaard's forces and the bulk of the
Salamanders martial strength in Canticus.

If the two had met as planned...

'Oh, merciful Vulkan...' Zantho whispered.

Both vox-links to Kor'ad and Colonel Redgage were non-responsive.

'Drek'or,' he called down to his comms-operator below, 'establish a
column-wide link.'

After a few seconds, Drek'or replied, 'Ready now, commander.'

Zantho nodded, and addressed the entire column.

'All tank commanders, change heading to east now. I repeat, all armour
is to proceed eastwards immediately.'

A direct route would take them through the city. They would be vulnerable to ambush. They would lose vehicles to the terrain. Some, most,
would likely not make it through. Desperation had forced the commander's hand, robbing him of choice and sound tactics.

'Brother-Sergeant Zantho,' Drek'or began, 'across that rubble and debris,
we risk–'

'I know the risks. If we have to bulldoze our way through this accursed
city to reach our brothers then that is what we'll do. We have no time left
for caution. Warriors are dying, Drek'or.'

CHAPTER THIRTY-FOUR

Heletine, Canticus, inside the ravine

Redgage's Chimera was on its side and trailing smoke. One of its tracks had been torn off and the front section was ablaze. Still groggy from the crash, he could feel the heat prickling his skin and smell the burning crewmen trapped inside. Mercifully, they were dead before the flames had taken hold but the fat of their bodies crackled and spat all the same.

Blood was leaking down his face from a gash in his forehead. No doubt his helmet had saved his skull, but Redgage couldn't find it now and wasn't about to look.

A ravine had opened up in the heart of the city, a yawning abyss that swallowed the allied Imperial forces whole at the exact moment they combined assets. The concerted push by Captain Drakgaard had ended in dismal failure. As far as Redgage could tell from his smoke-choked death trap, everyone in a Cadian uniform or drake-scale battleplate was fighting for their lives.

The enemy had been waiting, goading Drakgaard just enough to keep him eager. Weeks of bitter attritional fighting had led to this moment, though why the plan had been enacted now was anyone's guess at this point.

Redgage struggled from the half-crushed cupola hatch, surprised at his own clarity. Perhaps his imminent death had ramped up his situational awareness in an effort to save him. Survival was really all that was left to him now, though judging by what was going on below the Salamanders weren't ready to capitulate yet.

He had heard that said about them, that they refused to admit defeat, willing to fight in the face of impossible odds.

Though he could discern little through the smoke and heat haze, Redgage ventured only two possible outcomes: retreat or destruction.

He crawled out through the narrow hatch on his stomach, dragging his wounded leg behind him. It hurt like the damned Eye, but reminded him he was still alive and kept him awake so he could try to stay that way. Something snagged his belt on the way out and he reached down to find out what it was. He touched skin and looked back into the murky hatch to see what appeared to be Hansard's fingers grasping at him.

Incredibly, Redgage's gunner had survived.

'Hold on, Hansard,' Redgage told him. 'I've got you,' he said, grabbing the man's wrist and heaving even as he lurched from the cupola himself.

Hansard came loose, but only from the elbow. The rest of the poor fool was still in the tank, severed from his limb in the crash.

Redgage gaped at Hansard's forearm, distraught, before casting it down in disgust and muttering a prayer for the man's soul as he reconciled himself to an uncomfortable truth. Of his crew, he alone lived.

Free of the wreck, coughing up black tar from his lungs as the smoke intensified, Redgage limped away into cover.

Dirt and debris from the collapsed city block was strewn all around him. Some of his comrades had been crushed by it. He had his back against a pillar and was trying to look up through the grey clouds at the summit of the ravine. It was a hard climb, but even with his leg it was doable.

Redgage started to move. If asked, he would not have described himself as a corpulent man. Several decades had passed since he had taken his physical training seriously, though, and he wished he had recently put more time in on the endurance yard.

Very few Cadian tanks had avoided the sinkhole. Those that did stood proudly on the edge of the ravine, speaking loudly through their cannons. Less than half the Thunderers and Demolishers Redgage had brought with him remained. The rest were broken and on fire like his Chimera. Clambering up the ruined slope, Redgage fixed a point in his mind where a stout wall of armour still resisted and aimed for it. So intent was he on reaching salvation that he failed to notice the cultist until it was almost upon him.

Dressed in whatever rags they had worn when forfeiting their immortal souls, cult worshippers had poured into the ravine like vermin. Driven to the point of desperate fanaticism, ordinary men and women had become murderers by the insidious promises of Chaos.

Salvation, status, vengeance, retribution, a man's sins were varied enough that the gods of Ruin knew what to offer in return for eternal servitude. Moral corruption was, by its nature, a choice. Every cultist scrambling into the ravine had made theirs – some, Redgage noticed with disgust, were even wearing ragged Cadian uniforms.

One such traitor leapt at him now, combat knife already bloodied and hungry for more.

Redgage had enough time to throw up his arms in defence and managed to seize his assailant by the wrist before the frothing trooper bore the colonel down beneath his weight.

Hot breath, rancid with halitosis, washed over Redgage and he fought not to gag. The blade nicked his cheek like a wasp sting and he roared to push it back again.

Eyes sunken, hair falling from his scalp in clumps, the trooper looked like he was rad-poisoned. But it wasn't radiation, it was the taint. Redgage barely recognised the man as one of his own. Only the uniform gave weight to the lie that all the Cadians had stayed loyal or died to remain so.

'Traitor!' spat Redgage, kneeing his assailant in the chest and using his anger to throw him off. Seemingly fuelled by unnatural vigour, the trooper sprang to his feet and was about to lunge again when Redgage drew his service pistol from its black leather holster and shot the man dead.

A second cultist a few metres away was lining up a rocket tube when the colonel spotted him. Steadying his aim with his free hand, Redgage killed him too. He executed a third who was scrambling up the slope below. He wanted to kill them all, to vent the anger and the horrific sense of frustration threatening to unman him. So many slain – no amount in return could balance those scales. The accountancy of war didn't work like that and Redgage knew it.

His brief, but frenzied, bravura brought the attention of others and made the colonel regret his lapse in composure. For after the deluge of cultists had stormed the ravine, the genuine warriors of the heretic cause had shown themselves.

Black Legion, the name held terror for most who heard it. For the men and women of Cadia, especially those who stood watch at the Cadian Gate, it promoted a stern but resigned steadfastness.

Said to descend from Horus himself, the sons of old Cthonia were rightly feared throughout the galaxy, at their head a leader so venerable he could remember the days of the primarchs. Such history, millennia old, was little more than fiction for those who lived in the Time of Ending, but not by him, nor his sworn warriors.

Redgage watched as three hulking, armoured bodies muscled through the rubble. Each had drawn a chainblade, their impassive faceplate masks unable to convey their relish of the kill. Skulls hung from their breastplates on spiked chains. Human hair dyed red served as topknots for their horned helms. Eager, murderous fire blazed within their flat, rectangular eye slits.

Redgage knew he couldn't outrun them. He did the only thing he could – he levelled his sidearm at one of the power-armoured monsters and declared with more courage than he felt, 'Come on then, scum!'

Then fired.

The bright flare of laser discharge lit up the slope for a few seconds as Redgage drained the pistol's power pack. Barring a few scorch marks, the warriors emerged undamaged and undeterred. More than that in fact, they were laughing at him.

Lost somewhere during the crash, Redgage had no close combat weapon so he picked up a length of pipe instead, and tried to prop himself up against the rubble so he could swing it.

'Bernadetta, my love...' he whispered to the wife he would never see again, 'I am so sorry.'

The growl of hungry chain-teeth filled his senses as Redgage faced down the three traitors.

Uselessly brandishing the pipe, Redgage prepared his soul for the end. The prayer died in his mouth as the first warrior evaporated in a ball of actinic blue light. The others turned at once, recognising a worthy foe.

Huge, imposing and horrendously powerful, Kor'ad strode amongst them. His plasma cannon was recharging for another burst, but the Dreadnought still had his thunder hammer and smashed a second warrior aside with it.

The third went in close, shouting for reinforcements in his own crude language, aiming for the Dreadnought's weak points with his chainblade.

Sparks spitting from a ruptured power cable in his casket, Kor'ad backed up and knocked the warrior down with a punch from his massive fist. Then he quickly stepped forwards and crushed the traitor underfoot.

Two more were coming, and Kor'ad shifted his massive bulk into their path.

'Rise, colonel,' he bellowed through his vox-emitters. 'Return to your men.'

The reinforcements looked tougher than their predecessors. Both were clad in hefty suits of war-plate, larger and more formidable than power armour. As one of the warriors stood firm, he unleashed a long-barrelled cannon. Redgage threw himself down as a hail of shells filled the air. Kor'ad bore the brunt of it, staggering as several dense rounds pierced his thick armour. There was no respite.

In the wake of the salvo, the second warrior drove into the Dreadnought, chainfist swinging. Kor'ad reacted on instinct, striking a glancing blow that took off the warrior's helm and sent him sprawling. Beneath the blood and the mass of shorting cables, the warrior wore a face of flayed skin.

Kor'ad advanced on him when a second burst ripped from the long-barrelled cannon. This time the Dreadnought could angle his body without fear of Redgage being hit and avoided most of the shell storm. Turning back, aware the warrior with the chainfist was coming at him, Kor'ad fired off a bolt from his plasma cannon and the Black Legion shooter disappeared from sight.

Dead or smashed back down the slope by the impact, Redgage didn't know. He saw the other warrior hit Kor'ad again though, and heard the ominous clunk of a grenade being attached to the Dreadnought's casket.

The detonation came seconds later as Kor'ad's plasma cannon exploded, taking his left arm with it and severing the cables in the right so the Dreadnought dropped his thunder hammer. Kor'ad had enough power left to reach for the unhelmeted warrior and crush his skull in his fist before throwing him bodily into the air and back down into the ravine.

Redgage had never seen a Dreadnought kneel; he didn't know they could until that moment. Close up, he realised it wasn't just the arm that had been damaged when the krak grenade had gone off. Part of Kor'ad's casket was split too, and he could see the remnants of the warrior the Dreadnought once was languishing within.

He was just a man inside, a withered torso and head, whose flesh was puckered with cables and venting fluid, a war-maker no more.

'What can I do? Tell me,' Redgage pleaded, his knowledge of Dread-nought repair woefully lacking.

Kor'ad was bloody, struggling for breath. Dying. Without his vox-emitters, he sounded frail and rasping.

'You've stood with me... colonel,' said Kor'ad haltingly. 'That is... enough. Run... save your–'

The whine of rocket propulsion cut off the end of the sentence, followed by the ear-shattering explosion of the missile striking the Dreadnought's back. There was a scream, half mechanised through the emitters, half croaked by the failing lungs of the withered corpse entombed in his dying machine.

Kor'ad fell face forward. His back was a smoking ruin. The Venerable was dead, slain by an honourless blow. Redgage thrust out his pistol, searching for a target but it was an empty gesture. His enemy was lost to him through smoke and fire. He paused, holstering his pistol as he regarded the wreck of his saviour, once so formidable but now laid irrevo-cably low.

Then he ran, scrambling, up the slope.

CHAPTER THIRTY-FIVE

Heletine, nearing the border of Solist

The screaming began about forty kilometres out from Solist. Sitting quietly in the gunship's troop hold, Stephina had the vox frequency switched to that of their so-called allies. In that moment, surrounded by the solemn figures of her Seraphim whose heads were bowed in prayer and guilt, she wondered if that word could really be used for betrayers.

As abhorrent as that truth was, it was also irrefutable.

Sister Helia went to cut the link but Stephina's raised hand stopped her.

'No,' she uttered flatly. It was the first time any of them had spoken since the vox-feed had been opened.

'We need not listen to that,' said Helia, her seraphic appearance at odds with her obvious discomfort.

Stephina looked up to meet her fellow Sister Superior's gaze.

'Does it bother you, my Sister, to hear their cries of pain and curses against our Order?'

The voices conveyed by the vox not only screamed their death agonies, they also vowed revenge upon the Ebon Chalice and the daughters of the Emperor who had chosen to abandon them.

'Craven men will oft lay blame at the feet of the blameless,' Helia replied.

Stephina quickly got to her feet, causing several of her fellow Seraphim to look up from their devotions.

'Your own words betray you, Sister, and barely convince yourself!' she snapped, but then calmed down. It would not be proper to act thusly in front of the others. 'We have both seen them fight. They are not craven men.' She let that hang in the air for a moment to gauge Helia's reaction and see if she dared refute it.

Helia's mouth shaped a response but the words died on her lips, and she shook her head.

'No.'

'Nor are they savages, deserving of savage treatment.'

Helia lowered her gaze and let out a resigned breath.

'Our orders come from the preceptor, she who is the will of the–'

'The will of the Throne, yes I am well aware,' said Stephina, reaching out to gently lift Helia's chin. She spoke with a quiet intensity. 'Whatever work Canoness Angerer is engaged in cannot be worth the souls of thousands of Imperial servants, the very angels of the Emperor Himself!'

The vox-feed cut to static as whoever was broadcasting the signal could do so no longer. A brief silence followed.

Helia's eyes were pleading, tearful.

'We must have faith in Angerer's plan…'

'Even if that plan is to leave our allies to slaughter?'

Stephina turned away, not waiting for an answer as she contacted the transport's pilot.

'Sister,' she began with authority, 'we are turning around.'

There was a short pause as the pilot tried to comprehend the order.

'Superior?'

'Do not question. Obey. Make heading for Canticus at all speed. This is my order: you are my Seraphim. Let it not be said that we too abandoned our God-Emperor sworn honour.'

The vessel slowed with the dull roar of turbo fans, banking sharply as the pilot changed course.

When Stephina had relayed the same order to Avensi and Cassia in the second transport, who were both wise enough not to argue with their commanding superior, she addressed the hold.

'Know who you are,' she said, shouting above the engines as they pushed hard and complained loudly. 'Know your purpose is divine and that there is no greater expression of faith or loyalty to the Throne than in battle against the enemies of the Ecclesiarchy. We are less than forty souls aboard these two ships, but we will fight as more than four hundred.

'Our allies are dying on the battlefield, our promise to them ash in the wind. Take up your arms and follow me. The righteous have no fear. A holy wrath descends upon the perfidious and the traitor – it falls on ebon wings, your wings. I would have them occlude the very sun.'

Stephina gritted her teeth, stirred by her own rhetoric.

'If any here believe we follow an unjust path, that I lead you to damnation in the eyes of Throne and God-Emperor, speak and let us all hear your condemnation.'

None did.

And none looked down to their feet anymore, either. Every Seraphim aboard the vessel had raised their eyes, blazing with holy fury.

Betrayers no longer, they would be avengers and honour their oaths to the Salamanders.

'Canticus...' Stephina snarled through clenched teeth. 'Blood and fire await us!'

CHAPTER THIRTY-SIX

Heletine, Canticus, inside the ravine

The Serpentia moved through the ravine as one, fighting all quarters and surrounding Drakgaard as they went. Elysius was amongst them, roving between warriors and shouting canticles of retribution against the traitor. In the tight scrum of bodies slowly filling the ravine, resolve was everything. The Chaplain used his gifts to strengthen that resolve with hate. If vitriol was a blade, his would have cut through power armour.

The earth had collapsed beneath them, demolished by charges set against fragile foundations by the heretics. The explosives had exposed the weakened surface of Canticus, upon which were built its temples, shrines and domiciles, dropping the majority of the Salamanders into the catacombs below.

This subterranean world was vast, only hinted at in maps and impossible to accurately chart through geological survey and sensorium probes from low orbit. Tunnels threaded the catacombs like arterial veins, leading to vast chambers and antechambers where the bulk of the heretic forces had mustered and lain in wait. Goaded like fools, the Imperial army had been drawn into the trap based on the belief that the enemy was defeated. It had merely been saving its killer blow for that moment.

Recalled dimly through the smoke and dust, Elysius saw an immense sinkhole open up. As they were at the vanguard of the army, the fire-born fell first, dragged down against their will as the dirt and rock piled on. Then came the tanks, an entire company of Cadian heavy armour raining down on the heads of the fragile infantry like a vehicular landslide.

After the first blow, the enemy made itself known. Cultists swarmed from the ridge, weapon emplacements were established. Solid shot, las and shells descended in a storm.

Most of the Kasrkin were dead, and those that had survived were getting picked off as they tried to haul their severely wounded captain back up the slope. Half the Cadian tanks were lying broken and on fire at the bottom of the ravine in a slurry of unrecognisable machine parts.

The fire-born held their ground. No Salamander would ever retreat, unless in extremis. Even then they would solemnly lay down their lives if it meant denying victory to the enemy, self-sacrificial to the end. It was a bitter, self-destructive creed but it had hardened them well.

Few remained though – Devastators, some remnants from Tactical. There was no sign of Kor'ad or his brother Dreadnoughts. Zantho and the armour was cut off from the main army.

Escorted by the Serpentia, Elysius surveyed Drakgaard's operational assets and knew they were vastly outmatched. They had got so much wrong, made so many mistakes it might not be possible to rectify.

It wasn't the fall that had killed the fire-born, it was what was waiting for them inside the ravine that opened up beneath them. This was the third blow.

Not only Black Legion, but a massive host of sworn Renegade Astartes. A veritable army of deserters and civilians turned cultist served as cannon fodder, weak but armed and numerous. One man alone with a stubber was barely worthy of notice. A mob armed with cudgels and blades could similarly be dismissed, but a horde of thousands arrayed with rocket tubes and heavy cannon... Such an enemy posed a genuine threat, even to Adeptus Astartes.

It was the fanatic masses that attacked first, a second host spilling from the tunnels to join up with those scrambling down the slopes of the ravine. Only once the dregs had been engaged, the fire-born committed to what they had seen as a desperate but still costly ambush, had Black Legion emerged from the tunnels.

Then the real killing began.

The attack was well-crafted despite its savagery, intended to split the Salamanders up and destroy them piecemeal.

So far, it was working but not without resistance.

Elysius caved in a renegade's skull with his mace, splitting it apart in a shower of crumpled armour plate and bone. He barely paused to register the stink of hyper-cauterising blood caused by the energy surge from the powered crozius, instead turning to see Tul'vek die.

A chainsword was lodged in the warrior's throat. Dismayed, Elysius reached out for him but the churning blade had chewed through enough flesh and sinew to nearly remove the Serpentia's head. As Tul'vek fell, gouting blood, Elysius snatched his banner so it wouldn't touch the ground.

Kaladin slew Tul'vek's killer, coring the Black Legion warrior through the torso with his melta. The dragon mouth of the weapon roared as he fired, given voice by Kaladin's anguish.

'Brother Her'us…' Elysius called above the battle din, causing the Champion to pause in his hammer swings and look up.

Elysius gestured to the gap in their defensive circle left by Tul'vek.

Her'us nodded and took the dead banner bearer's place to close it.

Apothecary Sepelius had already departed with the injured Sergeant Bar'dak. At least, Elysius considered bitterly, there would be someone left to harvest the Chapter's due. So, without Tul'vek, Drakgaard's command squad numbered six warriors.

They fought like sixty.

Drakgaard led them, hacking and cutting with his kaskara. There was a certain savagery to the captain's blows, a wild abandon brought about through desperation. In spite of everything, he wanted this victory, believing solely through force of will and aggression he could still obtain it. Whatever injuries blighted his once strong body were forgotten during the ferocity of close combat. Though not skilled beyond any expected level for a ranking fire-born, Drakgaard was tenacious and hard to kill. His wound-ravaged flesh was testament to that.

He took blows that would finish lesser men, shrugging them off and gutting his surprised opponents with typical brutality. A kaskara was a noble weapon, a blade forged by artisans. Drakgaard had afforded it every flourish but wielded it like a slaughter-man's cleaver, and to great effect.

'We are dying in this grind,' Elysius voxed to the captain during a brief respite.

From its initial sprawling melee, the battle had broken up into smaller but still brutal skirmishes. Occasionally, two or more would merge and a larger fight would erupt only to break apart again when warriors were slain or routed.

At the nadir the ravine smoke and settling dust from the earth collapse reduced visibility, and with enemies in such close proximity to one another, combat was dominated by short-range firefights and hand-to-hand engagements. Farther out, where rubble and the shells of tanks littered the slopes, artillery from both sides was being employed to even the odds. Shell impacts from the heavy guns sent plumes of earth and bodies skyward, adding to the horrendous carnage.

'Let the screw turn,' Drakgaard replied, forging onward through the chaos, 'let it gnaw our bones, Chaplain. I won't yield until I am dead!'

'Ur'zan, listen to–'

Drakgaard cut the feed, his violent threshing of the enemy unabated.

Elysius could respect a death wish – it spoke to the Promethean Creed – but not one that could lose a war and kill dozens of fire-born into the bargain. He briefly clutched Her'us's shoulder guard. The Chaplain was close enough to speak to the Company Champion without the aid of comms.

'Stay close to him. He dies and I'll be the one who brings you to account.'

Her'us nodded. He parried a chainaxe with the haft of his hammer before throwing the renegade back and obliterating the right side of his torso. Blood flecked his draconic faceplate as the traitor's flank crumpled, ruddying the inlaid ivory teeth of the helm.

'On my honour, Chaplain,' Her'us replied when he was clear of foes. 'I die before he falls.'

A Company Champion's place in battle was by the side of his captain. Her'us fought on Drakgaard's left, where their different fighting styles would complement each other. Zetok positioned on the captain's right, shoulder to shoulder. Zetok was a pyre warden and protected Drakgaard's off-hand with his storm shield. The three of them formed the Serpentia's vanguard, cutting through the throng of heretics and supported by their brothers in formation behind them.

A bolt-round struck Zetok's shield square on and would have staggered him if not for Vervius leaning in from behind with his shoulder to help set his brother back on his feet.

'Hold as one,' said Vervius, and shot a sustained burst from his plasma pistol. Crackling spheres of energy left an actinic smear in their wake, indiscriminately rupturing flesh and ceramite.

Having recovered his composure, Zetok drove forwards again, and the circle of Serpentia hit hard into the Black Legion ranks that were swelling with every second as more warriors poured from the tunnels with their cultist retinues.

Warriors of like-for-like skill and ferocity met and were bloodied.

Tseg'un broke apart a traitor's breastplate with a power fist, crushing bone and organs, as another warrior lodged a chainblade in his clavicle. His cry of agony drew the attention of Her'us, who lashed out at Tseg'un's attacker and split the warrior's chainblade apart in a storm of broken teeth. Elysius finished the traitor with a crushing blow from his power glove.

'Ave Imperator…' he snarled breathlessly.

They had been fighting for several minutes already, but had barely begun. More were coming.

Tseg'un lived but was badly wounded. His part of the circle was now weakened.

Elysius moved alongside him to bolster Tseg'un's strength and resolve as further enemies loomed out of the half darkness.

Drab, grey smoke choked the battlefield. If it was day above, no one within the ravine would have known it. The sun was utterly eclipsed. Fire illuminated the oily clouds, spat in sharp flashes from promethium-based weapons or rendered in dull smudges from slowly burning vehicles.

Onagar lit his own flame and it cast him and the other Serpentia in a feverish wash of amber. He was the squad's pyroclast, an old term from the Heresy War, since fallen out of fashion but still remembered by some in the Chapter. Burns ravaged Onagar's exposed skin, making it leathern and tough. He was gnarled like a petrified tree but scowled with an arsonist's pleasure as he spewed hellfire from his Nocturne-forged flamer. Silhouettes, smears of dirty brown and grey, stumbled in the blaze. Onagar laughed as they seemed to shrink inside the fire. His dark humour was cut short when a bolt-round took apart half his cheek and battle-helm. Retribution was meted out by Kaladin who reduced the renegade to a noisome slurry with his melta.

'How do I look?' Onagar slurred to his avenging brother, bone visible through his ruined and bloody cheek. It was a miracle he could still speak.

'Ugly,' replied Kaladin.

Onagar laughed, a reedy, guzzling sound. 'I was always ugly.'

For every warrior slain, another two took his place along with an entourage of cultists that came on in deranged hordes. Zetok hewed at them with a butcher's grace, cleaving limbs from torsos and severing necks with a drake-fanged axe. On Nocturne it was a called a 'burning blade' because the edge glowed hotter than a furnace and fire licked its savage teeth.

One cultist violently combusted as the axe touched him, the fire of his immolation spreading to his confederates. Only the Traitor Space Marines, girded by their power armour, weathered the blaze and were able to engage.

In seconds, Zetok was hard pressed and on the defensive. Beyond the edge of his storm shield, which was being hammered by mauls and chain-teeth, he saw a Havoc in black war-plate stand to and steady a missile launcher.

'Brace!' Zetok roared, throwing back his attackers so he could thrust forwards with his shield and meet the threat.

Elysius was ahead of him, in both reaction and commitment.

The incendiary streaked from the launcher tube, flying scarcely ten metres before it struck a shimmering barrier of force generated by the Chaplain's rosarius. It dissipated in a firestorm, throwing hot orange tendrils around Elysius's protective dome and scattering metal shrapnel from the casing that struck the field and bounced off harmlessly.

In three strides, Drakgaard reached the Havoc and struck him down before he could reload or draw a weapon.

The Serpentia quickly reformed but had to wade deep into the enemy's ranks to do so.

Somewhere amidst the carnage, Kaladin went down. Elysius missed whatever it was that had killed him. Only the stark evidence of an indent-rune turning crimson in his tactical display told the Chaplain they had lost another.

With so much black armour surrounding the chosen of Drakgaard's warriors, the deaths came swiftly after that.

Zetok, his shield arm severed at the wrist. He parried the first thrust, blood spitting from his wounded stump, but the second took him in the side and chewed up his body. A third cut parted his gorget and took his head. The three traitors who had killed him then hacked apart his body.

Onagar died by immolation, his promethium tank struck by a tragically unlucky ricochet. He went up in a flare of magnesium-white before collapsing in a bone-charred and fire-blackened heap. The explosion blew the heart out of the Serpentia, smashing the defensive circle and scattering them. Mercifully, it also threw back their enemies.

Elysius felt his body lifted by the pressure wave, the heat and impact force registering in violent warning spikes on his armour's integrity display. It was breached in several places but ultimately it had saved his life.

Drakgaard was nearby, sprawled onto his front but rising heavily onto his hands and knees. With a trembling hand he ripped off the faceplate to his battered helmet and spat up a thick gobbet of blood. Elysius saw his face through the smoke and heat haze. It was pained, Drakgaard's old scars and permanently snarling mouth contorted in a rictus of agony.

The Chaplain was about to call out to him when something lumbering and swathed in feverish heat loomed though the grey fog. It moved silently, despite its bulk, and Elysius realised he had been temporarily deafened by the blast.

'Ur'zan!' he cried, but felt like he was shouting into the void. He stumbled, weak in his left knee, and saw the greave was split, the kneecap reduced to a broken crevice thick with partially clotted blood.

Drakgaard was still on his knees, but had dragged off his ruined helm. The scalp beneath was also scarred, and scraps of badly healed flesh colonised his skull. A trickle of dark fluid ran from his left ear.

'Ur'zan!' Elysius was on his feet, staggering as if in slow motion towards his captain. He couldn't see Her'us. He caught Vervius in his peripheral vision, reaching for the fallen banner that was streaked with mud and gore.

Up ahead, beyond Drakgaard but closing, was a monstrous form. It was part flesh, part machine, bone plate scabbing over metal, sinew and exposed viscera entwined around pistons and cables. A single black ivory horn sprouted from its back, arcing between two fluted exhaust pipes.

Insane and screaming, the warrior slaved to the diabolical engine glared out from an aperture just above the torso that glistened wetly and was studded with sharp teeth.

The warrior's skull was shrunken and emaciated, his vitality surrendered to fuel the machine. It was no noble Dreadnought, no venerable Space Marine clad for all time in an armoured war-casket. Those in service to the Omnissiah called it abomination. Elysius knew it by it a different name.

'Helbrute!' Sound returned in a cacophony of pain, the warning shout and the battlefield noise rushing back to the Chaplain in a flood.

Still dazed, hurt and bleeding, Drakgaard turned and saw the danger. He rose, scrabbling up his sword from the dirt and brandishing it at the monster.

Elysius cast around for Her'us, even as he staggered to Drakgaard's side. He found the Champion surrounded by a growing circle of corpses, whirling around his thunder hammer in reaping arcs. Vervius stood beside him, holding up the banner. Defiance like that, so Elysius believed, was uniquely Nocturnean.

Elysius couldn't help either of them now, so he stayed with Drakgaard.

'You might get your wish,' said the Chaplain, bitterly. 'Death before surrender.'

Drakgaard raised his sword, saluting to the mindless Helbrute as it crossed the last few metres to them.

'Would you have it any other way, brother?'

Elysius could not suppress a fatalistic grin. His power fist might crack the abominable war machine's armour but he and the captain were running on reserves of strength.

'I would not, brother.'

They were not, and would likely never be, friends but the war on Heletine had made them better allies. Elysius was glad they would face the Helbrute as such. It was something traitors would never truly understand.

Before they could engage the monster, a pair of hellfire missiles streaked out of the gloom on burning contrails. They struck the Helbrute's centre mass simultaneously and tore the wretched machine apart in a spray of gore and metal. Only its smoking feet, severed at the shins, remained. The rest was scattered across the battlefield.

Elysius craned his neck as the roar of stabiliser jets overhead broke through the clamour of the battle. He looked up to see the descending shadow of a gunship, its embarkation hatch lowered and warriors standing upon the ramp.

Drakgaard collapsed alongside him, finally succumbing to his wounds.

'Death from above...' he rasped, flat on his back. As Elysius rushed to his side, Drakgaard laughed at the Wyverns taking flight.

CHAPTER THIRTY-SEVEN

Heletine, Canticus, inside the ravine

Iaptus was first onto the Thunderhawk's ramp, his thunder hammer gripped firmly as the turbine engines of his jump pack started to ignite. His weapon's crackling energies illuminated the mouth of the troop hold, casting the eight warriors waiting to disembark in a cerulean glow.

Smoke shrouded, littered with bodies and the burning wrecks of tanks, the ravine would seem a daunting prospect to many soldiers. It was meat and drink to the Wyverns.

'We are outnumbered and cannot be everywhere,' Iaptus shouted to his warriors above battlefield noise that had intensified with the dropping of the ramp. He took a further step upon it. 'Defend Brother-Captain Drakgaard and Brother-Chaplain Elysius. We have orders to effect their egress from this chaos.'

'We are retreating?' Arrok ventured, foolishly.

Va'lin exchanged a look with Dersius who rested a hefty gauntlet on Arrok's shoulder.

'No, brother. But we need to regroup. We can't do that if our commander is knee-deep in enemy dead, swallowed in that mess below.'

'We are the ones that are going to be swallowed, Arrok,' said Naeb with ironic cheer.

Va'lin exchanged another glance with him, but Naeb shrugged unapologetically.

'Wyverns…' Iaptus declared, 'on breath of fire!'

He lifted his hammer and was about to make the leap when the gunship's left side exploded. It pitched immediately, throwing Iaptus and the rest of the Wyverns against the right-hand side of the hold. Through a ragged gap in the fuselage, Va'lin could see the left wing had been sheared off and the engine was trailing smoke. Fire lapped at the edges of the tear, guttering with the passage of air as Brother Orcas piloted them through it at speed, whilst trying to keep them aloft.

Iaptus got on the vox. 'Orcas!'

The reply was halting and marred by static.

'Rocket hit… Attempting to correct, but we've sustained critical damage. Don't think I can… bring her back, sergeant. Suggest emergency disembark.'

The vox went dead as the communications array failed. Klaxons were wailing inside the troop hold, which was washed in crimson emergency lighting.

'Everyone out,' roared Iaptus as the high-pitch whine of the engines told him they were descending fast and about to crash. 'Now!'

The ramp had jerked back up a fraction when they were hit, so he kicked it back down with his boot and began to usher his warriors out.

Arrok went first – he and Xerus had been right behind Iaptus in formation. Then Dersius and Ky'dak jumped, the latter taking off from the ramp at a furious sprint. Va'lin quickly lost them to the smoke. He was next in line with Naeb and barrelled through the open hatch as flames from the burning engine washed across his sight.

Va'lin broke through and hit a bank of thick smoke that occluded optics so he switched to auto-senses. Naeb was gone, but he kept a track of him and the others on the tactical display flashing upon on his right retinal lens. Six were free of the gunship, in the wind. Two were still aboard, Vo'sha and Iaptus.

A missile burst through the cloud layer, an instinctive twist of his body saving Va'lin from its warhead and a short flight. He turned, head facing downwards towards the ground and looking back up. He had yet to ignite his pack in case the enemy had heat-seekers trained on the sky. The missile was still visible, arcing towards the stricken gunship with rocket-fuelled intensity. Va'lin saw the future and felt a cold ball of ice rise up into his gullet. He had one attempt to shoot the missile down. His flamer was no use. Preferring his sidearm, he ripped the bolt pistol from its holster and took aim. Buffeted by the wind and the force of acceleration as he reached terminal velocity, his hand was shaking. The missile was moving fast, closing on the gunship.

Va'lin fired off a three-round burst, hoping the spread would improve his chances.

Two shells missed, but a third hit the target. Va'lin's triumph turned to anguish when he saw the bolt-shell detonate but only throw the missile slightly off course. It struck the gunship in the ramp instead of the underside, tearing off the hatch and throwing the two warriors who were about to leap out back into the hold. The gunship pinwheeled, plummeting now as it spun around prow to aft, trailing fire. Thick black smoke poured from its fuselage and engines, choking the hold and enveloping the gunship in a dirty pall. The glacis protecting the cockpit was shattered and exposed to the elements. As he fell, still yet to ignite his engines and watching in morbid fascination, Va'lin thought he saw Orcas on fire, wrestling with the controls.

The gunship disappeared from view, only to return a few moments later as it struck the slope and went up in a massive fireball.

Va'lin crushed down his guilt and tore his gaze away. Smoke and cloud parted, and the ground came rushing up to meet him. He fed all power to the jump pack's turbines, barely arresting his descent in time with a huge burst of ignition.

He landed hard, buckling at the knees, and heard his powered joints protest at the rough treatment. Then he was moving, shooting at targets with his bolt pistol. A cultist's head exploded. A renegade armoured in heliotrope purple went down with two shell holes in his torso.

Despite the frenetic chaos of the battle around him, Va'lin realised he had landed far from the intended drop zone. He couldn't see his fellow Wyverns, let alone Drakgaard or Elysius. They were scattered, thrown apart as their Thunderhawk had pitched and yawed in its death throes. Though the smoke cover at ground level wasn't as thick as it was in the sky, the ravine was massive and overrun with clashing warriors from both sides. He was alone, though not for long.

Having witnessed Va'lin's descent and subsequent arrival, a swathe of heretics were converging on him led by a warrior of the Black Legion.

Two warbands, Va'lin realised, recalling the conflicting sigils he had seen during the Canticus street battle when the Wyverns had lost Sor'ad. An alliance explained the sheer numbers of troops the heretics had in reserve. They had been waiting here, under the earth, to attack. A rudimentary trap. It was sprung by a desire to end the war quickly and inspired by the erroneous belief that the heretics were all but defeated. Blind, without proper reconnaissance, the Salamanders had rushed into an unknown part of Canticus and denied all of their methodical instincts into the bargain.

As the heretics came for him, Va'lin brought to mind the words of Zen'de.

He who knows himself, knows truth. He who knows himself and acts to his own strengths shall deny all lies that might bring about weakness.

A pity they had not heeded their own natures, but it was too late now.

Va'lin stowed his sidearm and brought up his flamer. A long, fiery plume ignited on the air and struck the baying mob with enough force to knock down the heretics who burned horribly.

Not the Black Legionnaire, though. He emerged from the conflagration wreathed in fire and spitting curses to salve his obvious pain. Two dark eyes glared out from a pallid-looking face etched with the eight-pointed star of Chaos and promised pain and suffering for the Salamander.

Clenched in both gauntleted hands, the warrior hefted a flanged mace that exuded a strange, aetheric mist. Images formed and collapsed in that mist, the faces of the damned and the claws of their tormentors. He would need to be wary of the mace.

The flamer would be useless in close combat and didn't look like it would stop the Black Legionnaire. Va'lin drew his sidearm and gladius, letting the flamer fall. That made the warrior smile, though his eyes shone with murderous intent, and he saluted the Salamander for his reckless bravura.

'Vorshkar,' uttered the traitor, nodding to Va'lin.

He had surged through the flame storm like a mad dog but now gave his name as part of some strange honour ritual. Va'lin had heard of the capricious nature of the warriors of the old Legions, those poor souls trapped out of time, their sanity gnawed away by daemons but had never experienced it before. Regardless, he answered the warrior with the same contempt he would any traitor.

'Death to the slaves of Ruin,' he spat, and adopted a fighting posture, leaning forwards in preparation for a small burst of ignition. A sudden attack might provide a sorely needed edge.

The warrior's smile faded. His reply in Gothic was hard for him to form but he delivered it with certitude and malice.

'Yours will be slow and lasting, Vulkan's son.'

Va'lin gunned the throttle, boosting into an abrupt but rapid charge. His transhuman mind had already analysed the traitor's defences and found his face and neck to be his weak points. The Salamander aimed for them, firing off a snap shot into the warrior's torso to distract from the intended killing stroke with his gladius.

But where the blade should have cut through jugular and carotid artery, it only sheared through air. The warrior had evaded him, moving faster than the jump pack's propulsion capacity was able to move Va'lin.

A blow resounded against Va'lin's shoulder, crumpling his guard and carrying on into his jump pack. The left jet turbine exploded, ripping apart much of the protective housing and spraying it over the side of Va'lin's armoured face. Shrapnel from the sundered intake vent embedded in the side of his battle-helm crazing the visual feed from the left retinal lens and effectively ruining depth perception.

A second blow hammered against Va'lin's ribs, denting the plastron and shearing the jump pack's quick-release strap. Pain resounded through his body, felt in his shoulder and chest at once, so acute they vied for dominance on the scale of Va'lin's agony.

He was sunk to one knee before he had even managed to raise his sword weakly in defence.

Vorshkar's mace was invested with the sorcery of the warp but it did not just grant him deadly potency, it also imbued the warrior with preternatural speed. It was a boon that Va'lin had no power to counter. He reacted but it was as if he had been drawn into a well of extreme low gravity and every movement was slow and laboured.

A third blow shattered Va'lin's standing knee, breaking his armoured pad apart and sending him crashing to the ground. He tried to look around and find his enemy but injury warnings were streaming across both retinal lenses – the right clean and grim with severity, the left a cracked and hazing mess.

In the end, Va'lin felt the traitor's boot slammed atop his chest. He met Vorshkar's gaze, the warrior looking down on his defeated opponent with amusement. Another smile twisted his ivory-pale face.

'I lied about it being slow and lasting,' he admitted, 'at least in this realm of existence. I am about to end your flesh, Vulkan's son, but your soul... well,' he let out a long, malicious breath, 'that is for the neverborn to decide.'

'Never... born?' Va'lin croaked, not understanding, as consciousness began to leave him.

Vorshkar's eyes narrowed. 'Let me show yo–'

A flash of light overloaded Va'lin's optics, rendering him blind. In the second of vision he was afforded before blackout, he saw Vorshkar thrown onto his heels, his neck snapping back as he unleashed an agonised scream.

It was the last sound Va'lin heard as he faded – his body shutting down, his mind suddenly awash with visions of the fire canyons.

Rest, the figure in his dream said again.

None can come back. Zantho's words resounded, echoing the Promethean belief in the Circle of Fire. None can come back.

CHAPTER THIRTY-EIGHT

Heletine, Canticus, inside the ravine

Elysius dragged Drakgaard's prone form across the battlefield, Her'us and Vervius guarding their retreat. These two were the last of their kind – the rest of the Serpentia were dead. Not even their bodies could be recovered. The battle was over, the Imperial forces defeated. Tenacity met its equally potent counterpart in a Nocturnean's cultural psychology, pragmatism, and lost.

Fight on and they would certainly be destroyed utterly. Retreat now and regroup, at least they could muster whatever was left of their forces and salvage some kind of military response.

With Drakgaard incapacitated, command fell to Elysius, and the Chaplain had no hesitation about giving the order to fall back. Most not clad in drake-scale armour already had, though precious few Cadians were left alive to be ashamed of the fact.

Armour had come in from the east, a ragged assembly of Space Marine tanks under the charge of Sergeant Zantho, battered and bruised from shouldering their way through the rubble of a city. Elysius could not comprehend how many vehicles Zantho had lost or what sort of damage had been done to the ones that were currently bombarding the heretics to curtail any meaningful pursuit, but would have laid oaths that it was grievous.

'We are clear of the third vector, brother-sergeant,' voxed Elysius, his bionic arm and power glove making light work of hauling Drakgaard up the slope.

'Understood, Brother-Chaplain,' came the reply from Zantho a moment later.

Three more seconds elapsed before the area of the ravine Elysius and the remains of the fire-born had just evacuated was engulfed in a hail of explosive shellfire.

On the opposite side of the battlefield, the Sisters of the Ebon Chalice were still engaged in a fighting retreat themselves. Of the promised reinforcements, a vast Ecclesiarchy warhost, only these Seraphim had answered the call. There was no time to question that now, but Elysius was determined that if he lived he would have an answer, one way or another. The betrayers, whoever they were, would be punished.

As he reached the ridge line, a Rhino armoured transport was waiting with a rough bodyguard of fire-born outside it firing off shots into the ravine to deter any last ditch attacks. Elysius got Drakgaard aboard, sending him off with Her'us by his side in the troop hold. A Thunderhawk was waiting to take them back to Escadan, one of the few that could still fly.

Elysius stayed behind with Vervius to oversee the retreat. The Chaplain's jaw clenched at the sight and the thought of such utter defeat.

'Chaplain,' uttered Vervius.

Elysius turned to face him.

'You are bleeding, sir.'

Elysius looked down at the many wounds he had sustained that had penetrated his battleplate. In truth, it was a ruin and in dire need of a Techmarine's ministrations.

'It's a small matter, brother,' Elysius replied, lifting his gaze to the ravine again. 'Upraise the banner, Vervius,' he said as the last few survivors made it to the ridge line and safety, 'let our enemy know we are defiant even when we are beaten.'

Elysius spared a last glance in the direction of the Seraphim who were now embarking aboard transports. These few had defied whatever order had condemned the rest of the Imperials to defeat. By blood or torture, if it was necessary, he would find out who gave it.

CHAPTER THIRTY-NINE

Nova-class frigate, *Forge Hammer*

Xarko's strength was at its end. He saw the kine-shield flicker once and then dissipate. Alone in the access corridor, exhausted to the point of collapse, he faced down the four Black Dragons who had come aboard the ship intent on murderous vengeance.

Every fractional movement was bone-gnawing agony, but Xarko still drew his sword. The edge crackled with ionic charge. He doubted he could do much with it beyond lift it.

'Don't make me kill you.'

The sergeant in war-ravaged black plate laughed, seeing through the weak facade.

'I shall not afford you the same courtesy, Salamander,' he replied, exposing the sharp fangs in his snarling mouth. 'You sealed your fate when you murdered our captain.'

Xarko frowned.

'Murdered? You are mistaken. No blood has been shed on this ship that you did not bring about yourselves.'

'Liar!' spat a warrior with bone nubs jutting from his ugly pate. Another beside him snarled, clenching and unclenching fists that ended in calcified blades. The fourth was a cold storm. He'd lost an eye but the one that remained was like a chip of ice as it regarded the Librarian, and he carried the Prime Helix of the apothecarion.

'Who are you? What are you doing aboard this ship?' Xarko asked, stalling.

Silencing the beasts in his retinue, the sergeant came forwards.

'We are the wrath,' he declared in a menacing undertone, 'here to claim our vengeance...' As he raised his bone blade to strike, a stentorian voice echoed from the opposite end of the corridor.

'Trouble yourself no further with him,' said Adrax Agatone as he moved into the light with bolter raised, 'you have much worse problems now.'

The captain had returned with a small war party. Sergeants Lok, Clovius and five other warriors all armed. One of them stepped in front of Agatone, seeing the familiar trappings of the infiltrators aboard the *Forge Hammer*.

'Brothers...' said Zartath, disbelieving. 'Who sent you?'

The sergeant's anger bled away instantly and he took a knee. So too did the others he had brought with him.

'Don't you know us?' asked the sergeant, seemingly confused by Zartath's attire but more concerned that he didn't recognise them. 'I am Urgaresh. This is Skarh, Haakem.' He gestured to each in turn.

'Thorast, my lord,' uttered the Apothecary.

Zartath sneered, confused. 'Lord? I am no one's lord.'

Urgaresh rose to his feet. His eyes narrowed. 'We are your wrath,' he said. 'And have searched long and far.'

'To what end, warrior?' Agatone interjected, reminding the Black Dragons of his presence and the bolters aimed at them.

'To find our captain,' said Urgaresh, as all eyes fell on Zartath.

'Do you trust them?'

Agatone looked up from his vigil and met Issak's gaze.

'They boarded my ship and killed several of its crew. No, I don't trust them.'

They were sitting in the darkened confines of the *Forge Hammer*'s apothecarion, the unconscious form of Exor laid down on the medi-slab in front of them. Vitals were steady but the wound he had taken from the traitor's sword in Molior was grievous. Given the extent of the injuries and Exor's augmentations, Agatone considered they might have been better off with an enginseer rather than a ship's medic.

'What will you do with them?' asked Issak.

Agatone looked down again. The Black Dragons had been incarcerated in the brig. They went willingly, in part due to Zartath's presence but also on account of the sheer number of bolters levelled at them.

Zartath had no knowledge of them, and had spent every moment since his brothers' imprisonment watching them from an observation chamber. Agatone resolved to go and check in on him after he had finished visiting Exor.

'Why did you come with us, medicus?' he asked, answering Issak's question with one of his own.

'Because you allowed it.'

Agatone looked up at that.

'It was more than that,' he said. 'And don't tell me you just wanted out of the hive.'

'I won't. I experienced something in the archive, a sense of being there before but not knowing when or how. It led me to a name.'

Agatone raised an eyebrow, questioning, and Issak continued.

'It was amongst the wreckage in the archive. The uppermost level before we got in the lifter. I don't know why I was drawn to it, but I was. I think it was what your errant warrior and his companion were looking for.'

'What name?'

'Draor.'

CHAPTER FORTY

Heletine, beneath Solist

Angerer awoke to pain and an alarming lack of feeling in most of her body. The lids of her eyes were heavy and difficult to lift, so what she saw when she first tried to open them came in slivers.

A dark chamber, somewhere underground and lit by flaming torches…

The brooding presence of my monstrous captor, hulking and vile as it regards me from the back of the room…

Warriors, clad in armour, the same traitors we met at Solist…

A wretched figure, robes clinging to her body, knelt and praying before me…

She is hunched, shivering, but does not relent in her murmuring benedictions.

Looking up at me, our eyes meet and I recognise the kinship in them.

It is Revina. It is my sister. And she is praying for me.

'Reunited with your sister,' uttered the monster, its voice resonant. 'How long has it been?'

Angerer glanced at it but only glanced. To do anything more would be to invite damnation. She tried to focus on Revina, on her sister. Despite her conditioned revulsion for the witch and the heretic, Angerer had tears in her eyes when she answered.

'Years…' she said, her tone low and faint, 'it has been years since I last saw my sister.'

'I forgive you,' said Revina. Her voice had recovered, losing the reedy croak from when she had been staked down in the desert.

Angerer had no words. She warred between familial compassion and what was demanded of her by the sacred creed of the Ecclesiarchy.

Suffer not the witch and the heretic to live.

It was tattooed across the back of Angerer's partially shaved scalp, just above the nape of her neck, scribed in High Gothic.

'I forgive you, Maelisia.'

No one had called Angerer that name since before the Adepta Sororitas.

'And I am so sorry…' said Revina, bowing her head.

Incredulous for a moment, Angerer found her voice stronger. 'For what?'

Belatedly, the canoness realised she was pinned. Her limbs, waist and neck were shackled to some kind of wrought iron edifice. It stank of old blood and the foulness of decay, but was impossible for her to see whilst she was bound to it.

Rage supplanted pain as Angerer fell back on her training. All those hours of excoriation and penitence had honed her into something more and at the same time less than human.

'Release me!' She snarled at the monster, spitting her zeal from cracked lips.

'I too have siblings I wish to be reunited with,' it answered, stepping into the light and letting the lambent glow from the torches wash over it.

It wore a thick sheath of war-plate, but rather than fit perfectly over its body like the armour of a Space Marine should, it was stretched and malformed like wax exposed to heat. Between the glossy black plates, pale ivory trimmed with ocean green peeked through like an aperture into another world. Its face was false, the simulacra of one of the Emperor's Angels rendered into artistic stillness.

'Unlike you,' said the monster, coming in close so Angerer could smell the corpse-stench of its breath and feel her skin prickle at the proximity of its unnatural aura, 'I won't cast them out. They are lost. Your sister,' it gestured to Revina, whom Angerer glanced at, 'is going to help me find them.'

Its eyes briefly changed from two pure black voluminous orbs to having corneas, retinas and irises. Perhaps it was her pain-fuelled imagination, but Angerer swore there was something vaguely lupine about them.

'I was formerly a Wolf,' the monster confessed, tearing open Angerer's thoughts as easily as it would her flesh. 'One of Luna…' it said resignedly, 'but no more.'

'Sister,' Angerer was weeping, her wrath and despair colliding ambivalently, 'what have you done?'

'What I had to do,' Revina replied calmly, though her eyes betrayed the depth of anguish she felt for her sister, 'what I was born to be. If you didn't want me to see, you should have taken my sight.'

'Would that I could, dear sister.'

The monster clamped a meaty gauntlet around Angerer's chin, forcing back her attention.

'Strange, isn't it, that only when we are faced with losing something or someone do we appreciate its true value.' There was scorn in its voice now, and Angerer suspected some part of it despised her for what she had done to Revina.

'She has a gift, your sister,' the monster went on, though it did not loosen its grip which had begun to wear at Angerer's jawbone. 'I shall see it used to bring about a reunion between my brothers and I. They are here... somewhere, and blessed Revina and her witch-sight are going to peer beyond the veil for me, so I can know exactly where, so I can determine where in the skein of the flesh-world I need to make my cut.'

Revina was a seer, an augur of sorts. Her latent gift had been discovered in her infancy, manifesting as an uncanny ability to know things before they had happened. The first time had been the death of their mother. A virulent illness had destroyed her from within, eating the poor woman alive whilst her children could only watch. Revina wept. Once on her own, before her mother had passed, and again with her sisters – both for the parent she had lost and the orphan life as part of the Sisterhood they were about to be forced into. She had seen everything.

Though she was only a child, Revina saw the drill abbot arriving at their domicile before he had arrived. Through her sorrow she was afforded a glimpse of him.

Later, when the three sisters had been inducted to the Order of the Ebon Chalice as neophytes, Revina had lost the penitent cup she used for prayer and ablution. Without it she would have been severely beaten and chastised by her superior. Her tears revealed the location of the cup, sparing her the lash but eventually opening her up to more serious censure. It was Angerer who had discovered her 'taint', and Angerer who brought her to the attention of the then canoness. Once Angerer had been cleared of any suspicion, her genetics deemed pure, it all but assured her rise to prominence in the order but condemned her sister at the same time. Laevenius rose with her, whilst Revina languished in a cell, her existence known only to a few, a dirty secret the order kept at its heart. It was a circle that shrank to two when the old canoness died and Angerer replaced her.

Decades old, the memories resurfaced like fresh wounds. It might have been the presence of the monstrous warrior or just pent up and repressed emotion. The revulsion, the disgrace of having a mutant for a sister and the purifying vindication she felt when she had exposed her to the order. It was empowering.

'Witchling!' Angerer cursed Revina, tears streaming from her eyes now, 'Laevenius and I should have strangled you as a child.'

But Revina was no longer there. She had been ushered away by the monster's warriors. Angerer turned to it instead, hawking a gob of phlegm onto its pristine, false face.

'Abomination!'

'I wasn't always,' said Faustus, and tightened his grip until the Sister's jaw broke. His name was no longer Heklion Faustus, it was Gralastyx, daemon lord of the Eye.

Lufurion watched the brutalisation of the woman with detached interest. He kept to the shadows, out of Gralastyx's immediate sight and gathered with his trusted warriors, ostensibly strategising. These three had been hard to find. Amongst the Children of Torment and the remnants of his own Incarnadine Host, Lufurion had discovered entire nests of betrayers. But these three he had fought with, bled with, pledged oaths with. It wasn't brotherhood – he had abandoned that long ago, but it was something close.

'Reports are coming in,' uttered Klerik, keeping his voice low, 'Vorshkar has led the army to victory against the Imperials.'

'I heard he was injured in the act,' whispered Juadek.

'No need to sound so conspiratorial, you idiot,' snapped Klerik, looking askance at the Black Legion warriors standing to attention around the chamber and waiting on their master.

'It has been agreed,' said Lufurion. 'We deliver the daemon's kin and he will give us the witch. From there we part ways.'

Preest angled his head up slightly.

'He knows, Preest,' Lufurion told the sorcerer.

'Can we trust him, though?'

'Of course not,' Lufurion told him, 'but his mind is no longer entirely his own. He's a slave to that thing he has become, but he's also driven by sentiment and an outdated sense of fraternal honour.'

'A true son of Cthonia then,' laughed Juadek.

'So he claims, yes,' Lufurion replied.

'Are we certain we still need the witch?' asked Klerik. 'In the wake of Vorshkar's triumph we could take our ships and be gone.'

Lufurion looked to the sorcerer again. 'Preest says we do.'

All eyes went to him for an explanation.

'Our brothers we sent to Sturndrang are all dead.'

Juadek leaned in, a sour look on his face as he regarded the sorcerer.

'You're sure?'

Preest gave him a disparaging glance.

'I spoke unto a servant of the Eye,' he said, as if it were a rudimentary thing he was describing and not a rite of incredible difficulty and peril.

'Claimed by the warp then?' asked Klerik. 'I had wondered what happened to Ryos and the others.'

Preest shook his head. 'They arrived, only several years ago.'

'Temporal displacement,' said Klerik. 'The tides really didn't favour them, did they?'

'Something else killed them,' Preest continued. 'Even now their souls are in torment.'

'And I have no desire to join them,' said Lufurion, nodding to Gralastyx as the daemon allowed his prisoner to sag in her chains. She would not die yet – he still had use for her.

The gathering parted swiftly. Preest would be needed to 'encourage' the witch's auguring. His mortal worm would assist, the one that still lived. As the sorcerer was summoned by one of the Black Legion warriors, Klerik hung back to whisper in Lufurion's ear.

'We both went on bended knee before the Warmaster. We pledged oaths in front of Devram Korda. If they discover our plan to betray them, the daemon will be the least of our worries.'

Lufurion smiled, the patchwork of his stitched face straining to perform the gesture.

'We always knew it would come to this. Either Ryos and the others found the archive on the hive world or we secured the witch. Ryos is dead, so that leaves us. I've seen her work. She'll give us what we seek.'

Klerik's eyes narrowed. 'Is it real?'

'Ten thousand years ago, it was.'

'But can it do what Preest claims?'

Lufurion gave the facial equivalent of a shrug. 'Something that old, with that kind of provenance... We'll have to acquire it to find out.'

'They'll hunt us. The drakes, what's left of the Iron Tenth... Abaddon.'

Lufurion smiled thinly. It was a viper's smile, deadly. 'You sound scared, Klerik. Have I misplaced my faith in you?'

Klerik didn't respond to the threat. He knew Lufurion was just testing him.

'I merely point out the list of our enemies should we pull this off.'

'If we do, Klerik,' said Lufurion, 'with the storm we'll unleash, none of them will matter anymore. They'll all be too busy... drowning in their own blood.'

EPILOGUE

A future truth…

Kinebad struck up the lamp's igniter and a stark light lifted the darkness. Old stone, layered with dust, was revealed. The chamber was based on a hexagonal structure, a vast outer ring that led to increasingly smaller ones.

So far, Kinebad and his companion had passed through five circles. He hoped the sixth was the last.

The lamp hissed and flared, reacting to something in the air, before settling into a pulsing glow that gave off an actinic stench.

'That thing reeks foul,' uttered a deep, belligerent voice behind Kinebad.

Kinebad was stooped over, trying to avoid a section where the ceiling had partially caved in. Dust cascaded languidly from the gap with the natural shifting and settling of the stone above. It did not look as if it was going to come crashing down any time soon – in fact, this place barely looked disturbed in years – so Kinebad was content to proceed.

'It's phosphor,' he said.

Kinebad turned the lamp on the speaker to reveal a tall, thick-set warrior clad in loose-fitting carapace. The grey armour was bespoke and had sigils on it scrawled by the wearer in ash. A mesh layer underneath the plates hinted at a muscular frame, far larger than that of an ordinary human man. The hood attached to the mesh was drawn up over his head, but couldn't conceal his eyes. They were fiery red, burning like hot coals.

'Sadly, it is also necessary,' answered Kinebad. 'Despite my many gifts, I

313

don't have your enhanced sight or physiology,' he said, and took the lamp light off his protector.

He didn't need protection, per se. Kinebad was trained: both armed and unarmed, and in a variety of fighting disciplines. He carried a folded long rifle in a case cinched to his back and a snub-nosed automatic pistol, the Redoubter, in a holster on his left hip. His right thigh was strapped with a mono-molecular kaisen blade. It was a relic, as well as his birthright, from an ancient human dynasty.

Compared to the other warrior's heavy slugger that he had strapped across his immense back and shoulders, Kinebad's weapons were practically an arsenal. He had offered to furnish his protector with better materiel but had been refused. Repeatedly.

The light picked out the details of the chamber. It was mainly granite but there was also some ouslite, marble and even obsidian, though the volcanic glass had tarnished over the ages. The air was cold too, and it made the light grainy. The slightly brisk atmosphere was in sharp contrast to the world several hundred metres above them. On the surface of Draor, it was a blisteringly hot night and the sulphur rain was falling in sheets.

Kinebad had searched for this world and then this chamber, or series of chambers, for almost half a decade. Using the power and influence granted him by the rosette he carried beneath his armoured tunic, he had scoured obscure histories, references on forgotten parchments and proscribed knowledge vouchsafed by the Holy Ordos of Terra. A common archeotech could not have come as close as he – likely they would have been silenced for even asking the question. But here he was, on the very threshold of a significant discovery. Shogu master he might be, but it was the beating heart of a scholar and a theologian that fed the blood around Kinebad's veins and gave him vigour.

'What is this place, witch?' asked the warrior, casting about his surroundings as bare stone gave way to lapidary inscription.

Kinebad had moved beyond the sixth ring and was into the seventh. A pair of columns separated it from the rest, between them the only entrance. Faded frescoes had been worked into their smooth stone but the meaning had all but been obliterated by time and entropy.

'I do wish you wouldn't call me that.' Kinebad moved further, slowly casting the lamp around to find his footing. There was much debris on the ground, which made crossing the chamber slightly hazardous.

'It's untrue?' The warrior sounded nonplussed.

Kinebad turned his gaze on him. A scrutinising lens flicked from under his headgear across his right eye. It gave off a faint whirring sound as the analysing rings calibrated.

'It's derogatory.'

'I didn't think you had me in your company for my manners.'

'Your bearing suggested nobility, Scar-borne.'

'You say that like it isn't my name.'

'I know it isn't. It's what the overseers called you on Sturndrang, a slave name. Are you a slave?'

'To you, witch… no.'

Kinebad laughed. 'You're fortunate I have need of you.'

The warrior named Scar-borne took a step forward. In the light from Kinebad's lamp, he seemed to increase in size. And threat. The shadows across one side of his features deepened, his face a cleaner version of the volcanic glass in the chamber.

'Am I? Am I really, inquisitor?'

There was a brief moment when Kinebad felt the irresistible urge to reach for a weapon. But even with an arsenal as formidable as his, and with all the dynastic training from his shogu instructors, good sense told him this would be a mistake.

Scar-borne was testing his boundaries again. He harboured a deep anger, a sense of injustice and volatility Kinebad had found useful, but occasionally it needed marshalling.

Not rising to the bait, he turned away and went back to his work.

A large circular hall stretched in front of the inquisitor, held up by more columns. And something else…

'There,' Kinebad hissed, and gestured to a shaft of light.

An opening high up in the vaulted ceiling fed back to the surface almost three hundred metres above them. Thin veils of sulphur rain were coming in through the gap and hissed against an obelisk as they struck it. The obelisk was marble, three metres high and its six faces each carried an illustrated slab of varicoloured minerals. At the summit there was a statue of a massive warrior, similar in build to Scar-borne, and another, smaller warrior kneeling down in front of the first.

They looked like ancient knights, armed and armoured as such.

From the look of the breach in the ceiling it was recent, and rather than diminishing Kinebad's find, the caustic action of the rain was actually revealing the begrimed tablets around the obelisk. Script had begun to form at the base of each. A closer inspection revealed the language to be old, some form of archaic Gothic no longer spoken in the Imperium.

As a student of history, Kinebad had mastered many dead tongues as well as the extant conjurations of languages that had evolved over time. Though obscure, he found he could read what had been inscribed on the tablets.

'You asked what this place is,' said Kinebad, as he knelt by the tablet that was facing the entrance and therefore in his line of approach. The image on the tablet was of the same warrior depicted by the statue, his gauntleted fist held up in triumph. 'It is history, Scar-borne. It is legacy and the truth concerning a myth ten thousand years old.'

'You're wrong, inquisitor,' said Scar-borne, his voice darkening as he drew the heavy slugger from his back.

This time Kinebad turned, his right hand reaching for Redoubter out of instinct and conditioned reflex.

It would be too late. Scar-borne had him cold. The ugly maw of the slugger seemed to gape and mock. Little more than a blunderbuss, it would, nonetheless, shred the inquisitor's storm coat, light body armour and flesh.

'We had an agreement,' he snapped, more a reminder than a threat.

'Down,' said Scar-borne.

Kinebad obeyed.

Thunder shattered the silence of the temple, broke it apart with two raucous booms of the warrior's massive cannon.

Hot viscera splashed against the inquisitor's storm coat. He looked around, still crouched down, and saw the steaming bodies of two skels. The wire-furred canines shone black in the half-light, their mail coats glossy with their exploded blood and innards. Massively muscled, with fur as resilient as mail and the unerring silent approach of the very best apex predators, skels were a deadly xenos breed. They were also the dominant and prevalent form of life on Draor.

Scar-borne went over to both carcasses, stamping down on their skulls with an armoured boot.

'It's a lair,' he told Kinebad, before thrusting an outstretched finger at the opening. As the light came in, the summit of a ziggurat was revealed. 'More skels will fill this place within the hour. Whatever you need to do, do it quickly.'

Skels were also adept climbers, their long dewclaws strong enough and sharp enough to gain purchase in solid rock. Before planetfall, Kinebad had conducted extensive observation of the indigenous xenos population. That learning had proved extremely useful in getting them this far.

Kinebad gave a mute nod of thanks in Scar-borne's direction as he remembered the many reasons he had offered him a position with his group.

Turning, he began to read.

'On the eighteenth day of Nureg, the Guardian of Terra did alight on Draor…' Kinebad began.

Scar-borne's gaze went to the statue, the great armoured warrior. There was something familiar, archaic about the design of his battleplate.

'…and there was a great star-fire in the heavens as seven ships of gold descended.'

The fabled landing described was depicted on the second tablet.

On the third was a host of warriors, knelt down in fealty.

'And, lo, did the men of Iron kneel to his will and the will of the Avenging Son.'

On the fourth tablet was a huge figure wearing a politician's robes and carrying a heavy book under the crook of one mighty arm. His head was arrayed with a laurel wreath and a white 'U' symbol served as a clasp for the garments he wore in place of his armour.

'He brought his word and his bond, but it was the gift of bone the men of Iron took heed of.'

The fifth tablet depicted the so-called 'Guardian' handing a box to one of the men of Iron, a leader judging by his sword and banner.

'And so reunited with their patriarch was a pact with the men of Iron sealed and the Imperium of Man reunited.'

A skull, its eyes rendered in dull, lifeless jet, dominated the final tablet and it was there the inscribed legend ended.

'Never again would it be put asunder.'

Kinebad was shaking. He wiped a bead of sweat from his forehead, despite the chill.

'Do you know what this means?'

Throughout the recitation, Scar-borne's gaze had not left the statue. Now it fell to the inquisitor.

'They raised a monument,' he said, 'the people who once dwelled on this world.'

'Almost ten thousand years ago, yes they did.' Kinebad shook his head, scarcely believing what he had discovered. 'This is real Imperial history, Scar-borne, from the days of the War.'

'There have been many wars. I've fought in several.'

'The Heresy War that ended the first Great Crusade.' When Scar-borne's interest wasn't piqued by Kinebad's rhetoric, the inquisitor grew irritated. 'It was a formative period in your Chapter's history.'

Now it was Scar-borne's turn to be angry.

'I have no Chapter,' he said. 'Not anymore.' Scar-borne's shoulders slumped as he briefly relived bitter memories. 'I am unworthy of it,' he added quietly, allowing his gaze to fall.

As Kinebad revisited each tablet, pict-capturing with his scrutinising lens, he heard Scar-borne speak from the other side of the obelisk.

'Why have I never heard about any of this before? I know my Chapter's history. I have read of every battle the Legion fought in, and studied them. But this… I have no knowledge of this.'

'Even I was ignorant of it. History is full of lacunae, especially after so many millennia. Much is lost, like the people who raised this monument and committed this truth to indelible stone for others to find. Here we are unearthing some of that truth, the same truth that our enemies seek to use.'

Recording the image of the final tablet, Kinebad walked back around the obelisk to find Scar-borne looking right at him.

'The cult you and I destroyed on Sturndrang. That was not the end of it?'

'It was the beginning.'

Scar-borne shook his head and scowled, gesturing to the obelisk.

'Do you even believe this?'

Kinebad's gaze, much like his conviction, was unwavering. 'I believe we are a step closer to achieving our ends and finishing the Incarnadine Host for good.'

The vox-link in Kinebad's ear crackled, interrupting them.

'Go ahead, Skaed.'

A woman's voice answered, patchy but still audible across the feed. Torrential rain served as a backdrop behind it.

'Indigenes are moving in. So we need to be moving out. Right now.'

A brief break in connection prompted Kinebad to crouch and press the receiver bud in his ear. 'Skels?'

'Hundreds of the ugly bastards, and some larger xeno-forms we haven't seen before.'

'Effect egress at once, Skaed. I want you on the *Reckless* and back with Heckt immediately.'

'I am in no immediate danger, inquisitor. My vantage is still good. I could provide you with some cover.'

'Unnecessary. Scar-borne is with me.'

'That is what concerns me.'

'Retreat to the *Reckless*, Uanda.'

Uanda Skaed gave the affirmation tone and cut the link.

Scar-borne was racking two immensely large shells into the breach of his slugger.

'I knew she didn't like me.'

'Do many?'

'No.'

Kinebad raised an eyebrow. 'I don't know why you favour that monstrous cannon. It's badly weighted, the aim is poor and the reload slow.'

'Because it kills whatever it hits.' Scar-borne grinned and one side of his face, one that was severely scarred, contorted into a terrifying scowl. 'We have an understanding, it and I.'

'So it seems.'

Through the gap in the ceiling, the howling had begun.

'We need to move,' said Kinebad.

Scar-borne nodded and led them out.

Outside, the deluge intensified. Sulphur rain was lashing straight down in burning little tears of acid. The refractor field generated by one of Kinebad's several rings flickered with the constant hammering of the rain. Scar-borne had no such protection. He did not need it. His armour was acid-proofed and his skin was inviolable against it. He endured the heat

too. Kinebad used his psychic gifts to maintain a comfortable temperature; Scar-borne was simply used to hotter.

Underneath the tumult of the storm, the low howling of the skels was
just audible.

A flash of lightning cut a jagged path through the night sky. It lit up a
barren landscape, a place of ruination and a people long since deceased.
Skels dominated now and their eyes flashed like hungry sapphires as they
gathered in packs around the inquisitor and his warrior.

Scar-borne counted almost three hundred skels. The larger xeno-forms
Skaed had mentioned were further back and harder to make out. Porcine
perhaps, with an almost simian gait? When encountering the alien, it is
mankind's natural instinct to try to make sense of it, to look for parallels
within his own sphere of knowledge. But one cannot impose the natural
upon the unnatural, the familiar on the alien. The things waiting for them
out in the rain adhered to no natural template. They were monsters, but
Scar-borne knew monsters and their kind very well indeed.

'You expect me to fight all of them?'

'I know you probably would,' said Kinebad, producing a small lozenge-
shaped object from his many trappings, 'but I had something less messy
and more effective in mind.'

'The fealty the tablet spoke of,' said Scar-borne, showing some interest
in what Kinebad had discovered for the first time, as the inquisitor began
to activate the aetheric beacon, 'it was to Guilliman, wasn't it? He was the
Avenging Son and the pact he had Dorn make was for the Codex.'

'I believe it was, yes.'

As if scenting that their prey was leaving, the skels began to move and
their howling increased in pitch.

'And the gift he gave? The one to force the men of Iron onto bended
knee...'

Dematerialisation was in process, and both Scar-borne and Kinebad felt
their bodies and immortal souls being slowly surrendered to the warp.

The skels were rushing now, shrieking and baying as the prey-scent
began to fade. Saliva-wet fangs glistened in their hyperextended mouths.

Kinebad spoke a silent prayer as he felt the first pull of aetheric wind,
the skin-tingling charge of corposant.

'It was the skull of their primarch,' said Kinebad as the screaming of
the skels and the tearing of reality merged. His voice trailed off, partially
lost to the warp but lingering long enough for Scar-borne to hear what
he said, 'the head of Ferrus Manus.'

TO BE CONTINUED IN
INFERNUS

ABOUT THE AUTHOR

Nick Kyme is the author of the Horus Heresy novel *Vulkan Lives*, the novellas *Promethean Sun* and *Scorched Earth*, and the audio drama *Censure*. His novella *Feat of Iron* was a *New York Times* bestseller in the Horus Heresy collection, *The Primarchs*. For the Warhammer 40,000 universe, Nick is well known for his popular series of Salamanders novels and short stories, the Space Marine Battles novel *Damnos*, and numerous short stories. He has also written fiction set in the world of Warhammer, most notably the Time of Legends novel *The Great Betrayal* for the War of Vengeance series. He lives and works in Nottingham, and has a rabbit.